By Elizabeth Moon

The Deed of Paksenarrion

Sheepfarmer's Daughter
Divided Allegiance
Oath of Gold

Paladin's Legacy

*Oath of Fealty**
*Kings of the North**
*Echoes of Betrayal**
*Limits of Power**

The Legacy of Gird

Surrender None
Liar's Oath

Vatta's War

*Trading in Danger**
*Marque and Reprisal**
*Engaging the Enemy**
*Command Decision**
*Victory Conditions**

Planet Pirates (with Anne McCaffrey)

Sassinak
Generation Warriors

*Remnant Population**

The Serrano Legacy

Hunting Party
Sporting Chance
Winning Colors
Once a Hero
Rules of Engagement
Change of Command
Against the Odds

*The Speed of Dark**

Short-Fiction Collections

Lunar Activity
Phases

*Published by Ballantine Books

PALADIN'S LEGACY

LIMITS
OF
POWER

PALADIN'S LEGACY

Limits
OF
POWER

ELIZABETH MOON

BALLANTINE BOOKS • NEW YORK

Published in the United States by Del Rey, an imprint of The Random House Publishing Group, a division of Random House, Inc., New York.

DEL REY is a registered trademark and the Del Rey colophon is a trademark of Random House, Inc.

ISBN 978-0-345-53306-7
eBook ISBN 978-0-345-53307-4

Printed in the United States of America on acid-free paper.

www.delreybooks.com

2 4 6 8 9 7 5 3 1

First Edition

Dramatis Personae

Fox Company (formerly Kieri Phelan's mercenary company)
Jandelir Arcolin, commander, Count of the North Marches
Burek, junior captain of first cohort
Selfer, captain of second cohort
Cracolnya, captain of third (mixed/archery) cohort
Stammel, veteran sergeant of the Company, now blind

Tsaia
Mikeli Vostan Kieriel Mahieran, king of Tsaia
      Camwyn, his younger brother
Sonder Amrothlin Mahieran, Duke Mahieran, king's uncle
Selis Jostin Marrakai, Duke Marrakai
      Gwennothlin, his daughter and Duke Verrakai's squire
      Aris, his son and Prince Camwyn's friend
Galyan Selis Serrostin, Duke Serrostin
      Daryan, his youngest son and Duke Verrakai's squire
Dorrin Verrakai, Duke Verrakai, formerly a senior captain in Phelan's company, now Constable for kingdom
      Beclan, Kirgan Verrakai, formerly Beclan Mahieran
Oktar, Marshal-Judicar of Tsaia
Seklis, High Marshal of Gird

Lyonya
Kieri Phelan, king of Lyonya, former mercenary commander and duke in Tsaia, half-elven grandson of the Lady of the Ladysforest
Arian, Kieri's wife, queen of Lyonya, half-elven
Aliam Halveric, commands Halveric Company, Kieri Phelan's mentor and friend
Estil Halveric, his wife

elves
Amrothlin, the Lady's son and Kieri's uncle
Elven ruler of the Lordsforest

Fintha
Arianya, Marshal-General of Gird
Marshal Cedlin, Fin Panir
Marshal Sofan, Crossways

Aarenis
Arvid Semminson, former thief-enforcer, now Girdish convert
Marshal Porfur, Ifoss
Marshal Steralt, Valdaire
Jeddrin, Count of Andressat
      Filis Andressat, Andressat's third son
Visla Vaskronin, Duke of Immer (formerly, Alured the Black)
Samdal, Chancellor and Regent, Horngard

Kuakkgani
Ashwind, itinerant Kuakgan, Tsaia
Elmholt, grovemaster Kuakgan, Tsaia
Larchwind, itinerant Kuakgan, Lyonya
Pearwind, itinerant Kuakgan, Lyonya

Gnomes
Dattur, kteknik gnome and Arvid's companion/servant
Aldonfulk Prince

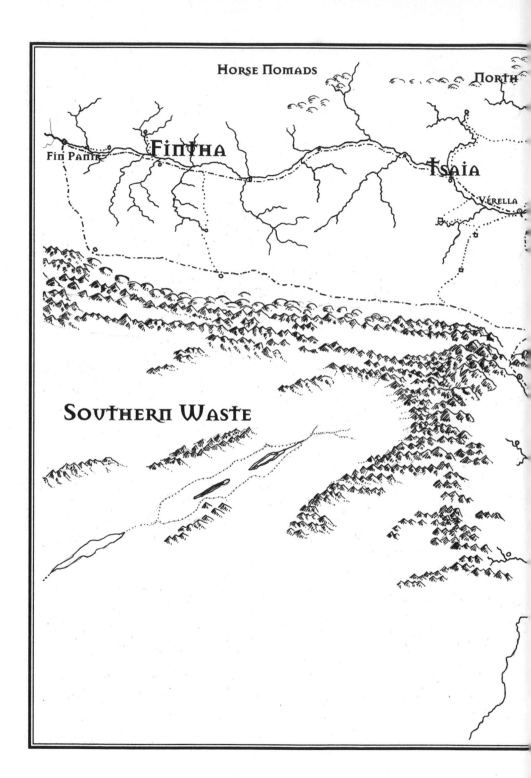

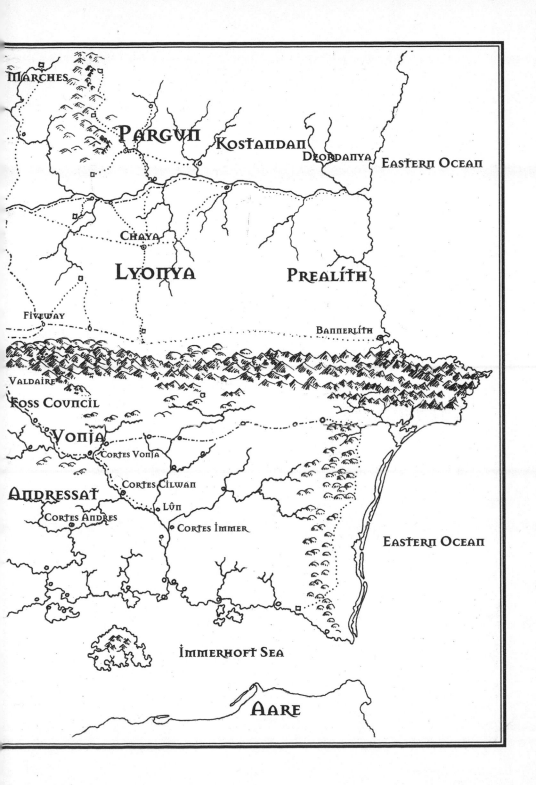

MARCHES

PARGUN

KOSTANDAN

DZORDANYA

EASTERN OCEAN

CHAYA

LYONYA

PREALÍTH

FIVEWAY

BANNERLÍTH

VALDAIRE

FOSS COUNCIL

VONJA

CORTES VONJA

CORTES CILWAN

ANDRESSAT

LÛN

CORTES ANDRES

CORTES IMMER

EASTERN OCEAN

IMMERHOFT SEA

AARE

PALADIN'S LEGACY

LIMITS
OF
POWER

CHAPTER ONE

Chaya, in Lyonya

Y ou killed her!" That first voice, instantly joined by others, rose in a furious screech of accusation. "*You* killed her! You killed *her*!"

The angry voices penetrated Kieri's grief and exhaustion, and he looked back over his shoulder to see at least a dozen elves, some with swords drawn, his uncle Amrothlin among them. Behind them, more Squires pushed into the room.

"I did not," he said. "I tried—"

"She's dead! You're alive; you must have—!"

"I tried to *save* her," Kieri said. "I could not." He stood up then, automatically collecting his weapons as he rose.

"Let me see that!" Amrothlin strode forward, pointing at Kieri's sword. "If it has her blood on it—"

"Of course it does," Kieri said. "You saw: my sword lay in her blood, there on the floor." He had knelt in her blood, he realized, and his hands were stained. No wonder Amrothlin suspected him, though the blood that spattered his clothes had come from others.

Amrothlin reached out his hand. "Let me smell it. I know her scent; I will know another's scent, if indeed another's blood is there. Give it to me."

"No," Arian said before Kieri could answer, blocking Amrothlin with her arm. "You will not disarm the king," she said. "Not after what has happened."

"You!" Amrothlin glared at her. "You half-bred troublemaker, child of one who should never have sired children on mortals—"

"*Daughter* of one who gave his life to save the Lady," Arian said. Kieri saw the glitter of both tears and anger in her eyes. "There he lies, and you would insult him?"

"And you know you cannot hold this sword," Kieri said, forcing a calm tone through the anger he felt. How dare Amrothlin insult Arian—and where had he been all this time? Was he the traitor? "You remember: it's sealed to me. Smell if you wish, but do not touch it."

Amrothlin glared at them all, then fixed his gaze on Arian. "What should I think when I find three mortals around my Lady's body with swords drawn and her blood run out like water from a cracked jug? I see no other foe here. It is you, I say, and this—this so-called king."

Kieri glanced past Amrothlin. The ring of elves stood tense; behind them were Squires who hesitated to push them aside, and behind those the hooded figures of two Kuakkgani. He met Amrothlin's angry gaze once more.

"I am the king," he said, keeping his voice as steady as he could. "I am the king, and my mother was your sister, and this Lady was my grandmother. So we are kin, whether you like it or not. If you can indeed detect identity by the smell of the blood, then you will smell another immortal's blood on this—and on the queen's sword and Duke Verrakai's as well."

"Do you dare accuse an elf?" Amrothlin asked. He still trembled like a candle flame, but his voice had calmed.

"The one who did this could appear without walking through a door. Its mien seemed elven at first and also its magery, a glamour of the same sort as the Lady was wont to cast. Yet it was like no elf I have known in its malice and determination to kill the Lady. I believe you name such iynisin; in Tsaia we called them kuaknomi."

Amrothlin glared. "We do not speak of them." He looked over his shoulder, then back to Kieri. "Who was here at the time?"

"Later," Kieri said. Voices rose in the corridor: angry, frightened, demanding. Time to take command. "Uncle, this is not the time for

questions. I am the king, and I am not your enemy, nor the Lady's. People are frightened; I must speak to them."

Before Amrothlin could answer, he raised his voice and called to those beyond the room. "The danger is over for now: I, the king, am alive, and the queen is safe here with me. Those of you in the corridor: fetch the palace physicians for the wounded. The rest disperse, but for the Queen's Squires assigned to the queen today and one Kuakgan. Put by your swords." The elves by the door looked at Amrothlin, who said nothing, and then at Kieri again and finally put up their swords. Two Queen's Squires made their way into the room and edged through the elves to Arian's side.

Dorrin had already moved to one of the wounded Squires. "This one first, sir king. Both are sore wounded, and though I tried, I cannot heal them."

Kieri knelt beside her. When he laid his hand on the man's shoulder, he felt nothing but a heaviness. "Nor I," he said, standing again. "I must be more worn than I thought."

The noise outside diminished. "I will tell the whole of it to Amrothlin," Kieri said to the elves. "Two may remain; the rest of you go and make what preparations you need make for the Lady's rest." He knelt beside the other Squire yet felt no healing power in himself. Sighing, he stood again.

Amrothlin's stony expression did not change, but he did not contradict Kieri; with a wave of his hand he sent most of the elves away. Now the carnage showed more clearly—the pools of blood, the stench of blood and death, bloody footprints on the fine carpet, what looked like scorch marks, the dead: the Lady, Dameroth, another dead elf whose name Kieri did not know, Tolmaric's twisted and shrunken body, and the two iynisin Kieri and Arian and Dorrin had killed. Arian's clothes were as bloodstained as his own, and Dorrin, though she had not knelt in any blood, still had splashes on her shirt and sword hand.

"More dead elves," one of the other elves said, bending to examine them. Then he stiffened, turning back to Amrothlin. "My lord! These are not elves! They are . . . what the king said."

Amrothlin, still looking at Kieri, said, "Is this what you fought? Did you kill it?"

"That is another it split from its body after it killed Sier Tolmaric," Kieri said. "Look at Tolmaric, look at its body, and if you can explain how that was done, I will be glad."

Amrothlin turned and walked over to Tolmaric's remains. "This was human?" He sounded more worried than angry now.

"Yes. The iynisin did that with a touch of its blade to his throat. He was already bespelled by the Lady, as I said, and helpless."

"Where were you?"

"There." Kieri pointed. He told of questioning Sier Tolmaric, the Lady's interruption, and then the appearance of the iynisin—he insisted on using the name, though Amrothlin flinched every time—and its taunting of the Lady and attack. "I had just taken such a blow on my shoulder as almost threw me down. It was almost invisible; I could not see to parry the blow—and then it made for poor Tolmaric and did *that* to him, whatever that is. Then from the iynisin came two more, and each of those split into two."

"A formidable foe indeed," Amrothlin said. "Few of . . . such . . . can do that, and only with fresh blood and life taken." He moved over beside the elf looking at the other body. Kieri saw his shoulders stiffen. Amrothlin crouched beside the body and touched the blood staining its dark clothes, then sniffed at his fingers. He stood and faced Kieri again. "You brought this on us."

"What?" That accusation made no sense to him.

"You could not survive such a one unless it willed it so. The— these beings—" Even now Amrothlin would not use the word. "You know their origin? Traitors who once were elves, in the morning of the world, and who turned against all because of *those*." He pointed at the Kuakgan now standing near the door. "You called Kuakkgani here; that must be why the evil ones came. We do not speak of them. We do not acknowledge them."

"And yet these iynisin exist," Kieri said, once more using the elven name for them. "And they—or one—killed the Lady. Are all of them that powerful?" This, he was certain, was one of the secrets the elves had withheld from him; how could they think that not speaking of danger meant it did not exist?

"So you say, that she was killed by such." Amrothlin made an obvious attempt to calm down, but did not answer Kieri's question.

He sniffed his fingers again. "It is more likely a lord of the Severance could kill her than a half-human like you," he said. "These dead are certainly ephemes, split from such a one. And that—" He glanced at Tolmaric's remains. "That is what any living thing looks like that they destroy to make ephemes." He nodded to Kieri, now apparently calm. "I accept your story of the fight, but still—it is your fault that the Lady came here unescorted and such evil followed her. You knew what she thought of the . . . the Kuakkgani." He nearly spat the last word, his voice full of venom again.

"What *I* see is that you are determined to blame the king," Arian said. Kieri had never seen her so angry before. Flanked by her Squires, she stalked over to him. "Where were you when I was poisoned and my child never had a chance to live? The Lady did not come. None of you came. It was a Kuakgan who found the poison concealed in a block of spice: you elves did nothing. And you blame us for that?"

Amrothlin stared at her, speechless in the face of her anger.

"So now," Kieri said, taking over once more, "let us clean up this mess and confer." The palace physicians bustled into the room; he pointed to Binir and Curn, the two wounded Squires. Linne, another of the King's Squires, handed him cleaning materials for his sword; he began wiping it down. Arian handed her blade to one of her Squires. "Who is now the ruler of the elvenhome?" Kieri asked Amrothlin. "Will it be you, her son, or had she named another in her stead?"

Amrothlin shook his head. "There is no elvenhome."

"What—? Of course there is . . . must be." At the look on Amrothlin's face, Kieri said, "How can it be gone?"

"Do you not *see*?" Amrothlin gestured to his own grief-stricken face. "Do I look the same? Do you feel the influence of the elvenhome? It was hers—*her* creation—and it died with her. She alone sustained the Ladysforest; she had no heir. We are unhomed, Nephew. We are cast away, and nowhere in the world will we find a home now."

"That cannot be. The taig is still here." Kieri could feel the taig, the strength of it, even in its grief.

"The taig, yes. It is the spirit of all life. Where there is life, there is taig, greater and smaller. The taig nourishes elvenkind, and elvenkind nourishes the taig. We encouraged it, taught it, lifted it toward more awareness, according to the Lady's design. But it is not the elvenhome."

This was the longest explanation Kieri had ever heard about the relationship of elves and taig. "Then what *is* an elvenhome? Did the Lady then maintain the elvenhome with her own power? By herself?" And if so, how could such a power be stripped away?

"At first, yes," Amrothlin said. "But after we left the great hall below, in the time of the banast taig . . ." His voice trailed away; he looked down and away. "I cannot talk of it now, Nephew, please. Her power diminished, and now she is gone; the elfane taig is gone; I must prepare to lay her body to rest."

Kieri felt tears rising in his eyes and blinked them back. "Why didn't you ever tell me? Why didn't Orlith? If I had known—"

"You would have tried to interfere," Amrothlin said, his voice harsh again. "And what could you, a mortal, do? *You* had no power to lend us. You could but cause the Lady more anguish, to know that you knew her shame."

"And this is better?" Kieri asked. The familiar irritation with elven arrogance overrode even his fatigue. He waved at the room, at the bodies and the blood and the stench of death. "Her pride cost you dear, Uncle. You were so sure we could not help, you did not even seek understanding, let alone alliance—"

"How could such as you understand?" Amrothlin said. He looked more weary than angry now, his grace diminished. "What we live— what she lived—is beyond your comprehension. It is no use to explain; you do not have the mind for it."

Kieri's anger grew, but he knew that for a postbattle reaction as much as a fair response to Amrothlin. He glanced around the room. Everyone but the physicians working on the wounded Squires was looking at him. This was not the time to continue a quarrel with Amrothlin.

"Are any others wounded and in need of care?" No one answered. Arian's Squire returned her blade, now cleaned, and Arian slid it into the scabbard. Kieri had almost finished with his own.

"We will need to make a bier to move her," Amrothlin said. "And . . . and the others."

"Is there any menace in Sier Tolmaric's remains?" Kieri asked.

"No," Amrothlin said. "The evil destroyed him but does not remain. Do what you will with . . . that." He gestured toward Tolmaric's body but averted his gaze. "But beware the iynisin ephemes. Even their blood taints anything alive or that once lived. You must burn such things in a safe place away from here."

"Sier Tolmaric was a brave man from a family that had suffered much at elven hands," Kieri said, ignoring the rest for the moment. Amrothlin's arrogance grated on him. "Had the Lady not pressed her glamour on him, he might have fought at my side."

"What injury had he from elves?" Amrothlin asked, brows raised.

Kieri regretted mentioning it; this was something else that would be better discussed later. But if he wanted answers to questions, then he must answer those asked of him. "When my mother was killed, and I abducted, Tolmaric's father and grandfather were taken away by the elves—possibly by you yourself. Were you involved in that?"

Amrothlin scowled. "We thought humans were, of course. How else?"

"Perhaps today you see another possibility," Kieri said. "Elves took some of his family, and they came back damaged, with no apologies or recompense made. Nor, though I asked the Lady, was any recompense made for his losses from scathefire. Nor was that family the only one injured in your search for my mother's killers." He slid his sword home in its scabbard, picked up the dagger, and wiped it down. "But we will talk of this later, when you have taken the Lady away. For now, tell your people what happened—what *really* happened— and give those who died whatever honor you can. Where will you lay the Lady?"

"In that valley where the elvenhome below was," Amrothlin said. "She loved that valley. It is not in Lyonya as you know it, but you would be welcome to come there."

Kieri shook his head as he slid the dagger, now clean and oiled, into its sheath. "With this menace hanging over us, I cannot leave, Uncle. It would be better, indeed, if you found a place for her nearer to Chaya, since you lack the protection of the elvenhome. Why not the King's Grove, where the symbol of our alliance is? You say, I understand, that your people have no existence beyond death—though truly I do not understand how you can know that—"

"We were told," Amrothlin said in a low voice.

Kieri wanted to ask, *By whom?*, but this was not the time. "Linne, please tell the steward or Garris—whomever you find first—to summon the Council to the large dining room. They may already have heard, but I will formally announce Sier Tolmaric's death there. And we will need a bier for Tolmaric's body." He looked at Amrothlin again. "The palace can furnish biers for your dead. I will want two elves at the Council. You, unless your duties to the Lady's body require you here, and whomever you choose."

"Yes," Amrothlin said. His sword hand moved weakly, as if he could not decide on a gesture. "Yes, to all. Is there—is there any place we could take the bodies to wash them? I do not wish to parade the Lady through the streets to our inn."

"Of course. We will use the salle for them. Arian?" Kieri turned to her. "What is your desire in this?"

"That it not have happened," she answered, her voice choked with grief. "But it did. I would stay with my father's body, if you can spare me." Her expression was grave and resolute.

Kieri nodded. "Of course I can. You are his kin; it is your right."

"You said you were hit on the shoulder," Arian said. "I see the cut in your clothes—"

"And the blade did not touch my skin thanks to the mail. I will have it seen to when I can, but not now." He laid his hand on her shoulder. "I will come, Arian. But first I must speak to the Council, and then I will come to the salle."

"Then I take my leave," Arian said. "But you will be seen by physicians, Kieri—I insist on it." She gave a little bow and turned away, going back to her father's body. Kieri watched the set of her shoulders. He had lost his parents so long ago . . . he knew the pain of having none but not the pain of recent loss. And with the loss of their child . . . she had lost so much in so short a time.

He moved away from the iynisin's body to Tolmaric's. He could hardly recognize this ugly twisted relic as human remains. "You were brave," he said to Tolmaric's spirit in case it lingered. "You were not afraid to speak out the truth you knew and would have fought if you'd had the chance. I am sorry I could not save you from this fate. I swear to you, I will do my best by your family. Your sons and daughters will have a father in me." Tolmaric, he knew, had no living brothers.

Out of the corner of his eye, he saw movement near the door and turned to look. Two servants came in with one of the net-covered frames used to move the injured and lifted Tolmaric's body onto it. "Don't move him until I am with the Council," he said. "They should hear it first, not see it. And the elves will need enough for these—" He pointed to the other bodies. Then he went to the door, where the Kuakgan had been waiting, and stepped into the hall.

"Do you blame us?" the Kuakgan asked, speaking softly. For the moment, Kieri could not think of his name.

"For what?" Kieri asked. He could think of nothing the Kuakkgani had done that day worth blame.

"It was our song to the One Tree, they say, that began the Severance and the evil that followed, when some elves rebelled against the Singer and chose destruction."

Kieri huffed. "The Severance happened long ago, and your responsibility lies with your own acts. Today you did us more than one good service. I am not angry with you, nor do I blame you. But I would ask what you can add to my knowledge of these iynisin, as the elves call them."

"The kuaknomi have some powers beyond ours," the Kuakgan said. "We depend on the bond of kinship with trees and the taig and can do no more than kinship allows. The kuaknomi draw their power from hatred—from Gitres Unmaker."

Kieri had heard the iynisin called kuaknomi before, in Tsaia. "Did you know what it was without seeing it?"

"Oh, yes. We feel the taig all the time, you see, as elves do, and the trees felt their most dire enemy near."

"I thought fire was their worst enemy—or the scathefire at least."

"Fire is the nature of dragons and their young," the Kuakgan said. "The young do not burn out of malice, but joy. Kuaknomi, though, hate trees especially and delight in tormenting them." The Kuakgan paused, looking past Kieri around the room. "Kuaknomi blood is corrosive to living things and to things that were alive. See where the carpet is blackening as with fire? And your wounded—if such blood touches an open wound, that is very bad. Do your physicians know about the dangers—?"

"I doubt it," Kieri said.

"You and others have much blood on you—some of it kuaknomi by the smell. If you are wounded even slightly, you need treatment now."

"I'm not," Kieri said. A bruised shoulder was not a wound. "Can you help my physicians with the wounded?"

"We will try," the Kuakgan said. "I will call the others. We were going to ask if we could visit the ossuary and the bones of your ancestors, but this is more urgent."

"The ossuary? That seems a strange desire for those who live in groves," Kieri said.

"It may seem strange, but to us . . ." The Kuakgan paused, frowning. "I am not sure I can explain it. When we find bones in the forest, they . . . they tell us things. Not only how the animal died but who has passed. I felt an urge to visit your ossuary."

Kieri thought suddenly of the connection he'd discovered between the ossuary and the King's Grove mound. His face must have shown something, because the Kuakgan's gaze sharpened and he said, "What is it, Lyonya's king?"

"We must talk," Kieri said. "But first I must speak to my Council. Please help with the wounded, as you can, and I will talk to you later."

The Kuakgan was silent and motionless a long moment, then he nodded, his eyes bright beneath his hood. "I have called the others; we will do what we can."

Kieri turned and went down the passage to speak to his Council. The mumble of conversation stopped when he entered the room; the men and women all turned to look at him.

"My lord king! You're hurt!" That was Sier Halveric, just a beat ahead of the rest.

"No," Kieri said. "It's not my blood." Most looked scared, startled, shocked. Across the room, Aliam Halveric's brows went up; the glance between them conveyed the years of comradeship and shared experience in war. "Sit down, please," Kieri said. He felt the postbattle letdown even more now, but they needed his steady confidence, as they had needed it before he rode away to war. He hoped that this time they would respond better. He waited until they were seated and silent. Amrothlin came in just then, his expression strained, followed by another elf. Kieri waved them to their seats as well.

He began with a terse recital of events leading to his confrontation with Sier Tolmaric.

"Then it's true you know what the poison was?" Sier Davonin, of course. Women losing their children would interest her more than a fight in his office, however bloody.

"Yes," Kieri said. "And there's no more danger of contaminated food here. But let me go on—what comes is as important." He told it in order, ignoring all signs that someone wanted to ask a question. "The queen and I are alive, unharmed," he said as he finished. "Lord Amrothlin—" He nodded to Amrothlin. "—as you know, is the Lady's son. He has told me that the elvenhome is no more. He and I will discuss later what this means for Lyonya, for the remaining elves, and for us, who have long been partners here. I counsel you all to be vigilant. If you have doubts of something you see, tell a palace official or a servant. I must go to the salle, where the bodies are laid for the night. Those who wish may pay respects later." With a short bow, he left them and headed for the salle.

In the passage near the salle, he met Sier Tolmaric's wife, escorted by one of Arian's Squires. Lady Tolmaric's face, normally pale, was blotched with crying, her graying red hair loosening from its braid.

"My lady," Kieri began, but she burst into more tears before he could offer any comfort. He knew it had been her first visit to Chaya— she had not come for the coronation—and he had seen her wide-eyed joy in the splendor of the court and her shyness around other Siers' wives. Now she was bereft here in this strange place with strangers all around and no husband to guide her.

She sobbed out her misery, her fears, her certainty that nothing would ever come right. "The children—they'll starve—who'll take the land? And the farms—what will I do? Salvon knew it all; he worked so hard for us—"

"My lady, listen to me," Kieri said when the fit seemed like to go on another turn of the glass. "Your children will *not* go hungry, nor your house be taken away . . . I promise you, as I promised him—"

"Do you . . ." A gulp and cough interrupted that. "Do you really mean . . . you'll help?"

"Yes," Kieri said. "A king keeps his promises, and I have promised. Before a witness here—" He glanced at Arian's Squire, who spoke up on cue.

"I witness the king's promise," she said. "Now, Lady Tolmaric—"

"You should not go in yet," Kieri said. "It would distress you— and where are the children?" He knew that one son and two daughters had come, as wide-eyed and shy as their mother.

"At—at the house. This—this lady, this Squire said the queen had sent word, so I would not hear it from gossip, but I do not listen to gossip, sir king, truly I don't. And she said I should wait, but I could not, I must come, he was my husband. Oh—" She broke into sobs again. "Oh, what will I do?"

"You will listen to me," Kieri said with more force. Her mouth opened, and she stared but was quiet. "Listen carefully now. A dangerous being killed him, and the killing defaced him. What was done to his body was evil. You should not go in now but wait until those whose business it is have sewn him into a shroud for burial."

"But I must see his face one more time—must kiss his hands, his feet—"

"No, you must not. Remember his face as it was. Hold that memory and do not degrade it with how he now appears."

Her eyes were wide, fixed on his. "But . . . it is what a wife should do . . . it is what his mother did when his father died. What my mother did . . ."

"Yes, if his death was natural. This is not. Trust me, your king, to know what is best. You will have enough distress when you see him in the shroud, for the evil that was done distorted what was left. You must not remember him as he is now."

"Then what—how long—?"

"Your children need you. Do you have servants in the house where you are?"

"N-no. It is not our house; we paid to use one for three hands of days. No need for servants; I can cook as well as any."

"Yes, but you should not be alone now." He sent the Squire to arrange an escort and someone to stay with Lady Tolmaric for a day or so. As soon as Lady Tolmaric and the two servants headed back to her rented house, Kieri went on to the salle.

CHAPTER TWO

here he found Arian with her father's body. Dameroth's bloody clothes had been removed, his body washed and clothed in white. Arian sat on a low stool, one hand on his forehead. As Kieri walked toward her, she looked up but did not speak. One of his Squires fetched a stool for him, and he sat beside her.

Arian crooned some tune he did not know, but he could feel power being used. She reached her other hand out to him, and he took it. He glanced around. The other dead elf, the one he did not know, had also been dressed in a white robe. Elves were still working over the Lady's body, wrapping her in silvery lace with fresh flowers woven through it.

Arian's song stopped. He glanced at her. "I knew him so little," she said. "When he quit coming . . . the years passed, and I was busy, and then my mother died. I did not even know all of his name or all of mine. Or why I was not told before. He said he would tell me later."

"I'm sorry," Kieri said. He could think of nothing else to say.

"At least I had him when I did. More than you had of your parents." She drew a deep breath and faced him squarely. "I sent one of my Squires to Lady Tolmaric, when I found she was not in the palace."

"That was well done," Kieri said. Tolmaric's contorted form, now sewn into a shroud, lay against one wall of the salle. "She wanted to see him. I convinced her to go back and sent servants with her as well."

"What will you do for her?"

"Find out if they have a good steward, and if not, find her one. Make sure she has land to plant."

Arian was looking at her father's face again. "I cannot believe he is utterly gone, that there is no place for their spirit to dwell. They are so alive when they are alive—"

"We are not like you, lady," Amrothlin said. Kieri had not heard him come in. Amrothlin looked at Kieri. "It is time to return them."

"At night? Will you not wait until dawn?"

"No. In our custom, as soon as it may be, it must be. For the sorrow of their violent deaths, we clothe in white, but still it must be swift, the return to the taig. And—lord king—I know I said yes when you suggested they be laid on the mound in the King's Grove, but—but that is not right."

Kieri's memory of Midwinter night came to him again. "You fear what is below," he said.

"She deserves better," Amrothlin said, not answering directly. "If not the high mountain she loved, then a glade she loved almost as well. Two days' journey, carrying her without the aid of the elvenhome, and a day and night of singing, and two days' return. I swear to you, lord king, I will return here in five days, six at the most, if you permit."

Kieri nodded. He had many questions for Amrothlin, but this was not the time to press them. "What of the others?" he asked.

"We would take them there as well, but if the queen wishes—if the king wishes—the queen's father could be laid straight nearer."

Arian shook her head. "My father died trying to save the Lady's life; he should lie where she lies."

Amrothlin bowed deeply. "Arian daughter of Dameroth, you are a daughter of the taig as well. I thank you. Forgive me for my earlier discourtesy."

Arian nodded without answering, stroked her father's face one more time, and folded her hands in her lap.

"Very well," Kieri said. "Know that you take my sorrow as companion—for the Lady's death and for the deaths of these others.

Will you at least tell me the name of this one?" He gestured to the other elf. "I want to honor them properly when I tell of this day."

"Silwarthin," Amrothlin said. "I have known him since my own childhood."

"I am sorry," Kieri said. He could not think of more to say that would not diminish the moment.

He and Arian rose and moved back as more elves came into the salle carrying frames of branch and vine. Though Amrothlin said the elvenhome had passed away, a similar silvery light brightened around them as they lifted the bodies onto these biers and then the biers onto their shoulders. Four each carried Dameroth and Silwarthin, and eight carried the Lady, with more elves before and behind. Kieri and Arian followed this procession out of the salle and across the palace courtyard to the gates and there halted, seeing the glow of it vanish into the trees across the way.

Now only Tolmaric's body remained in the salle, a single King's Squire keeping watch. "Now," Arian said, facing him, "you will take off that mail and let us see if indeed you have no wound."

"It's only a bruise—"

"We do not know that, and you have looked more exhausted every moment. I insist."

Kieri looked at the King's Squire watching over Tolmaric's body. "I will send another to relieve you," he said. "I must go." The stench of blood on his clothes sickened him suddenly.

"Of course, sir king."

He gave orders on the way through the palace for the nightlong vigil by Tolmaric's body and asked after his Squires. The physicians and Kuakkgani were still with them, he was told.

"Send one to the king's quarters," Arian said to the steward.

"Arian—"

"No, Kieri. We have had treachery and mortal danger in this palace; I take no chances with the king's life."

"Your baths are ready," the steward said. "And a hot meal will be sent to your chamber, sir king—or would the queen wish to eat in her own?"

"With the king," Arian said. She leaned a little on his arm as they went.

Upstairs, Kieri found Aliam and more Squires waiting for him.

"Estil will be with the queen," Aliam said. "And we have plenty of Squires; no assassin will get past all of us."

Kieri grinned in spite of his fatigue. He hung his sword on its rack beside the bed, then Squires helped him off with the blood-stiffened clothes and the mail. He could feel that his arming shirt had stuck to his shoulder.

"That's a notable bruise," Aliam said. "And you've bled, too. Might have cracked a bone as well. I'm surprised the padding didn't protect you better."

"I could fight, once I caught my breath." Kieri frowned, trying to remember every detail of the day, but his head felt stuffed with old wool.

Aliam chuckled. "Kieri, you could fight if you were half dead. Go take your bath; it'll need a poultice and bandage after."

When he was finally bathed, bandaged, and clothed again, he found a meal laid on the table. Arian came across from the queen's chamber. "So you were wounded after all," she said. She looked pale, violet shadows around her eyes, and Kieri wondered if she'd also been hit. "I didn't have any breaks in my skin," she said. "But you— are you sure that poultice is enough? Remember what the Kuakgan said."

Kieri nodded without speaking, though he didn't remember; his concerns about the Lady's death, about Amrothlin, filled his mind now. He felt almost too weary to eat. As often with injuries, his shoulder hurt more now than it had when it was hit; the poultice stung, and the bandage itched.

"At least we found out about the poison," Arian said after her first swallows of soup. "That pin-pig—"

Kieri put down his fork. "The Kuakkgani," he said.

"What about them?"

Kieri told her about his conversation with the Kuakgan. "I was supposed to meet with them—I forgot. You know what I told you about Midwinter. I think they should visit the ossuary and perhaps the mound in the King's Grove as well."

"Perhaps. But not tonight. Tonight they need to see to your wound; I'm not satisfied—"

Kieri shook his head but then agreed. He felt more than simply tired, he realized, and the Kuakgan had said—something—about iynisin and injuries. Was it fever coming on? Had the iynisin poisoned him, or was this an effect of the poison they had all eaten at the feasts?

When the Kuakgan Elmholt arrived, he looked keenly at Kieri. "You *are* injured, king—I thought you said the blood was not yours."

"I thought it was only a bruise."

"I will be back shortly," Elmholt said, and left as swiftly and silently as he had come.

Arian looked at Kieri with wide eyes. "What do you think?"

"I don't know," Kieri said. He shifted in his chair, trying to find a comfortable position. Then Elmholt returned, his hands full of greenery, both the other Kuakkgani at his heels.

"It's been poulticed," Kieri said, eyeing the greens.

"That is well," Elmholt said. "But as I said before, we have some skills your physicians are not like to have, and with the Lady's death no elves are here to aid. Would you permit?"

"Yes," Arian said before Kieri could say anything.

"But what about my Squires who were wounded worse than this?" Kieri asked.

"We spoke to the physicians, sir king, but it was too late for one; the other we hope will live, and we will continue to give aid."

Kieri nodded to the Squires who had come in with the Kuakkgani and tried to stand, but his knees trembled and he had to lean on the table. Arian slid her arm around him while his Squires helped him shed the robe and the shirt under it.

"You should lie down," Elmholt said.

He lay facedown on his bed; Elmholt cut the bandages and lifted the poultice. "This poultice was well done," Elmholt said, "but not enough. Look: the poultice is black, the leaves withered. That is kuaknomi evil the poultice drew out." Kieri felt the poultice being pulled from his shoulder.

Kieri turned his head; Elmholt showed him what looked like rain-rotted leaves. "How?" he asked. "The kuaknom's blade did not touch my skin—the mail held—the arming shirt wasn't ripped."

"It's full of holes now," one of the Squires said from across the room. "And they're spreading."

"The shirt was once alive," the Kuakgan said. "Wool, linen, silk— all were once alive, and on anything alive the touch of a kuaknom's finger or blade or curse has deadly power. Once you bled, your blood was tainted by that same curse. If it is not properly treated, you would slowly wither and die."

"Can you heal—?" Arian began.

"Yes. This wound is not deep, and it has not been that long. Pear- wind, you know what herbs we need: gather a good amount."

Kieri heard Arian give the orders for a basin, for hot water, her voice steady. He thought of the blood on her clothes—was she in danger? He tried to ask; she put her hand over his. "My clothes were riddled with holes like yours," she said, "but I had not so much as a scratch." She took her hand away and moved back as the Kuakkgani went to work.

He felt peculiar lying there and doing nothing, but he found it hard to summon the energy to speak. He could not feel whatever the Kuakkgani were doing to his back and shoulder. Shadows crowded his mind, as they had at Midwinter, visions of death and dissolution. Then Arian's living face appeared in his sight, and her warm live hand touched his face, stroked his forehead. As before, he clung to her—the hope of her and the reality of her. A sharp, clean smell came to his nostrils, the scent of a forest in winter, firs and spruce and pine. Some errant current of thought wandered from firs to Paksenarrion— from Three Firs, he remembered—and he remembered how she had healed him . . . after a Kuakgan healed her.

The dark shadows and portents faded, replaced by visions of a crackling fire, Arian's face, Paksenarrion's face, and the sound of humming. Humming? He felt his body now, felt the bones within, the blood running through his veins, his heart steadily beating, the air moving in and out of his lungs. The humming seemed to be within and without, and his awareness of himself moved outward through sinew and muscle to his skin. Now he could feel the pressure of hands on his shoulders and a sensation rather like the direct touch of the sun on a spring day.

"That's better," a voice said. Aliam, he thought.

Kieri opened his eyes. The familiar coverlet, a slice of vision that included Arian's face. He tried to smile at her and speak. She laid a finger on his lips. The feeling of sunlight went away; he felt a sudden chill on his shoulder, dampness exposed to the air. Quickly, something warm replaced it, almost too hot for comfort. He watched Arian; her gaze shifted to someone above him, someone he could not see without turning over. He had no desire to turn over, though he felt stronger and more awake every moment.

Finally the humming died away. He felt no pain.

"Help him rise," a woman's voice said. Larchwind, he remembered after a moment. He tried to push himself up; Arian's arm slid under him, helped, as did Larchwind herself. Larchwind leaned close. "I must see his eyes," she said; someone brought a candle close. Then she moved back. "His eyes are clear; the kuaknomi poison never reached his center," she said to the others. Then, to him, "You must drink this infusion tonight and thrice a day for two hands of days. I have already told your servants to burn every garment you and the queen wore in that room. None can hold your weapons, but they must be cleaned again as well, ritually cleaned."

Kieri nodded. He took the cup she handed him and drained the bitter brew; his mouth tingled when he had finished. "I feel well," he said to her. "Need I stay in bed?"

"No," she said. "Though as it is after the turn of night, sleep would not harm you. Tomorrow is soon enough to talk about this."

"Thank you," Kieri said. It was not enough, but all he could think to say. She smiled.

"One of us will be nearby, and the queen will stay with you. Rest well, king, and rejoice in the morning to come." With that, she took the cup and turned away. Others in the room—Aliam, Dorrin Verrakai, his Squires including Garris, the steward, the other Kuakkgani—filed out by ones and twos. At last he and Arian were alone.

"They burned my clothes, too," she said. "And those of the Squires with you, and Dorrin's. The touch of iynisin blood, even after death, could carry the taint. I did not know that. We are all to drink the same draft—I've already had one cupful—because you and I and Dorrin wore our bloody clothes so long and touched that thing's blood with bare hands, cleaning our blades." She yawned. "I am tired, Kieri. Too much happened today."

"I wonder if it was an iynisin who brought the poison that killed the unborn," Kieri said. He sat up, swung his legs over the side of the bed, and stood. He felt perfectly steady. He snuffed the candles still burning, all but one. Together they turned down the covers. Arian put off her overrobe and climbed into the bed. Kieri followed. "I don't think I even told you how glad I was to see you and Dorrin come rushing in, swords out," he said. "That was a bold stroke. I should perhaps scold you for outpacing your Squires, but on the whole—you saved my life, beloved."

"I was very scared and very angry," Arian said.

"They often go together," Kieri said. He blew out the last candle. "But at this moment I am neither scared nor angry. Quite the contrary."

Next morning, he woke feeling perfectly well, but—mindful of the Kuakgan's warning—he drank down his medicinal draft before breakfast. He asked Elmholt if he could carry his sword as usual, and the Kuakgan handed him a jug of sharp-smelling stuff.

"If there's any hint of kuaknomi blood or taint, this will cleanse it. I heard from others that both sword and dagger might have some healing properties, so this should take care of any residue."

"Thank you," Kieri said. "What about my mail?"

"Kuaknomi have no power over metals," Elmholt said. "Only the blood on it could make it dangerous. Nonetheless, it must be dipped in the same infusion of herbs you drank and then pulled through a fire. The carpet and any other cloth or leather that touched the kuaknomi or its blood must be discarded entire. Your steward is even now removing the carpets in the entrance hall so that the one in your office can be removed without risking any contamination of others. Only one chair need be burned."

"You wanted to visit the ossuary," Kieri said, changing the subject. "I agree you should, but first I must tell you what happened at Midwinter." He told the tale; Elmholt listened with full attention. "I am sure there's something under the King's Mound, something human:

bones, I suspect, dead of some treachery. But I am not sure what to do. Be wary. I would not have you trapped in death."

Elmholt chuckled. "Lord king, we are as trees, whose roots extend beneath the ground. It is not death to us there, but the source of nourishment and connection. We will ask the trees what is there and whether Kuakkgani can help. I suspect, though, that as you are both king and half-elven, you are the one to cleanse any evil there. Do you think kuaknomi were involved?"

"I have no idea. The Lady held it to be a sacred place; the Oath-stone there is where we both swore oaths and where I was crowned. If kuaknomi had done whatever was done, would that invalidate the oaths?"

"No . . . the lords of all hold all true oaths in their keeping," Elmholt said. "If you swore truly, then your oath holds until you break it. We will seek what answers we can from the taig and the roots of the trees. When we have done that, we will await your convenience." He smiled. "I know that kings are busy men."

"Thank you," Kieri said. Elmholt bowed and left the chamber.

Breakfast was subdued. Kieri felt naked without his mail. He wore his heavy quilted gambeson under his clothes—poor protection against an iynisin's blade—and his heaviest doublet over it, hot as that was on a spring day, and went to the salle to ask Carlion about armorers. There he found Maelis, who reported that Lady Tolmaric was calmer but wanted to know if she could take Sier Tolmaric's body home for burial.

"I must talk to her," Kieri said. "I do not want her leaving without some understanding of what I intend for her and the children. She will need help on the journey, as well. Do you think I should visit there, where the children are, or ask her to come here?"

"Here," Maelis said. "If the children are in the room, she will break down again, and then they will cry."

"Then, since she knows you, it would be better if you were her escort. I will speak to her in Garris's office, mine being unusable at present."

"I heard you were injured after all, sir king," Carlion said. "You must not train today if you were."

Kieri nodded. "I need to ask you for advice on new mail," he said.

"If I face such an enemy again—and I expect I will—I don't want to be left without mail while a damaged or tainted suit is being purified."

"Your father's mail is in the armory," Carlion said. "And other pieces from earlier. It's all kept sound, cleaned regularly. It would be quicker to modify that, I'm thinking, than to have someone make you a new suit."

His father's mail did not fit as well as his own, but he could wear it. When he came back into the palace, he found Lady Tolmaric already there.

He could see the effort she made to stay calm, and she answered his questions about the estate, about the children. Clearly she had been involved in management of the steading; she knew how many farms they had, the harvests of each, and how much land had been lost to the scathefire. Dealing with practical matters like this, she seemed much more competent than she had the day before.

"Much of our steading is swamp forest, you see," she said. "It is large, I know that, but not all can be farmed, and the products of the swamp, valuable as they can be, are scattered and time-consuming to harvest. I would ask, sir king, if you find it in your power to extend our grant, if we might have some higher ground, not just that along the river to the east."

Into Kieri's mind flashed the proposal made by Master-trader Geraint Chalvers. Some of the land he'd proposed for a port overlapped Tolmaric land. "I will certainly recompense you for land lost," he said, "and grant you good land, suitable for farming. But I have a thought—would you be interested in a venture, you and the Crown together?"

"A venture?" Her brows furrowed.

"Master-trader Chalvers, who is now on my Council, suggested digging out a harbor in that swamp and trading directly with the coastal cities and all the way south to Aarenis, as Pargun and Kostandan do. No more need to transport goods by land across Tsaia, paying their tolls. His best estimate of location included some of your land. If he is right, a town or even city there would bring income from the trade—and you, as part owner, would have money to improve your new lands."

"I don't know anything about making a harbor."

"Nor do I, but Chalvers seems to. I am not asking an answer now, but only that you consider it."

"If it brought a way to pay for a new house for that family the Pargunese burnt out . . . cattle . . . farm tools . . ."

"Those you will have from the Crown," Kieri said. "But such a project as this could profit us both."

Her back straightened. "I . . . I think it might be a good idea."

"Good. I will talk more to Chalvers. It cannot be done in a day or ten hands of them—perhaps a year or two—but it seemed a good idea to me." He reached out and laid his hand over hers. "Now . . . you can of course take Sier Tolmaric's body to bury in your own burial ground, but we have a ground here where he could be laid with all honor, and when his bones are raised, you could take them instead."

"You said he was bad to see. Maelith and Naren told me it's better not to look sometimes. I thought it was my duty." Her eyes filled with tears once more, but she did not break down this time.

"I think not in this case," Kieri said.

"Does he look . . . normal . . . in the shroud?"

"No," Kieri said. "And that, besides the honor due him, is another reason I offer the royal burying ground, to prevent distress to your people."

"The children," she said. "Do you think they would notice?"

"We could not lay him straight," Kieri said, hoping such bluntness would not start another storm of emotion.

Her lips trembled, but she did not sob. "Then . . . to spare the children . . . lord king, you are so gracious . . . let him be laid in the ground here, and maybe Alyanya will mend his bones."

"That is my hope as well," Kieri said.

"I will dream badly," she said, "if I do not at least see him in his shroud. Let it be as unnatural as you say, for me—I am a plain woman—it is better to know than to imagine."

"Very well," Kieri said. "Come with me, then."

She stared a long time at the crooked bundle, lips pressed tight together. "He was a good man," she said finally. "A good man to me, a good father to our children, a good Sier to our people."

"He was indeed a good man," Kieri said. "I honor him."

She bent her head and turned away. "Tomorrow?" she said.

"Yes, tomorrow. I will send for you when all is prepared."

"Thank you, my lord."

Kieri found the Kuakkgani in the rose garden, humming with the bees. Pearwind, he saw, was having a lesson in controlling the flow of springtide, letting her staff leaf out and then restraining it. Kieri found the sight disturbing. They stood up when Kieri appeared, but he waved them back to their seats and sat down on a bench himself.

"You have told the others what I told you?" he asked.

"Yes," Elmholt said. "And we have learned a little that may help you."

"You were correct that treachery was done there," Larchwind said. "The oldest bones in the ossuary itself had no memory of it, but the roots we could feel beyond the ossuary did . . . and elves had a part in that treachery. They raised the mound to hide all evidence: underneath is a place sacred to old humans, who lived there before the magelords came from the south. The Oathstone was theirs first. Against elven magery they had no power but endurance, even in death."

"What must I do?" Kieri asked. "Do they desire my death?"

"No, sir king. They desire to be restored to their rightful place. We do not know how you will accomplish that, but we know it should be done at Midsummer. Perhaps the usual rites there, without the Lady present, will be sufficient."

"The rites . . . I do not know all the rites without her," Kieri said. "She and I sang together."

"And the power of her singing and the elvenhome silenced them. Without her, they may be able to speak to you."

"I will do what I can," Kieri said.

"No one can do more," Elmholt said. "We will stay another few days, if it please you, to be sure your Squire continues to mend."

"You are welcome," Kieri said.

In the palace, the work of cleaning his study continued; furniture not damaged by iynisin touch or blood had been moved to another room; the carpet was gone, and Kieri met servants carrying away buckets of water from cleaning every speck of blood from walls and floor. The floor, patterned in squares of green and gray stone, with a central design of more colors in a complicated interlacing pattern, had been impervious to iynisin blood that leaked through the carpet. Kieri looked at the design he'd never seen, since it had been covered by carpet. It teased his gaze, almost as if it moved, forcing his eye to follow.

Elven, no doubt. Annoying, in the way it compelled the gaze; no wonder someone had chosen to cover it with a carpet. He turned to his Squires—this day, Jostin and Harin. "Do either of you know what this pattern is? Some symbol sacred to elves, maybe?"

"No, sir king," Harin said. "I have no elven blood. Maybe one of the part-elves would know."

"Nor I, sir king," Jostin said.

"It may be in the palace records," Kieri said. "I'll ask the steward."

The steward, Garris told him, had gone out with the party that had cut up and removed the carpet for burning. Kieri went out into the courtyard. A column of smoke led him to the site.

"Sir king!" the steward said. "As you see, we have been careful, as the Kuakkgani told us." He pointed to a stack of turves set well to one side.

"You have indeed," Kieri said. "Tell me, do you know anything of the history of the stone floor in that room?"

"No, sir king. That carpet has never been lifted for cleaning in my lifetime; it has always seemed unnaturally clean. There was not even dust beneath it when we picked it up this time. I supposed the elves who made the carpet had bespelled it so."

"I expect they did," Kieri said. "To me, the pattern underneath— that one in the middle—looks elven as well. Yet as far as we know, the palace was built for humans, the first of the human kings. Is there any carpet that could cover it? I will find it distracting when I move back in there."

The steward shook his head. "No, sir king. We have no elven

carpets in storage, I suppose because they never needed to be taken up for cleaning. We have smaller rush-mat carpets I could put down, but nothing as large as this one—" He tipped his head toward the burning pile.

"That will do, as long as it covers that central design," Kieri said. "In the hot weather to come, the stone floor will be cooler anyway."

"You don't think that pattern had meaning, do you?"

"I don't know," Kieri said. "I know elves use patterns for various things, but I don't know what they are. Orlith was supposed to teach me that when I was advanced enough, he said."

"Do you want me to come back with you and have a mat put over that one right away?"

"No," Kieri said. "It's not that urgent. When you're through here, or even tomorrow, will be soon enough."

He walked back to the palace, thinking. A pattern laid down by elves. And then covered by elves with a carpet. Why would they lay such a pattern in a palace meant for humans? And why cover it up? It must be connected in some way with the joint rulers, but how?

He found something to write with and went back to his office. Before another mat or rug covered it, he wanted a record of that pattern. Someone might know what it was.

He found it hard to draw. As his eye followed the lines and colors to mark them down, he felt a pull from the pattern, and he could not remember, except in the briefest glances, how the pattern fit together. Even the squares of green and gray that had seemed so flat and simple before now seemed to move, as if flowing down into the central pattern.

How, he wondered, did the elves see such a pattern? Did it move, for them, or did it stay still? He did not hear Arian approaching until she spoke his name.

"Kieri—what are you doing?"

"Trying to draw that pattern on the floor," he said. "I think it means something, but I don't know what. And it seems to shift about." He turned to look up at her; her expression showed surprise, even shock. "Do you know what it is?"

"I think that's the same pattern I saw in that underground place where the Lady was trapped," Arian said. "I had to mend it so that she and the others could come out. That one had the power to allow movement." She took a step forward and stared at it. "Does it suggest that to you?"

"Other than an urge to go stand on it and turn certain ways, no," Kieri said. "Is that what you feel?"

"Yes. I think this must be the same. The Lady's power could take her anywhere from that one. If we had her power, we could probably go to Vérella or Fin Panir or anywhere."

Kieri frowned, thinking. "I wonder if these mark destinations as well as origins. I did not see it, but when I went to Fin Panir to speak for Paks, I heard that the expedition to the far west had returned by means of some ancient elven pattern. They arrived in the High Lord's Hall there to find a pattern graven in the stone like the one they'd started from. Their archives said Luap used it to help the magelords in Fintha escape to the west."

"So if we tried this, there is no certainty where we would arrive?"

"You weren't thinking of trying it, were you?"

"No-o. But should we not know where the other end is or if this can be used by someone . . . ?" She looked at Kieri; when their gazes met, uncertainty faded from her eyes.

"The Lady," they both said. Arian nodded.

"She came here whenever she willed it," Kieri said. "I always thought the elvenhome brought her, but the elvenhome emanated from her: she brought it, as well. And the iynisin—was it using the pattern?"

"Yes," Arian said. "Unless it focused on the Lady herself and her power. Elves must have put the carpet here to hide the pattern from human eyes. I never sensed anything strange in this room until now, but elves must have been able to feel that pattern even when it was covered."

"Or perhaps only the Lady," Kieri said. "Perhaps other elves need to see or touch it." He stood, shaking his head. "We don't know enough. It's been like this since I came—what I did not know brought great harm, and what I do not know now might bring more. I will press Amrothlin when he returns and make clear to him—I hope—how dangerous these secrets are."

"Indeed," Arian said.

He looked around. "I wonder if there are more such patterns, though I cannot imagine the Lady needing to arrive directly in every room and outbuilding. But before I have a mat put over this, can you draw the pattern, do you think, without looking at it?"

"Yes," Arian said. "Although if it is a pattern of power, it might have the same force on paper."

"We must chance that," Kieri said. "Or you can leave a break in some of the lines—that might be enough to make it useless. We need a record of it in the palace archives." He touched her shoulder. "You came with a purpose—what was it?"

"That journey to the Tsaian court," Arian said. "Duke Mahieran is anxious to leave soon; he says he will have stretched his king's patience as far as it will go, being here with his younger son so long. Do you still want me to go, or have these other happenings changed your mind? It would be half-summer before I could return, and we both want a child."

"And you are still recovering from losing our child," Kieri said. "Are you sure you're strong enough after the poisoning? We should not rush—either the child or the visit—if you are not."

"I'm sure," Arian said. "I talked to Estil Halveric and a midwife who has cared for other half-elven. They said it was not too soon if I truly wished it. And I do; the taig agrees." She looked down. "Estil reminded me . . . you lost children before, as well as your . . . as Tammarion. I have been thinking only of my own feelings . . ."

"We both grieve," Kieri said. He closed his eyes a moment, those two child faces floating clear in his memory, then fading again. "And we will both rejoice when our child is born. Whenever that is. I trust Estil's experience and a midwife's, but—this was poison."

She nodded. "Now is a safe time—we know there is no poison here right now. And that is why I want to try and then travel at once, while I can. If I were carrying a child at this moment, I would leave today, before that traitor or another brought more poison or something else . . ." Her voice trailed away, then strengthened again. "I don't want to be away from you—but I don't want to be here, waiting, uncertain—"

"You won't stay away the whole time!" Kieri stared at her.

"No. No, my love, I will not. But long enough to—perhaps— convince a traitor that the chance has passed."

"I will talk to Sonder, then," Kieri said. "Your visit can certainly be delayed until we engender another child. Sonder will understand that and can explain it to Mikeli if he returns immediately. But perhaps he would stay until you could travel if Dorrin and Beclan left. I'm sure she's anxious to get back to her steading, and it's the king's command that he and Beclan have little contact that makes him anxious to leave. It should not take us long . . ." He looked at her, and she looked back at him. They both grinned, though he saw the glitter of tears in her eyes.

CHAPTER THREE

North Marches, Tsaia

"Welcome home, my lord."

Jandelir Arcolin, Count of the North Marches, nodded his thanks. His face was near-frozen with riding into the north wind. It bit even through the layers of wool.

He dismounted, handed his horse over to the grooms, and stamped, banging his hands together until he could move his fingers. The courtyard was almost empty; he had seen the recruits drilling far out on the plain as he rode up from Duke's East. At least here, the rest of the stronghold broke the wind's force, and he could look forward to a hot bath soon.

"Any news?" he asked one of the servants.

"Not up here, my lord. There's a message for you from the Duke—I mean King Kieri, my lord, sorry." More than a year since Kieri had left on his last journey, and he was still "the Duke" to most here in the north. Probably always would be. "Come across country by Lyonyan courier, not ours. He's gone these hand of days."

What could be important enough for Kieri to send his own courier so far? Rumor in Vérella had it that Kieri had pledged to one of his Squires at Midwinter, but Mikeli had said nothing about it. An unmarried king, as he and Mikeli both knew, would collect gossip and rumor. But maybe it had been true. He couldn't himself see Kieri courting one of his Squires: not the man who had been so careful to distance himself from his troops. Except for Tammarion, of course, but that was only the once.

Inside the officers' courtyard, his household staff waited, and soon he was warm, clean, and refreshed by two mugs of sib and a hot meal. Now for work.

The green velvet sack with the gold-embroidered arms of Lyonya lay alone in the center of his desk; lesser messages were stacked to one side, a courteous gap between them and the royal missive.

Arcolin opened the sack. A letter from Kieri, in his own hand, and a wedding invitation in multicolored inks, clearly the work of a palace scribe. He read the letter first, brow a little contracted. Kieri was marrying one of his Squires but no youngster—she was his age, half-elven like Kieri but on her father's side, not her mother's. Dark-haired, dark-eyed, a Knight of Falk . . . Arcolin nodded slowly. He understood: a king must wed and get heirs. So should he himself. A king must consider a queen differently than a light-of-love. And yet . . . Arcolin's gaze blurred as he thought of Kieri's first marriage. That had been love, combined with character. Would his second be only character?

He looked at the next passage in the letter.

Do not fear, old friend, that this marriage is mere statecraft. For beyond my hopes, Arian has true affection for me, and I for her. I have not been so happy for a very long time.

Well. If it was not too late for Kieri . . . perhaps it was not too late for him. Though where he'd find a wife, what with spending near-half his time in Aarenis or on the road and the rest up here in a fort, he did not know.

The wedding, he saw as he worked his way through the fancy scrolls in scarlet, gold, green, blue, and silver, was to be on the Spring Evener. Arcolin shook his head. He wanted to go, but Kieri knew the schedule he must keep to get his troops to Aarenis on time. Four hands of days to and from Chaya he simply could not afford.

The other messages were routine. Marshals of the two granges on his domain, reporting on the membership and training schedule of each. Captain Valichi, reminding him that he intended to retire as soon as the troops left for Aarenis, reporting that the neighboring

Count Halar had agreed to let Fox Company recruit in his domain and shared more gossip about Dorrin Verrakai. Mayors of Duke's East and Duke's West, their usual reports, including—from Duke's West— a request for one more Count's Court to hear a case that had arisen while he'd been in Vérella. Best to get that over before he took the troops south.

Before the afternoon was over, the gnome estvin arrived seeking audience.

"It is that the stone is welcome," he said.

"It is large enough?" Arcolin asked.

"It is," the estvin said. "And the lord's king? It is that the king agreed?"

"Yes," Arcolin said. "By Gird's Code, as I said." He paused, wondering whether he should mention the dragon's appearance at court. But why not tell the estvin something that concerned the gnomes? "Before I came," he said, "the dragon visited the king."

The estvin paled. "Dragon said to king?"

"That the land the dragon claimed must be released. The king agreed—"

The estvin muttered something Arcolin could not understand.

"And the king agreed to the grant of those hills to you and yours forever," Arcolin said. "You will be safe, in your own home, I hope. Did my steward give you the food I promised?"

"Yes, lord," the estvin said. "It is that in . . . in new stone kapristi have no need of as much. By midsummer at earliest will need no more from our lord."

Arcolin started to say he did not grudge their need and was not their lord now that they had moved out, but the estvin's expression was set. Better not to argue now, he thought. "You will have food until you say you need it not," he said. "Do not, I beg you, go hungry. I want you to prosper and grow."

"It is that my lord is . . . is beyond the Law," the estvin said.

"Beyond—have I broken the Law?" Arcolin asked. To a gnome nothing was more serious than their Law—as far as they were concerned, the only law that mattered, rigid and immutable.

"No! Not to break. My lord is . . . is . . . more fair than fair."

"It is Gird's command," Arcolin said, having found that a useful phrase before in dealing with the gnomes' intent to exact precise trade between them.

"Yes, my lord," the estvin said, bowing. "Will my lord come with me to the cellars to see if they are now acceptable?"

Acceptable? What could the estvin mean? Arcolin went with him into the space the gnomes had occupied. He had assumed they'd leave it clean, but he had not imagined that they would leave it polished, plastered, and whitewashed as well. The stones of the floor gleamed; a little frieze of dark red foxheads ran around the top of the white-washed walls. When had they had time to do this?

"It is pleasing?" the estvin asked.

"It is very pleasing," Arcolin said.

Back upstairs, he explained that he would be gone almost a half-year on campaign, not to return until after Autumn Court. "For whatever you need, ask Captain Arneson or the steward. They have my orders to supply you."

The estvin bowed again. "My lord goes to serve the king?"

"To fulfill a contract made with Foss Council," Arcolin said. "And to obey the orders of my king that I find out more about the danger to the South. A very bad man seeks to gain power he should not. I will be sending reports to the king during the summer and at least one or two all the way here, to Captain Arneson. If you wish to send me word of your welfare or any problem, you can do so using the same couriers. Only tell Captain Arneson."

"It is not to write language of men," the estvin said. "It is that my lord reads kapristi writing?"

"Um . . . no, my pardon. I will endeavor to learn," Arcolin said. "But Captain Arneson or one of the scribes here would write down your words if you spoke to him."

The estvin bowed again. "If my lord permits, it is time for this one to return."

"Of course," Arcolin said. "I do not know yet the exact day I will leave, but it will not be for another three hands of days at least. I hope you will come again before then."

"As my lord says," the estvin said. With a last bow he withdrew.

In the next days, Arcolin worked through all the reports, held

Count's Court for both Duke's East and West, conferred with Captain Arneson on the readiness of the recruits, and discussed with him and with those who had been on recruiting duty before the likely intake for the coming year.

"The king wants to be sure we have enough troops in case of invasion," Arcolin said. "I know the Marshals are keeping the civilians and retired in at least basic training, but I'd like to see larger recruit cohorts even than Kieri had. We have the space, and with Foss Council's contract this year I'll have the resources."

"We'll need cloth to replace what the gnomes used," the quartermaster said.

"Already ordered when I was in Vérella," Arcolin said. "You should have it in plenty of time to make the tunics before the new recruits arrive. The weavers said they'd have it on the way by the Evener."

"Thank you, my lord."

"And I have permission from the king to recruit this far afield," Arcolin said, pointing to the map. "Valichi has talked to Count Halar and has permission for me to recruit there. I'm going to leave you an extra recruit team, Captain, to handle the larger numbers. Don't hesitate to release the ones who don't work out, but let's try to retain at least a hundred ten. On the basis of past recruitment, you'll need to start with at least twenty more."

"Yes, my lord," Arneson said.

"I will be short of senior enlisted," Cracolnya said.

"I know. We'll discuss that later."

Cracolnya nodded.

"This year's intake is looking good," Arcolin said to Arneson. "Are there any you have doubts of now?"

"Barring serious injury in the coming days, no, my lord. We'll be ready to march when you give the word."

On that final morning, the new troop—now in Fox Company maroon tunics, newly sworn to Arcolin—marched out to the tune of "Gird at Greenfields," with the yeomen of the nearest grange arrayed beside the road singing with them. Another change, Arcolin thought as he rode in the lead, persuading his chestnut not to caper about like a colt. In Kieri's latter days, there'd been no notice taken when the recruits left the stronghold for the south.

He ticked off in his mind all he had accomplished—he had already written it down back at the stronghold, but it made a goodly recital. He hoped he would not be delayed long in Vérella, though he was eager to find out what had happened with Beclan Mahieran. Somewhat to his surprise, Count Halar met him at the border of their domains with two of his men-at-arms and a pack mule.

"I'm on my way to Vérella," Halar said. "I wanted to ride with you if I might."

"Of course," Arcolin said.

"I told your Captain Valichi you might recruit on my land."

"Valichi wrote to me; I thank you for that," Arcolin said, hoping the man hadn't changed his mind.

"Wanted to be sure you understood I wasn't just shipping off troublemakers," Halar said.

"I didn't think you would," Arcolin said, though it was common enough for local lords to encourage their wilder youth to enlist in someone else's militia.

Halar cleared his throat. "In fact, I have a son—he's too young this year, but he asked me to ask you—would you consider taking on a squire?"

Arcolin frowned. "You do realize it's not like squiring here in the north. There's real danger. Kieri lost squires to war."

"I know. My father hated him for it, though it wasn't one of his own."

So that was the cause of the former count's enmity. Arcolin wondered if that was all of it.

"Friend of his," Halar said.

"But you would risk your son?"

"Kaim's going to run off and sign on somewhere under a false name if I don't find him some place," Halar said. "He says the training at the grange isn't enough. I'm hoping a year in a real military unit will cure him of his ideas—or make him a good leader if this war the king worries about comes to the north."

"It could," Arcolin said. "And we'll need as much training as we can put into our people." He thought for a long moment. "Would you consider sending him as a junior squire to my recruit captain up at the stronghold? He'd learn how soldiers are trained, but he wouldn't be at as great a risk. Then, if he still wanted to go and you were willing, perhaps next year or the year after . . ."

"I thought Valichi was your recruit captain."

"He was; he's retiring later this spring. Arneson's a veteran from the south, blind in one eye but a good man. Look at this troop—" Arcolin pointed to the cohort first in line.

"I saw. Fairly young, aren't they? How long have they served?"

"They're last year's recruits—well, we still count them as recruits until they've been in battle. It takes almost a year to make a soldier from a raw youth." They rode on a little way, and Arcolin said, "If you're willing, I'll tell Arneson when I next send a courier—you can await his reply."

"Thank you," Halar said. "I—that's very generous of you."

"Not at all," Arcolin said.

"If you permit . . . I could send one of my men to your stronghold now."

"Your son's that eager?" Arcolin said.

"Yes. And his mother's that worried that he'll run off and get himself killed right away."

"Very well," Arcolin said. He signaled a halt, reined off the road, and spoke to Cracolnya. "March them on, Captain; I'll catch up within a half-glass. I'm sending a message north by Count Halar's man."

"Yes, my lord." In a moment, the cohorts were moving again, marching steadily past Arcolin and Count Halar. Arcolin wondered if Halar noticed the older troops in the mixed cohort. He dismounted, rummaged in his saddlebag for writing materials, and scrawled a note to Captain Arneson, suggesting that he take on Count Halar's son as his squire but giving him the choice and bidding him send word either way to Count Halar.

Halar's man saluted and rode off at a brisk pace. Arcolin mounted, and he and Halar caught up with the troop. "You should have an answer by the time you're back from the city," he said. "And if he goes, he should have no more than two mounts and clothes he can work in. We're not fancy up there."

Halar nodded. "Kaim's not one for fine clothes and dances. I'll say this for him, father as I am: he works and doesn't quit once he's started a task."

"Sounds as if he'll suit," Arcolin said.

Once in Vérella, Arcolin reported to the palace while the recruits marched on through the city and out onto the south road to wait for him.

At the palace he was quickly immersed in all that had happened with Beclan Mahieran.

"And he's now Duke Verrakai's kirgan," the servant leading him to the king's study said.

"Count Arcolin," the king said. "Welcome. You're on your way south?"

"Yes, sir king. If possible, I should continue on today. It's best not to overnight a cohort of inexperienced troops next to a city."

"Understood. Are the gnomes well settled?"

"Yes. And as the dragon promised, we've had no difficulty with Pargunese to the east. I've asked my recruit captain to enlarge the recruit cohort this year—"

"Excellent," the king said. He shuffled some papers on his desk, then looked up. "I must thank you, Count Arcolin, for your advice in the matter of my cousin Beclan. Even though it did not turn out as I hoped—your advice was sound. He is not invaded, but after the High Marshal's relic proved that, we—I—chose to use him as bait for those who might hope he was. It was a bad decision, and many died as a result. In short . . . he has some mage powers, and it was necessary to alienate him from the royal family. He is now with Duke Verrakai, adopted by her as her heir."

"I gathered something like that from the page who brought me," Arcolin said.

"I cannot stop that gossip," the king said. "It had to be publicly done to preserve the Crown. With my aunt Celbrin in house arrest now, there's less new gossip about Duke Verrakai; I'm hoping the Duke will be more accepted. You should know that although I'm still not comfortable with her magery, I chose to trust her with my cousin.

And she is still Constable for this realm and will be until . . . unless . . ."

Arcolin said nothing, waiting the king out.

"It is possible," the king said, "that the regalia she found and gave to me may create such a danger for this realm that it must be taken away. And if so, she is the only one who can move it. It answers to her will, not mine or the High Marshal's or even a paladin's."

"I think," Arcolin said carefully, "that she will not go until you command her, sir king."

"You may be right. In that case, I hope I choose the right time." The king sighed. "You must be on your way; you know what I want from you in the South. Go with Gird and send me word as you can."

"Yes, sir king." Arcolin bowed and withdrew.

Within the hour he had ridden through the city and out the south gate, and spotted his troops ahead, having their noon meal under Cracolnya's watchful eye. Cracolnya saluted. "Leave now, my lord?"

"No. I didn't eat in the palace. Any extras?"

Cracolnya grinned. "I thought you might miss lunch. Ham or beef?"

"Beef," Arcolin said. Cracolnya handed him a fat beef roll, and he ate it standing up beside his mount. They were on the way shortly, this time with Cracolnya's cohort in front.

The rest of the trip south, through alternation of watery spring sunshine and miserable cold rain, as the days lengthened and the Dwarfmounts loomed ever higher, Arcolin and Cracolnya discussed the Company, the situation in Tsaia, what might have happened in Aarenis over the winter, and made plans for every contingency they could imagine. Behind them the two cohorts marched along, the novices learning from Cracolnya's veterans how best to keep themselves comfortable in overnight bivouacs. And not to dice with veterans.

"Not," Cracolnya said one day at a midday halt, as they leaned on a rail fence together, "that we won't be beaten on the head by something we never thought of."

"True enough," Arcolin said, though he privately thought Cracolnya put the worst face on things he could. "But I hope not."

CHAPTER FOUR

Chaya

Dorrin Verrakai eyed her squire and heir with a mixture of amusement and severity. "Beclan, you have now been invited to dinner at *how* many Siers' houses?"

"Five," Beclan said. "This would be the sixth. Is that bad, my lord?"

"No, not bad, but—I think it's annoying your—Rothlin." She tried not to say "your brother" or "your father," though she still thought of them that way and was sure Beclan did as well. "The princess fawning on him went back to Falk's Hall; he's had only one invitation I know of."

"He'll have his choice of the girls at court in Tsaia," Beclan said.

Dorrin shook her head. "Not the right attitude, Kirgan Verrakai. He's not your enemy; you should wish him well."

"We're not supposed to be together," Beclan said. "Unless you think I should ask the families who invited me to invite him." That with a challenging look, almost pert.

"Enough," Dorrin said, firmly enough that he wilted. "You know better than that, but you could have made him seem like someone they might invite."

Beclan looked thoughtful. "I didn't think of it. I just thought—"

"How pretty the daughter of the house was and how much the family seemed to approve of you?" Dorrin asked.

"Well . . . yes."

"And I had said you might find the girls here interesting. Yes. Well, you're too young to marry, and I would like to see you a knight. If the king permits, and I think he will, you could go to Falk's Hall. By then, it would be appropriate. Tell me, did any strike your fancy more than another?"

Beclan's enthusiastic descriptions of all the girls made it hard for Dorrin to keep a straight face. Every family had offered an opportunity to chat with the girl or girls, a stroll through a garden, a reason to sing or dance or both. Considering his confinement most of the winter, his lack of experience at court before, and all that had happened, his exuberance seemed inevitable.

"Well, then," Dorrin said when he finished, "you've made friends here, and in the next few years, your choice may settle. Let me know at once; I will need to speak to the family or families."

A knock came at the door; Dorrin said "Enter," and Kieri came into the room. Dorrin and Beclan rose and bowed; Kieri waved them to seats and took one himself.

"I have a request that may seem unfriendly but is not meant that way," he said. "I know that you and Duke Mahieran were to ride together with Arian to Tsaia, but with all that has happened—"

"It would be better if we left separately," Dorrin finished. "Do not think I will misunderstand, sir king." In front of Beclan, she could not be other than formal. "We have stayed longer than planned already, and we do not wish our king annoyed. Arian has told me of a direct way to Verrakai Steading. We might reach one of the rangers' shelters if we left now."

"Not until tomorrow, at least," Kieri said. "Arian wants to speak with you first, and there is something you must see in my office. But if I have your agreement to leave tomorrow or the next day, I may persuade Duke Mahieran to wait a few more days for Arian in case she should be able to travel that soon." His expression shifted for a moment, and Dorrin realized what "able" meant. He went on. "All the preparation for this visit to Tsaia was undone by the poisoning."

"Of course," Dorrin said. She turned to Beclan. "I leave you to supervise the packing, Beclan. It would be best if you sought no last meeting with Rothlin unless Duke Mahieran suggests one."

Beclan nodded. "Yes, my lord. We have said . . . what we could say, anyway."

Dorrin followed Kieri to his office and looked in when he opened the door. "That was a beautiful carpet," she said. "It looks quite different this way . . ." Kieri did not answer, and she walked on into the room, aware of his attention behind her. Something she should see? The floor was the most obvious, but though different, it was all clearly a stone floor, squares of green and gray. She looked around and caught her breath at the pattern of colored stone in its center.

Once having looked, she could not look away from it. Colored bands formed a pattern of curving and intertwining lines, forcing her gaze to move along them. She shut her eyes with an effort; against the darkness, little bright lines now writhed as if attempting the same pattern.

"What *is* that?" she asked. "That pattern . . . I can't watch it." She turned away. When she opened her eyes again, she was facing the end of the room and Kieri's desk. She felt the pattern behind her still pulling at her.

"Arian says it's an elven pattern of power," he said. "She saw one like it in an elven place; they used it to move a distance without walking. She and I feel it, and you do, but the palace servants seem oblivious."

"But this was never an elven place, was it?" Dorrin asked.

"Not that I knew, but I am sure they put it here. They gave the carpet that hid it, a carpet my steward said never needed cleaning."

"And those with magery sense it . . . and use it? Is this how the Lady came and went?"

"So I suspect," Kieri said. "But any other elf could use it, and more to the point, I believe that is how the iynisin came here. I suspect there might be more such patterns under other carpets the elves gave. When Amrothlin comes back, I will ask him that and how to block them short of ripping up the floor."

"What do you think he'll say?"

"I don't know that he will answer at all," Kieri said. "Elves usually don't, but I have to try."

"Why did you want me to see the pattern?"

"The box of regalia—you said it had a pattern that you traced with a finger and the box opened. I thought perhaps this was the same pattern."

Dorrin frowned. "A pattern to open things?"

"Yes. A door . . . or a way . . . ? It might be different, of course. I wish now I had gone into the High Lord's Hall in Fin Panir. The Girdish told me about a pattern there and another in Kolobia; the expedition returned using them. But I was so focused on Paks, I never took the time. Now I need to know: are those patterns like this one? And are there such patterns in Vérella?"

"I hope not," Dorrin said. "Assassins in the palace were bad enough: kuaknomi would be worse. If there are more of these—and in places we do not know, where none recognize them—" Verrakai House? She could not imagine elves as Verrakai allies, but . . . kuaknomi? The palace in Vérella . . . some parts of it were certainly old enough. "You must tell Duke Mahieran about the pattern," she said.

"I intend to," Kieri said. "But what about the pattern on that box?"

"I don't think the pattern on the box is exactly the same," Dorrin said. "But it's complicated; I'd have to see them together to know for sure."

"You can take a drawing of this one with you," Kieri said. "Compare it to that one if you have a chance."

"Anything more?" Dorrin asked.

"No," Kieri said. "Only remember, Dorrin Verrakai, that you have a friend in me whenever you need one."

"Thank you." Dorrin took a deep breath and pushed away the wish that her duty, her lands, and her oath had been in Lyonya. "My oath is to Mikeli now, as you know—"

"Yes. And you have never broken an oath; I know that as well. But I care about your welfare."

"And I about yours," Dorrin said, making her tone as light as she could. She bowed. "I should go to Arian now and then check on my kirgan. He has learned much, but I am not sure packing my court clothes is a task within his competence."

"Go with my blessing," Kieri said.

Dorrin bowed again and walked out of the office without a glance at that pattern.

She found Arian in the rose garden, pacing the paths. More roses had come into bloom, pink and gold and peach, with a blood-red one in a corner. Others were thickly covered with buds.

"Duke Verrakai," said one of Arian's Squires near the garden entrance. Arian turned. Dorrin could see the marks of tears on her face, but otherwise her expression was calm.

"I was thinking of my father," Arian said before Dorrin could say anything. "And of the loss of the elvenhome . . . and our child."

"That would bring tears to anyone's eyes," Dorrin said. "But how are you feeling? Do you really want to travel now?"

"I would if I were bearing," Arian said. She sat down on a bench and gestured for Dorrin to sit with her. "Staying here will not bring my babe alive again or bring back my father or the Lady and the elvenhome. I have seen nothing but Lyonya—that brief visit to your steading hardly counts. I want to learn, and for that I must travel." She leaned back, lifting her face to the mild sun. "But it is a long trip, and being away from Kieri so long means . . . well . . . the nights. And the chance for another child."

"Mmmm." Dorrin put the pieces of conversation together. "I am allowed to know that if the inconvenient Duke Verrakai and her even more inconvenient kirgan can be persuaded to leave, then the queen's Tsaian escort, the noble Duke Mahieran, might be persuaded to stay . . . until the queen has a chance to . . . catch a touch of baby?"

Arian snorted. "You put that bluntly, but yes. I told Kieri I didn't want to leave until I was bearing again, and the timing being what it is . . ." She looked at Dorrin. "It is discourteous to you."

"No, it is both practical and convenient. You know how it is with my kirgan and his natural father and brother. It's become more awkward every day. It strains my oath to my king, as well. I would rather be on my way. I'm sure I'm needed at home, as I suspect Gwenno and Daryan have gotten into some mischief or other."

"You mean that?"

"Arian, one of my besetting faults is that I do say what I mean, whether it is in order or not. Be sure I do mean what I said. I like you;

Kieri is one of my oldest friends. But I have other responsibilities, and Kieri's given me leave. We're riding tomorrow morning."

"I'll miss you," Arian said. Dorrin heard the matter-of-fact tone and knew that Arian had, in spite of everything, made the adjustment to her new role and duties. She hoped the queen would find other friends here, women she could relax with. The Queen's Squires might become such, but that would take time. "And did I ever thank you for what you said when I came to you before?" Arian asked.

"No need," Dorrin said, shaking her head. "We are both Knights of Falk, sisters of the ruby and the blade, who have fought evil together. Come visit me whenever you please. Though I must be at Midsummer Court and probably again at Autumn Court, you would be welcome any time."

"I will not be running from anything when I come," Arian said, grinning. "And I hope you will visit here again."

Dorrin chuckled. "If Beclan had his way, I imagine we would be here many times a year. He has enjoyed the attention from Lyonyan girls, but the boy has much to learn before I approve betrothal. For myself, I like to know I have friends across the border. I will come back, be assured, and not just on Beclan's behalf."

"I hope your problems with your king's court are over," Arian said.

"As do I," Dorrin said. "But I suspect suspicion will not die so quickly. And now, I really should go check on Beclan. He's supposed to be packing for us." Dorrin rose.

"And you fear for that gorgeous formal robe?"

"A little," Dorrin said. "I'll need it later."

"I'll come in with you," Arian said.

Early the next morning, Dorrin checked the girth of her horse as Beclan held the reins.

"A moment!"

She looked at the palace entrance. To her surprise, Duke Mahieran was coming down the steps.

"Yes, my lord?"

"I wanted to say goodbye to your kirgan," he said formally.

"Of course," Dorrin said. She nodded at Beclan, who had been holding her reins. "Go on, Kirgan."

"I will report to the king," Duke Mahieran said, "your correct behavior in this situation. It pleases me and will please the king, who granted us leave to speak, that you have adhered to the restrictions. Your—my kirgan, Rothlin, wishes you to know that he admires how you have borne yourself throughout."

"Thank you," Beclan said. His back straightened a little.

"And you, Duke Verrakai, have . . . have done all you ought for the king's honor and your kirgan's welfare. I wish you well."

"And I, my lord, wish you and your family well, including the king. You should know that we do not ride to Harway, but along a trail the queen told me of—a more direct route to my domain." He would realize by this that there would be no chance meeting along the way no matter when he chose to leave with Rothlin.

"Go with Gird's blessing," Mahieran said.

"I should mention," Dorrin said, "that I propose sending my kirgan to Falk's Hall, where I went, to take his knightly training. Will you inform the king and ask his permission?"

"Of course," Mahieran said. He bowed and turned away.

"Well," Dorrin said to Beclan when Mahieran was out of earshot. "That was . . . not expected. But now we ride. For now, you will take rear guard." She mounted and turned her horse toward the gate without a backward look.

They made good time through the springtime forest. Dorrin used the time to think about the mysterious pattern as well as about the equally mysterious patterns of power operating among the people of the Tsaian court and between the elves and humans in Lyonya. Would Duke Mahieran's current attitude hold, and would it have any effect on lesser lords? While they were both gone, others would have attended the court at the Spring Evener in Vérella. Were any of them but Arcolin on her side? And would the elves decide to help Kieri, or would they disappear somewhere, using those patterns of power?

CHAPTER FIVE

Six days after the elves left with the Lady's body, Amrothlin returned to the palace in Chaya alone. Other elves, he said, were still singing the Lady's life in the deep forest, though a few had come back to Chaya with him.

"But I promised the king I would return swiftly, and here I am," he said to Arian. "Do you know where he is?"

"He rode out with Aliam Halveric this morning," Arian said. He turned away, but she spoke again. "I have my own questions for you about those things my father promised to tell me later. Now he is dead, I will never know from him. You, however, know more of him than I do."

Amrothlin stiffened. "Arian—lady queen—you cannot ask me—"

"I can and I do," she said. "For the good of the realm, for the good of my future children, and for the good of Lyonya's elves, I must know those things I am sure you know."

"You have no right—" His eyes flashed; he looked the same as before the Lady's death, all arrogance. She felt the pressure of his glamour but resisted it.

"I have every right," Arian said. "As queen, as Dameroth's daughter, and as one who was kept in ignorance far too long, I have the right. Your mother quarreled with my father, but that is no reason for you to continue that quarrel with me."

"For her memory—"

"For her memory, explain why she made such tragic mistakes," Arian said, scorn edging her voice. "She admitted one the day I freed you all from captivity underground. You cannot deny that; you were there."

Amrothlin passed a hand over his face as if to wipe that memory away. Tears glittered in his eyes. He nodded slowly. "It may be easier to tell you than the king," he said. "What you choose to tell him after—I suppose you will not promise to withhold anything?"

"Indeed not. It is his responsibility and mine to do the best for Lyonya, both taig and people, human and elven. I will not keep secrets from the king. So: why did the Lady hate my father? And why, if she did, did he stay here? Was he another of her children?"

"No," Amrothlin said. Arian waited. Finally he said, "He stayed because he was commanded to stay. By his father. And I cannot— *must* not—tell you who that is, not without his permission. I have no doubt you will meet him when he learns of your father's death."

"I do not need more mysteries," Arian said. She heard the anger in her voice and tried to soften it. "I need answers, Amrothlin. What was my father's full name? For that matter, what did he name me?"

"His name . . . Damerothlyarthefallibenterdyastinla." He rolled it out quickly, the syllables blending together like water over stones, then looked at her for a reaction.

Arian worked her way through the name even as she understood why he'd not told her before. "He was the son of an elvenlord? Son of someone who had founded an elvenhome?"

"Yes."

"But he sired many children on humans . . . That is not common, is it?"

"No." For an instant, Amrothlin seemed angry, then his expression softened again. "It is not. An elf of his . . . rank . . . would usually mate with elven women, and that is what the Lady thought he would do when he came here. Instead, he dallied with one human after another."

"Why?" Arian asked. She watched Amrothlin flush again and kept her gaze hard on his. However much he might stop and start, she was determined to find out more about her father and more about the Lady from the one person who clearly knew.

In the end it took hours to drag out what still seemed meager information, though far more than she'd known before. Amrothlin, still his mother's loyal son, made every excuse he could for the Lady and laid every fault he could on others. Had Dameroth or his father really intended insult to the Lady by refusing to mate with one of her elves? Or had they some other reason?

Some questions he would not answer at all; to others he professed not to know the answers, but instead went off into long explanations of relationships she did not understand at all.

She did understand that he was still angry with Kieri's mother for her choice of a human partner, for marrying Kieri's father.

"She was the heir and carried the seed of a new elvenhome; to mate with those who cannot possibly engender an elvenhome—to bring forth only children who cannot—is irresponsible, utter folly. If my sister had not chosen to marry a human, she could have revived the Ladysforest when the Lady died. As it is, her decision doomed us."

"I suppose she thought she would outlive Kieri's father and could then mate with an elf," Arian said. "It was her death that doomed the Ladysforest, not her first marriage."

"Chance comes to all," Amrothlin said. "As events proved. Besides, she had sworn she would not. She doubted herself after—" He stopped abruptly. "I cannot say all. Not yet. You might as well know that she was determined to pass it to her son, but *we* knew that was impossible. She quarreled with the Lady about it, insisting she had done so."

Secrets indeed! Arian stared at him, silenced for a time as the new possibilities tumbled through her mind. Kieri's mother had intended him to inherit the elvenhome gift? Why? And how? And . . . most important . . . had she done it or merely talked about it?

"Do you think she—?" Arian began.

Amrothlin interrupted. "It is impossible, I tell you." He ranted on for another half-glass about the impossibility of such things, about Kieri's mother's rebellious foolhardy nature, about the elven estimate of Kieri's own character when he had escaped from bondage and returned to Lyonya an abused waif.

"It would have been better had he died; nothing was left of whatever the prince had been."

Arian's own anger erupted. "Can you say that now, to the king's face? *Nothing* left? He has taig-sense, he has the healing magery—"

"He did not have it then."

"And you did nothing to help him! How could you leave any child to starve in the winter forest, let alone your sister's son? How is *that* creating harmony and song?"

"I did not," Amrothlin said. "I was not the one who found him first. When I heard—" He closed his eyes a moment before going on. "I argued he should be taken to some human settlement, placed there. I went, in fact, to where he had been found, but he was gone."

"And how long did you search?" Arian asked.

"The second time? Until I found bones," Amrothlin said. "You do not understand. The first time—when he was taken—I found his mother's—my sister's—body. We never found his—we thought animals had scattered—we did not know he was taken." He shuddered. "The second time—I found the bones of a child perhaps twelve or thirteen, clearly mangled by animals. I know now they were not his. At the time . . . I thought they were. A half-year, perhaps, later, someone reported a waif taken in by the Halverics. The Lady sent an elf to visit. He was not sure; there was no memory, no sign that this boy was certainly the prince. The boy was thriving in Halveric hands. Later still . . . from the description, it was clear who he was, but all reports had him too broken to be worthy of a throne."

"And yet he is," Arian said. Amrothlin bowed assent.

She started to ask again about her own father but stopped short. If her father had been his father's heir, had inherited the ability to form an elvenhome, could he have transferred that to his half-elf children? To . . . to *her*? No, certainly not. On reflection, an elvenlord would not have sent his only heir so far away and forbidden him to mate with elven women. He had mated with human women precisely to prevent fathering a child who could receive the Lady's elvenhome gift and continue the Lady's domain. He—or his elvenlord father— had wanted it to fail.

She asked instead about the length of time the other elves might be gone before returning to Chaya. What seemed to her like a simple question resulted in another half-glass explanation for uncertainty—and soon he took his leave, saying he would be back in the morning to talk to the king. When Kieri rode in shortly before dark, she told him what Amrothlin had said.

"Elves!" Kieri said, stripping off his gloves and tossing them on the table. "Why can't they just tell us straight out? Why is everything so . . . so complicated?" Then he looked thoughtful. "Orlith . . . could that be why he was murdered?"

"Because if you had such ability, he might know it? That suggests someone else already knew. Unless he found out and told someone else—" Arian frowned.

"Orlith's wounds could have been made by elven arrows. And we never heard more from the Lady about his death."

Arian stared at him, and he stared back. "If he told her—"

"Or any elf. Any elf who was against us—against me—a traitor—" Kieri's voice darkened. "My mother—"

Arian reached out and touched his shoulder. "Kieri—the rest of it—" She told what she now knew about her father, little as it was. "Amrothlin says your mother tried to pass the elvenhome gift to you; I believe that even if *she* did so, my father's choice to mate with human women had no such intent. I cannot imagine he was his father's heir; he simply wanted to prevent the Lady's use of him to engender a child to whom she could transfer it."

"But you don't know for certain she could have done so."

"No. And nor do you, though I think in your case—despite Amrothlin's belief—your mother might have succeeded. If you *could* create an elvenhome, then the elves would feel more at home here."

"I'm not an immortal," Kieri said. "After I die, it would disappear again."

"Not if you could pass on the gift to a child—and that child to another."

"If I have the talent . . . which I don't know and have no idea how to use . . ." He stood and moved around the room. "Another puzzle. Every time we drag an answer out of them, it leads to more questions.

I would like just one thing I'm supposed to do to be straightforward and obvious."

"I can think of something," Arian said, chuckling.

"What—oh. *That*."

She laughed aloud. "Your duty, sir king. Straightforward, obvious, and easily attained. Shall we begin?"

CHAPTER SIX

Vérella

Prince Camwyn Mahieran had witnessed the expulsion of his cousin Beclan from the Mahieran family; his brother, King Mikeli, had explained all the reasons that lay behind that ruling, and he understood them—intellectually. Imaginatively, he felt unexpected sympathy for Beclan, whom he'd never really liked. How could Beclan be a Verrakaien now? Families were families: related by blood. If blood meant anything, how could someone be alienated from that relationship? He posed the question once to the Marshal-Judicar during a lesson on Girdish law, and the look he received from those frosty gray eyes stopped the rest of his protest in his throat. The Marshal-Judicar recited the relevant law and its reasoning, a process that at least relieved Camwyn of the need to discuss the day's assignment, involving the kingdom's economic base in relation to Gird's beliefs about earned and unearned income. Camwyn knew that the royal household was not thought to earn its income, though with Mikeli spending most of every day on the realm's business, why not?

He nodded at the end of the lesson and escaped with relief to a session with the royal armsmaster. He was finally learning to use a real sword—real, that is, in being a longsword almost as long as his brother's. He had grown much taller in the past year—an earlier growth spurt than Mikeli's—and he lacked but a few fingerwidths of his brother's height.

The armsmaster greeted him with the familiar scowl. "What did you do to have the Marshal-Judicar hold you beyond your time?"

"Asked him a question, sir," Camwyn said. "He wished to make sure I understood it fully."

"And do you?"

"Yes, sir," Camwyn said, thinking meanwhile that understanding did not mean agreement.

"Well, let's see if you understand this." The armsmaster handed him.a hauk, not the blade he'd used in the last two practice sessions. "Do you know why?"

"No, sir," Camwyn said. He held the smooth wood, polished by many hands over the years.

"Your parries are weak with the longsword," the armsmaster said. "Your height is one thing; the strength of shoulder, arm, and wrist is another. You will build up strength before you pick up a long blade again. In the meantime, you will learn the moves with a reed-blade."

Camwyn opened his mouth to protest, then thought better of it. Armsmaster Fralorn won most arguments with his students, and Camwyn did not wish to invite a negative report to his brother.

"Yes, sir," he said.

"I will show you the exercises I want you to use," Fralorn said. "And if you can find a glass in your busy day to work on your own, I will see by your increasing strength whether you are following my instructions. Or, if you prefer, we can spend the next five tendays working with hauks in your weapons class."

"I will do it, sir," Camwyn said.

The armsmaster nodded. "I thought you would say that. If you wish, you may come here, or you may take hauks with you. If you wish to improve your friends' fighting skills, invite them to join you."

For the next half-glass Camwyn worked with the hauk, the arms-master insisting on correct form at every point. "Until I'm certain your body has learned the forms, we will spend a short time every session in review, but I will depend on you to do most of the work on your own," the armsmaster said. "If you do not improve soon, we will do more of this here."

"Yes, sir," Camwyn said, trying not to pant. His shirt was soaked with sweat.

After that, he rose early each morning and put in the time with hauks. He was soon bored with the exercise; he knew the armsmaster expected him to give it up. Instead, he invited his friends in the palace to join him. Aris Marrakai, as he might have expected, was the most faithful of the others. Camwyn had long since understood the king's reason for attainting his former friend Egan Verrakai and no longer blamed Aris Marrakai for taking Egan's place. Aris was lively and mischievous, very much a kindred spirit.

Yet it was Aris who raised the question of magery. "I do not understand how the king is so sure only Beclan has mage powers," he said one morning as he tossed a hauk back to Camwyn, who caught it, twirled it, and tossed it back, this time to Aris's heart-hand.

"No one else has shown any," Camwyn said.

"But Beclan didn't know he had it, so how does the king know someone else doesn't? He might have it himself. You might."

"Duke Verrakai says we don't."

"But she didn't think Beclan had it, did she, until he used it? Does it just come when it's ready, like beard hairs?"

"I don't think we should talk about this," Camwyn said.

"Why not?"

"I don't think Mikeli would like it." He was sure Mikeli would not like it after the lecture he'd had from the Marshal-Judicar. He could see from Aris's expression that the younger boy was about to ask why. "Besides . . . surely if I had it, I'd know."

"You had something that made that dragon give you a ride," Aris said. Of all Camwyn's friends, Aris had been the only one who seemed envious of that. The others had shuddered.

"Nothing makes a dragon do anything," Camwyn said. He was sure of that.

"Then why did it choose you and not the king?"

"I wanted to. I asked."

"Would it come if you called it?"

"No," Camwyn said. "And it's 'he,' not 'it.' "

"I wish I could see it—him," Aris said. He said nothing more for a time as they went into one of the armsmaster's more complicated drills involving simultaneous cross-throws. Finally, one of Aris's thrown hauks hit one of Camwyn's with a clatter and bounced loudly on the stone floor of the Bells' training hall, where Camwyn had permission to practice these early mornings. That brought a yeoman-marshal out of the Bells' offices.

"Oh—it's you, prince. A little more careful if you please. I thought we had an invasion of orcs."

"We didn't drop them on purpose," Aris said.

"With more purpose and attention, you would not drop them at all." The yeoman-marshal, Camwyn knew, reported to the Knight-Commander of the Bells and was therefore no one to annoy.

"Sorry, Yeoman-Marshal," Camwyn said. "It is a new drill the armsmaster gave me but a tenday ago; this is the first time we've tried to speed it up."

"Slow it back down, then," the yeoman-marshal said, and went back to the offices.

"Something simple," Camwyn said. "We can't afford to anger him. I can't."

"I think you should try it," Aris said when they paused again, this time without any dropped hauks.

"Try what?" Camwyn mopped his sweaty face with a towel.

"Calling the dragon. Just to see if you can. You might need him someday."

Camwyn stared at him. "Aris, if I could call the dragon, that would be by magic, wouldn't it? And that's treason."

Aris scowled. "I never thought of that. I just thought—maybe if you've ridden with him, he listens for you, and then it would be his magic, wouldn't it? I didn't mean I wanted you to commit treason."

"That's good," Camwyn said, feeling much more mature than Aris. "Because if you did, I'd have to report you to the king, and then you'd be the one doing treason."

"I didn't think of that, either," Aris said. "But anyway, you're not going to be king. Once the king marries and has children—"

"I don't want to be king," Camwyn said. "It's too much work being king."

"Will you be Knight-Commander of the Bells?"

"I don't know. I'll be whatever the king wants me to be, and he hasn't said. I don't think he will until I've earned my knight-hood."

"I wish I were your age. You'll be two years ahead of me whatever I do."

"It matters less when we're grown," Camwyn said. He punched Aris in the shoulder, not too hard. "We'd better get these hauks back to the salle. Have breakfast with me?"

"I can't," Aris said. "Page duties. But I'll be at riding, of course."

"Good—I'll see you then."

Camwyn cleaned up and then went to breakfast with his brother the king—he had a standing invitation now whenever he wasn't breakfasting with a friend. He had begun to understand Mikeli's sense of urgency about his education since Beclan's disgrace—or adventure, as he preferred to think of it.

When Camwyn came into the king's quarters, he found Mikeli staring at a parchment roll embellished with colored inks and gold leaf.

"You should see this," Mikeli said. "It's from the king of Kostandan. He thinks I should marry his daughter Ganlin."

"I thought Rothlin was interested in her," Camwyn said, reaching for a hot roll. "He said she seemed to like him." Then he remembered he'd heard that via Aris, his sister Gwenno, and Beclan, which made it gossip. He stuffed the roll in his mouth.

"Close to the throne isn't the throne," Mikeli said. He put the scroll down and picked up a tumbler of juice. "I hate this, you know. Girls are all very well, and I must have a wife, but I understand how Kieri Phelan felt when they pressured him. And now he's married and happy with it. I suppose I will be."

"Will you marry this girl, then?" Camwyn tried to sound more adult and sensible than he felt. Girls—Aris's sisters or the others he knew—were just people as far as he was concerned. Pretty or plain didn't matter as much as whether they were lively or dull. He liked what he'd heard about Gwenno, Aris's older sister, but he also liked Temris, a year younger than Aris.

"I don't know," Mikeli said. "I am supposed to do what's best for the realm. Kieri has advised me that I must marry someone who will sustain my interest and not be overwhelmed by dynastic considerations, but the Council want me to marry soon. Kieri has inspired them, it seems."

"Have you met her?"

"Ganlin of Kostandan? No. Her father suggests a state visit similar to that on which she was sent to Tsaia—but you know what happened then."

"Will she finish at Falk's Hall?"

"I don't know. From what Kieri's told me, she's eager to marry. She thought she wanted to run away with Elis of Pargun; now she thinks she wants a husband, as high ranking as possible. She's still young—a few years younger than me—so who knows what she'll want in another few years?"

"Surely any woman would be happy to wed the king of Tsaia," Camwyn said around a large wedge of ham roll.

"It's not the wedding but the time after I'm concerned about. Think of our uncle Mahieran, Cam. He loved Celbrin; he thought she loved him. Perhaps she did. But through her has come all this trouble with Beclan. And by the way . . . are you really questioning my decision?"

"Um . . . no."

"It sounded like it to the Marshal-Judicar."

Tattletale, Camwyn thought, and then tried to unthink it. Mikeli was too good at reading faces.

"And he should have told me," Mikeli said, making it clear he had figured out what Camwyn was thinking.

Was that magery? Or just an older brother's understanding of a younger? Camwyn wasn't sure. "I'm sorry," he said. "It's all this emphasis on bloodlines. If blood matters, then whatever you say, whatever the law says, Beclan's still in our family. He's Uncle's true-son, not Duke Verrakai's."

"Camwyn, you're old enough to know that physical truth and legal truth aren't always the same thing."

"They should be."

"In this instance, the physical truth would have required me to order Beclan's execution when he broke his oath to me."

"But the law that demanded it is just the law—not the physical truth."

Mikeli shook his head with a rueful grin. "You *are* arguing with me, Brother. And here, in the privacy of my apartments, that's legal. Just don't upset our new Marshal-Judicar with it—or anyone else. You want the physical truth, but the most important truth is political. And we do not *want* it to become physical: we do not want a revolt against the Crown, bodies falling in the street, blood flowing. Enough of that right after the assassination attempt. The political truth is that the people do not want a magelord king, and we cannot afford to let them think the Crown's bloodline is tainted with magery." Camwyn started to speak, but Mikeli held up his hand. "You and I can talk about the details later, Cam, but I'm hungry and need my breakfast, and so do you. The armsmaster tells me you're strengthening into your height—doing it on your own. I'm proud of you."

"My shirts are getting tight around the chest," Camwyn said. "The shoulders and arms as well."

"I can see that. Tell me, Cam—what are you considering for your own future marriage?"

"Me?" Camwyn felt his blood run cold. "You're not thinking of that Kostandanyan princess, are you? She's older than I am. And anyway . . ."

"Time to start looking. Until I get an heir, you're next in line. You're doing better in your studies, I hear, and soon fathers will be trailing their eligible daughters past you."

"I like Aris's sisters," Camwyn said. "They ride really well."

Mikeli laughed aloud. "If you're still thinking of girls in the context of how they ride or fence or draw a bow—"

"Kieri Phelan did."

"That's King Kieri of Lyonya to you, Cam, until it rolls off your tongue as easily."

"Yes, sir king," Camwyn said, and quickly filled his mouth with another ham roll. Mikeli feinted a punch at him, and he dodged.

"So . . . try to put your mind to more about girls than their athletic skills or your body will do it for you—very soon now, I think."

"Did that happen to you?"

"Yes, of course. But I could not think of marriage until after my coronation. This—" He tapped the scroll still open on the table. "This must be answered one way or the other, and soon. And you, Brother, must not speak of it."

"I won't." Camwyn finished that roll and scooped a large spoonful of stirred eggs onto his platter. "But don't you think it would be better to marry someone from here?"

"The difficulty is what we were talking of earlier." Mikeli set his elbows on the table and tented his fingers. "The Council and I have been looking into the bloodlines of all the great families and most minor ones. All have a magelord background; latent magery could be in any of them. We know it's in ours because of Beclan. It's likely that Celbrin never knew it and may not be able to manifest it herself. So marrying away from magelord bloodlines would be a good idea."

"You could marry someone not from the peerage," Camwyn said.

"Except that many such families also have a blood connection to the mageborn. We suspect it cropped out in Beclan—strong enough to be triggered by his ordeal—as a result of minor influences from both sides. That's another thing you must not speak of."

"I won't . . . So you think even you and I might have some?"

"That's not something I'm going to admit even to you, Cam, and you would be wise never to mention the possibility. We still have enemies; we think most of the Verrakaien traitors are gone, but we're not sure. At any rate, there's a reason to consider marrying outside this realm. Marrying into Kostandan joins the Seafolk and ourselves and might ensure lasting peace in the north, something we certainly want."

Camwyn nodded. "We want peace, I know. But if war comes, like that new ruler in Aarenis I've heard about?"

"Then perhaps an ally." Mikeli sighed. "But I could wish she had not set on our cousin first. He has seen that before. And I do not want a queen who is no more than a flirt."

"You think this princess is?"

"I don't know," Mikeli admitted. "Not for certain. But both Duke Verrakai and Kieri say she was clearly putting herself forward to Rothlin. If she was using my cousin just to get closer to me, that's not the right kind of woman to be queen."

"She's not the right kind of woman for Rothlin, either," Camwyn said.

"No, but that's his choice, his and his father's. If she stayed at Falk's Hall and got her ruby, that would prove something of her character. But if I tell her father that I will only consider her if she is knighted—what if then I do not choose her? It would be considered an insult, and that would not be good at all."

"So—"

"So I must think how to say 'Not quite yet' while I find out more about her. The Knight-Commander of Falk's Hall will not tattle to me but might share something with Kieri, who might then think to mention it to Duke Verrakai, who might share it with her king."

"That's not tattling?"

"No. Everyone's within a chain of obligation, loyal to an oath. Something to think about when you tell someone something—to whom might they feel obligated to tell it?"

That day the riding instructor led them north of the city for a gallop in fields separated by hedges and patches of woodland. Rain two days before had left water in the furrows; they rode along the margins until the instructor found a drier pasture on higher ground. When the riders had completed their exercise and dismounted to walk the horses cool in the shade of a hedge, Camwyn stooped to look at some bright red mushrooms that had come up after the rain—unfamiliar to him, as were the trees they grew under. He touched them but knew better than to eat one without asking someone.

When he came back into the palace, he did not expect to be taken immediately to his brother the king, who was in no good mood.

"I thought you knew how to keep your mouth shut," Mikeli said.

"I didn't tell anything," Camwyn said. "What do you think—"

"You didn't tell anyone that we discussed Ganlin, that her father had written me?"

"Of course not. You said not to, and anyway, who would I tell? I was out riding. What happened?"

"Rothlin. He knows about the letter, and he knows you know. I thought you were the only one who could have told him, but someone else must have." He sighed. "Roth was not pleased to find that Ganlin's father had involved himself, though he said that he knew her brother was even more ambitious for her than a king's cousin. He thinks Ganlin really likes him but would defer to her father's wishes." He rubbed his head. "It's such a tangle. We need time to straighten things out here after Beclan; rushing into a marriage—either of us— is not the best plan."

Camwyn went off to his supper thinking about all this and wondering who else could have known about the Kostandanyan king's letter and its contents—and who would have talked. He knew he hadn't mentioned it. Only later, as he lay in bed, did he think of magery. Someone with magery might have known . . . or could magelords know what others said—or thought? Mikeli had told him that Duke Verrakai claimed the mysterious crown she'd brought spoke to her. Did it speak to anyone else? If Duke Verrakai knew things about the Kostandanyan princess . . . would the crown know what she knew, and could it tell anyone else?

Or what about elves or their dread cousins the iynisin? Iynisin had killed the elven queen . . . but no one in Tsaia had reported anything like that. He lay in the dark, imagining what it might be like to be an elf, master of strange magicks, able to shape growing things . . . or an iynisin, able to kill with a spell. Or a magelord . . . able to make light.

He put up his hand, staring at it in the faint light from his window. What would it look like if he could make light with it? Would there be a flame flickering from his fingertip? Or would it look like a hand held before a flame, with that red glow through the skin? Or would there be light around it, like the pictures of paladins? Or more heat than light, like the dragon? Would there be a smell, a forge smell?

He fell asleep wondering about all that and woke sometime later, wide awake, as if startled, but he heard no noise. He felt too warm and threw off his covers.

Only then did he notice the dull glow, like a dying coal, moving in the dark not far from him. He gasped, rolled over to the opposite side of his bed, clutching the covers as he did, and stared where it had been. Nothing. He licked dry lips and stared around the room. What? Where? Slowly, he let the covers drop and backed toward his door. His heel hit the rack where his sword and practice armor hung; he reached for the armor, and a blur of dim red caught his gaze.

He stared. When he moved his hand, the glow moved. He relaxed suddenly. He knew what it had to be. Some fungi glowed in the dark. He had touched those mushrooms, and though he'd washed since, he knew he'd done so hurriedly. He brought his hand nearer his face to smell his fingers. His one finger. It glowed from the knuckle to the tip . . . surely he hadn't rubbed his finger on the mushroom that far down.

As he looked, the glow strengthened. Now it lit the rest of his hand. Fear returned; he felt an icy chill down his back . . . though his hand, as he brought it closer yet, warmed his face.

Was this what had happened to Beclan? Did it mean some dire threat was near him? An evil mage? An iynisin? Was someone fooling him, making him think he might have mage powers when he didn't?

Mikeli would be so angry. So would the Marshal-Judicar. And that reminded him of Gird, who had made the law against magery. He thought then he should pray, but the only prayer that came to mind was the Ten Fingers, not really a prayer. He recited it as fast as he could. The glow did not disappear, nor did it brighten. "I'm sorry, Gird," he muttered under his breath. "I didn't do it on purpose." Whatever it was. But so often things he hadn't done on purpose still earned him blame.

He shook his hand, hoping the glow would disappear. It didn't. He thought at it: *Go away.* Nothing happened. Well, if it wouldn't go away, could he make it brighter? He stared, concentrating. Nothing for a time, then it brightened for a moment, enough to light the way from where he stood near the door to his bed—to the window beyond.

The window—Gird's cudgel, someone might see the light and wonder why he was up! He scrambled to the bed and stuck his hand under the covers. It brightened again, an obvious light showing through the fabric. And it was hotter. He put his knee up, holding the covers away from his finger lest they catch fire. He couldn't sleep like this. And what if it stayed lit until morning? What would he do then?

He imagined himself being sent away, forced to live with Duke Verrakai . . . But no, it was worse than that. Beclan had been only the king's cousin. He was the king's brother. What would they do to Mikeli if he were found with light on his finger? Would anyone believe it came from Gird?

Just how hot was his finger? He thought about that for a moment, then touched it to the wick of the candle in the stick by his bed. After a moment the wick caught, and simultaneously the light in his finger disappeared.

That was easy. He fell asleep in the instant of that thought, waking only in the gray dawn with the bedside candle burnt down to a puddle of wax. His hand looked perfectly normal. "Thank you, Father Gird," he said. "I will never do that again." Whatever it was he'd done, since he had no idea how he'd done it.

He cleaned the puddled wax out of his candlestick and off the chest beside it, so no one would accuse him of leaving a candle burning, and put the wax in the bowl used for such scraps. As he was dressing, he heard his friends gathering out in the passage. He was late for his early morning hauk practice already.

That morning's practice went badly; he could not keep his mind on the more complicated patterns, and after dropping a hauk the second time—bringing the same angry yeoman-marshal out to scold them—he pleaded bad dreams that had kept him awake and went to breakfast with Mikeli only because Mikeli would expect him. He prayed steadily on the way that his hand would not light up in front of the king.

"What's wrong?" Mikeli asked the moment the servants withdrew.

"I had dreams," Camwyn said, and stuffed his mouth with a meat pasty. He nearly choked and had to spit out some of it and quickly drink water.

"Bad dreams?" Mikeli asked. "What about? Not the crown, I hope." He said it almost as a joke, but Camwyn felt his face heat up. "Cam?"

If only he'd had a big brother who ignored him—or was not the king. "Not exactly," Camwyn said. "I mean—I had been thinking about it when I went to bed—you said it talked to you, and I wondered how, and if it was a kind of magery, who had put it there—but it wasn't in the dream, or I don't think so. I can't quite remember. Just that I woke up sometimes and it was hard to sleep after." Which was a lie, and lying was, according to the Code of Gird, wrong, so no wonder he still felt the telltale heat of his face. But what could he do? And maybe his hand *had* been a dream—the whole thing.

"You're maturing enough to start dreaming about girls," Mikeli said. "That can be embarrassing the first time it happens. Finding that in the bed." He wasn't looking at Camwyn now. "If that happens, don't worry about it. It happens to all of us."

Camwyn felt his blush deepen. It already had happened more than once, and he hadn't mentioned it to anyone. "So . . ." he said, hearing his voice waver. "It's not—it's normal?"

"Yes. Uncle said if our father had lived, he'd have explained it. He told me and told me to tell you—so now I have. Was it that?"

"I . . . guess so." Partly. But he remembered now that magelords sometimes came to their magery about the same time.

"When I was your age, I started needing more sleep," Mikeli said. "If you need to sleep later, just let me know so they don't bring breakfast for two. You can tell your tutors—they'll understand."

"It was hard to get up this morning," Camwyn said. He applied himself to a plate of stirred eggs. "And some days it's hard to concentrate."

"I know," Mikeli said. "It was the same for me. You'll get through this."

Having Mikeli sympathetic was new and troubling; Camwyn was used to being merely tolerated or in trouble. And he was in trouble . . . unless the glowing finger really had been just a dream, a very vivid one. He was on his way to his drill session with the armsmaster when he remembered the candle. That puddle of wax had been no dream this morning. He refused to look down at his hand to see if a finger glowed. *Please, Gird: no more of that. I didn't mean to.* No answer. He didn't expect an answer. He hadn't expected the glowing finger, either.

That day's drill and lessons went by without incident; the armsmaster said his strength was growing as fast as it likely could. "The trick's to keep the balance," he said. "Too much strength isn't good for growing bones, but neither is too little. You're not to go beyond your training until the growth slows—is that clear?"

"Yes, Armsmaster," Camwyn said. He'd heard that before.

"No playing around with a blade without me present."

"No, Armsmaster."

"Well, then, let's see what that extra muscle's done for you." He nodded to the chests by the wall. "A banda and a practice longsword. Number three."

Camwyn forgot he'd been tired and worried. As he put on the banda and took the assigned practice sword, he heard the armsmaster refuse the same to Aris Marrakai and Jami Serrostin. "You're not ready yet. And you, young Marrakai, you're muscling up more than you should right now. Do you want to be a head shorter than your brother?"

"That can't happen," Aris said.

"And you know everything about physical conditioning, I suppose," the armsmaster said. "Bide you there, lads, while I see how the prince is coming along."

Camwyn found the sword lighter than it had been before. He brought it to salute, as the armsmaster, now with his own practice blade, faced him in the middle of the salle.

"Drill," the armsmaster said. "Distance first: tip to tip. On guard."

Camwyn moved as the armsmaster moved—forward, back, sideways. He scarcely felt the sword's weight.

"Better," the armsmaster said. "Now, half speed on my count." He began the count, and Camwyn responded with the correct parries and combinations. Then he began to feel it in his neck and shoulder and arm. "Halt," the armsmaster said. Camwyn grounded his blade. "Your wrist has strengthened out of proportion to your shoulder on your strong side. Switch hands and let's see if it's the specific exercises or something else."

With his heart-hand, Camwyn felt the weight sooner but equal stress from shoulder to wrist. He said so, and the armsmaster nodded. "Good. You're becoming more aware of your body."

Camwyn felt his face warming again. The armsmaster's expression didn't change. "It's no shame, lad," he said softly. "And you need to know your reactions to control them. It's no harm to have your wrist strengthening a little faster than your shoulder, but you need to balance it across both hands. You've done well with the hauks—keep it up—but enough with the sword for today."

After that came unarmed combat, then footwork drills, and then it was time for other lessons. Camwyn told Aris and the others about his brother's suggestion that he sleep later.

Jami Serrostin hooted. "I wish *my* brother would tell me that."

"I'm not sleepy in the morning," Aris said.

"You're also two years younger," Camwyn said. "Just wait. It'll happen to you."

"Is that why you were dropping the hauks?"

"The king thinks so," Camwyn said. "He said he got clumsier for a while and needed more sleep."

"Nobody thinks pages need more sleep," Teris Konhalt said. "And if I don't leave now, I'll be late for my duties. Pardon?"

"Of course," Camwyn said. The others soon followed—all had duties in the palace as well as with him. He uttered another silent prayer that Gird would ward him from any further excitement with his hand and went to his own session with the Marshal-Judicar.

Details of the law regarding the way money could be transferred between gnomes and humans seemed to have nothing to do with him, and it was hard not to yawn as the morning warmed. His eyelids sagged.

"Wake up, Prince Camwyn," the Marshal-Judicar said. "Did you not sleep last night?"

"Sorry, sir," Camwyn said. "I had dreams and . . . and other things."

The Marshal-Judicar looked hard at him and muttered something Camwyn couldn't hear. "I suppose it's natural," he said aloud, and then, "You need a cup of sib, I daresay. Get more sleep tonight and come tomorrow ready to learn."

"Thank you, sir," Camwyn said as he rose and bowed.

His other tutors seemed to have heard something, for all of them gave him an easy time for once. He found that a mug of sib at midmorning, lunch, and midafternoon helped, but he suddenly felt twitchy and wider awake than usual, as if someone had pulled his eyelids up into his head.

"Too much sib," Mikeli said when they met before dinner. "You're not used to it. Keep it to one or two a day. Best go for a brisk ride or another session with the armsmaster or you won't sleep tonight."

The extra session with the armsmaster, who made him run back and forth the length of the salle, must have helped, because he rolled over only once before falling asleep.

Only to wake in the dark with his finger once more glowing like a coal in the night. Lighting a candle had turned it off last time— would it this time? He tried it. The candle flared, but his finger did not go dark. Now what?

He stared at his finger, willing it to darken. Instead, it brightened. Well, then . . . he willed it to brighten, and it flared even brighter. He sat on the edge of his bed, arm propped on his knees, and wondered what he should do now. Clearly he had mage powers from . . . from somewhere. Clearly that was against the law and imperiled his brother. He needed to not be a mage or . . . not be.

The thought of that made him cold again, but his finger did not dim with his fear. It glowed on, steadier than any candle. His thoughts stumbled on. If he did not exist, Mikeli would not be in danger because of him. *Should* he die to protect Mikeli? Could he . . . the thought lay a cold black shadow over his mind . . . could he kill himself? He'd heard the story now of the old sergeant who had killed himself to save Beclan, but he, Camwyn, didn't want to die. Not even for Mikeli, not this way.

Yet . . . how else could he save Mikeli from the stain of this magery? He could . . . well, he could run away. But how? And where? Where in the whole world would his magery not condemn him? And where would he not be found and dragged back to be imprisoned or executed?

These thoughts tangled in his mind, chasing one another around and around. He must not have magery—but he did. He must not be Mikeli's downfall—yet he was, if discovered. So he must not be discovered—but without the ability to control the magery, someone would eventually see his hand glow, and then . . . it would be too late. He should leave now, at once, this night.

But *how*? Again, the impossibility of that—where could he go, how would he live?—stopped him even as he stood and moved toward his clothespress. He thought of the dragon first: could Aris have been right? Would the dragon come to his rescue if he called? But no: he could not believe the dragon would even hear him. That was a child's wish. Into his mind came the thought of Duke Verrakai— she hadn't killed Beclan and would not, he was sure, kill him. But Mikeli might kill her if he thought she had known and not told him. He didn't want that. She fascinated him—a magelord, a soldier, and a woman, unlike anyone else at court—and he didn't want to cause her trouble. Where else? Not Fintha, of course, and not Lyonya . . . but he might go south, to Aarenis. Could he get there before Mikeli tracked him down? He wasn't sure.

He blew out the candle, stared at his finger again, and then lit the candle again. This time his finger dimmed a bit. So . . . the magic could be used up? Again he blew out the candle and again lit it. Now his finger seemed normal, just a finger. And he was awake enough to blow out the candle a last time before he fell asleep.

CHAPTER SEVEN

Lyonya, between Chaya and the Tsaian border

As Dorrin and Beclan rode west along the forest track, Beclan's mood shifted; Dorrin could see it in his posture as well as his expression. Those days in Chaya had been fun. Pretty girls had flattered him; he had been able to talk to his father and brother. But now he was going back to Tsaia, where he had been stripped of his own name and rank and lived under a cloud of suspicion.

She understood that better than he could realize. And the best thing for him would be work. While still riding through Lyonya's forest, he might as well start working on his magery.

"Beclan, do you feel the trees?"

He turned to her. "My lord? You mean . . . the way the elves do?"

"Yes," Dorrin said. "Apparently, those of us with magery can feel the taig. Queen Arian taught me—it would be helpful, she said, in healing the damage done to the trees in Verrakai lands. And I hope you can learn it. Best to start here, where the taig is strong."

"What would I use it for?"

Wrong question, but if it stuck in his mind, she must answer it. "My ancestors did much damage to Verrakai lands—you will see when we've come to our borders. Working with the taig, we can heal such injury. The Lyonyan forest has been maintained in its beauty by those who served the taig—I'm sure you heard about that."

"Yes, my lord."

"The queen—Arian—says I can learn to do that. So as soon as we're over the border into Verrakai lands, we're going to try it. Meanwhile, I'm working on my skills at sensing the taig, and I want you to start as well."

"Is it like making flowers bloom in winter?"

Dorrin reminded herself that he was very, very young. "Elves can do that but rarely do. I heard that the Lady did it at Aliam Halveric's steading. But that's unnatural. What we need to learn is how to restore and sustain the natural growth and health of living things. What do you feel closest to, Beclan? Any particular tree or plant from your childhood?"

"No . . . but I had a dog once. I knew what Hunter was feeling, what he was going to do next. He died two winters ago."

"My people—*our* people now—are afraid of dogs, you know, all but the shepherds' dogs. My uncle used dogs to scare them and hurt them as well as for hunting, so I haven't brought any in. Kieri didn't use them in the Company. Would you like a dog, Beclan?"

"I don't know, my lord. Hunter was so special . . ."

"What about horses?" He said nothing, and Dorrin went on. "If you have never had a feel for plants, I was wondering about animals . . . a dog, a horse, anything that would help you make that connection to the taig."

"I thought the taig was all about trees."

"Hmmm. I should have had you talk to the Kuakkgani while we were in Chaya. If I can find Ashwind, I may ask him to come and instruct both of us. My understanding is that the taig is formed of all living things."

"My lord Duke!" That was one of the King's Squires Kieri had sent to guide them through the forest. "We could spend the night in a ranger shelter if it please you."

Dorrin nodded. "It does. The queen told me about Verrakaien brigands who'd been killed, and my king would like to know which of the attainted they were. Will rangers be at the shelter?"

"Yes, we expect to meet some there," the Squire said.

The next morning, before resuming their journey west, she and Beclan followed one of the rangers to the grave site, but the ranger's description of those killed did not give her enough information to identify them for certain. The grave was covered with a dense growth of a vine she did not recognize.

"We planted that," the ranger said. "It is good for such places, where evil is buried. Its roots hold fast, and it devours without being tainted. Later it will die, and by its death we will know any evil has been cleansed."

"I am sorry my kinsmen caused you such trouble," Dorrin said, "but glad you have taken precautions with their remains."

When they reached the border; their Lyonyan escort turned back. Dorrin and Beclan rode on with only the two Verrakaien militia. The spring sun, the fresh scents of the forest, raised Dorrin's spirits, and she saw that Beclan was taking an interest as well. After a glass or so, Dorrin felt the taig weakening. "Something's wrong here," she said.

"It feels . . . sad," Beclan said. "If I'm feeling what I think I'm feeling."

The feeling worsened as they rode on, and then they saw the first deformed tree. Only half the limbs had leafed out; the branches and trunk had lost bark. Others stood beyond, grotesque parodies of healthy trees. Under them grew only a few twisted shrubs and stunted flowers, the blooms pale and already wilting.

"This is what Gwenno reported last year when she patrolled in this area," Dorrin said before Beclan asked. "Why my family cursed the trees, I don't know—unless it's possible that some form of blood magery works with trees."

She turned to her militia. "Ride on until you find a healthy stand of trees and make camp there. I want to study this and see if anything may be done." The guards saluted and rode ahead. Dorrin dismounted; Beclan followed her.

"It's horrible," Beclan said. "Can we do anything?"

"We can try, though I suspect it would take a Kuakgan or an elf— or a group of them. Pick a tree."

Beclan chose a tree with a few tufts of spring-green leaves on twisted limbs. They both laid hands on it; Dorrin felt its living essence, frayed and sad, through the palms of her hands. "Alyanya's power," Dorrin said. "Lady of Flowers, Lady of Peace . . . if we can help this tree, show us how." To her senses, the tree seemed to warm, as if a little more life flowed into it.

Beclan looked at her. "I feel something, my lord," he said. "It's not like a pulse, but a . . . a flow." He looked up. "But no more leaves."

"It will take time, I suppose," Dorrin said. She sighed. "Do you feel tired, Beclan?"

"Yes. As if I'd been running."

"Enough for today. We'll eat and rest before riding on."

As they sat in the thin shade of the crooked tree, Dorrin felt a tremor in the ground, much like a horse shaking a fly off its skin. Beclan dropped the bread he was holding. They both heard the groan that followed. Then shade thickened; they looked up, and Dorrin saw thrice as many leaves as before and a few sprays of apple blossom, its scent drifting down to them.

"We did that?" Beclan said, his eyes wide.

"I would not say so," Dorrin said. "The taig and the Lady of Plenty did that, but we opened a way for them to work. Come, let us try another."

But the next attempt exhausted Beclan; he crumpled to the ground, pale to the lips. "I'm sorry, my lord," he said when his eyes opened again.

"It is not your fault," Dorrin said. She felt tired, too. "You are new to this; you did very well. When you're able, we'll ride on to camp." Her guards had set up tents and had hot food waiting when she and Beclan arrived. She wondered as she ate how many trees were damaged and how long it would take to heal them.

O n the last day, dusk was closing in as Dorrin caught sight of the house. Her guards picked up a canter, riding ahead to announce her return. Dorrin held her mount to a walk. The guards had not reached the house yet, but lights flickered in the windows of the great front room. They had not known when to expect her . . . Who was there at this hour?

Torches appeared on the porch, and mounted torchbearers rode out of the stableyard as she came to the ford. Light glittered on the moving water; rain had fallen here, and swifter water tumbled over the stones, knee-high on the horses. Torchlight lit someone . . . a visitor . . . in red and silver. A royal? Then she was close enough to recognize Duke Serrostin. Had he come to demand his son's return?

"They thought you might not be back for days," Serrostin said, sounding more cheerful than she expected. "I'm on the king's business, my lord Duke. He's decided to make a progress, and you are the fortunate first domain he will visit."

Dorrin had a moment of stark panic. The king? Here? When? Surely not before Queen Arian's visit to Tsaia . . .

"He plans to come between the queen's visit and Midsummer Court," Serrostin went on. "And perhaps he'll have time to visit Konhalt, depending on when the queen leaves."

That left time to prepare. "Thank you," Dorrin said. "We will welcome him, of course. Do you know how many will travel in his party or how long he will stay?"

"Not certainly, though he said he did not intend to impoverish his people; he will bring supplies with him. Possibly the prince, certainly one or two peers, a small staff; he'll send a courier with details a tenday before he leaves." Serrostin turned his mount to parallel hers and lowered his voice. "I've seen Daryan."

"He's matured," Dorrin said.

"Yes. He informed me very firmly but with perfect courtesy that you had jurisdiction here and I could not take him away without your consent since there was no proof of maltreatment."

"He thought that's why you had come?"

"Yes. I finally got a word in to reassure him. Since then he's been a gracious host in your absence, since both your kirgan and Gwenno Marrakai were out of the house." He smiled at Beclan. "Hello, Beclan. Daryan said you were wife hunting in Lyonya."

"I was not! I was just . . . I had the chance . . ."

"He was teasing," Dorrin said. Beclan subsided.

"So tell me, my lord, do you know when the queen will come?" Serrostin asked. "We had thought she planned to leave Chaya within days after the marriage."

He must have missed the courier sent to Mikeli, Dorrin realized. "I have news both good and bad," she said. "But let me save that for a private conversation."

"Of course."

Later that night, after a pleasant dinner at which Daryan served, his wrinkled brown thumb uncovered as he handed platters around, Dorrin took Duke Serrostin into her office and related all that had happened while she was in Lyonya.

"The elf queen dead! I cannot believe it—they're immortals—"

"Not with a sword in their vitals," Dorrin said bluntly. "It will change Lyonya; Kieri doesn't yet know how, but it's clear the elves are in disarray, with no elvenhome. What King Mikeli needs to know— though he should have had a courier by now—is that King Kieri intends no change in his own policy toward Tsaia."

Next morning Serrostin started back for Vérella. "I've had a very pleasant several days here, my lord Verrakai," he said. "It's not what I expected, very homelike." The laughter of children sounded from the kitchen garden as they spoke. "Our king will enjoy his time here, I'm sure, and I'm glad I had this chance to meet with Daryan and reassure him I was not as upset with his . . . his Kuakgan influence as I had been earlier. A father's panic, for which I hope you will forgive me."

"Of course," Dorrin said. "Any father would be upset—and angry—to have a son first injured and then defiant."

When Duke Serrostin and his escort had ridden across the ford, Dorrin turned to her squires. "We have work to do," Dorrin said to them. "In addition to the usual patrols, we must prepare for a royal visit, and I find no record of any such in the rolls. So you, and Gwenno when she comes back from patrol, will be helping me with this. Food, housing, supplies for the king's entourage, fodder for the extra animals, some kind of welcoming ceremony. And safety, of course. Beclan, you're to find a place to go on legitimate business while the king's here . . . the new middle road, perhaps. Have you ever surveyed anything?"

"No, my lord."

"Time you learned. Since you're going to inherit all this—" Her arm swept out, indicating the entire domain. "—you'd best know how big it is and every part of it. I'll start you with Sergeant Natzlin: she's good with a rope."

"A rope?"

"For measuring distance. You can practice with the house and stableyard for a day or two. Daryan, it would be good for you to learn this as well, but I have another errand for you."

Gwenno arrived back from her patrol that day; Dorrin was in her office, examining accounts, and saw the girl ride in, straight-backed and steady. She counted quickly. No one missing: no need to ask questions yet. Dorrin ran her finger down the page, checking every line. She trusted Grekkan well enough, but the Verrakai domain still bled money, and her reserves in gold had dwindled with frightening speed. So much needed to be done, so many gaps mended.

She turned at a knock on the door frame. Gwenno bowed.

"My lord, could I speak with you?"

"Come in," Dorrin said. "You look troubled; what is it?"

"Beclan," Gwenno said. "It's not fair."

Dorrin had expected this eventually. "That he's kirgan?" she asked just to be sure.

"No, my lord. Well, not exactly . . . It's not fair what the king did to him, making him give up his family. It wasn't his fault any more than Daryan's thumb—"

"It's different," Dorrin said. "The king did what he must to protect the Crown and realm."

"But it wasn't Beclan's fault, and he's punished—"

"He could be dead," Dorrin said. Gwenno shut her mouth, eyes wide. "By the laws of the land, Gwenno, he could have been charged with treason and executed. Not only was he in the line of succession and showing mage-power, but there was an oath between him and the king—"

"He was too young to swear—"

"He chose to swear as an adult. The king warned him what that would mean. And then—then he admitted his magery. It could not be left as it was, Gwenno. The other peers—the people—would not have accepted that."

"It could have been a secret."

"A secret such as my family kept?" Dorrin shook her head. "It would not do. Not so close to the Crown. The king did the best for Beclan he could while doing his duty to the realm." Gwenno looked thoughtful now. "And though Beclan's inherent mage ability is not his fault, his choices led him to this end. He knows that; he has admitted that. His grief, Gwenno, is not just that he had to leave his family but that his own choices led to the deaths of all those men . . . his escort and, later, the guard put around him. He might have gone through life with unwakened magery, with no one—including himself—the wiser."

"But if Gird waked it—"

"We cannot know for certain," Dorrin said. "It may have been Gird—I think it likely—but it might also have been Beclan's own fear." Before Gwenno could say more, she went on. "And you are right in one thing—it is not fair. But here is a truth to ponder: many things are not fair. You will have unfairness in your life, and you will then decide how to handle it. Will you bleat 'Unfair, unfair' like a child or make the best of the situation you can like an adult? Like a knight of Gird or Falk?"

Gwenno said nothing for a long moment. "Beclan does not complain."

"No. He was shocked, and hurt, and frightened, but he has chosen to make the best of it."

"I just wanted to . . . to help . . ."

"You have a good heart, Gwenno. As you learn, you will find other ways to help Beclan—or anyone else. What he needs now from you and Daryan is respect and acceptance. Nothing more. He will fight his own battles."

"It comes of being the oldest sister in my family," Gwenno said, flushing a little. "Mother warned me. I—I thank you, my lord."

"I'm not scolding, Gwenno. I would rather have squires care about one another, defend one another, want to help one another, than be at odds. And all three of you have grown since last summer—remember that quarrel about grooming horses?"

Gwenno laughed. "Yes, my lord. We were prickly then, for certain."

"I do caution you, Gwenno, as I cautioned Beclan: he is not to practice his magery around you or show you how it is done. Your father does not think there's any magery in his family, but if you have any buried talents of that kind, we do not wish to wake them. It will be tempting, I'm sure, but do not try."

"No, my lord, I won't."

"Good. Now, is there anything else?"

"No, my lord. Oh—just that I finished the stable supplies tally you asked me to do—" She fished a group of tally sticks from a pocket and handed them over.

"Thank you," Dorrin said. "If that's all, I need to finish these accounts."

"Yes, my lord." Gwenno bowed and went out.

Daryan came next to report on the patrol he'd been on most recently. Everything had been calm, he said; no sign of brigands or vagabonds. "About Beclan," he added.

"Yes?"

"Shouldn't we call him kirgan? I mean, when I meet Kirgan Mahieran or Kirgan Marrakai and I'm a squire, I have to give them the honor—"

"It's different here," Dorrin said. She had explained this once to all three squires, but then Beclan had gone off to Lyonya with her. "He's my kirgan, yes, but he's also my squire. And since he has not grown up here, with the knowledge of this domain he would have if he were my son, he cannot take on the responsibilities of kirgan without more time and experience. As far as you and Gwenno are concerned, he's a squire—the same as you two—and you owe him no deference, only the courtesy due a fellow squire."

"It's sad," Daryan said. "I didn't realize that at first."

"Yes, it is. But it's also sad that you were captured and tormented and had to have Kuakkgani healing."

"I don't know . . ." Daryan looked down at his hands, the scar on one and the peculiar-looking thumb on the other. "Nobody else I know has a thumb with bark. I hope the other one buds. Dressing will be easier with two thumbs."

Dorrin struggled not to laugh. "I'm glad you accept it that way," she said. "Though if you turn Kuakgan, your father will be angry with us both all over again."

"Oh, no," Daryan said. "I want to be a knight, like Roly. I don't think Gird will mind."

After he left, Dorrin wondered if Beclan would be next but remembered he was off learning surveying with Natzlin. She had seen them start out that morning with a collection of ropes and sticks and other necessary gear. With no more interruptions, she finished the morning's work with the account books.

In the kitchen she found Farin Cook chatting with Sergeant Natzlin. Natzlin looked brighter than she had since Barranyi left the Duke's Company. She saluted Dorrin. "My lord, Squire Beclan has learned to make square corners three ways this morning and will show a creditable plat of the orchard."

"Excellent. If my kirgan can learn accurate surveying, I may not need to hire anyone. Did you come in to report to me?"

"Yes, my lord. I just stopped here to . . . to . . ."

"You're a soldier; it's a kitchen," Dorrin said, chuckling. "You notice where *I* am—we eat when we can, eh?"

A look passed between Farin and Natzlin, and then Farin said, "She was telling me about the old Company. And I said, stop a bit and have a bun. Those scars she's got—takes good food to heal up."

"Indeed," Dorrin said. She felt she was intruding, but it was her kitchen. "Any leftover buns for your duke?"

"Always something," Farin said. She looked at the kitchen workers. "Efla—fetch the duke some sib and a plate of those pastries with honey and nuts." She looked back at Dorrin. "In your study, m'lord?"

Go away, that meant. Dorrin leaned back on the main worktable. She valued Farin—and Natzlin—for the years of her service in the Duke's Company, but she was not going to be driven out. She glanced at Natzlin, whose expression she remembered from years before. So. Farin and Natzlin? Unlikely as it seemed—veteran soldier and cook—Farin would be a far better companion than Barranyi had been. If it gave Natzlin peace . . . well enough.

"If the two of you wish to partner," she said, staring Farin down, "that's fine with me. It's not my business. However, with the king coming to visit, this kitchen *is* my business."

"The king is coming?" Farin said, turning pale.

"Yes. After Queen Arian leaves Vérella—and we don't know when that will be—he's coming here with an entourage. I need your best estimate of our reserves and what we can expect in eggs, milk, and garden produce tenday by tenday until Midsummer—he's coming before then. There'll be no more use of any fancy foods—nuts, preserves—we can't replace within, say, two tendays."

"Yes, my lord. Sorry, my lord. I thought . . ."

"Even if you'd thought correctly, Farin, I won't be rushed out of my own kitchen."

Efla came out of the pantry with the pastries. Dorrin took two. "I'm going to miss these," she said as she nodded to the kitchen as a whole and walked out.

Natzlin and Farin—an attachment would, she realized, solve a persistent problem with her old veteran. The wounds suffered in Kieri's defense more than a year ago still affected her. Dorrin had promoted her to sergeant—the only clear choice after Vossik's death—but Natzlin struggled in that position—mounting was increasingly difficult, for one thing. Partnering with Farin might be a reason she'd accept for moving from patrol duties to something less strenuous. And Farin would keep watch on her physical well-being.

Dorrin ate the pastries, looking out over the fields below where cattle grazed and wondered how long it would take Kieri to get Arian pregnant.

CHAPTER EIGHT

In a Pargunese forest

"It is done," the dragon said. "You have completed your tasks."

"All of them?" Stammel asked. He took a breath of the fresh spring air, still chill this morning but alive now with growing things.

"All in that phase." The dragon had explained that its solid eggs were filled with crystalline shards each capable of hatching into the first immature form of a dragon. "I must now convey the eggs and unhatched shards to a safe place far away. You have done me great service, Stammel, and now I can return you to your home."

"I could still help," Stammel said.

"No." The dragon's voice was gentle but implacable. "What I must do now, you cannot do."

"I have trained raw boys and girls," Stammel said. "And I can see the dragonlets—surely I could help train them—"

"No," the dragon said again, a tone final as the ring of hammer on iron. Then in a gentler tone, "What is it, Stammel? I would have thought you'd be glad to return to those you know."

Stammel thought of the past quarter-year and wondered how to explain. It seemed at first no words would come for the longing to be useful, needed. But the dragon waited, that great shape of fire, and finally he could say it. "When you took me away," he said, "it was from the only home, the only friends, I had had in my adult life. I thought I would be lonely; I thought I would yearn for them."

"And you do not?" the dragon asked.

"What I yearned for then was no longer possible," Stammel said. "I will never be what I was. Who I was. I had come to realize that, and yet I saw no other future. You showed me another future. New places, new people, new challenges. A reason to live, with something to do . . . something worthwhile."

"You have changed," the dragon said.

"I had changed before, not by my will," Stammel said. "And now I have changed again, with your help. I can change again . . . but not back into what I was. If I return, I will be poor blind Stammel, someone with a past and no future."

"You are still oathbound to your commander," the dragon said. "And I think you are not an oathbreaker."

"No . . . but death breaks all oaths," Stammel said. "If you told them I was dead . . ."

"I do not lie," the dragon said. "And nor should you. Your commander will release you if you ask and he trusts you have a place to go."

"Then carry my request to him," Stammel said. He hated the roughness in his voice, but grief trapped him once again. "Please . . . take me somewhere I have never been, somewhere I might be of use, and take my word to him."

"That I can do," the dragon said. "Though your commander would rather see you again, I know, and judge of himself whether your new home was safe."

"It is just his care I do not want," Stammel said. "They will visit if they know. Someplace far——"

"Aarenis?" the dragon asked.

Stammel shook his head. "I have marched all over Aarenis, one war and another. Someone might know me."

"I know a place," the dragon said after a moment. "An island in the sea, summerwards of Aarenis but not as far as Old Aare, where I am known a little and you will be welcome. Can you write your letter?"

"It would be better to use a scribe," Stammel said. "My hand was always crabbed after I broke two fingers years ago. Are we near a town?"

"Yes. I will go with you."

Stammel dictated his letter to a scribe, speaking of "good friends" who had found him a home and asking release from his oath. Then he gave the dragon his uniform, folded into a neat bundle, and the dragon walked away from the town to change and fly away.

Stammel strolled about the market with his stick and bought himself a sweet pastry at one stall and then a tankard of ale. He felt emptied of his old life, the shape of himself waiting for something else to fill it. He sat on a bench listening to ordinary people talking about weather and crops and the market for wool and answered a few questions about himself with pure invention, feeling no guilt for the tale he spun. He would never be back here. Someone offered him another mug of ale; he accepted it and then followed his nose to a stall where he bought two rolls stuffed with fried mushrooms, onion, and ham.

It was evening before the dragon returned, walking up to him in man's shape there in the market square.

"You are sure?"

"Yes." That empty feeling still made him ache, but he also felt certain as stone that his decision was right.

"Do you want to know what he said?"

He did and did not, but only one answer would serve, in courtesy to both the man and the dragon. "Yes."

"He released you," the dragon said, "and said you had a home there if ever you chose to return. He gave me a ring for you to show, should you have need."

"He is a good man," Stammel said. Into the empty feeling came another, a lift of joy. "I hope he does not worry." He knew Arcolin would; he knew he had to bear that.

"Are you ready, then?" the dragon said without answering the implied question.

"I am," Stammel said. They walked out of the village, a distance away the dragon chose, then the dragon shifted into his own form, and Stammel walked into the dragon's mouth until the tongue moved beneath him, drawing him in to the same comfortable place he had sheltered so many times since he'd left the Company.

He slept away the time—whatever time it was—until the dragon woke him, and in his mind the voice said, "We are here." Beneath him the surface moved, lifting him, pushing him toward the open mouth. Scents rushed in—not the delicate scents of a northern spring but summer smells he remembered from here and there in Aarenis: oilberry trees, pungent herbs, roses, a whiff of goats and pigs, the tang of the sea . . . a strong breeze carrying all of that and more. Here it was warm, as warm as the dragon's mouth, with sunlight he could see as a bright blur though he could see nothing else.

"You are facing the rising sun," the dragon said. "I am changing and will walk with you down to the village. We are on the mountain above it."

Stammel waited, turning his head . . . if that was sunrising, then this way was summerwards . . . it would be a view over water toward Old Aare, and that way would be north—he sensed something there, some dark looming mass.

"The mountain," the dragon said. "The people here say sometimes the mountain blows fire. They believe a fire dragon lives deep within it. And they say *I* am a wizard. Take my arm."

It took them some time to come to the village; the trail was rough, and the dragon took care that he did not fall. Stammel did not try to memorize the way; he let himself think only of the sounds and the scents . . . the *clong-clong* of some belled goat or sheep, the clatter of small hooves on rock, dung-smell and fox-smell, the cries of seabirds, and then the stronger scent of the sea as they descended and a sudden whiff of baking bread. Voices now: children shouting, a woman scolding in a southern dialect he had learned to understand back in Siniava's War, in Sibili or Cha or some other place south of Andressat.

"It's the wizard! He's come back!" someone said from a small distance. A youth, he thought. Footsteps, coming nearer, more than one pair, and a lighter step running away, and a child's voice crying out "The wizard! The wizard!"

"Well, wizard, who is this you've brought?" A man's voice, good-natured but firm.

"A friend," the dragon said. "A good man who lost his sight and now needs a quiet place with useful work to do."

"He has the look of a soldier," the man said.

"I was," Stammel said. "But no more."

"We have no soldiers here," the man said. "But if you are the wizard's friend, we welcome you. I work with wood; my name is Cadlin."

Soon others arrived, some introducing themselves at once to Stammel while others talked to the dragon . . . the wizard, he reminded himself. The wizard was still talking to them when a woman named Sulin offered him food and led him a little distance, putting his hand on a bench. He sat down, and she brought him bread smeared with oil and salt, then handed him a pottery cup of water.

"I see you'll do well here," the dragon said after Stammel had finished the bread and was listening to the woman explaining to a child how to wind yarn properly. "I may be back from time to time. Be well, Stammel."

"Thank you," Stammel said. He could see the man-shaped fire move away and did not try to follow; he turned his face once more to the sun.

"Can you see at all, then?" the woman asked.

"Only the light, nothing more," Stammel said.

By the next day he had a home of sorts—a bed in a lean-to at the back of the woodworker's shop and a line strung to help him find the jacks pit out back and the way to the front of the house. From there, someone's child was always ready to guide him where he needed to go. He learned their names quickly, having mastered that art training recruits.

Soon he needed neither guide nor twine to find his way around. Many simple chores were still within his ability; as he learned the routes from home to home, to and from water, he found ways to make himself useful. He sharpened the woodworker's tools, carried anything that needed carrying, put out his hands for one of the women to wind yarn, held up one end of a board while someone else lashed it in place, helped with whatever crop was being harvested. He ate what food was offered him—always enough and always cheerfully offered.

And for a time each day, in the freshness before the day's heat, he practiced the exercises he had practiced his entire adult life. He was not a soldier any longer, but he could not give up that habit. He told himself it kept him fit for the work he did now. Soon he knew by the sound that he had a gaggle of children trying out the same exercises. Then the heavier footsteps of adults.

"Why?" he asked them.

"Sometimes there are pirates."

"I am done with war," Stammel said. But he knew as he said it that war might not be done with him. He hated the thought. For so many years, he had gone to war almost every campaign season; he had endured what that meant. Blindness had freed him from war, as it caged him in darkness, and he had finally come to treasure that freedom. And these people, hardworking all of them, and most of them kind . . . he had seen more than enough of war and what war did to lands and people. He did not want that here.

"There are rumors from the mainland," Cadlin said one day, his plane hissing along the wood. "Trouble there. Maybe it's why the wizard brought you here, because we need a soldier."

"There are always rumors," said Rort from the doorway. "And the wizard would have brought us a soldier, not a blind man." He spat; Stammel heard the gobbet hit the stone beside the workshop door. "No offense to you, Matthis, but you're not a soldier now."

"True," Stammel said. He was sharpening Cadlin's tools, his thumb as good a guide to angle and sharpness as his eyes had been. For a moment he was tempted to throw the best-balanced knife so it would stick quivering in the door frame next to Rort's head, but that was foolish. He knew Rort to be honest and kind, though rough in speech.

"But maybe you know things we should know," Cadlin said. "If trouble does come here, I mean."

"Has there been trouble before? Pirates, someone said?"

"Only once in my life. Mostly the villages on the coast. Where our fish comes from." The salted fish traded up the mountain for fruit and oil and leather.

"You should run away," Stammel said, setting aside one tool for another. "Up the mountain. Pirates, renegades, they will not want to climb very high."

"But last time they came, they broke everything—looms, pots, benches, beds—and then set afire what would burn."

"Did they kill and rape?" Stammel asked. On the blur of his vision memory painted sharp images of one campaign after another, bodies strewn in fields, in cottages, in such workshops as this.

"No, we ran away," Rort said. "But all had to be built again, and it was a hard winter. It would be better to fight, to have our homes, our tools."

"It is true," Stammel said, "that death makes winters easy. There is no hunger or thirst in death, no pain, no anger, and no sorrow. If that is what you want, then stay next time." His words and the tone of his voice surprised him; he had not known he felt that way.

"I thought a soldier would want to fight," Rort said. He sounded aggrieved, but then Rort often did.

"I did, when I was a soldier," Stammel said. "It was my life, and I do not regret it. Now . . . I am no longer a soldier, and I exercise to keep myself fit for work, not . . . not killing."

"The wizard left a gift for you," Cadlin said. Stammel heard him get up from his stool and walk across the workshop. Something scraped—and as if he could see, he knew what it was that Cadlin had lifted down from a peg overhead. "He told me you were blind but not helpless, that you had used this to save others from harm. You might want it, he said." Footsteps came nearer. "Here," Cadlin said from close beside.

Stammel put out his hand and took the crossbow, running his heart-hand down the stock, checking the binding and the string automatically. He heard Rort draw in a sharp breath but did not know what expression of his face or movement of his hand had caused it. Slowly he stood up, careful not to bump the stool on which Cadlin's tools lay waiting for sharpening, and walked to the back entrance. The men were silent.

"Did the wizard leave bolts?" he asked, even as he wondered why he was doing this. Why not put it down, refuse to hold it, refuse to use it ever again? He had no gods, like Paks, to tell him what to do.

Tir had left him, when he could no longer see; Gird had never been his patron.

"Yes," Cadlin said. "I'll bring them."

"Rort," Stammel said, using the least tone of command he could while holding a weapon. "Find a rotten fruit and set it on that stone between the oilberry trees." The stone he knew by touch, by walking to and from it, feeling around it. Shoulder-high on him, and behind it a rising slope with more oilberry trees. Rort went out the front and was back before Stammel had felt through the bag of bolts for one he wanted.

When Rort had placed the fruit, Stammel said, "You stand two paces to one side, and Cadlin, you stand two paces to the other." He heard them moving into place. Then he took his own five paces to the center of the little yard behind the workshop, feeling with his toes for the dip in one of the stones there. He spanned the bow, set the bolt in the groove, and faced them. "Now," he said, "both of you— count to three."

From their voices, from the minute reflections of sound from the stone, from whatever instinct made him the Blind Archer at need, his inner sight built an image of the stone and the fruit. At the count of three he raised the crossbow and touched the trigger; he heard the hum of the string, the flight of the bolt, the soft explosion of the rotten fruit . . . then the bolt's thwack into the trunk of the oilberry tree some paces behind it.

"You—that's impossible," Rort said. Stammel heard longing in his voice as well as disbelief.

"I am the Blind Archer, sometimes," Stammel said. "But it is not enough for war. And you should run away up the mountain if trouble comes." He stroked the bow, then walked back inside and laid it on one of the benches.

"But why did you show us that if you won't—if you can't—" Rort said.

"What I showed you," Stammel said, "is what skill all my years of training gave me. Without those years, without the discipline of a soldier's life, I could not do it. You cannot do it, not having had those years. I am one man; I could not stop them. Run away, I tell you. Store food and some necessities somewhere up there, hidden away: that would be sensible, if you think more trouble is coming. But you are not soldiers, and I cannot make you soldiers, though I have trained many young men and women."

"Will your exercises help us run faster?" Rort asked.

"Yes," Stammel said. "And carry more when you run. And plan what to take and ensure that you can survive until you rebuild. I can help you with that, if you will."

"That is worth learning," Cadlin said. "But we have work to do now. Shall I hang the bow back up, Matthis, and the sack of bolts?"

"Show me the peg," Stammel said. Cadlin led him around, told him where to reach up for the peg. Stammel hung the bow there, then went out and found the bolt he had shot dangling from the bark of an oilberry tree, it had had so little force left. When he came back in with it, Rort was gone. He sat down at his own workspace and checked the point on the bolt before going back to sharpening Cadlin's tools.

CHAPTER NINE

Chaya

"We ask formal audience, sir king," Amrothlin said. Behind him, a group of elves nodded. He looked tired but determined. "It is a matter of importance."

"Of course," Kieri said. He was in a better mood this bright morning; even the prospect of dealing with elves didn't daunt him. A good night's sleep. An early morning session in the salle. Both had left him feeling in tune with spring. "I have matters of importance to discuss with you, as well."

"Sir king, we wish to leave."

"Leave?" He certainly had not expected that.

"Yes. As there is no elvenhome for us here, we find only sorrow where once we found joy. The memories of what we have lost gall us every moment and make the days that should be brief long. If you and the queen had less ability with the taig, we would stay out of duty to tend it, but it is our belief you can do what must be done."

"Is this really all about your sorrow or is it that yesterday you told Arian things you wish you had not?" Kieri asked. She had told him that only direct challenges and questions kept Amrothlin talking. "Perhaps you wish to keep other secrets you know I would ask about."

A faint flush darkened Amrothlin's cheeks. "It is true I spoke too freely to the queen. I did admit there were things I could not say. Not yet, anyway."

Kieri scowled. "Your time is not as our time, Uncle, I know that well. So what seems hasty to you may be a lifetime to us, who must deal with things as they come. I am not a hasty man, save in war and at great need, but even I can see death on the horizon. I am still your king, bound by the oath the Lady and I shared, and you are bound by your oath as well. You owe me the knowledge you have withheld." He paused; Amrothlin glared. "Was it not through lack of knowledge that my mother died and I was taken? That you could not rescue me from those years of torment?" He pushed away the lingering suspicion that the elves—or some of them—might have left him there on purpose. "Withholding knowledge can cause as much harm as knowledge untimely given."

"Are you telling us to stay, sir king?" Amrothlin's expression was challenging, but Kieri felt a subtle lessening of the elf's resistance.

"Yes," Kieri said, putting all the warmth he could into his voice. "Exactly that. Your actions have shaped this realm; your experience and wisdom will help me." He paused. "There is also the matter of the iynisin."

All the elves looked away. "You cannot pretend they do not exist," Kieri said. "Do you think you will be safer elsewhere? Do you have entry to another elvenhome?"

"No," Amrothlin said. "Not yet, at least, though we might hope. But *you* cannot protect us from iynisin."

"I might, if you tell me what I ask," Kieri said. "My magery was growing when Orlith was yet alive; if you help me, perhaps it will become—"

"My lord—" one of the other elves said, looking at Amrothlin.

Amrothlin's expression silenced them both. Kieri saw surrender in his gaze. "You are the king," he said, bowing to Kieri. "You are my sister's son, the Lady's grandson, all we have left. I will stay and assist you as I assisted the Lady."

"But we agreed—" one of the others began.

"I cannot command you," Amrothlin said without turning around. "But he *is* the king."

The others nodded slowly, and Kieri relaxed slightly. They needed something to do, he thought, some assignment. He had no idea what they were capable of, what tasks best suited them. But he had one of some urgency in which they could be helpful if they would.

"These patterns," he said. "I need to know if there are more in the palace, what power they confer, who can use them, and if they exist anywhere else in Chaya. Can they be changed so iynisin cannot use them, or must we rip up the stones?"

This got the elves moving; Amrothlin assigned some to seek out patterns in the palace and others to look at other buildings where— Kieri was sure—the elves already knew such patterns existed. Others were told to paint reversal patterns on heavy cloth to lay on patterns found so anyone attempting to use a destination pattern would be sent back. That left Kieri alone with Amrothlin, who now looked wary.

"So, Uncle," Kieri said. "Sit down and let us continue."

Amrothlin at first was as hesitant to answer Kieri's questions as Arian had reported, but Kieri kept insisting, and finally Amrothlin's resistance gave way. But it was less helpful than Kieri had hoped.

"I should tell you about the Lady's first heir . . . before my sister, your mother."

"I am listening," Kieri said.

That was not, however, where Amrothlin's story began, for he started long before. The tale chilled Kieri's blood; it made sense at last of Paksenarrion's story about the underground stronghold where she had nearly died. Vanryn ago—the vanryn of the elves, ten thousand winters to humans—the elves had lived in the far south that humans called Old Aare, and fewer vanryn ago they had moved north, finally over the mountains. And there the Lady's first heir had chosen the Severance over his mother's obedience to the Singer, turning inexorably into the vicious being imprisoned in the banast taig.

Amrothlin went on—and on—with the tale, telling it as elves did, in great detail, connecting every action to its cause and its consequence. Hours passed, the sun's light shifting from window to window, but Kieri was afraid to break into that torrent of speech now revealing so much he had wondered about. It was nearly dark, and Amrothlin finally had come to Kieri's mother, when Kieri held up his hand at last, and Amrothlin paused.

"Another day, Amrothlin. You and I both need food and rest, and I have other duties, as you know. Come, if you will, the day after next."

Amrothlin stood and bowed. "I will come," he said. "The Singer's blessing on you."

"Take care, Uncle," Kieri said, standing as well. He felt stiff as a log and stuffed with knowledge he needed time to understand. "We know we have enemies still."

That night Arian said, "Did he tell you anything useful or more roundabout tales?"

"I learned that his brother—my eldest uncle—was a traitor and turned iynisin," Kieri said.

"It took him all day to tell you that?"

"That and everything leading up to it, connected with it, and . . . It's no wonder they won't answer simple questions, Arian. They don't think anything is simple." He shook his head. "I suppose it's not, if you're looking at ten or twenty thousand winters as a short time; they can see the beginnings and endings, the connections." He laughed, mocking himself. "So much for elves being peaceful lovers of harmony and song. I heard about quarrels that lasted thousands of years, and grudges held from before the Dwarfmounts were lifted up and set in place. I will never remember it all."

"I suppose you could tell it to a scribe—"

"And get half of it wrong? No. No, I'll deal with the days as they come, use what I can remember. Oh—I didn't ask the steward—did the other elves keep on with the jobs Amrothlin gave them?"

"Yes," Arian said. "They said all the patterns in the palace are on the lowest floor, and there's one in the courtyard, lightly incised into the stone. None in the cellars or pantries, none in the salle or in the entrance to the treasury and ossuary. They said they will have the reversal patterns painted in a few days."

"Amrothlin's coming back in two days," Kieri said. "I hope I don't have to listen to a single elf about anything tomorrow."

Arian laughed. "Let us talk of other things, then."

"Or not talk . . ." Kieri stroked her hair. "We have a child to invite, do we not?"

"We do."

CHAPTER TEN

Arian woke one morning some ten days after Dorrin had left, aware of the taig's intense regard. She felt perfectly healthy, in no need of the taig's care, and wondered why she was feeling its interest so strongly. Then she realized the taig's attention was not concern but a richly braided song of joy from tree and flower and every form of life outside the palace windows. Kieri still slept, but she could not sink back into sleep. Instead she rose and was half dressed when the sense of joy lifted in a dizzying cloud around her.

Delicately, she touched herself with taig sense and found two trembling sparks within. Healthy, yes—no shadow of the earlier poison. As she came into Kieri's bedroom, he woke.

"You had a reason for rousing so early?" he said mildly enough.

"I did," Arian said. "More than one, in fact. Two in particular, but also—"

"Two . . . in particular?" She had his attention, no doubt about it.

"Two."

"Do you know yet what—"

"One of each."

"You're sure . . . of course you are. Let me—"

She came closer; he put his hand on her belly. She felt his attention, his hopes and fears, and then the joy as he knew for himself.

"Thank Falk and the High Lord and the Lady of Flowers," Kieri said. He held her close. Arian nodded against his chest. "And you, my brave queen, so ready to risk again . . . we must be vigilant. We must not fail these children. Are you sure you wish to travel?"

"We still don't know who sent the poison, how the iynisin knew about the pattern here," Arian said. "So my going to Tsaia should be safer than staying."

"I suppose." Kieri had been increasingly reluctant to send her.

"I know I will want to be two places at once." She twined her fingers in his beard and changed the subject. "I wonder how many of the supposedly powerless magelords still have *their* talent."

"It would be best not to find any more in the royal family," Kieri said, shaking his head. "I'm serious about that: we need stability on our western border, and if the government falls apart . . ."

"I won't mention it if I do sense something," Arian said. "Not to them, at least. Now: do we tell anyone about our good news or wait?"

Kieri thought about it a long moment. "We must think of your safety and theirs," he said. "It might be safer to wait—though the way you're grinning—"

"And you!"

"Both of us, then—we can't hide that we're happy, and someone is sure to guess and say something even if we denied it. So I suppose we must tell them. But not everything. Twins! That can be a surprise for later."

"We must go to the ossuary," Arian said. "If your sister has more warnings for us, we must hear them."

"Indeed," Kieri said.

But the bones had no message other than a vague sense of satisfaction, which Arian took as good news. "So: I will leave as soon as Duke Mahieran is ready, and return as quickly as courtesy allows." She pulled on her boots, glancing at Kieri.

"And you will be careful," Kieri said again as he stood and offered her a hand.

"As careful as courtesy allows," Arian said, laughing.

He held her hand. "As careful as our offspring require," he said, not smiling.

"Yes," Arian said, nodding. "That careful."

By the end of breakfast, news had spread through the palace, and

Arian was certain that already someone had slipped out the gate to the city. How long would it be before an elf arrived? And would it be Amrothlin?

The first elf, as it happened, was not Amrothlin but a woman who arrived shortly after breakfast, when they had gone upstairs to change. A Squire brought word that the elf had asked an audience with Arian alone, but Kieri shook his head. "On this day of joy, I cannot be parted from my wife," he said. "Tell her that, and we will receive her in my office." When the servant had left, he turned to Arian. "I do not want you meeting any elves without protection, including the women."

"But Amrothlin—"

"Amrothlin may be true as gold, but he does not control them all. I still think it possible—no, likely—that one of them killed Orlith and may have invited in the iynisin who killed the Lady."

Arian and Kieri came into his office to find the elf standing quietly, a Squire nearby. The elf made a courtesy as graceful as a leaf in the wind. "My lord king," she said. "My lady queen. All the taig sings of your joy, and I bring a gift—" She held out a crystal bottle stoppered with a pale green stone. "This potion combines rare and precious herbs; its action is to cleanse and cool the blood. Should the queen take a fever, a few drops in a cup of wine will ease it and save harm to the babes within." She smiled at them. "I would rejoice to see the grandchildren of my friend," she said.

"So . . . you are not one of those who wish to leave?" Kieri asked.

"Oh, no," the elf said. "I will not leave this land, though others may." She handed the bottle to the Squire, bowed, and withdrew.

"You are not drinking that," Kieri said.

"No," Arian said. "But we may as well see if it smells of the poison we know."

The liquid had only a sharp herbal smell. "It may be harmless," Kieri said, sniffing again.

"But I take no chances," Arian said. "We will pour it out." She frowned. "I have no reason," she said, "and perhaps it is only a form of jealousy for her beauty, but I have no warm feelings for her."

Kieri chuckled. "Perhaps you are remembering my feelings when she suggested we might marry. Yes—this was the same one. A friend of my mother's, she said, and my mother was no elf-child when I was born."

Amrothlin was surprised to hear of the elf woman's visit when he arrived. "But then," he said, "she was your mother's friend, and she would want to congratulate you."

"I have another task for you," Kieri said. "Orlith's murder—his wounds were not made by crossbow bolts or longbow arrows. It is possible he was killed by another elf, and if so—we may yet have enemies among the elves in Lyonya."

"Iynisin use the same bows and arrows as elves," Amrothlin said. "That is more likely than that anyone I know would kill someone so respected—"

"I hope that will prove true," Kieri said. "But I would know for certain. Consider the possibility, at least. If you hear anything, tell me."

Amrothlin nodded. He left after a few minutes, and the rest of the day was a constant stream of visitors come to congratulate the king and queen. Arian was glad she had already readied her clothes and equipment for the trip, because she had no chance to supervise the last-minute packing. She made sure, however, to see the bottle the elf had brought emptied out down one of the kitchen sinks.

CHAPTER ELEVEN

Vérella

S leeping later in the morning helped Camwyn stay awake during his lessons, and extra exercise seemed to keep his hand from lighting up every night. One mug of sib at midday kept him alert through his lessons and supper with Mikeli when that was required. His brother treated him more as an ally, less as a child, as if discussing a maturing body and marriage made him older. Mikeli even brought up the problem of the old regalia and his own difficult dreams. "It's talking to me every night now. Telling me to let it go. I tell you, Camwyn, I do not know what to do or whom to ask for advice. It wants to be with Duke Verrakai, and it wants her to put it on. Should I release her from her oath? Even command her to take it? But then who would take over in her place? Beclan is too young and not yet in control of his magery, according to her letters."

At that last, Camwyn twitched. Mikeli glanced at him, one eyebrow raised. "Can he learn that, do you think?" Camwyn asked, doing his best to feign only mild interest.

"He had better," Mikeli said, in what Camwyn thought of as his king voice. "We cannot have a magelord in Tsaia who is not both master of his magery and committed to the Crown and to Gird's law." His voice softened once more from king to brother. "Duke Verrakai thinks he can, and she learned to, so I suppose it can be done."

Camwyn wondered if he could learn to control his own magery

before anyone found out about it. If only there were someone he could ask . . . but Duke Verrakai was an inconvenient distance away.

"Do you think it's . . . sort of . . . leaking magery?" he asked instead.

"Leaking? What do you mean?"

"Well . . ." Inspiration struck. "Beclan had been where it was, in Verrakai House, when he showed magery. And it's talking to you, you say. What if, because it's old and was a magelord thing, it's so full of magery that it leaks out? And it can seep into people, making them mages when they weren't."

Mikeli looked thoughtful for a few moments, then shook his head. "I don't think that's how magery works, Cam. Not the magery in people. I think that's different from the magic in magical items like a sword."

"Are you sure? How would you know?"

Mikeli shook his head again. "I don't know for certain. How could I? But it just seems like they ought to be different. Do magical items have a will?"

"Magic swords can light up when they are near something dangerous. Didn't Duke Verrakai's magic sword make a light—?"

"She was holding it, and she's a mage," Mikeli said.

"But it was magic before she owned it. Gwenno Marrakai wrote Aris that Duke Verrakai said she saw it light up when another soldier had it."

"I suppose," Mikeli said. "But it still needed a person to wield it. Making a light isn't the same as making magic . . . I don't think. Though magelords can make light. I saw Duke Verrakai . . ."

Camwyn did not want to pursue that thought. "Do magelords make magic things like swords, or can other people?" he asked. "Can wizards make a sword or a dagger magic?"

"Not that I know of," Mikeli said. "The only magic swords I've heard about were dwarf-wrought or elf-wrought."

"So that crown must've been made by a dwarf or an elf, whatever they say," Camwyn said.

"Nooo . . . I don't think they're lying," Mikeli said. "Which means that magelords might have such magicks. Some of them. Maybe no one now alive." He looked hard at Camwyn. "You're asking a lot of questions about magery, Cam. I hope you're not wishing you were like Beclan."

"I'm not!" That much was true. He had no wish at all to be like Beclan. He sent another silent passionate prayer to Gird to keep his hand from betraying him. "I wouldn't want that. I just—I just can't help being curious. It's like the dragon that came. I want to know things—about dragons, about magic, about . . . about everything."

"Except, apparently, about the monetary policy of Tsaia," Mikeli said, grinning now. "Master Danthur blames it on your being an overindulged prince who's never had to learn the value of money, but he says he's very glad you're not in line to succeed unless I fail of siring an heir."

"I try," Camwyn said, feeling sulky all at once. "And I do know the value of money. I know what my allowance covers and how much I can spend, and I haven't overspent in a long time . . . at least a half-year, and that was only to get presents for my friends."

"I know you're learning, Cam. I'm not scolding you. But until I do get an heir, the more you know . . ."

"The better. I know. I'm trying, really I am. But all that about exchange rates . . . if they stayed the same, I could understand it, but not when it changes. Market law is easier. Fair weights, fair measures: that makes sense. Master Danthur says it's not enough."

"It's not," Mikeli said. "But I know you're trying, Cam. I wish it weren't so hard for you. You know the Lyonyan queen is coming to visit; you will meet her. You'll want to impress her, I'm sure."

Camwyn felt a telltale warmth in his hand, and he was trying more than anything else to keep that hand hidden under the table. Was the finger glowing now? Right here? Where Mikeli might see it? He did not dare look.

"Are you dining with Council tonight?" he asked.

"Yes. Since word got out—and I believe what you said, that you weren't the source—I need to talk it over with them. Some of them. You?"

"I'm fine," Camwyn said, sticking both hands deep in his pockets as he stood. The right didn't feel any hotter than the left, actually. "I'll try again with the exchange rates. After supper, maybe."

"Don't stint your sleep," Mikeli said. "It's not that serious."

Maybe. Or maybe it was. He could not put thoughts of the strange regalia out of his mind . . . and as soon as he lay down that night, the image of the crown he'd never seen appeared. Blue stones, white stones . . . well, clear, but sparkling. It was a beautiful crown . . . and the ring . . . the bracelet . . .

Let us go. Let us go home again. Let us free.

The voice—how could a crown have a voice?—seemed to ripple in his mind like water chuckling in a stream. Camwyn felt less frightened than he thought he should. The crown had spoken to Mikeli: why would it not speak to a prince?

Our sister is held captive by evil.

Sister? The crown had a sister? How could a crown have a sister? Another crown, a crown for a queen? Camwyn was puzzling over that when another image came into his mind: not a crown but a necklace, star-bright in the darkness of his chamber.

Torre's necklace, it must be.

No. Our sister, of the same making.

Camwyn wondered if he thought he saw these things only because Mikeli had spoken of them. He'd never seen the regalia himself. Only Mikeli, the Marshal-Judicar, and his uncle Mahieran—and Duke Verrakai, of course—had that he knew of. He lay still, trying to convince himself it was his imagination, that same imagination he'd always been told would get him into trouble. But he knew there was such a crown, a real one. And a necklace, now he thought of it: the one stolen from Fin Panir. So if there could be a real crown, a real necklace . . . and a dragon in the world, which he knew absolutely to be true . . . *was* it just imagination?

Without any warning, his entire hand lit up like a candelabra, making the room bright enough to see clearly from end to end.

Such magic would open the chest.

He shoved his hand under a pillow, blinking against the afterimage of light, before the words sank in. Open . . . the chest? The sealed chest that no one but Duke Verrakai had been able to open? That not even the paladin had been able to move?

The voice had not sounded like the crown's voice, but it was clear as if spoken in his ear. He could not have made it up. He would not have made up something like that. He pulled his hand partway from under the pillow. No light. It had gone out. Thank Gird. He put his head down on the pillow and then sat up again. The pillow smelled scorched. He lay awake, sweating and trembling, thinking.

Guards patrolled the palace all night. Someone was stationed at the door of the treasury all the time, day and night. There was no way he could get in there unseen . . . and he had no legitimate reason to go there at all. He tried to imagine the steward's reaction if he asked to see the treasury. The man would want to know why, and whether his brother the king had sent him, and if he'd asked . . .

Another thought came unbidden. He was supposed to learn about exchange rates and values of things . . . perhaps Master Danthur would want him to see . . . whatever was there. Perhaps if he asked the right questions . . . the answers would be in the treasury.

On that thought he fell asleep and did not wake until morning.

The Lyonyan queen's coming visit had already begun to upset the usual routine. Even his instructors seemed less alert than usual, and he found he could gain both information and time. Judicious questioning about counterfeiting and the difficulty of distinguishing counterfeit coinage and false jewels led to Master Danthur suggesting a trip to the treasury.

Camwyn approached the treasury doors with vivid curiosity but, once inside, found the great room boring. Windowless now, it had once been a ballroom with a portico overlooking the street far below, catching the cooler breezes. Now it was stuffy and smelled like any storeroom. Soft light filled it; Camwyn looked up and found a skylight far overhead.

"Two full stories up, inside," the steward said. "Was a gallery up there one time, but they tore it down when they blocked up the windows. Outside now it's a sheer drop, four stories at least, and not a ledge or nub to cling to."

Camwyn remembered looking up as he rode down that street; the wall here was far higher than on the other sides of the palace complex, and there was, he knew, a long blank stretch between windows. Still . . . surely the best thieves could climb up to the roof. From another part of the wall?

"You're not here to gape," Master Danthur said. "Pay attention."

Camwyn looked around again. Nothing but boxes, chests, shelves of smaller boxes and chests, cabinets . . . The steward and his tutor joined in opening boxes filled with sacks of coins old and new, counterfeit and true. The castle's own expert, Master Junnar of the Moneychangers' Guild, arrived to show him how to test coins for gold or silver, how to use fine scales and displacement to determine whether a coin had the right amount of a precious metal.

Camwyn found that part moderately interesting, though he was tempted to ask why Master Junnar didn't just smell the coins. To him, each had a distinct odor, and he saw no reason for the tests. He did not ask, suspecting that this was yet another sign that he was developing powers he should not.

He did learn more about the Tsaian coinage than he'd known before, and his ability to pick out the counterfeits impressed Master Junnar, but it was not until near the end of the lesson, when he walked about the treasury and asked what was in this or that box or chest, that he found the one containing the regalia.

The closer he got to it, in fact, the more he wanted to approach. It was a plain box—not finely finished, carved, or inlaid—and its only distinguishing feature was a lack of any: no hinges, no hasp, no discernible line where lid met body.

"What is this?" he asked, though he already knew. "A box without any opening?"

"It's a puzzle," the steward said. "It houses the gifts Duke Verrakai gave the king at his coronation."

"It's none of your concern, Prince Camwyn," Master Danthur said. Master Junnar nodded. "Such a thing, even if it could be seen, would have no place in your education."

That was too much. "Surely, sir, a foreign crown in our treasury—one that has both affected our history and is like to affect our future—should be part of my education. The king—" He stopped, thinking how to say anything useful without breaking Mikeli's prohibitions. "Any king," he said, "or any king's advisor, must understand the implications of such a thing, should he not?"

Master Danthur looked down his nose, more difficult as Camwyn was now his height. "Well, prince, you certainly are showing more interest in foreign affairs than you were a few days past."

"Mikeli—the king—explained to me why it was important, especially with the Lyonyan queen visiting," Camwyn said, attempting a mix of naivete and humility and seeing from his tutor's face that he'd failed.

"Hmpf. And I see you apply that advice to what interests the boy you are, not to what may be needed by the man you might become. Explain to me, then, what you see as the 'implications,' as you call them, of these objects."

That he could do, having thought about them since Duke Verrakai first brought them. "Possession of them must have affected Verrakai policy," he said. "If only in keeping them secret so long. We do not have all the records of Tsaia during the Girdish war, but I would guess—"

"Guessing is not history, Prince."

"I know that, sir, but it's all we have. The Verrakaien had these things and might well have thought to be kings when the old king fell in the war—only they weren't allowed. They would resent that; anyone would. They kept the things secret and used blood magery to bind them—"

"And no blood magery binds them now—so why are they bound?" asked the steward, coming nearer.

"They bound themselves," Camwyn said. "At least that's what I heard—" And his sources, he knew, would be dismissed by his tutor as mere gossip.

"So it seems," the steward said. "But why? Was it part of a Verrakai plot to move their influence here, into the heart of the realm?"

"I doubt it," Camwyn said before his tutor could get a word in. "If we stipulate—" A word his tutors used often; he was proud of himself for using it now. "—that the former Verrakaien were hostile to the Crown, they were doing their best to keep the regalia and knowledge of it secret. I think the king thinks that keeping it secret was treasonous and handing it over was not."

"True," his tutor said. "But that does not explain how the box sealed itself. Or why."

"To keep anyone but Duke Verrakai from opening it," Camwyn said. "And—there's that necklace people talk about, the one stolen from Fin Panir. If the magicks in this box—" He patted it and felt his hand tingle. *Oh, please, don't let it light up!* He rushed on. "If the magicks in this box somehow know that the necklace was stolen—if the regalia have a will and want to be together—then it might fear having pieces stolen here."

"But it's in the treasury," the steward said. "It's safe here."

"The Marshal-General thought the necklace was safe in the treasury in Fin Panir," Camwyn said.

Silence for a moment; they all looked at him as if they could see his thoughts. He hoped they couldn't.

"I did wonder if it was Duke Verrakai's magery," the steward said. "That she did not trust me—or the king—and wanted it to open only in her presence. But she said it talked to her—I heard her say so."

Camwyn held himself still with an effort. If it talked to her, and to Mikeli, and to him . . . that had to be its own magery somehow. "If the other Verrakai held it bound in blood magery—then they weren't listening to it."

"That doesn't necessarily follow," his tutor said. "Maybe they forced it to talk."

"Duke Verrakai could ask it," Camwyn said. They all stared at him again; he felt his face heating. "She could," he said. "Why not?"

So could you. The voice was so clear in his head he expected to see them all react to it, but no one did.

"What was that?" his tutor asked.

"Um?"

"You looked as if you'd sat on a hot horseshoe nail."

"I just thought—if it can talk to Duke Verrakai, whom else can it talk to?"

"What, do you think it would talk to *you*? Isn't it more likely to talk to the king, if anyone other than the Duke?"

Camwyn felt the heat on his face.

"Now don't sulk," Master Danthur said. "You surely realize the king is more important than you are—you may be a prince, but you're only a boy. Did you really, seriously, think a magical item would prefer to talk to you?"

"No," Camwyn muttered. The men all stared at him; he felt himself going redder by the instant. He would have to say something more to divert them but couldn't think of anything that wouldn't make things worse. "I just . . . I just worry that if it can talk to one person, it could talk to another. What if it did talk to the king? We don't know whose it was or what its purpose is. Is it even safe to have it here?"

"That's what I said," the steward said. "Granted it's not a Verrakai plot. But just that it's here . . . If it started talking to the king—or the prince—or you or me—and no one else could hear it, that would be a foreign influence."

All the men were staring at the box now, not at him; Camwyn edged toward the door but made only two careful steps before being noticed. "Where do you think you're going?" Master Danthur asked.

"I'm hungry," he said. "And I thought I heard the gong."

"You're always hungry," Master Danthur said. "But enough of this time wasting. Back to the schoolroom with you this instant."

Camwyn didn't argue. He now knew the way to the treasury and the order in which its locks must be unlocked. He had seen the keys for each lock; he had seen them hooked back onto the steward's belt. The guards didn't have keys; no use befriending them. The treasury had no windows, of course . . . but it did have, high overhead, what looked to him like a skylight. Lucky the dragon hadn't landed there, Camwyn thought.

CHAPTER TWELVE

Arian arrived in Vérella after a journey far different from what she had expected; the forest she was used to dwindled quickly to strips of woods, giving long views of cultivated land. But nothing compared to Vérella. At Westbells, where they paused to greet Marshal Torin, Arian first heard the faint sound of bells.

"Yes, those are the bells the elves gave," Marshal Torin said when she asked. "You will hear them all the way to the city, I expect."

"Then we had better ride on," Duke Mahieran said, "or the whole city will go deaf."

As they rode, more and more people stood by the road to watch and shout greetings.

"Look there—you can see the walls now. And the bridge."

Arian stared at the looming gray shape. Walls, towers, more towers, the tops of buildings just visible. She could not even guess how tall the walls were, or the towers within them. She saw buildings outside the walls on the downstream side—ramshackle structures, part stone and part wood, petering out into mere hovels. Her nose wrinkled at the stench of filth draining into the river, something no elf-born could ignore or tolerate.

A bridge, massive as the walls, spanned the Honnorgat, which ran deep and swift. Buildings clustered around its near end as well and stretched along the road south. Kieri had told her about that road to the Dwarfmounts that led over the pass to Valdaire and Aarenis. As they came between the buildings—inns and taverns and shops crammed together—the lines of people watching them pass thickened. The air smelled of people and cooked food and more animals.

Most had flowers to throw in her path; others waved flowering branches. Arian had never seen so many people at once in her life. Their cheers and the sound of the bells together were deafening; she could not tell what they were shouting for the noise. As they neared the bridge, Arian saw a party riding toward them, escorted by more of the Royal Guard, one in the lead bearing a great banner.

"It's the king," Mahieran said, shouting in her ear. "He's come to welcome you."

The heavy white horses Kieri had told her about, the Tsaian Grays, pranced over the bridge. Arian's mount trembled; she soothed it as she watched the others come nearer. The king's party stopped when the king had cleared the bridge. Someone—Arian could not see who—bellowed, and the crowd nearest them fell silent. Overhead the bell chime continued, sweet and inexorable. The king wore the Mahieran colors, with a long crimson cloak, its silver embroidery glittering in the sun, draped back over his horse's rump.

Two mounted trumpeters blew fanfares, and the king rode forward another two lengths. Beside Arian, Duke Mahieran bowed almost to his horse's crest. Arian merely inclined her head as Kieri had advised.

For a moment, all was still. King Mikeli looked at her, and she at him; she was sure he was making the same assessment she was. He was young—very young—and the family resemblance to Duke Mahieran and both Beclan and Rothlin was strong. He had darker hair and eyes than his cousins but the same bone structure, the same nose. And when he smiled, which he did then, the same smile.

"Be welcome here, Arian, Lyonya's queen," he said then. "We greet you in all honor and wish you all joy of your visit."

Arian had her first speech memorized, formal and full of praise for Tsaia and the courtesy of her escort. She delivered it smoothly, and the crowd cheered.

"If it pleases you to ride with me to the palace," the king said, "my escort and yours will join together."

"Thank you, sir king," Arian said. She nudged her mount closer; the king wheeled and came up on her heart-side. The rest rearranged themselves; Arian noticed that the king looked straight ahead. "King Kieri sends his greetings," she said. "He wishes you every health and joy."

He glanced at her from the corner of his eye. "Things are more difficult without him," he said.

"It is a difficult time," Arian said.

"I understand that you are also half-elven," he said.

"Yes. My father was an elf; he died not long ago."

The king turned to look at her. "Died? I thought elves never died."

"A blade through the heart will kill even an elf," Arian said. "You have not heard the latest, then?"

"No—my uncle sent word that you—that poison had killed—"

"Our child, yes," Arian said. Here in public, she must hide the grief that even new life could not extinguish. She kept her voice steady, her face immobile. "And others' babes as well. I hope Duke Mahieran bade you take care and have expensive spices examined for adulterants."

"He said it was in food, yes. We have taken precautions. More of this at the palace," the king said, just as one of the Royal Guard said, "Ready, sir king." Ahead of them, the king's banner bearer moved forward, and behind him one of Arian's Squires with her banner. Their horses stepped off in stride.

Arian glanced at the river below. Dark, swift, with little streaks of white foam. Ahead, the streets were thronged with people and closed in by tall buildings. They passed streets leading off to her right. More buildings crowded shoulder to shoulder down all of them. She recognized Dorrin's house by its pennant; from its upper windows one of Dorrin's people threw down rose petals. One caught on Arian's nose; she blew it off, and it landed on her horse's mane. On the other side, the wall of the palace complex stood much taller than the palace wall in Chaya. The clamor of the bells stopped suddenly as they turned the corner into the wider street that led to the palace gates, but the cheering continued.

"The bells have their own timing," the king said without looking at her. "They always ring at noon—but also when they feel like it."

"You have no ringers?"

"No. Legend says the elves installed them and told the king to leave them alone. We have no way to ring them—they are sealed into their tower."

Once in the palace courtyard, paved with the same pinkish stone as the ashlars of the wall, servants swarmed to take the horses and unload the pack animals. This was the courtyard Dorrin had told her of where the battle of magelords had taken place.

Arian followed her escort through the palace to the apartment set aside for her, the former queen's chambers. The bedroom overwhelmed with heavy furniture, all covered in rose-colored velvet under lace, velvet draperies and bed curtains, tapestries depicting flirtatious maidens and fond lovers in lush gardens, and a strong scent of dried rose petals. What had the king's mother been like to choose such decor? The room felt stuffy and warm; Arian's headache—born of the noise and bright sun outside—worsened.

Servants in palace livery bustled about—maids unpacking Arian's clothes into a closet the size of a small room, bringing in ewers of hot and cool water, filling the pink stone tub in the bathing room, scattering rose petals on the water. "Refreshments are on the way, milady queen," one of the maids said. "You will want to refresh yourself and rest after your long journey, we know. Your ladies-in-waiting—"

It took a moment for Arian to realize the maid meant her women Squires. "Not ladies-in-waiting," she said. "These are my Squires, my guards. They are all Knights of Falk."

"Oh!" The maid looked frightened. "Beg pardon, milady queen . . . we thought—"

"No matter," Arian said. "They will not trouble you."

She had no idea how to get rid of these strangers without offense. Lieth, who had been to Vérella before, gently shooed the maids all the way out of the chambers and came back with an armload of towels scented heavily with herbs.

"I'll stay while you bathe," Lieth said. "And Maelis can watch the door. They're strange." She set towels on one of the benches in the bathing room as Arian undressed.

"Strange?" Arian stepped into the tub.

"Yes." Lieth put the clothes Arian had worn into a basket to one side. "They were surprised that women could be King's Squires when we came before. Few of their women become knights."

Arian slid deeper into the water, savoring the feeling of travel grime coming off and muscles loosening. "What about Paksenarrion?"

Lieth frowned. "She's a paladin. And Girdish women do train as soldiers. But not the nobles."

After her bath, Arian pulled on her thinnest nightshirt, climbed the steps to the bed, and pushed aside some of the cushions. The lace coverlet looked scratchy, the velvet too hot. Maelis helped her turn back the covers to linen sheets below. Arian lay down; though she was tired, she could not relax at first: she had no connection to the taig. She had seen no trees, no grass, within the city, only stone and brick and people and their things. She lay quietly, persuading her muscles to relax one by one, and breathed carefully, imagining a cool green breeze out of the forest. She could feel the new life within her. For the moment, safe. Perhaps the moment was enough.

Arian woke clearheaded and refreshed. The rose-colored room, though still stuffy, was less oppressive. She dressed in one of the outfits she and Kieri had devised both for her own comfort and to lessen animosity toward Dorrin's choice of clothes at court: dress shirt with ruffles at throat and wrists, dark green trousers with their subtle woven pattern of leaves tucked into low boots of russet leather, brocaded vest bright with multicolored flowers, open-fronted lighter green coat with the Lyonyan royal crest embroidered on the back.

Outside in the passage, a man in a Royal Guard uniform waited. He bowed to Arian.

"Milady, queen, the king requested that I show the way to the small dining room. I am Sir Aldan Menisor, and it is my honor to be assigned as your guide wherever you wish to go."

"Thank you," Arian said.

He started off; she moved with him; her Squires followed. Then he glanced back. "Are these coming with you?"

"My Squires . . . yes. They go with me everywhere."

Two more Royal Guards flanked a doorway ahead of them. Sir Aldan spoke to them; one stepped inside and announced Arian: "Sir king, the right royal queen of Lyonya, Arian."

Arian gave her Squires a hand signal, and they let her go into the room alone. Mikeli stood beside a table laden with trays of food. "I hope you feel as refreshed as you look," he said. His gaze lingered a little too long, she thought, but Tsaian customs might be different.

"Your people provided every comfort, and I do indeed feel refreshed," Arian said.

"I thought a quiet evening for your first." He gestured to the table.

"Thank you," Arian said again, and sat in the chair he indicated.

For the rest of that meal, she was aware of the king's youth and of his fascination with her. Though perfectly polite in speech, his expression revealed a boy half enchanted by the mere idea of meeting an elf-maid. Which she wasn't.

"You know I am with child," she said finally. He blinked, and a little color came to his cheeks.

"I—I can scarcely believe what I am told, that you are of age to bear children, let alone the king's age."

"A year older, in fact," Arian said. "Or so I was told by my mother; we half-elves do not attend as much to actual age as you do."

"And a wife and soon to be a mother," he said, as if instructing himself to remember it. "When your king was a duke here, he seemed much older than you look."

"Because he was reared among humans and away from the elven-home," Arian said. "My early life was very different from his. And, my lord, he now looks younger than he did."

"With such a wife, of course he would."

An attempt at gallantry but not welcome; Arian frowned. "Not

so, my lord. It is the taig and elven magery combined that have restored his body."

"I'm sorry." The king flushed again. "I didn't mean any
rudeness—"

Arian relented. "I am not offended; do not fret yourself."

"You sound like my aunt," he said. "Now I can believe you are
older than I." He ate another pastry and let silence build briefly. "Do
you always go armed?" the king asked suddenly. "You have your
Squires to protect you."

"I'm a Knight of Falk," Arian said, touching her ruby. "And we,
like you, have been attacked in our own palace. Are you ever far from
your sword?" She had seen it hanging at his side.

"No, but—but you're the queen."

"And you're a king, and so is Kieri. Perhaps it is not the custom
here for noblewomen to bear weapons, but it is with us. Sier Davonin, who's gone completely gray and is old enough to be my mother,
trains with us as well."

He left that topic for another, and another, and finally invited her
to take a brief tour of the palace that evening. Rather than return to
the stuffy suite, Arian agreed. A chance to see the royal salle and
meet the Knight-Commander of the Bells would give her an opportunity to look for the elven patterns Kieri thought she might find.

Their path through the palace's labyrinthine tangle of passages
brought them at last to the Marshal-Judicar's office.

Arian wondered if this was the same place where the assassination attempt of the previous spring had taken place but did not ask.
As they passed through an outer room, obviously an office, she
heard, "Is that you, Mikeli?" from the next.

"It is, Marshal-Judicar, and I'm bringing Lyonya's queen with
me."

"Wait just a moment." A thump as of chair legs hitting the floor,
a mutter too low to understand but for the tone, which was clearly
one of dismay. Then, "You should have let me know . . ." and the
Marshal-Judicar appeared in the doorway.

Arian had met Marshals on her trip along the River Road; Duke
Mahieran had stopped at every grange. Would a Marshal-Judicar—
arbiter of the Code of Gird in Tsaia—be more like a Marshal or a

noble? Marshal-Judicar Oktar reminded her at first glance of Arms-master Carlion: square-set, moving with the controlled power of a fighter. Aside from that, he was dressed like any other Marshal.

"Lady," he said to Arian, bowing. "You will pardon me, I hope, for not being ready to welcome you properly. I was sure you would be resting this evening after so long a journey."

"Readily, if you will pardon my ignorance of what a Marshal-Judicar actually does," Arian said, smiling. "We do not have many Girdish in Lyonya, and thus few Marshals and no Marshal-Judicar."

"You have heard of the Code of Gird?" Oktar said.

"Yes, but I know little of it."

He leaned forward a little, eyes gleaming with the joy of any expert who finds a novice to instruct, and launched into what promised to be a long lecture.

Even as Arian reconciled herself to this, the king intervened. "Another time, please, Oktar," he said. "I'm taking Queen Arian around the palace this evening. You're welcome to come with us if you wish. I thought I'd show her the royal salle and the Bells' training hall and have her meet the Knight-Commander."

"Certainly. Be glad to." Oktar gave up his lecture, went to the weapons rack on one wall, and took down his sword. Over his shoulder, he said to Arian, "I saw you carried a sword and wondered if it was ornamental."

"No," Arian said. She considered telling him that she'd killed with it. Instead she said, "I am a Knight of Falk."

"Ah. Like our Knights of Gird."

As they neared the salle after another confusing trip through crooked passages and stairways, the clash of blades sounded clearly down the passage. The long high room had polished mirrors on two walls and a floor whose inlaid pattern, Arian saw at once, was not the elven one, merely the Tsaian Rose.

The two young men fencing in the center of this space had not heard the party arrive, but Arian recognized Duke Mahieran's son Rothlin seated on a bench across the room. He came to his feet. "The king," he said. The others grounded their blades at once and turned to the door.

"I was hoping some of you would be here," the king said. To

Arian he said, "My closest friends. You know Rothlin, of course, but here is Juris Kirgan Marrakai—" The black-haired young man reminded Arian at once of Gwenno Marrakai. "And Rolyan Serrostin." Rolyan had lighter hair, a ruddier complexion. To them he said, "This is Queen Arian of Lyonya. She wished to see the salle, with a view to practicing here."

"Honored, milady queen," Juris Marrakai said. He and Rolyan both stared—the same wide-eyed look of wonder the king had first given her. "Rothlin told us about your royal salle. It has different levels, he said."

"Yes, it does," Arian said. She looked around. "And a very fierce armsmaster whom even the king obeys—do you practice alone, then?"

"Rothlin's being our instructor this evening, milady queen," Rolyan said. "He said he was too tired to fence himself, so we didn't bother Armsmaster Fralorn."

"And has Rothlin been approved to supervise your practices?" the Marshal-Judicar asked. From the guilty looks on all three faces, the answer was clear, and Oktar had known it.

The king turned to one of his escort. "Go tell Armsmaster Fralorn that I'm in the salle with Queen Arian and ask him to attend."

When the man had left, the king turned to his friends. "Do not get me in trouble with Fralorn. The rules are rules for all. Quickly now; fetch bandas for us."

By the time Fralorn arrived, the entire party, including Arian's Squires, had donned bandas.

Fralorn was a tall, lean man with thinning dark hair and a gray mustache. He wore clothes Arian had not seen before: short full breeches over stockings, thin slippers of gray kid, and a close-fitting gray tunic embroidered with the royal arms in rose and crimson. "Sir king," he said, bowing. His gaze swept the room and snagged momentarily on the swords lying on the bench where Rothlin had been sitting. "How may I serve?"

"Milady," the king said, "may I present Armsmaster Fralorn." Fralorn bowed. "And this is Queen Arian of Lyonya," the king said. "Queen Arian asked if it would be possible for her to practice in the salle daily."

Fralorn smiled and bowed again. "My honor, milady queen,

would be to have you share this space. May one ask what time of day the queen prefers to drill?"

"King Kieri and I drill before breakfast," Arian said. "It improves the appetite."

"Indeed, milady, so it would, and the swordplay as well. And would that be with your own escort, or would you wish to drill with others?"

"Either would suit me," Arian said. "I wish to cause no more work for my hosts than necessary."

"Never mind that," Fralorn said. "Perhaps—I see you are wearing a banda—you would enjoy a brief session this evening? Then, should you wish other partners, I will know which might suit you best."

"Yes, indeed," Arian said.

"Perhaps you would like to work with your own escort first," he said.

"Certainly." Arian turned to Garrion. "Shall we?" He nodded and she led the way to the center of the salle.

Fralorn turned to the others for a moment, his tone crisp and commanding as he said, "Kirgan Marrakai, Nigan Serrostin, I see you laid your blades ready; you two and the king may warm up with footwork exercises on the targes at that end. Sequence five from Mathalion's Classics. Remember to keep time accurately."

"Yes, Armsmaster," they said, meek as mice. Arian laughed to herself. They knew they were caught.

"Now, milady, if you permit, a brief warm-up. Keeping distance; I will call the pattern for your escort. Will that suit?"

"Excellently," Arian said. Garrion followed the armsmaster's instructions; Arian inverted them, and after a very short time Fralorn nodded. She and Garrion squared off, beginning with one of their standard drills. They had sparred many times; they knew each other's tricks and rarely got a touch on each other on level ground.

"Hold, please," Fralorn said. "Milady queen, you are the equal of any blade in the kingdom, and so is your escort. Have you ever instructed?" His voice held no flattery, only a professional assessment.

"Yes, but not recently."

"Would you consider crossing blades with me someday?"

"Yes, certainly."

"At the moment I believe the young gentlemen need an instructor's eye on them. The king should accompany *you,* of course . . ." Fralorn approached the three, who were keeping a reasonably good tempo and distance in what Arian saw was a complicated footwork pattern.

"Sir king, your guest would appreciate your guidance. I am certain, however, that Kirgans Marrakai and Mahieran and Nigan Serrostin would enjoy continuing their exercise with me. Perhaps Marshal-Judicar Oktar would care to join us?"

Arian stifled another laugh. The young men looked anything but eager for the exercise, but they bowed and said, "Yes, Armsmaster."

The king led the way out of earshot of the salle and then turned to Arian with a mischievous grin. "They will regret they broke the rules," he said. "I myself would not dare to drill without him or one of the approved auditors present. Not now, anyway. I did that with Juris once when I was a boy Cam's age, and it didn't end with a footwork drill. I had bruises through the banda."

"At Falk's Hall, we students tried to get in some practice time when the instructors weren't hanging over us. Punishment was footwork drills while holding a pike overhead."

"You broke rules?" He sounded disbelieving.

"Not very often," Arian said. "But enough to know what would happen when I did."

"I'm surprised at Juris and Roly; I suppose they thought everyone would be busy with your visit."

"Perhaps they learned something new while Rothlin was away and wanted to show him."

"Still, they shouldn't. They're dukes' sons; they should set an example." *If I have to,* that meant. Arian reminded herself that this king was very young, had lost both his parents early, and only the year before had been nearly killed in his own palace. He went on in a different tone, "Though if I set them a better example, maybe they wouldn't do things like that."

"Do they often?"

"No. That's why I was so surprised. We're going to the grange-hall for the Bells now—it's the other place you could practice. The Knight-Commander would need to know you were coming—it's the training hall for the Knights of the Bells, and sometimes it's full."

"I understand," Arian said.

The Knight-Commander was in his office when they arrived, writing in a ledger. "Sir king," he said, rising and bowing. "Milady queen." Juris Kostvan was a man of the king's height with light blue eyes and honey-colored hair. He wore a long blue surcoat with the symbols of the Knights of the Bells embroidered in silver on the breast. He was new to this post, Arian knew; one of the king's uncles had been the previous Knight-Commander, killed the same night as the previous Marshal-Judicar.

He gave Arian a tour: the armory with its racks of swords of different styles, the polearms, the battle-axes and maces, the crossbows hanging from hooks, the longbows on racks. "And now the grange-hall," he said. This hall was much larger than the royal salle, with ranks of seats along one side. "We hold the trials of arms here—so we needed more space for witnesses."

Arian started to ask a polite question, but as he moved forward, the light from his torch picked out a faint incised pattern on the floor, a pattern she recognized. It pulled at her less strongly than the one in Chaya, but she felt it nonetheless. "What is that?" she asked, bending to touch it. Her fingers tingled.

He looked embarrassed. "I don't know," he said. "Some knight-candidates have asked, but it must be accidental, some flaw in the stone. The surface is smooth, as you felt, and it's all one block of stone—you can see the joints to the next."

Her heart sped. How could they think that, when to her vision the pattern grew clearer every moment, colors beginning to show through the stone's own pale gray. "Interesting," she managed to say. Kieri had been very specific: if the pattern existed in the Tsaian palace, the king must be told—but discreetly. She thought back to that conversation. This man was a Konhalt and supposedly loyal to the Crown, but some Konhalts had not been. She would have to tell the king when they were alone.

The king led her back to the corridor off which her suite opened and bowed to her there. "As we are to meet early at the salle, I will leave you now. You must surely be fatigued." He bowed again.

"Sir king," Arian said before he could turn away. "I have a message from Kieri that I must give you now."

"Now?" His brows went up.

"Yes." She looked up and down the corridor. Only her own Squires and two of his palace guard. "It is of utmost importance."

"Well, then . . ." He looked around him and motioned his guards to move away. "Can you tell me here?"

"Yes." In courtesy, she gestured for her Squires to move away, and when they had retreated to the same distance as the king's guards, she spoke. "That pattern in the Bells' hall—that your Knight-Commander thinks is natural to the stone—is instead a pattern of elven devising, permitting those who know its use to travel from one pattern to another. Have you heard how such patterns were used for the Girdish to travel from Fin Panir to the far west and back?"

"It cannot—are you *certain*?"

"Yes. It is by such patterns that elves traveled to our palace in Chaya, and the iynisin who attacked and killed the Lady came through one in Kieri's own office. He suspected one might be here and asked me to look for one and tell you—but privily—if I found it."

"And humans can use them," the king said, scowling.

"Yes, if they know how. But more dangerous, the iynisin use them—the kuaknomi," she added, since he did not react to the elven term.

"Could there be more than one?"

"There were in our palace, sir king. They can be blocked, the elves told us, with a reversal pattern that prevents entry. I brought a drawing of such a design with me, for your use."

"Does my uncle know about this?"

"That such patterns exist, yes, and can be used by kuaknomi, yes. But not more than that."

"You could have waited until tomorrow—"

"No one knows when another attack might come," Arian said.

His lips tightened for a moment. Then he bowed again. "You are right, milady queen. Thank you. I will have a guard set this night, and we will speak more of this another time."

When Arian entered her suite, she told all the Squires what she'd seen. "I told the king; he says he will set a guard."

"One of the palace secretaries came by with a tentative schedule for tomorrow just after you had left to meet the king," Darvol said. He handed it to her. "We also received a note from Armsmaster Fralorn, who said he'd be pleased to open the salle for you at dawn."

"I met him," Arian said. "We will drill as usual." She looked at the paperwork they handed her, including their own rotation. "This will do," she said. "And if we're meeting the armsmaster for drill at dawn, we should retire now."

Arian found it hard to sleep at first; the heavy scent of rose petals and lack of air movement stifled her. She woke to the sound of tapping on her door. "Come in," she said. Maelis entered with a candle and a tray.

"Thought you might like sib before drill," Maelis said.

Arian and her Squires arrived at the salle just as Armsmaster Fralorn pulled the door open. He smiled. "You're very welcome this morning," he said. "The young men you met yesterday evening will join us, as will the king. Just let me light the lamps."

Arian began her stretches while her Squires helped Fralorn light lamps and lay out bandas. Soon the king appeared with his escort of guards and his friends. Fralorn called for all to line up for footwork drills.

"If it please you, Queen Arian," he said.

"Certainly," she said. No one, she'd been taught, could spend too much time on footwork, the foundation of effective swordplay.

Fralorn proved as exacting as Carlion or Siger: position of the foot, length of a half pace or full pace, all the other details. Before it became tedious, he called for seven of the group to do point-control drills on the pells at one end of the salle and the other six to pair up: Arian with Rothlin, two of her Squires with the king and one of his escorts.

Practice did not last as long as in Chaya; Arian's schedule for the day did not permit it even with so early a start.

K ieri had described the chamber where the Tsaian Royal Council met. Now Arian faced them, recognizing only the king, Duke Mahieran, and Marshal-Judicar Oktar.

King Mikeli introduced her and then said, "If you would, the Council would hear your account of the recent war and any information you can give us about the current state of Pargun."

Arian knew Kieri had sent letters to Mikeli giving details of the war but gave a quick review. "The last I know for certain," she said finally, "is that Torfinn, their king, survived his brother's attempt to take the throne and kill him. He did not order the invasion, and we no longer consider him a threat. His daughter Elis, the elder of his surviving children, is at Falk's Hall, in training for knighthood. She is also his ambassador to our court."

"You have met her?"

"Oh, yes. Last summer I was one of the Squires assigned to her when she was sent to marry Kieri. We had two princesses last year: Elis of Pargun and Ganlin of Kostandan."

"Ganlin seemed very interested in Rothlin," Duke Mahieran said. "And he was flattered, I think."

"Her father, the king of Kostandan, would like an alliance south of the river," Arian said. Let them figure out the implications themselves.

"What of the Pargunese princess?" the king asked, drumming his fingers on the table.

"She is not like to marry," Arian said.

"And Dzordanya . . . do they even have any convenient princesses?"

Arian started to make a jest, but the look that flashed between Duke Mahieran and the king stopped her. The king . . . the young *unmarried* king . . . had an interest in princesses. "Not to my knowledge," she said instead. "They sent an elderly woman to our wedding—a grandmother of the longest of long houses, she was announced. No mention of princesses or a king. Of course, it might be that there are. The Sea-Prince of Prealíth is of an age to have children, but he did not mention them."

"Is it true, Queen Arian, that the curst webspinner, Achrya, was destroyed by the dragon, with all her evil servants?"

"So the dragon said," Arian said.

"The dragon came here," the king said. "I had not believed the rumor from Lyonya until then, not truly."

"Too many new things," someone muttered.

"Count Tivarrn, you wished to speak?" the king said. Tivarrn, a man Arian judged to be in his thirties, with a narrow face, flushed.

"Sir king, it just seems to me that there are too many new things." He looked around, challenging. "Those mysterious jewels we heard of but no one can now see, the gnomes moving into Count Arcolin's domain, the dragon, the war with Pargun. All that started with the return of magery . . . with Duke Verrakai."

The king shook his head. "My lord Count, you were not here last year when we learned Duke Phelan was the rightful king of Lyonya. To my mind, the changes started when the paladin Paksenarrion went on quest to find that king . . . and the quest led to him. But I would guess some forces were already at work beyond our knowing."

Tivarrn did not look convinced, but he said nothing more. He was one of the newest on the Council, Arian remembered.

"If I might—" Master-trader Palloton held up his hand; the king nodded. "I heard from a trader in Harway that King Kieri is considering improving the River Road into Lyonya and also reopening the Middle Way that crosses Verrakai lands."

"Indeed we are," Arian said. "We would like to see easier travel between our realms." She said nothing about the port. Had he heard rumors of that?

"With the Pargunese weakened, do you think it might be possible to transport goods from your river towns all the way to the sea? Even to Aarenis? Does the river freeze over below the great falls? I suppose you know that the pass to Valdaire cannot be traveled in winter or even half of spring."

"As to that, I have little knowledge," Arian said. "The Pargunese traded that far in their ships, I do know. The river freezes in winter between us and Pargun, but not solidly until near Midwinter, and flows again by the Spring Evener. We, too, have thought of attempting to use it for trade."

"You certainly have the timber to build ships," Palloton said. "I'm sure a shipwright from Aarenis would be glad to get his hands on such trees."

Arian had not thought of that. Build their own ships? Cut down Lyonya's precious forest for ships?

"What about a place to load and unload?" Duke Serrostin asked. "Do you have river ports?"

"Not real ports," Arian said. "Lyonya had not engaged in river and sea trade before. Torfinn told us of a port the Pargunese built up one of the tributaries." Kieri had not wanted her to bring up the idea of a port until theirs was well under way.

Arian could almost see the thoughts in Serrostin's head. Tsaia had the large city, the riverside developments, but no maritime trade because of the falls that made downriver shipping impossible. Lyonya had access to the river below the falls, with no barriers between there and the ocean, but no city on the river itself and no development.

"If I might, sir king, lady queen—" Palloton began. The king nodded. "I might suggest that it could benefit both Tsaia and Lyonya if Lyonya were to build some kind of port—landing stages, warehouses— with access to the River Road, passable for wagons in most weathers."

"Are you suggesting a joint venture?" Arian asked.

"I cannot do that, lady queen," Palloton said with a look at the king. "I can say only that a river port, if it existed, could profit both of us."

"Master-trader, I believe this is something you and this Council may wish to discuss without a guest present. But it is something that—if the Council made a proposal—King Kieri would be pleased to know." She paused. No one said anything for a long moment, glances going back and forth. "If you wish, I can excuse myself now—"

"No, no," the king said. "We can discuss this later. This morning's meeting is intended to give everyone a chance to meet you. Most of the Council knew King Kieri when he was Duke Phelan."

Another pause, another set of looks back and forth. "Queen Arian, you were visiting Duke Verrakai when the Pargunese invaded, were you not?" That was Baron Brenvor. He and Destvaorn were both looking at her. "Did you see her work magery? Is it like elven magery?"

"No to both questions," she said. "If I had not been told she was a magelord, I would not have known it. As far as I know, the magery of full elves is different from that of magelords. I never heard of a magelord producing an elvenhome, for instance, or shaping the growth of trees the way elves do. I have seen a Kuakgan do something similar, however."

Duke Serrostin shifted in his seat. "Have you heard about my son Daryan, Queen Arian?"

"Yes," Arian said. "He was healed by a Kuakgan, was he not?"

"Indeed so. His new thumb is still wrinkled and brownish but no longer stiff. Do elves heal injuries by grafting them with plants?"

"No," Arian said. "Elves think Kuakkgani magery is disgusting. The elves were appalled when we invited the Kuakkgani to come help us find what had poisoned me and the other women with child."

"I thought perhaps—as elves claim that bond with trees—"

"It's different," Arian said. How could she explain about the taig to those who had no taig-sense or the Severance to those who did not live among elves?

The king rose then, signaling the end of the meeting; the others rose as well, and the king offered Arian his arm. "A quiet luncheon— or as quiet as my younger brother allows it to be. I would have you meet Camwyn, my heir." He grinned then. "At least until I marry and get one. Camwyn assures me he does not want to be king."

CHAPTER THIRTEEN

Arian had already heard gossip about the boy's wildness and knew from Dorrin that he had been the target of assassination attempts. As he bowed over her hand and greeted her courteously, Arian sensed a vibrant energy in him that seemed stronger than the king's. He had the family look in coloring and bone structure, and as they ate lunch, he showed he had the family charm as well.

"I have told Cam about the pattern in the Bells' hall," the king said as they sat to the table.

Arian was startled. The boy seemed too young to be trusted with such a secret.

"I don't tell secrets," the prince said.

"But you do talk out of turn," the king said; the prince flushed and busied himself slicing cheese. The king turned back to Arian. "I also told the Knight-Commander, of course, and had him set a guard, but from what I heard, a kuaknom might overpower even two or three."

"Indeed," Arian said. "The best thing would be to destroy or cover with reversal patterns any that you find."

The king nodded, his expression grim. "Do the Verrakai know this pattern?"

"Dorrin Verrakai saw it in Kieri's office when the rug was lifted.

She thinks it is similar to, but not quite the same as, the pattern on that box she showed you."

The king pressed his lips together and looked at Camwyn.

"I won't say anything to anyone!" the prince said. "You know that."

"Not even one of your friends," the king said.

"Of course not," the boy said. Then, with a change of expression, "I wonder where it goes."

"Cam!"

"I wouldn't try it, Mikeli—sir king. Last year maybe, but this year I know better. I can't help wondering, though. If it's the way the dragon moves, for instance. Would it feel like slipping through—"

"Cam!!" The boy sat back. "Just . . . don't."

"I said I wouldn't," the prince said. "And I won't tell anyone . . . especially not Aris, because he would."

"Aris Marrakai," the king said to Arian. "A mischief, but good-hearted; you met his sister at Duke Verrakai's." He paused for a swallow of wine. "Do you think Duke Verrakai knows about the pattern here?"

"No. I'm sure she would have mentioned it if she had. Kieri thinks it would be wise to compare the patterns to that on the box of regalia."

"My lord—" A palace servant spoke softly from near the door. "You asked to be reminded of the time . . . the reception . . ."

"Yes, of course," the king said. "The reception—we will talk of this again when the formalities are over."

"Of course," Arian said.

For the grand reception, Arian entered on the king's arm. This was her first chance to meet Tsaian ladies. Elaborate dresses, elaborate hairdos—no wonder they found Dorrin Verrakai strange. They found her strange, too, as she could tell from their expressions, but they seemed more puzzled than antagonistic. Flanked by the king and Duke Mahieran, she waited as they all—peers, wives, and older children—were presented for the ritual greetings.

Duke Marrakai's wife reminded Arian of their daughter Gwenno and a little of Estil Halveric.

"I am so pleased to meet you," she said. "Kieri was a friend in our house whenever he came to Vérella; I hoped so much he would find the right woman in Lyonya. Clearly he has."

Next came Duke Serrostin and his wife, short and plump. Lady Serrostin peered up at Arian with pale blue eyes but what seemed a genuine smile. "I've never met an elf before," she said. "And is that elven costume? How lovely it looks on you . . . on me, of course, it would be ridiculous." She bustled on to the king and greeted him with "Mikeli, lad, you get handsomer every day. You should find an elf like Queen Arian," and to her husband, "Yes, yes, I'm coming."

After her came the counts and their wives, then the barons and their wives, and then the older sons and daughters. Finally the line was done, and Arian wandered the room, flanked by her Squires and a servant ready to fetch food or drink. She imagined Kieri in this crowd as he had been when she first saw him or when he first became a peer. For all the trappings of the military about the nobility, for all their practice in grange and salle, none of them, she was sure, had Kieri's skill with a blade. Dorrin must have been a shock. For the first time she felt a little sympathy—not much—for these women when they first faced the new Duke Verrakai.

CHAPTER FOURTEEN

Vérella

Queen Arian's arrival put the entire palace in a frenzy. Except for the few brief formal moments when Camwyn was presented to her and made his own short speech of welcome (she could not, he was sure, really be as old as King Kieri), she had the welcome effect of removing even more attention from what the boy prince was doing. No one cared where he was as long as he was out from underfoot. He attended his lessons, but outside them, he explored. No one asked awkward questions.

Still, it took him days to discover a possible route to the skylight, a route involving a trip out onto the palace's complicated roof. The library held a large plan of the palace, but the librarians, remote from the ceremony of a visiting monarch and with Queen Arian having already made her appearance there, were the only ones who seemed to notice him these days. They'd already raised eyebrows at his interest in secret passages the year before. He did not want them remembering his new curiosity.

From the rooftop, it was much easier to see just how ridiculously complicated the palace was. The foundations—or some of them—might have been from the old palace from before the Girdish war. A wall here and there might go that far back. But since then, outbuildings had been constructed, added on to, and finally joined to the oldest parts, while the palace itself had grown, completely engulfing a few buildings and merging with others on the margins.

He could see the skylight from his first point of emergence—which he'd found by following signs of roof repair, a stack of tiles on a stairway. It was just over there, north of where he stood. He headed that way, but between his part of the roof and the other was a gap down to a stone-flagged passage between the main palace and the Bells' grange-hall. South of him was the bell tower in which the magical bells hung. For the first time, he wondered if their magic had any effect other than the bells ringing by themselves. A sweet sound came to him, faint but distinct in the bright air . . . not as loud as the bells but . . . was it the bells or elves?

Voices rose from below, and he leaned cautiously over the low parapet. A row of knight-candidates in training, voices echoing off the stone, moved from the grange-hall toward the palace, all talking at once. A face turned up to the sky; Camwyn jerked back. If he'd been seen . . . he slithered backward across the roof before standing and making for his exit. He would have to find a better way, but at least he now had an idea where the gaps between buildings were.

That night he ate alone in his own quarters, thinking about the regalia and his hand and the voices in his head. The thing about his . . . whatever it was; he would not call it magery . . . was that it wanted to be used, just as the crown and regalia wanted to be free and with Dorrin. It was like his body when he was restless and tired of sitting still in a meeting. His body wanted to move; it was natural for it to move . . . the moving itself wasn't ever bad, but he—anyone—could do bad things while moving. So if this—whatever it was—was natural like sight or movement, then the desire to use it was natural too. And surely it could be governed by his will in the same way as his movement.

But—by the Code of Gird—it was all wrong, except healing, and no one had that magery anymore.

Unless he did. Or Dorrin did. Paladins had healing magery. Marshals also.

The invitation to breakfast the next morning with his brother was not entirely welcome. He needed more time.

"Camwyn," his brother said as he wiped his mouth at the end of the meal, "what were you doing up on the roof?"

Camwyn's tongue clove to the roof of his mouth for a moment. He'd been seen? By whom? One of the knight-candidates, probably. What had they said? He'd been so sure— Then he was able to speak. "Exploring," he said, which was true enough. "I wanted to see if it made any more sense from on top than on the maps."

"Um. But you had no guard with you, did you? What if you'd fallen?"

"I was careful," Camwyn said. "And I went barefoot so my shoes wouldn't slip." Most of the time. Even in spring, sun-heated roof tiles were hot.

Mikeli shook his head. "Cam, that wasn't safe. And I suspect you had no guard with you because you knew they wouldn't let you that far out on the roof. You must not do that again."

"Have you ever been up there?"

"No. I wanted to, but I was caught before I found the way out. Where is it?"

"I can show you," Camwyn said. He had several ways out now, but he would show Mikeli only one. "We could go now—not all the places I went, but the way out. Just in case you ever need it . . . if something's chasing you." He meant it as a distraction, but the look of longing on Mikeli's face touched him. "It could be our secret," he said. "Just between brothers, you know. It's beautiful; the sky is so big, and you can see so far." Almost like flying in the dragon's mouth, and it lasted longer.

"Cam, I haven't time . . ." Mikeli looked at the scraps of paper on his desk, then pushed them into a rough stack. "Dammit, I'm the king. Why not? We'll just go look—but my guards are coming, you understand, and you're not to go out there alone."

"I understand," Camwyn said.

Preceded and trailed by palace guards, Camwyn and Mikeli made their way back to Camwyn's initial escape route and from there to the roof. One of the guards climbed out before either of them, then Mikeli went up and then Camwyn. Mikeli laughed. "I see why you like it, Cam. I can see right down into the city."

"And be a target, sir king, for any long-archer . . . you must not stand so." That was a guard. Camwyn was sure no one could shoot accurately that far.

"There's a chimney stack," Camwyn said, pointing. "It's just a little way, and you could put it between yourself and the city."

"Could you see like this from the dragon?" Mikeli asked softly.

"Only for a moment . . . but that's what gave me the idea." A twinge of guilt—part lie, part truth. Memory of that first aerial view had given him the hope the dragon might someday return and give him another ride; something quite other had driven him to find the roof.

Somewhat to Camwyn's surprise, Mikeli did negotiate the slant of the roof and then lean back on the chimney stack. Only one of his guards followed; the others clustered near the way out. Mikeli looked up at the sky, the clouds moving slowly and steadily westward, their shadows patterning the roofs and land beyond, following their movement with his eyes and then taking a long look in each direction. "It's beautiful," he said again. "I had imagined something like this, but— it's even better." He gave Camwyn a long look. "I changed my mind. I won't forbid your coming up here, Cam, but bring someone with you. Don't do it alone. A fall, a slip, could kill you, and I don't want to lose you."

"Does it have to be a guard?" Cam said. The guard still standing where Mikeli had stood looked uncomfortable, even frightened.

"No," Mikeli said. "If you've got a friend with a head for heights and some sense—both—that would do. No hanging from gutters or climbing drainpipes, though."

"I wouldn't do that," Camwyn said. "They might come loose."

"So they might. And if an enemy realizes you like to lark about up here, they might loosen one. Or set an ambush. Consider that, Cam. We still have enemies. Be careful. Promise me?"

"I promise," Camwyn said.

"I must go back—work. And you, as well. When you find your companion in roof exploration, tell me who it is."

"Yes, sir king," Camwyn said with a little bow to prove he meant it.

All the way back down he was considering which of his friends was most apt for such adventures. Not the real adventure, of course: he would not risk any of his friends with knowledge of his candle-lighting. But which of his friends, if something should happen . . . if his hand should start to glow, for instance . . . would not panic and fall off the roof?

The obvious candidate was—naturally—the first he saw after leaving Mikeli at a branch in the passages, Aris Marrakai.

"You're late for our class," Aris said. "Marshal-Judicar sent me to find out—"

"I was with the king," Camwyn said.

"Good. Then you'll get off the scolding he wants to give you for indolence."

"I wasn't sleeping later," Camwyn said, stung. "I was up betimes, but Mikeli—the king—and I had—had something to do."

"Lucky for you," Aris said, grinning. He led off at a brisk pace.

"Slow down," Camwyn said. "I wanted to ask you—"

"Yes?"

"Did you ever get up on the roof of your house—or anything else?"

"Roof-walking? Yes. I'm not supposed to, though. My mother says even the mischief of the brood is too valuable to lose with a fall. But in Fin Panir—" He stopped abruptly as they passed two guardsmen. Then he resumed in a lower voice. "One time I got out an upper window in the schools, onto the roof, and then onto the barn roof, and from there I made it all the way to the main buildings without touching the ground. Someone saw me, and the Training Master was waiting in my room when I got back in—and fair tanned my backside—but it was fun." He chuckled, then looked at Camwyn. "Why? Do you know a way to the roofs here?"

"Yes," Camwyn said. "And I have the king's permission to go up as long as I have a companion. Want to come?"

"Of course!" Aris's eyes sparkled. Then he sobered "But if we aren't both in class really fast, we're both in trouble."

Camwyn's excuse calmed the Marshal-Judicar, and he endured yet another lesson on the Code of Gird without doing anything to attract the Marshal-Judicar's ire.

His and Aris's first expedition came two days later, just before dawn. Camwyn had a night's respite from his hand's spontaneous flares and actually woke with the first light. He was half dressed when Aris scratched at his door. He let the younger boy in. Aris, like himself, was barefoot and had put on not his palace livery but an old pair of trousers with scuffed leather patches on his knees and a gray shirt with several mended rips.

Once on the roof, the world seemed lighter; all the stars had faded, and the sky was a peculiar shade of dull blue, brightening to the east, where a bank of clouds showed red at the upper edge. Below, the city made a dim pattern of lighter and darker blues and grays. They had not noticed the palace air as stale until they came out; here the air tasted of distant fields. Tiny currents set in the breeze like coils of wire in jewelry brought them here a wetter scent—mint, was it, or moss?—and then a momentary wisp of oak or wheat.

Camwyn thought of the dragon, always in the air, always drinking the wind, smelling and tasting all this. "Buildings stink," Aris said. They were sitting now, side by side, arms clasped around their knees. "Kitchens may smell good, but everything else—even the flowers they bring in and the herbs they strew—smells better outside."

"You like stables," Camwyn said.

"Horses smell better than people," Aris said. Then he said, "Sorry . . . I didn't mean *you*."

"I don't care," Camwyn said. The sky lightened moment by moment. "We can see well enough now, though." He stood. Under his bare feet, the roof was chilly and a bit damp.

"We should wait until the dew dries," Aris said. "I slid off the porch back home once on a shady bit I hadn't noticed was still wet. It's the only bad thing about early morning roof-walking."

"How long?" Camwyn asked. "We still have classes and chores."

"Not long after the sun comes up, in summer," Aris said. "Gwenno says it's not just the dew; it's the dew with the dust and moss and stuff on the roof. It's slippery like thin mud."

Camwyn sat back down. Together they watched as the edge of the cloud turned pink, then gold. More and more color had seeped into the world—enough to tell the greens and reds and yellows. But when the first spear of sun struck the palace roofs, the colors seemed to shout. "It feels like we should do something," Camwyn said. "Sing or pray or something."

Aris looked at him. "In the old times they did."

"You know that?"

"Yes. Before Gird, when the magelords worshiped Esea Sunlord, the priests would sing every morning, and special songs at the year's turnings. My father showed me an old book with a few of the songs set down. Not the special ones, the everyday ones." Aris closed his eyes and began to chant. Camwyn didn't know the words. After a moment, Aris opened his eyes and said, "That means 'Welcome, great light, and brighten our eyes, show us the truth and let no evil escape our gaze.' I don't remember the whole thing. Father said it was magelord language, but now all we know is Common, and it's mostly northern."

"How did he know it?"

"It's a family thing. We're all supposed to learn enough of it to read what's in that old book. I'm trying, but it's hard." He touched the roof. "Feel: it's drying now. As long as we stay where the sun's hitting and pay attention to our feet, we'll be fine."

That morning they explored in the opposite direction from the treasury, which suited Camwyn well enough, and were back down-stairs and in their proper clothes in time to escape any scoldings. Camwyn reported to Mikeli that Aris would be his companion on the roofs. Mikeli frowned a little. "I'm glad you like Aris better now, Cam, but he's younger and smaller. He's not going to be much help if you slip."

"He kept me from slipping this morning," Camwyn said. "He told me about roof-walking at the Training Hall in Fin Panir."

Mikeli blinked. "And did he tell you about the whaling he got for that?"

"Yes," Camwyn said. "I suppose Juris told you."

"He did." Mikeli sighed a little. "Very well, then. Juris also told me Aris has been out windows and up on roofs since he was knee high and only fell once . . . but here, once would be more than enough. And both of you are heavier now."

"We'll be careful," Camwyn said. Another few bites of stirred eggs and he said, "I . . . do understand now, sir king, why you took Egan away." He looked up to meet Mikeli's serious gaze. "He was making me not like some people . . . lying about them."

"Yes," Mikeli said. "I hated the necessity—he was only a boy, and maybe a boy could learn to change, but the danger was too great."

"I don't think he would have changed," Camwyn said. He dropped his gaze to his plate and stared at the last two sausages. "I think . . . I think he was one of those with someone else inside them."

"Why?" Mikeli asked.

"One time . . ." Camwyn had not been able to bring himself to tell anyone about it before; he had tried not to remember it in the days he thought of Egan Verrakai as his best friend. "One time he was close to me . . . very close . . . and his eyes . . . and his voice . . . he was saying things I could scarcely hear, just a murmur . . ." He shivered at the memory, the sudden jolt of fear, the instant of revulsion so strong that he'd jerked away from Egan. And Egan had grinned.

"Just a trick his brothers used to play on him, he told me," Camwyn said. "But I was cold—I shivered and shivered, and you remember the physicians said I had taken a chill." He looked up and saw his brother's face white as salt, a look of stark horror.

"Cam! And you told no one?"

"I—I was afraid. And I didn't know—"

"Bless Gird and the High Lord for protecting you," Mikeli said. "For I believe what you describe was an intent to take you over—to kill you, the real you, and insert a false you—whichever ancient Verrakai inhabited Egan—instead."

A sudden thrill of fear ran through Camwyn. "Could there be . . . anything left? Of them—him—it?"

"In you? I'm certain not," Mikeli said. "And Egan—his body and whatever lived in it—is very thoroughly dead."

Camwyn was not so sure. What if Egan had been trying to insert magery—just that? Or if the insertion or wakening—whichever it was—of magery had been only the first step in taking him over?

If it came from Verrakai, it was definitely evil. If not . . . maybe not. Beclan's had been awakened during an attack by Verrakaien . . . but was it by the Verrakaien or, as Mikeli had told him, by Gird allowing its use for his protection? Camwyn took that confusion to his lessons and wished he dared ask the Marshal-Judicar directly. Inattention earned him a rap on the head in the Marshal-Judicar's class and two bruises in weapons practice.

"I don't know where your head is today, my prince," the arms-master said, "but if you go fluff-minded like that when beset by an enemy, you'll be dead. Feel that—" He tapped unerringly on the bruised spot under Camwyn's banda on the left side. "Tell me now if you remember what lies under it."

Camwyn recited the relevant organs and admitted he would likely be dead after a while.

"And not soon enough, in that pain," the armsmaster said, scowling at him. "It would be a miserable sweating, groaning death you'd have, amply long enough and far too late to repent ignoring your lessons. You've improved this year, but it's no time to be letting your mind wander."

"Yes, armsmaster," Camwyn said. That was all one could say in such straits, and his rib still hurt.

CHAPTER FIFTEEN

By the end of the first few days of formal meetings, receptions, and dinners, Arian felt stuffed with new knowledge about Tsaia, its people, and its history. She very much needed a quiet day among trees and flowers where she could think and try to make sense of it all. But the palace complex had no quiet gardens, not even a tree-shaded walk. How could people live this way?

When she mentioned her desire for time outdoors, among trees, the king quickly arranged a picnic with peers' wives and children. The party, already a little boisterous, rode out to a grassy field bordered by trees, just off the main south road. Arian relaxed in the open air, smelling grass and trees instead of stone and fabric. She laid her hands on one of the trees . . . but it had no root-connection to others beyond the stone-paved south road, no communication with the eastern forest.

Family groups gradually dispersed in the shade of the trees, leaving Arian with her Squires. No one intruded on her privacy but the servants who replenished food and drink. After a while, Arian noticed two girls shepherded by an elderly woman: Mahierans, she overheard. Silence fell whenever they neared one of the groups sitting in the shade, and they looked miserable, not joining any of them.

"Ask them to come here," Arian said to Lieth. "They might sit with us awhile."

"Are you sure?" Lieth asked.

"I'm sure it's not fair for those girls to be so miserable."

Lieth walked down the field, spoke to the old woman, and then walked back with them. Arian rose to meet them.

"Queen Arian," the old woman said. She had a wary look in her faded blue eyes—as well she might, Arian thought. "I am Maris Mahieran; as a widow, I chose to take back my family name. You wished to meet my great-nieces?"

"Yes," Arian said. "Thank you for coming—you know I met your father in Lyonya?" She looked at the girls. One seemed to be near Beclan's age, and the other younger. Neither answered but looked to the old woman.

"This is Naryan," the old woman said, touching the older girl's shoulder. "And this is Vilian," she said, touching the younger. The girls curtseyed and murmured a polite greeting.

"Please, let us sit down," Arian said. "Have you eaten?"

"Yes," said the old woman, and "No," said the younger girl. Vilian . . . Arian tried to imprint the unfamiliar names in her mind. It took but a glance at the serving wagon for one of the servants to approach with a tray and another with mugs and a pitcher of chilled water.

Both girls glanced at their aunt and at her nod piled food on plates and began to eat. The old woman accepted water but ate nothing.

After a sip, she put the goblet down and folded her hands in her lap. "What do you want, Lyonyan queen?"

"At the moment, to be here among green things," Arian said. "I miss the forests of home."

"Ah. It is the elf blood, no doubt. You're not as young as you look. They say you are your king's age: is that true?"

"Yes. Did you know Kieri when he was Duke Phelan?"

Maris blinked. "I knew Kieri when he was a brash young soldier come to beg a commission from our king's grandfather. Hair like a flame, cocky as any barnyard rooster. I was married then; my husband died on that campaign. Not your Kieri's fault, so I was told."

"Did you think so?"

A shrug. "I know only that my husband died. Kieri Phelan was very young to end up in command, I thought. Many thought. And so many more experienced died."

"Old grudges grow stale," Arian said.

Maris's face relaxed into a grin. "Ah, my dear, there is no grudge. But you looked so like a picture painted on a plate—cool on such a warm day, not a hair out of place. It came on me to disturb that smooth surface if I could. You will say badly done, when you were kind enough to speak to us, but . . . it is my nature to prod immobility."

Arian stared for a moment and then laughed. "So you are *not* a poisonous old lady?"

Maris shrugged again. "That is not for me to say. I am old, no gainsaying that. I've been told my tongue's too sharp. But Barholt was willing to marry me—he enjoyed it, he said. He told me once it was like a currycomb, working the mud out of his mind. I've told these girls—" She patted Naryan's shoulder. "Told them many times not to copy my bad example. Dip your tongues in honey, I tell them: men want the honey, not the sting."

"Nobody's going to want me anyway," Naryan said, scowling. "Not now."

"Not with that look on your face, no," her great-aunt said sharply. "And if you can't smile when you're miserable, you'll have a life as miserable as you now imagine."

"You sit your mounts very well," Arian said to the girls, desperate to turn the conversation. "Do you ride often? I know your father breeds horses for the royal stud."

"We did," Vilian said. "But now we're in the city—"

"I used to ride with Gwennothlin Marrakai," Naryan said. "We sneaked into this field a few times, raced up and down, set up stakes, and tried to knock sticks off them with swords." She sat up straighter.

"Until you got caught," Vilian said.

"Until you watched us instead of the road like we'd told you," Naryan said.

"What happened then?" Arian asked.

"I would have ridden right out the far end," the older girl said. "There's a wall behind those trees, but it's not very tall and I knew my horse could jump it. Gwenno wouldn't leave the sprout behind, though, and her pony couldn't manage it." She shook her head. "They caught us. Escorted us back to the city, to our fathers. No more riding out without an official escort. Boring."

Arian could sympathize with that. At Naryan's age she'd been free to run loose in the forest whenever her chores were done.

"Did you also want to train in arms?" she said.

"We all *do* train," Naryan said. "In the family grange. Of course that's Girdish fighting: training with hauks and marching in lines. I like a longer sword better." She glanced at Arian's sword. "Like yours."

"Will you, then, continue your training?"

"I don't know." Her shoulders slumped. "I don't know if they'll let me."

"May we join you?" That was Lady Marrakai and a Serrostin girl of about Vilian's age.

"Certainly," Arian said.

"Gwenno wrote us about meeting you at Duke Verrakai's estate," Lady Marrakai said. She greeted Maris and the Mahieran girls, then turned to Naryan. "She also said she missed you, Naryan."

"Did she really?"

"Yes, indeed. You and she used to share secrets, did you not?"

"She didn't write *me* any letters," Naryan said. A mix of resentment and misery both in that, Arian thought.

"I understand she's being kept very busy, Naryan. For a time she was the only squire Duke Verrakai had."

"I know I'm not supposed to ask, but—but I have to—" Naryan looked at Maris, then at Arian, and finally at Lady Marrakai. "Do you think Duke Verrakai *really* tried to have my brother killed?"

Lady Marrakai's brows went up, but she answered calmly. "No, Naryan, I do not. Someone else has wished her and your family both evil and wanted her to have the blame. It is easy enough to get a bad reputation if you're not like everyone else."

"But my mother—" Another wary glance at Maris, who said nothing. "My mother isn't a bad person, milady. She's not. And they're lying about her—"

"And if they're lying about her, Naryan, do you not see that they could be lying about Duke Verrakai? That your mother could be mistaken, without being bad?"

"I want to go home," Vilian said suddenly. A tear ran down her face; her voice was choked. "Our real home. We can't visit Mother— we can't see Father—our friends won't speak to us."

"I will," the Serrostin girl said, putting an arm around Vilian's shoulders. "Vili, I'm still your friend. They told me I couldn't visit, is all, but I wanted to come over here, and Mama said I could come with Lady Marrakai."

Lady Marrakai turned to Maris. "You know, Maris, you could bring them to our house. It's true Gwenno's not there, so Naryan would not enjoy it as much, but at least they'd be around *some* young people."

"Charity," muttered Maris.

"Yes," Lady Marrakai said. "And you don't fool me, Maris: I've seen you extend hospitality to others in hard times. Whatever happened is not these girls' fault."

She turned to Arian. "My pardon, Queen Arian, for intruding our concerns on your space. I would have come earlier, but I find having five of my own to supervise—" She looked up, and her brow furrowed. "Oh, dear. I could always count on Gwenno to help me, and there they go—pray excuse me. Tiran, dear, just stay here; I'm sure your mama won't mind. I see that Julyan's about to run off with one of the cart horses."

"By all means," Arian said. Lady Marrakai was already up and moving toward a cluster of younger children around the horses. The servants, busy carrying trays of food and drink back and forth, hadn't noticed yet that a black-haired boy had swarmed up the harness and now leaned down to offer a hand to another.

"I never wanted to like her, but I always did," Maris said into the sudden silence that followed, nodding toward Lady Marrakai.

"Why not?" Arian asked.

"You will credit my sour nature with envy of her energy and competence," Maris said, but a smile shaped her mouth. "She has been like that—as if she were born entirely Marrakai, which she is not—since girlhood. Everyone thinks her children favor their father, but that so-called Marrakai character comes as much from her."

Arian did not want to think what Maris had been like as a girl. She turned to the girls of the day. "Naryan, you said you liked sword-play with longswords. Do you practice?"

"Not since . . . Beclan . . ." the girl said.

"Lady Maris, would you permit Naryan to engage in a brief les-son with my Squires and me?"

"Here?" The formidable brows rose.

"Here. We have blades enough. I know Naryan has riding gloves . . ."

"But no mail. Not even a banda. I do not choose to see her spitted and sliced."

"Please," Naryan said, her face alight.

"We will take great care," Arian said.

"My lady, we do have bandas," Lieth said. She grinned. "The thought came to us that you might enjoy a bit of swordplay out in the sunlight, on natural ground."

Maris threw up her hands. "Well, then, Naryan, if you choose to set yourself against those who are far better than you—take your chances."

"You?" Arian said, looking at the younger girls. Vilian and the Serrostin girl were head to head, whispering as fast as they could. They shook their heads.

The impromptu sword practice drew others to the area they'd marked off. Naryan, tense and serious, did a few preliminary stretches, then a few paces forward and back as Arian and the Squires put on bandas. The girl was stiff at first, but soon excitement took over. She had had, Arian decided, a little good instruction but not enough. She would benefit from more, but at the moment she would benefit most from being seen as both competent and acceptable to the foreign visitors.

Soon some of the other young people were eager to join in. Arian quickly assigned two Squires to serve as armsmasters—to have no more than two bouts going on at once, while another supervised footwork drills. Within the next two turns of the glass, more women and children moved closer. Lady Marrakai and Lady Serrostin had merged their broods, asking Vilian and Tiran to supervise the younger children so the eldest could take part. Other peers' wives chatted with one another and approached Arian when she was not fencing to ask questions about Lyonya and customs at that court.

By the time the shadows had lengthened and it was time to return to the city, Arian saw that Maris and the two Mahieran girls were no longer isolated at all—several peers' ladies were chatting with Maris and suggesting plans for including the girls in activities with their children.

A good outcome. She rode back to the palace beside a baron's wife, a tall angular redhead. "Did you have weapons training as a girl?" the woman asked.

"No, I grew up on a farm," Arian said. "Lyonyans are mostly Falkian, and Falkians do not train as young as you Girdish. I may suggest it when I return."

"Which of your parents was an elf?"

"My father was an elf," Arian said. "My mother wasn't. My mother died years ago; my father died recently, trying to protect the Lady of the Ladysforest."

The woman looked confused but then asked, "Are all the Lyonyan forest rangers knights?"

"By no means. My father paid my fees to attend Falk's Hall, where Knights of Falk train. That, in fact, is where I learned most of my weapons skills, that and in my years as a ranger. I'm a better archer than fencer: archery is the main weapon of Lyonyan rangers."

"I have used a crossbow," the woman said. "But that's not the same, is it?"

"No," Arian said. "I don't have my bow with me on this trip or I would show you."

"I'm from the northwest," the woman said. "Not so far from where Paksenarrion the paladin came from. We raise sheep, mostly." After a pause, she said, "You're not what I expected. Or most of us, I imagine. I was thinking half-elf, queen, she'll be haughty and hardly speak to us, but you're not like that."

"I should hope not," Arian said, laughing.

"Does your husband—the king—mind that you're half-elf?"

"Hardly. He's half-elven, too," Arian said. Surely the woman knew that. But it turned out this was only her second visit to Vérella and she had no real friends at court.

"It's a small domain," the woman said as they came into the city. "But I wanted to see you—" She grinned suddenly, and her face no longer looked bony and plain. "And I have. I've been to Vérella and heard the bells and met the king and a half-elf queen from a distant land . . . I'll never feel trapped again."

"You could visit us," Arian heard herself say. She had not meant to invite any of them.

"Oh, no. I could never be away so long. Once in a lifetime is enough for the likes of me. And I love our hills and streams. You understand; you grew up on a farm. I miss it in the city. But I thank you, Queen Arian, indeed I do."

"You're very welcome," Arian said.

CHAPTER SIXTEEN

Fintha

B ad news."
Marshal-General Arianya looked up. Marshal Kerivan held out a message tube.

"I've read this, Marshal-General. There's been a child found not a day's ride from here with magery—undeniable magery."

"And?"

"And he's dead. The people killed him. Girdish—all yeomen of a local grange. The yeoman-marshal led them, said it must be done."

"Killed . . . a *child*? What had the child done?"

"Made light with his hand, this says. And attacked the yeoman-marshal who held him. The light was true mage-light and hot; the man claims a painful burn."

Arianya clenched her jaw on the first words that came to her.

"There's more," Kerivan said. "They blamed the child's mother— she's not from there—so they beat her and drove her away."

"And what did the Marshal do?" Arianya asked in as level a voice as she could manage. From the glance Kerivan gave her, he was aware of her anger anyway.

"Marshal Sofan was away, he says, but he feels the actions were justified under the circumstances, as use of magery has always been considered evil, an offense punishable by death. He adds that he warned the child's father against marrying an outlander and that he always knew no good would come of the Marshal-General's new policies."

A second wave of anger roared through her. Arianya waited until the crest had passed and folded her hands, making sure not to clench them. "Did Marshal Sofan bring this himself or send it?"

"Sent it, Marshal-General."

"That's a mercy. For him." She could not sit still; she rose and paced her office. "So: we know nothing about the family except that the father was bred there and the mother not. We know nothing about the child except he made light. Gird's cudgel, *paladins* make light! Surely these people know that!"

"A child isn't a paladin."

"But paladins were once children," Arianya said, following that trail instead of the one that had a Marshal blaming her. No, she must deal with the real issues, and quickly. "I need to know exactly where this place is—we'll need maps—and everything about their Marshal you can find out. He'll have to be replaced, of course, and the yeoman-marshal as well. And we need to find the mother, if she's alive and not dead in a field."

"I'll send a patrol—and someone to the grange there?"

"Yes. Six knights. I want the Marshal and yeoman-marshal under guard here as quickly as possible. Perhaps I should go—" She stopped, considering. "If magery returns here—if it already has— have there been other children killed? I must send word to all the granges—"

"To . . . to let mages go?" His brows rose.

"To kill no more children, at least," Arianya said. "I'll write: you get those knights on the road and make sure they understand they're to bring the Marshal and yeoman-marshal here under guard."

She would have to convene a council of Marshals, she realized. Anger roiled her mind; she tried unsuccessfully to put herself into the minds of those who would kill a child for having a lighted hand. Magery was wrong, of course. No one wanted a return of the magelords—gods grant the sleepers in Kolobia never woke up—but even Gird had recognized that children with mage ability could be innocent of evil. He had hoped for a reconciliation between the peoples, mages using their powers for good.

She could not finish the letter. Not yet. She had to know why that Marshal had chosen to approve killing a child. Where did such hatred come from? Her mind threw up the memory of Marshal Haran and her hostility to Paksenarrion. Haran had seemed contrite, though she had resigned as Marshal less than a year later and left Fin Panir. What if she had kept the same opinion secretly? What if many of the Girdish Marshals were that angry underneath, that stubborn in their condemnations? The histories told of such, all the way from Gird's time—a strand of mingled envy, resentment, bitterness that Arianya considered evil. She had hoped her leadership had diminished its force . . . but Haran's behavior and now this proved her wrong.

She walked down through the back corridors, thinking of Paksenarrion and Arvid Semminson, of her own mistakes with Paks and the mistakes she hoped she had not made with Arvid. Through the kitchens and dining hall, out into the little garden that—they had learned from notes found in Kolobia—had been the favorite of a magelord priest who had known Gird.

Camwynya, one of the paladins then in residence, came in the gate from the main courtyard almost as Arianya entered the garden. "Gird's blessing," Arianya said. "Do you have time to sit with me? I have grave news and would appreciate your opinion."

"Certainly, Marshal-General." Camwynya settled onto the bench along one side. "I saw a company of knights heading out—is there trouble?"

"Yes, and unexpected. Tell me, what would you do if you saw a child's hand light up?"

"I would think the child had mage blood," Camwynya said. "I would wonder where it came from and if the child had contact with mages."

"What would you do about it?"

"Ask the child, I expect."

"Would you kill the child?" Arianya asked.

"Kill the child? No, of course not. Why do you ask? Has someone—"

"A yeoman-marshal and members of the grange killed a child two days ago," Arianya said. "The Marshal wrote to tell me: he approves, and he blames my laxity for the child's magery."

Camwynya stared. "That's . . . evil."

"Yes."

"That's not what Gird wants. What had the child done?"

"Nothing but have a hand alight. I sent those knights to bring in the Marshal and yeoman-marshal, but . . . I am not sure what to do. Stop this killing, of course, but how? I was heading for the High Lord's Hall to pray when I met you."

"They must be tried. A tribunal of Marshals?"

Arianya nodded. "That would be best, to start with. But I fear there are others of the same mind."

"May I tell the other paladins in residence?" Camwynya asked.

"Yes. Paladins may do better at convincing people this is wrong than a letter from the Marshal-General."

P rayers, Arianya reflected on her way back from the High Lord's Hall, were a necessary duty but did not accomplish the work of changing minds. She finished the letter—brief and firm—and sent it down to the scribes to copy and distribute to all the granges. She met with Camwynya and the other two paladins in residence, and then walked down the hill to the nearest grange to talk to Marshal Cedlin.

"Killed a *child*? For magery?" He looked as appalled as she felt.

"Yes, Cedlin. And they're apparently quite pleased with themselves for enforcing the Code of Gird."

He scowled, chewing his lower lip. "I won't say I don't have a few yeomen who might do the same, if they thought their Marshal approved," he said. "Most of 'em born and bred in little vills like that. There's pockets of meanness, Marshal-General. You know that."

"Yes, but I don't have to tolerate it."

"No more you do. There's not a grange here in Fin Panir will back killing a child even if the child does wrong. And making a light— that's not evil in itself."

"So, Cedlin—I want you as one of the Marshals in a court I'm convening and on a council later. If one child can show magery after so many generations, so could another. I can't count Duke Verrakai over in Tsaia, but there's that boy Beclan, a duke's son, but of a family thought to have no magery. If the gods are bringing magery back into the world—"

"Then there's a reason, and we've no call to be killing people that do no harm with it." Cedlin ran a hand over his head. "Though defining what is harm and what isn't—that's going to take some thinking."

"You've heard nothing about children showing magery lately?"

"No . . . but there has been more talk about the evils of magery. I blamed that on what's been said about Duke Verrakai—evil or not, her killing her father did not go over well here, as you know—and her squire showing magery, as well as the deaths of those knights cased in rock last year. We Marshals agreed it was rockfolk magic, but to many folk magery is magery whoever does it, and it's all bad."

Arianya visited every grange in Fin Panir that afternoon, with much the same conversation at each. Marshal Padlin, near the lower market, said he'd had to break up a fight. "They was hittin' and kickin' and sayin' the weaver's girl was a mage for some trick. I told 'em off myself and had my yeoman-marshal give all the young ones a good talking to about makin' up lies about people—"

"What was the trick?" Arianya asked.

"Lightin' a candle without a spill," Marshal Padlin said. "She said it was a spell she'd learned from a wizard in Tsaia a summer ago when she stayed with her great-aunt downriver. I asked the family; they said she'd been sent there, right enough, because she'd been feverish. Her great-aunt knew herb-lore. Came home healthy, with some tricks she'd learned."

"I must see her," Arianya said.

"Down Weavers' Lane, third door," Marshal Padlin said. "Light-haired girl, about so high—" He held out his hand. "Her name's Dalyin. Never any trouble in the grange until now. Family's old Girdish, been here since whenever."

Arianya found the house easily enough. Outside, on benches set either side of the door, four children were busy: a small boy struggling with a mass of wool he was trying to card, a slightly older girl instructing him while herself weaving a square on a lap loom, a girl about the size Dalyin should be spinning a smooth thread, and an older boy shaping a piece of wood into something that looked like the treadle for a loom. Through the door came the regular rattle and clack of looms at work.

"Are you Dalyin?" Arianya asked. "I'm Marshal-General Arianya."

"It's not her fault," the older boy said. "It was them kids—"

"I'm not here to blame anyone," Arianya said. "Dalyin, are your parents home? I'd like to speak to them—and to you."

The lower room held two looms; Dalyin's parents were as light-haired as their children. One was weaving plain Girdish blue, and the other a blue and cream stripe. Their faces were tight with worry. "She's done nothin' wrong," the woman said, reaching out to pull Dalyin close. "She's a good girl, she is."

"I heard she was set on," Arianya said, spreading her hands.

"She was," the man said. "Cruel mean, those boys are. She's not the only one they set on."

"I heard you were sick last summer," Arianya said, looking at the girl. The girl looked up at her mother before nodding silently.

"We sent her to my wife's aunt, just over the border to Tsaia, is all," the man said. "She's good with fevers, and we had a new 'un in the house, didn't want fever here."

"What did she do for you?" Arianya asked, looking at Dalyin again.

"She . . . made me drink things," Dalyin said, barely above a whisper. "I don't know what exactly. It was bitter. Then the fever went and I felt better, but she said stay until the cool weather or it might come back."

"And the wizard?" Arianya asked.

"There was a fair—with a show. Music, a song I never heard before, and then the wizard. He juggled balls of light. He made a wind blow and then stop. He had spells and potions for sale." Her voice had strengthened. "My great-aunt said it was nonsense and I should spend my bit on sweets or ribbons, but I can find sweets and ribbons here in Fin Panir. I wanted a spell for light, so Da and Ma could see better to weave in winter."

She stopped there; Arianya saw that the woman's fingers had tightened on Dalyin's shoulder.

"Did you buy the spell, Dalyin? Tell me truly now, on Gird's honor."

Dalyin bit her lip, looked down, and finally said, "No. It cost too much. But . . . but I really wanted it. I asked the wizard when my great-aunt was buying ribbons for herself, and he said . . . he said there was a trick. And that night I said the words and it didn't work, but on the third night . . . my finger lit up. Like this."

Her finger did light up—almost as bright as a candle.

"Dally—no!" That was her father. "Put it out, child, before anyone sees!" Then he looked at Arianya. "It's not forbidden magery—it's not, it can't be. We been Girdish a long time! There's no magery in my family or m'wife's. Just a wizard's trick, is all it is, and she's done no harm with it but to light candles and save a spill."

Arianya looked at the glowing hand. "What was the spell, Dally? Do you still use it?" Was there a wandering magelord pretending to be a wizard and implanting magery in children? Was that even possible?

"No'm. It's just a rhyme." She repeated it in singsong cadence: "If you want light/then late at night/wish hard and pray/the gods bring day. I thought it was silly at first. But . . . but I said it and wished hard, and the third night my finger lit up."

The rhyme made no sense to Arianya. A lighted finger wasn't "day." And yet there the finger was, glowing. "Light a candle," she said. The girl wriggled free of her mother and lit a candle; her finger's glow vanished. "Does it always vanish when you've lit a candle?"

"Yes—but it lights up again later when I want to light another one."

By all the old records, that had to be magery. But looking at the frightened faces—mother, father, and girl—Arianya could not say that, not without softening it. "Do you know the stories about Gird and the magelord priest?" she asked instead. They shook their heads silently. "When Gird was wandering, starting the first bartons, he found a man naked and beaten in a ditch. What do you think he did?"

"Helped 'im," said Dally at once.

"That's right." Arianya decided to leave out the rest Arranha had written and come to the relevant point. "Gird did not know the man was a priest of the old religion, the Sunlord, and they were sheltering under a log in a snowstorm when the man made light with his finger . . . and cooked bacon."

"An' Gird kilt 'im," said the father. "Didn't he?"

"No," Arianya said. "Gird did not kill him, and he and Arranha became friends. Arranha joined Gird's movement."

"A . . . a magelord?"

"Yes. And Luap, too, you know, was a magelord." She paused, watching their faces. "Gird did not hate mages," she said. "He hated meanness, lying, stealing: any cruelty. Arranha showed him that magery does not have to be cruel."

"But in the Code—"

"The Code allows certain uses of magery," Arianya said. "Healing—"

"But not makin' light." That was Dally's father.

"Not at the moment," Arianya said. "But laws do change. Dally wanted to make light so you could see better to weave, isn't that right?" She looked at the girl, who nodded. "There's nothing evil in wanting to help her family, not if it's not taking from someone else. As best I know, her making a light with her finger doesn't take light from anything else."

"Yes, but—" That was Dally's mother, her brow furrowed. "If someone can do things by magery, they will, won't they? And it's easier and not fair."

"Hmmm. I suppose if no one needed candles or lamps, then candlemakers would lose their job . . . but we don't complain if paladins make light. But Dally's just lighting the candles, isn't she? I don't see that doing any harm. As long as she's not setting fire to other people's things or burning them—"

"But if my finger's hot and they grab my hand, it burns—I can't stop it."

Arianya closed her eyes a moment and hoped they thought she was praying. It was too complicated—too difficult.

But you will do it anyway.

Her eyes opened even as her mind argued impossibilities. It could not be *that* voice. It had been *that* voice. "Just warn them," she said. "And I will call a council."

"A council?" the father said.

"If children start showing magery without malice, we have to change the Code," Arianya said. "It has been changed before, on other things. It will take time, so you, child, must be careful. I will tell all the Marshals here in Fin Panir, but they cannot be everywhere every second."

She began with Marshal Padlin. "It is magery, though they hoped it was not. The girl wanted to light the room her parents wove in, to help them. My order is that until a council has made a decision on changing the law, magery that shows no malice will not be punished. It must be reported to a Marshal and then to me, but such a child must not be harmed in any way—nor the family, either."

He bit his lip even as he nodded. "I see that, Marshal-General, but there's folk as will be frightened, and frightened people hit first."

"If you talk to them beforehand, they'll be less frightened. I want you on the council I'm calling—"

"Me! But I'm just—"

"A Marshal, one of whose flock has shown magery without warning. Exactly the person who knows what it's like for Marshals. Meanwhile: talk to your yeoman-marshals first and then the grange. I'm on my way to tell others."

The others, she realized, must include those in the Fellowship not only in Fintha but also in Tsaia, where magery had also appeared. Was Beclan Mahieran the only one? And why was this happening now? Everything had a cause; this must have a cause. If she could find the cause, maybe she could stop it. Change it back.

A cold breath ran down her backbone, a whisper as of drawn steel. To think of changing it back . . . how was that different from undoing . . . was she really contemplating an appeal to Gitres Undoer? No. The High Lord had gifted some humans with magery; the High Lord must have chosen to reawaken the gift. It was not her place to stand in the way. It was her place to stand between innocent children and those who would condemn them.

Two days later, she faced Marshal Sofan and his yeoman-marshal Rort across her desk; two Knights of Gird stood by the door. Downstairs, five Marshals waited to try them, but they had the right to hear the accusations from her and to make—if they would—such pleas of mitigation as they wished.

She remembered Sofan from his marshaling ceremony five years before, a thickset man, broad-shouldered, heavy-boned. His yeoman-marshal was a hand shorter, wiry. Both glowered at her; the knights who fetched them had told her the two had been angry to be ordered to Fin Panir and had protested all the way in.

"Gird never meant the Code to kill children," Arianya said at the start. "You have admitted to inciting to kill, and approving the killing of, a young child."

"That's not the way the Code's wrote," Sofan said. "Magery's wrong, against the Code, and them as use magery must leave or die." He leaned back in the chair and flexed his hands.

"And you gave the lad a choice, did you? A lad of—what? Five winters?" Arianya glanced at the report in front of her; the knights had interviewed some of the yeomen.

"Four," Rort said with a tone of satisfaction. "Best rid us of 'em young. Older is more dangerous. Look what he did to me." He held up his heart-hand, showing a few blisters on it. He glanced at his Marshal as if for approval. Sofan nodded.

"Not more dangerous than a mob you stirred up to kill a four-winters child," Arianya said. "And beat his mother and drive her away." The knights had not found her, but at least they had not found her body. Nor had they found the father; he'd run off, they were told. Sofan and Rort stared at her, smirking. "Gird's cudgel, can you not see that? Gird did not kill children! You know the story of Aris and Seri—"

"They 'uz traitors," Sofan said. "They chose that Luap and went away, didn't they? That's your proof, Marshal-General, and if you wasn't soft as custard, you'd see *that*." He smacked his hand on her desk, contempt in every line of his body.

"Show respect!" One of the knights at the door took a step toward him. Sofan ignored him, and Arianya waved the knight back.

"You got no right to drag us in here to scold like an old granna," Sofan went on. "I'm a Marshal; you gave me the touch yourself. If you think I done wrong, I want trial of arms. It's my right." He leaned back again, folding his arms across his chest.

"Child killers have no right," Arianya said over the rage fizzing in her ears. "You'll face a tribunal of Marshals."

Sofan laughed. "Tribunal of Marshals—Marshals you handpicked, I don't doubt. I'll tell you what it is—" He leaned forward a little and tapped her desk with his forefinger. "You're *afraid* to give me my rights. Afraid to fight, old woman as you are." He looked at the knights and then at his yeoman-marshal, nodding as if they'd all just agreed with him. "A woman's not fit to be Marshal-General, anyway. It's a man's job, ruling men. Wasn't a woman led us against the mage-lords. Gird was a man. This magery's come because the Fellowship's gone all to weakness: evil attacks weakness."

Arianya felt her control slipping but tried once more for reason. "And *you* attacked a four-winters boy. Evil attacks weakness: you said it yourself."

"Words!" Sofan waved them aside. "Magelords is evil. Magery's evil. Doesn't matter if a mouse squeezes through a tiny hole, it's still a mouse. Same with magery." He stood up abruptly; his yeoman-marshal stood with him.

Before the knights could move from the doorway, she was on her feet, hand on the hilt of her sword. Sofan's expression wavered; she had surprised him. That only fueled her rage. "Fine," she said. "If you demand a trial of arms, a trial of arms you shall have."

"Marshal-General?" That was one of the knights, frowning a little.

"Out of their own mouths," Arianya said. "They admit their deeds. Marshal Sofan does not trust a tribunal of his fellows. It is my choice to grant him the trial of arms he requests. High Lord's Hall. Now." When the others hesitated, she said, "Witnesses to the High Lord's Hall."

She did not miss the gleam of satisfaction in Sofan's eyes. He had intended this all along; he was sure he could take her. He meant to kill her . . . or his yeoman-marshal would. Both ten years or more her junior, both fit and weapons-skilled, as all Marshals and yeoman-marshals should be.

"Marshal-General—" The other knight, looking back and forth from them to her. "What orders?"

"Marshal Sofan," Arianya said loud enough to be heard in the passage, where she knew others listened, "has demanded a trial of arms to settle whether I am fit to lead the Fellowship."

"An' me!" Rort said.

Arianya ignored him. "See them safe to the High Lord's Hall. I will come with the required witnesses—"

"An' don't be takin' all day about it," Sofan said, sticking his thumbs in his belt. "If you think you can tire us out waitin' . . ."

"Within the glass," Arianya said. She turned back to the knight. "They are not to wander alone. They may have water at need. Escort them to the jacks at their request." And to Sofan, "I suggest you pray, Marshal and yeoman-marshal, asking guidance of Gird."

"You need it more than we do," Sofan said.

That was possibly true, Arianya thought, especially since Sofan wasn't going to take guidance of anything but a blow to the head.

O n her way through the complex toward the High Lord's Hall, Arianya gathered witnesses: the Marshals waiting for the tribunal, two High Marshals, Camwynya to represent the paladins, three yeoman-marshals, three Knights of Gird. She also considered weaponry. Traditionally, Girdish trials of arms used the weapons Gird himself had used: hauk, staff, and unarmed wrestling. But Gird at the Battle of Greenfields had a sword and used it. He wore a sword through the last year of the war, in fact. And Sofan had challenged her, insulted her . . . which under the Code meant she could choose any weapon she wished. Or, she corrected herself, that Gird wanted her to use.

Sunlight poured into the east window and south windows of the High Lord's Hall, painting splotches of color on the platform. Sofan and Rort, arrogance in every line of their bodies, stood on it already.

"Come down from there," Arianya said. "You know the ritual: first we pray."

Sofan shrugged and stepped down; Rort merely scowled and followed his Marshal. Arianya led them to the altar, where all the light was blue or silver. The witnesses knelt with her. Sofan and Rort waited and knelt after. Arianya ignored them, fixing her mind as best she could on Gird and the High Lord. Was there a way to end this without violence? She could think of none. Then how was she to proceed? She let the weapons run through her mind: hauk, staff, pike, sword, bow, ax . . . a phrase from a later revision of the Code came to mind: *Whatever custom is for a grange or group of granges, it is always meet for the commander to bear a sword.*

She sensed a touch on her head and then a presence moving away, but still within the hall, and stifled the part of herself that wanted to ask the outcome.

When she rose, the others did as well. Prayer had left her clear-headed, her anger cooled to a reservoir of determination. "You have challenged me," Arianya said to Sofan. "Do you renew that challenge in this holy space?"

"I do," he said. "And further: I intend to prove with your life's blood that you are no fit Marshal-General." A murmur rose from the witnesses, and he shouted at them. "She is *not*. She has brought magery on us by her weakness. She punished my aunt's daughter, Marshal Haran, for naught but telling the truth to that so-called paladin Paksenarrion. We saw that craven in our vill, saw her feared of the sheep she was hired to herd."

"Do you dispute that Paksenarrion is a paladin?" Camwynya said, her light filling the hall as if a sun had risen inside it.

"She was not a paladin then. She was weak—"

"Let it be, Camwynya," Arianya said. "His real quarrel is with me, not Paks." Camwynya's light lessened.

"Indeed it is," Sofan said. "But I am not surprised you bring in a paladin to take your part. You are afraid to face me alone."

"No," Arianya said. "The Code requires witnesses to any trial of arms between Marshals. High Marshals, bring forth the swords." She unwrapped her own sword belt; Sofan and Rort had been disarmed already. Now Sofan looked uncertain for the first time.

"Swords are not traditional—"

"They are when you challenge a Marshal-General," Arianya said. He made no more complaint. She took one of the three blades the High Marshal offered her after testing the balance of each. Sofan took one of the three offered him. They stepped up on opposite sides of the platform; the witnesses closed in around it.

Arianya expected Sofan to come in fast, but instead he shifted about, watching her reactions to his moves as she watched his. He handled the sword well, but how much experience did he really have

with it? Was he able to analyze while moving? She began a slow circle
to the left; he turned, balanced and almost in time with her. His previous behavior indicated a hasty man, a man who would want to
bring this to a climax quickly. He had expressed contempt—would
some instinct now teach him caution?

She closed the distance slowly, two steps on the circle, one diagonal that came closer. Again. Again. When would he notice? She let
her gaze soften, and in that instant, as she expected, he charged at
her . . . where he thought she would be with her next step. But she
had moved the opposite way. He was not quite in reach, but when he
whirled, their blades clashed.

Very fast, he was, and strong, as she expected with those shoulders.

"You're scared!" he said again, contempt in his voice, but his
slightly puzzled expression revealed that she had surprised him.
Then it hardened again. He thought he understood her now, Arianya
saw. That had been her trick, the spiral in, the reverse, the softened
focus of her gaze. His confidence returned, obvious in the way
he stood, the way he held the sword.

Arianya said nothing but smiled. She continued circling to her
right now, the mirror of what she had done before. This time he
moved in first, only one step on the circle before the diagonal. She
stayed on the circle, moving a little faster now. He seemed less concerned about his unprotected heart-side than most. Faster yet . . . but
he charged again, his sword's blade a blur, this time blocking what he
thought of as her retreat. And in his heart-hand, the knife he had
hidden from everyone, the knife that could cripple her sword arm or
kill her. She knew later that she had heard the gasp of shock from the
witnesses, that someone started to move, to say something . . . but at
the time she was not aware of these things.

It happened too fast for analysis; only experience saved her. She
moved into him, a high sweeping parry that forced his blade down
and away, between her and the knife strike, a long stride that took
her past him, her blade on reverse drawing a line of blood across his
thighs—he staggered—and finally, the stroke to the back of his neck
that severed his spine as he fell. The little knife clattered to the
boards, skittering almost to the edge.

A hand grabbed it; the yeoman-marshal Rort jumped onto the platform, eluding the hands that tried to stop him. "You must have used magery! He was the best swordsman I ever saw!" He had another knife—his own, she assumed, in his other hand. "I accuse you! I demand a fair trial of arms!"

"No," Arianya said. "Your Marshal's death decided his claim; under Code, you are bound to that outcome. You will face the tribunal for your own crimes."

For an instant, none of the witnesses moved. Then one of the yeoman-marshals from the training college swung a staff and knocked Rort down. A punch with the staff immobilized him, and the yeoman-marshals took him away.

"I apologize," one of the knights said. "I did not find that knife on him; it is my fault." He bent over the dead man, stripped back his sleeves, and found the strap from which the knife had come.

"Honesty is more easily deceived than dishonesty," Arianya said. "And he was a Marshal. You could not expect it; I did not. We must clean this up and hold a ceremony to purify the hall." And decide what to do about Rort, and convene that council, and consult the judicars about what new phrasing of the Code would exclude evil magery but allow children to grow up without violence if they lit candles with their fingers.

By nightfall much of this had been accomplished . . . not the solutions but first steps to what might become solutions.

CHAPTER SEVENTEEN

E xcuse me, Marshal-General—"
Arianya looked up from a report from Tsaia, where concern about the possible reappearance of magery was also growing.

"It's the elves, Marshal-General. They just . . . just appeared in
the High Lord's Hall, and they say they must see you at once."

"They traveled the mageroad from Kolobia?" Arianya asked.

"I—I don't know. They won't leave the High Lord's Hall . . .
they're standing in a circle staring at the floor."

"Gird's right arm," she said. "I wonder what it is now. Come with
me." At least this was unlikely to involve another dead or battered child.
She picked up the heavy chain of office she wore only when she had to
and put it over her head, settling the links automatically as she strode
down the hall, down the stairs, and out across the courtyard. Almost
normal activity, she noted, except that the yeomen posted by the entrance to the High Lord's Hall were peering inside instead of keeping
watch outside. At the sound of her boots on the stone, one of them
whipped his head around and jabbed an elbow into the other's ribs.

"We have visitors, I understand," she said to the more alert guard.

"Yes, Marshal-General. Elves. Just standing in there. Looking at
their feet."

"I doubt that last," Arianya said. She passed through the entrance and into the main vault of the High Lord's Hall. Esea's Hall it had been in Gird's time; Esea's window lit the eastern end. Now light splintered through the window, cut by the blue and clear glass into streaks of silvery sunlight and blue like flame that patterned the floor. Far up, near the altar, she saw a cluster of tall figures that glowed with a different light, a softer silver.

Before she could speak to them, one turned. In that silvery light— elf-light, as she knew—the shape of face proved beyond doubt this was an elf.

"Marshal-General of Gird," the elf said. "We are met at great need."

Their need or hers? she wondered.

The others turned to her now, stepping away from one who stood with his back to the window. The elf wore a crown; the jewels seemed made of light itself. Despite the light from the window streaming past him, she could see his face clearly. Power, majesty, wisdom . . . an elf king, it must be. Arianya felt her knees loosening and consciously fought the impulse to kneel. This was her place, not theirs.

"What is your need?" she forced herself to say even as the glamour beat on her will. She glanced down just for an instant: she stood on Gird's own stone and in that moment felt the pressure lift.

"It is not ours alone but yours," the elf said. "I am Master of the Kingsforest."

"The Kingsforest . . . ?"

"In the far western mountains. North of the land you know as Kolobia."

"Ah . . . and what is this need you speak of?"

"You must leave."

"Leave . . . here?" She hoped they did not mean that, for she would have to refuse, and then . . . She did not want to contemplate what might come of her refusal.

"No. There. The west. Leave entirely."

"Did you make Luap leave?" Arianya asked.

"He . . . broke his word."

"I do not think I understand," she said. "We were surprised, you know, to find records of his time there. We had not known—"

"You were not supposed to go there," the elf said. "All were to leave after his treachery. We sealed the patterns."

Arianya had realized for the past several years that local archives and the writings of Luap in the west did not agree, but was that what the elf meant by treachery? She asked.

"He found the place by mistake," the elf said. From his tone, this was a tale he did not want to tell and would tell only once. "We were never sure how he found the first pattern and came to the west. He brought his master Gird, and to our amazement, the High Lord, the Singer of Songs, the Maker of Worlds, and Namer of All, opened for him a way. So we guardians—we Sinyi, and the dasksinyi and kapristi as well—made treaty with Selamis, Luap of Gird, and gave him leave to make use of that place and bring others. We set limits on that right, which he swore to uphold, and warned him of dangers. But he opened his heart to evil and from the rock freed those imprisoned there, with great effort and danger . . ."

Freeing prisoners . . . Falkians laid great store by that, but Luap was not supposed to be Falkian. The Marshal-General's head began to ache. "Who was imprisoned?" she asked.

"Those we do not name," the elf said.

At a guess . . . "That would be iynisin," Arianya said. "Unsingers, haters of trees and elves and men, is it not so?"

"It is so," the elf said, through clenched teeth.

"And so more were loosed on the lands," Arianya said. "A great wrong; I understand that. He broke faith with you, is that it?"

"Yes."

"And so you prisoned his spirit in a wraith on the stone bridge?"

"No. That was not done by us. Nor were the men in the great chamber enchanted there by us. Had they been, we could have removed them. We cannot."

She felt adrift again. "Then . . . who? Luap himself?"

"No. We do not know . . . we could not tell . . . but they must go."

"How?" she asked. "If you cannot remove them, why do you think I could?"

"You must find a way. It is not . . . it is not safe. Not . . . stable . . . as it is. We must close the stone. There is evil—"

"There is always evil," she said. "Evil has existed since the beginning—"

"No."

The Marshal-General blinked. The elf must be wrong, but she realized arguing theology with an elf would not lead to anything useful. "When do you think evil began?" she asked.

"I do not know," he said. "But I know the Singer sang no wrong notes, and the Maker's hammer struck the anvil truly, and the Namer spoke true names. Some of us think it began with the coming of the lateborn—humans and others—and some think it came with the First Tree's response—but we do not know. It was long and long—it would seem the beginning to you—but it was not."

"And now you think more is coming."

"Dragon flies," he said, waving one arm sinuously. "The dasksinyi say Dragon removed his grace from them—"

She could not follow this, but it was not the time to ask questions. She had heard of the dragon that visited Vérella from High Marshal Seklis, though he had not seen the beast. He had also said something about Count Arcolin fostering a tribe of—was it dwarves or gnomes? She could not remember.

"We must close the stone forever," he said. "And all humans must leave first or we cannot do it."

"Do you have the iynisin confined again, then?"

"Not all. But your people must leave—both those you sent to study there and those enchanted."

"I can order my people home," Arianya said, "but I don't know how to wake the others."

"Someone alive now does," the elf said. "We can feel that."

"Who?"

"We do not know. Beyond—I have not been so far sunrising since the first years after we came north."

They had come north. That was more than Arianya had known. Questions sprang to her lips, but she held them back. Instead, she said, "Forgive my rudeness . . . we stand here talking when you could rest at ease and take refreshment. There is a garden."

The elves all looked at the one with the crown, who finally nodded. "I accept your offer."

They followed her from the hall, and she studiously ignored the looks cast at them by everyone in the courtyard. Instead she said, "It is a walled garden with fruit trees and flowers—the climate here is harsh for these things in the open. We will go through the building."

Once the garden had opened to the courtyard—larger then—but now the only way to it was down a hall, through the small dining area, and then—on the left—it appeared. As they passed through the dining room, she spoke to a cook's assistant swabbing down one of the tables. "We'll need cool water, fruit, and some of those spiced cakes in the walled garden."

When all were settled and had been served, Arianya tried to think what questions to ask. Enchanted magelords, yes . . . but how could the elves think that someone here knew how to wake them? And who could that be?

Dorrin, perhaps? Dorrin Verrakai, a magelord who still had mage powers. Could they have sensed Dorrin from afar? How? And should she tell these elves about Dorrin or send word to Dorrin herself, warning her?

"What do you know of the situation here?" Arianya asked. "Do you send messengers back and forth to the Ladysforest, for instance?"

"Never," said the king. His face expressed extreme distaste.

Arianya blinked. She had assumed elves communicated from one of their realms to another just as humans did. She could think of nothing to say for a moment. Then she said, "You do know Lyonya has a new king . . . Kieri Phelan. I met him when he was Duke Phelan of Tsaia and none of us knew his parentage. Did you?"

No answer to that. She felt pressure in her head, almost like the start of a headache before a summer thunderstorm.

"Stop that," she said without heat; the feeling vanished. She went on. "The king is half-elven; the Lady of the Ladysforest is his grandmother." Again he said nothing; she went on. "But to your main problem, as you state it—the mageborn in that hall. I have no idea how to break that enchantment. We Girdish do not deal in magery. There is but one magelord I know of who is presently capable of effective magery." Should she have said that? What would Dorrin Verrakai think if an elf king showed up in her house?

"You must tell the magelord to come to us and break the enchantment," the king said.

"Me?" Arianya felt her brows rising. "I am not her commander.

She is not Girdish but Falkian, and she is the vassal of Tsaia's king. You must go to her directly—or, better, to Tsaia's king—and gain his permission for anything she does."

He shifted in his seat. "I have never been to Tsaia," he said. "Is it far by road?"

Arianya had no idea what "far" meant to an elf who usually traveled from pattern to pattern. "Three hands of days, perhaps," she said. "Longer if the river has flooded; it does most springs."

He frowned. "I have no . . . no sight for Tsaia."

Arianya had no idea what that meant.

"Perhaps I should go instead to visit the Lady's grandson, the new king, in Lyonya."

"That would be a good idea," Arianya said. She would like to see that meeting of kings.

"But you must recall those of your people—the Girdish—from the west," he said. "For I do not know when we will be able to close the rock."

"We would like to bring back the archives," Arianya said. "I understand it was your land first, but what the humans there left—the writings, the things they made—are important to us. For our history."

"History!" one of the other elves said, with a dismissive wave of the hand.

"History to us," Arianya said firmly, "though but a blink of time to you. Since we do not live long, we need the records of past times to give us some guidance for the future."

"How long will that take?" the king asked.

"I will ask our archivist," Arianya said. "We have brought back some already. The archivist will know how much is left. How long can you stay? It may take a few days for the archivist to determine how many trips it will take."

"We will go . . . I must prepare my kingdom for the longer journeys to eastern lands," the king said.

"You could not send an ambassador?"

"I do not know," the king said. "Would he be believed? Respected?"

"Why not?" Arianya said. "From what I know, both kings have dealt with elves before. King Kieri certainly has."

The elven king frowned. "I will consider it. And for now we will leave open the patterns your people have used to go back and forth. Only you must bring them away as soon as you can."

"How can I tell you when we are all gone?"

"We will know. We are watching."

That was all he would say; the elves bowed courteously enough and then went back to the High Lord's Hall, stepped onto the transfer pattern, and disappeared.

"I wonder if it's their fault," Marshal Pedar said. "Whatever they're doing to close the rock—could that be what's waking magery?"

"Or was it our first expedition out there?" Arianya wondered. "It seemed so reasonable, with the scrolls of Luap Paksenarrion brought to us . . . a joint expedition of humans, elves, dwarves, just to find out what happened."

"So . . . Paksenarrion started it?"

Arianya shook her head. "I acquit her of that: whatever it was started long ago, before even Gird. But her finding those scrolls . . . that might be the shove that starts a boulder downhill."

"What now?"

"I don't know. We cannot wake those enchanted magelords; that, I'm sure of. I don't know why the combined skills of the Elders will not wake them . . . what enchantment could be stronger than theirs?"

"A dragon's?"

"Perhaps, but . . . why would a dragon cast embattled magelords into enchanted sleep?" She rubbed her temples. "I thought the return of magery more than enough challenge for the Fellowship. I suppose I had best write the letters to both kings and also Duke Verrakai. I doubt they will know any better than I what to do, but at least they must know what the problem is."

CHAPTER EIGHTEEN

Arian left Vérella with relief she carefully concealed from the king and court. They had been cordial; they had done everything they could think of—but to be surrounded by buildings and walls in spring, of all seasons—to be so distant from trees—stifled her. Besides, she had information Kieri needed, which she had not trusted to a courier, since at least one had disappeared between Chaya and Vérella.

Riding east with only her own Squires, her heart lifted with every league covered. Flowering trees, flowering hedges, drifts of flowers in some fields . . . Their perfume filled the air, and the various shades of spring green looked edible. It felt like a holiday—all the strain of trying to uphold Lyonyan honor in a foreign court past, and any duties to come days away.

At the border, the taig welcomed her, the sense of that living grace rising from the ground. Even riding up the scathefire track toward Chaya . . . Though the scar remained, ferns and flowers already grew along the margins where only natural fire had burned.

At last they came out of the forest track into the open and rode across the bridge onto the meadow just outside the palace. On the far side of the bridge, Kieri waited with his Squires. Behind them a small crowd stood waving flowering branches and cheering.

She and Kieri rode in together, showered with petals. It was hard
not to throw herself off her horse into his arms. From his expression,
he felt the same way. They made it through dinner and up the stairs
into the royal chambers. Kieri shut the door firmly in the Squires'
faces.

"I missed you," Kieri said mildly.

"And I, you," Arian said.

"I suppose I should ask you all the important questions," Kieri
said. "About Tsaia, about Mikeli . . ." He was undressing as he spoke.
"But the only real question is . . . are you too tired?"

"No," Arian said. "Not now. Not ever."

Later, Arian gave him a report of her visit, starting with the most
important. "They have at least one of the patterns. They hadn't noticed; apparently they saw only irregularities in the stone, like our
servants."

"Where?"

"In the grange-hall for the Bells. I didn't see any others, but I did
not visit every room in the palace; there wasn't time. I did warn King
Mikeli."

"The elves found more here after you left," Kieri said. "As we
suspected, under the elf-gifted carpets in the public rooms. They're
not all identical, however, and I don't know what that difference
means. Did you see the pattern on that box with the regalia?"

"No. It's sealed in an outer box they can't open. Only Duke Verrakai can, they said, and elven magery had no effect on it."

That night, Arian slept at ease, waking at dawn to find Kieri
looking down at her. "Are you all right?" he asked.

She stretched. "Very well, now I'm home. Did you enjoy living
there? In Tsaia? In Vérella?"

"I didn't live in the palace, though I visited . . . but yes, I enjoyed
it. What was wrong with it?"

"Not enough trees," Arian said. "And no gardens in the palace
grounds. It's stuffy inside." She looked to the window, the curtains
pulled aside to let in the early summer breeze. "I don't know how
they can stand it."

"It did not bother me then," Kieri said. "It might now. What
about the people?"

"At first they seemed very strange, but soon I saw they were much like us but for being all human. I saw no part-elves at all. Those who look young are young . . . it's almost frightening how young the king is. He's trying very hard, but no one that age can know enough. At least the present dukes are older."

"Don't underestimate him," Kieri said. "I knew him as a younger boy—and knew his father. How's his brother?"

"Impulsive, hasty, full of energy, eager."

"Envious of his brother?"

"No, not that. I think he wants adventure and considers kingship dull. A boy still. Yet . . . there's something endearing about him."

Kieri grinned at her. "You're going to make a fine mother, my love."

"What? Why?"

"Camwyn's a scamp, and our son may be one, too. Some women cannot love a scamp. I'm glad you can. Tell me, are you tired from your journey, or do you feel like practice this day?"

"Practice always," Arian said. "And that's another thing. *Our* royal salle is much better than their royal salle."

"Agreed. I've practiced there."

Arian rejoiced in the familiar morning routine, sparring with Carlion and Siger and the Squires. Breakfast with Kieri, catching up on the news: work had begun on the River Road extension and the river port. They walked in the rose garden, now a riot of fragrance and color.

"I cannot tell that the taig is much different without the elven-home," Kieri said. "What do you feel?"

"It certainly reacted when the Lady died," Arian said. She laid her hand gently on the stem of one of the old roses trained on a wall. From there to the trees beyond the wall, and the heart of the taig, the flow of energy felt easy, unrestricted. "You're right, though—barring the gaps and injuries done by the scathefire, it seems healthy and much the same. Has Amrothlin said anything about the taig in particular?"

"No. He's been helpful on other points, though it takes at least half a day for him to tell me one thing I need to know. I'm learning patience along with far too much about things that happened a van-ryn ago. He insists it's all connected, and I suppose it is, but I wish there weren't so much of it." He lifted her hand and kissed it. "And now, my queen, how do you feel about the burdens of queenship?"

Arian laughed. "I am not the same woman who was afraid back in the winter, my king. You said I would not find it as difficult as I feared, and so it has been. Oh—that reminds me—I met Duke Mahieran's daughters and their formidable aunt."

"Maris?" Kieri said. He shook his head, his expression rueful. "The first time I met her after being elevated to duke, she looked me up and down and said she didn't know how someone like me got to be a duke. I think she blamed me that her husband died in a campaign I survived when I was still very young and had no title at all."

"She seems very . . ." Arian paused, unable to think how to say it.

"Difficult? Yes. But honest, as well. How were Sonder's daughters?"

"Scared and rebellious both," Arian said. "They'd been confined—less closely than Beclan but forbidden most of the things they usually did."

"Are they living with their mother?"

"No, with Maris. And there's concern they may have the magery, as Beclan does."

"And so they're less likely to marry," Kieri said. "Could you tell?"

"No. I'm not sure I could, anyway; it's not our kind of magery. I could tell they were spirited and bored and touchy. I invited them to share the picnic with us—everyone else was ignoring them."

"Good for you," Kieri said. "I met them, of course, when I visited the house once or twice, but they were just children to me. They made their courtesy and went away while Sonder and I talked."

"What about Celbrin? His wife?"

Kieri chuckled and kissed her hand again. "Not my kind of woman. Very sure she knew exactly how everyone should dress, eat, stand, sit . . . impressive at court and very influential with the other ladies. Well, any wife in that family would be, but Celbrin was fond of the deference she got. Gracious with steel underneath. And yet I could not imagine her with a sword."

"What I heard was that she was elegant, regal, and always knew what to do."

"You heard that from——?"

"Several counts' wives. Not Lady Marrakai or Lady Serrostin."

Kieri chuckled. "No—they were never close friends, as I recall. Still, I'm sure it's hard on her being separated from her home, her daughters, and her chance to impress the wives of lesser peers."

Arian spent the rest of the morning wandering around the palace, simply happy to be home again. It seemed inconceivable now that she had been afraid she would not make a good queen, that she would find the duties too difficult. Glad as she was to be away from Tsaia's court, the trip had given her much more confidence. Queens and kings, she understood now, were merely guardians of the taig and the people . . . and she had trained as a guardian of the taig most of her life.

Amrothlin sought her out later in the day. "My lady," he said, the inflection making it clear she was not the Lady of his heart.

"Amrothlin . . . how are you?"

His eyes darkened. "Sun and stars both fade without the Lady."

"Is it so for all of you, or only for you, her son?"

"It is so for the whole world, if you could but see." He sounded angry but then shook his head. "I am sorry, Arian. You did not kill her."

Arian thought of asking him more about Kieri's mother and sister but did not feel like sitting through a long recital on this bright day. "I wish you more happiness than you now have," she said instead. "And I thank you for the loyalty you show Kieri in such a difficult time. Tell me, have you ever visited Tsaia?"

"Yes," he said. "At one time we sent elves there regularly . . . to . . . to watch."

"To watch Kieri? You knew then, did you not?"

He nodded. "We knew, and we watched, as the Lady bade us. At first we hoped to see some sign of his inheritance, but as you know, it did not blossom until he returned here."

"Where the taig could reach him," Arian said. "The taig there is so frayed, I doubt anyone not already trained could feel it."

"We did not think of that," Amrothlin said. "He had spent years with Aliam Halveric, after all."

S ometimes," Kieri said, running a hand through her hair, "I think the Elders are not what the dragon would call wise. Foolish, in fact. How could they think only of humans taking my mother? By all accounts she was a superb swordswoman, a skilled rider—" He had been telling Arian what he'd learned from Amrothlin while she was in Tsaia. "And to assume the child killed as well and not search for the body . . . unless . . ." He shuddered.

"What, love?"

"Unless, I was thinking, whoever did this killed a child, damaged the body so it could not be identified, and they found that—"

"Did Amrothlin say that?"

"No. But they've said nothing of a lot of things. My mother being the Lady's heir and having the power to create an elvenhome, for one." He sighed.

Arian looked at his face, now somber, almost angry. She had not wanted to think about his childhood after capture; the evidence of those old scars was bad enough. How had he survived to become the man he was?

"You are a good king, Kieri," she said.

"I hope so," he said, his expression shifting. He smiled at her. "If I become one, it will be because of you. You will not let me brood."

"Nor you, me. But I agree with you. For so long I had thought of the Lady as all-wise as well as all-powerful, but—"

"But not so wise as she might have been. What do you really think of Amrothlin? Could he be the traitor and still intent on fooling us?"

Arian thought a long moment before answering. "I think he is not the traitor. I think he felt his purpose missing after your mother died. I think he was loyal to your mother and then to the Lady."

"If I did become able to do . . . that . . . with the elvenhome, would he be loyal to me?"

"Do you think you can, Kieri?"

"I don't know. I never thought about it before. Orlith never mentioned the possibility. I have no idea how to try, even. But if I could . . . Annoying as I've found the elves this past year, they're still my responsibility. If I can be what they need, I would be a better king."

"How are the other projects coming?" Arian asked. "The road from Harway to Riverwash was certainly improved."

His face brightened. "I've talked to Master-trader Chalvers and given him permission to mark out a route from the border to Chaya. Work has begun on clearing for the port—that will take much of the summer, I fear, but at least it's a start."

"We should have some kind of agreement with the Pargunese," Arian said. "They're weaker now and have lost land; if raiders came up the river—"

"They trust Kostandan more than us," Kieri said. He frowned thoughtfully. "Then again . . . if Ganlin marries into the Tsaian royal family . . . if the three could all be allies some way . . . that would be a very strong position should Alured invade."

"They're a long way away if he comes over the mountains," Arian said.

"Yes, but he was a pirate first," Kieri said. "He controls the Immer ports now, and from what Andressat said, he may still control piracy in the Immerhoft Sea. I have worried about that. Tsaia would never suspect that—and he could not get past the falls—but he could wreak havoc on all of us below the falls."

"What did you think of the Sea-Prince?" Arian asked.

"Wary," Kieri said. "He's younger . . . Alured's age, I would say. And like him in some ways. He said nothing about it, but I would not be surprised if Alured had traded around the Eastbight to Banner-lith."

"Talk to Torfinn," Arian said, "and the Kostandanyans as well. If Ganlin makes a good marriage in Tsaia, they should be happy with you for giving her that opportunity."

"I can hope so," Kieri said. "But now—I need fresh air. Let's go for a ride."

The Royal Ride on a spring afternoon was pure delight for eye and ear and nose alike.

CHAPTER NINETEEN

Vérella

When the king called Prince Camwyn into his office before supper the day after Queen Arian left for Lyonya, Camwyn was sure he'd done something wrong.

"I've set the day to depart on my progress, Cam," Mikeli said. "At first I thought I would leave you here for your safety, but after what you told me about Egan, I can't do that. You'll come with me. We go first to Duke Verrakai, then—if we have time and the road permits—south through Konhalt and on to a town called Brewersbridge, where we'll meet the South Trade Road."

Camwyn's heart rose. "I'm coming with you? All that way?"

"Yes. I've just sent word to your tutors that you're excused from all classes until you return. It's a working trip, not just a rest period. I want you to be on the watch for things that may be kept from the king, and I'll expect a written report of what you see, day by day. Are you willing to do that?"

"Yes, sir king," Camwyn said with a formal bow. He felt like dancing.

"We'll be in tents some nights," Mikeli said. "Sharing a tent—and if I snore, you're not to complain."

Sharing a tent. Camwyn restrained himself from shoving his hands in his pockets. What would he do if his hand lit up and Mikeli saw it?

"You've never seen the royal tent," Mikeli said. "It's huge, big enough for a dozen or more to sleep in, so you'll have a little room of your own."

Thank you, Gird.

"Because you might snore and keep me awake." Mikeli laughed. "Oh—and you'll need a page. Someone I trust. You can have Aris. He'll have a pallet in your room."

Near panic again, except it was Aris. Aris was better than Mikeli. And maybe he slept very soundly.

Past that panic, his first thought was that he and Aris now had *three whole days* without lessons in which to explore the palace roofs and find a route to one particular skylight. They met at evening arms practice—not a regular lesson, he told himself, putting on his banda and lining up with the others. Just as he was about to tell Aris the good news, Armsmaster Fralorn arrived, and they all bowed. Fralorn scowled at him. "Prince, what are you doing here? Surely the king himself told you you're excused—"

"From tutors, he said, sir. Not arms practice."

"Here as well. You and Aris Marrakai. Put your gear away neatly and quietly and begone."

Aris, it was clear, had not heard the word; his lips were clamped tight and his expression stubborn. Maybe he thought they were in trouble. Camwyn explained on the way back upstairs, finishing with, "And you get to come with me. The king says I need a page—"

"I'm not your page! I'm your friend—I thought—"

"Of course you are. But I'm just a prince. I can't take friends with me. Only people with a job. That's why you'll be a page."

Aris's expression eased. "Are you going to order me around, then?"

"I am older," Camwyn said. "And if you were my brother, you'd be younger."

"Yes, but . . . all right." Aris gave in as quickly as a colt might. Now he grinned. "And no lessons or duties until we leave? Both of us?"

"That's right. They want us out of the way while packing, I don't doubt. We can go out on the roofs any time we want."

Early the next morning, they were up high in the palace, this time in the library wing, looking for a way out that would give them easy access to the north side roofs. One little windowless stair after another emptied only into attic storerooms, servants' quarters, or promising niches that might have been doors before having stones set firmly into the arch or square-cut gap. Once more, repair debris helped point the way: a stack of slates by a closed door in a blind passage.

By the time they made it up a ladder and out the trapdoor at the top, the sun was well up. The ladder, they discovered, had been on one side of a chimney stack that now hid them from anyone on the south palace roofs. They were dizzyingly high even for boys who liked to climb on roofs. Camwyn's stomach seemed to writhe inside him. Aris looked paler than usual.

"We're here," Camwyn said. Sitting down with his back to the chimney and one hand clasping the last rung of the ladder seemed a good idea. The roof here, shadowed by the chimney stack, was still damp; he ran his fingers over it. Yes, slippery.

"I didn't know it was this high on this side," Aris said. He looked straight out to the horizon, not down.

Ahead of them, the city roofs made jagged shapes out to the north wall; from up here, the places it had been breached in Gird's war showed clearly. Beyond were the pastures and then the forests and then higher hills and forests beyond. Up there somewhere, Camwyn reminded himself, was the northernmost part of the kingdom, the North Marches, where the dragon had come from.

He looked east and west along the ridge of the roof, trying to spot the skylight of the treasury. It should be . . . there. He forced himself to let go the ladder and scoot on his backside around the chimney stack to the ridgeline, telling himself he was less likely to be seen than if he stood up.

"Won't he be expecting you at breakfast?" Aris sounded scared. Camwyn turned to look, surprised. Aris was still sitting by the chimney stack, now more than his body's length away. "The king, I mean. Don't you have breakfast with him?"

"Usually," Camwyn said. He looked at the sun, then the distance to the skylight he thought was the right one. It would be quicker with just one. He looked back. "It will just take me a flick of time, Aris. You don't have to come."

Aris reddened. "I'll come. I'm not scared." He stood up; Camwyn could see at once that Aris had moved too quickly. His foot skidded on the damp roof; he grabbed for the ladder but raked his hand on the stone chimney instead and—his balance completely off—began the fall that could be nothing but fatal.

Camwyn flung a frantic prayer for help—*Gird! Falk! Camwyn!*— even as he moved, even as he knew he was too far away, too slow . . . and then he was flat on his front, his right hand around Aris's wrist, his left fisted in Aris's shirt. He had a moment to realize that he was lying on nothing but two handspans of air, and then he settled to the roof as gently as the dragon had settled back to the stones of the courtyard.

They were not falling to their deaths. They were not even sliding down the roof . . . here, out of the chimney's shadow, the roof had dried and the pitch felt less steep than it had looked. Face to face, eye to eye, they stared at each other. Camwyn could feel his heart pounding, his blood roaring in his ears, and he could feel—separate, distinct—Aris's pulse in the wrist he held.

"You . . . *flew* . . ." Aris said.

"I jumped," Camwyn said.

"You saved my life."

"Maybe. Let me see . . ." Very cautiously, without letting go of Aris, Camwyn squirmed a little uphill, using his hips and his toes. The roof under him felt rough, lumpy, and awkward, but stable. "I don't know if I can pull you, Aris, but I can steady you. Can you push with your feet? Squirm upward?"

It was an awkward retreat because Camwyn wouldn't let go of Aris at first.

"At least let go my wrist," Aris said. "Grab my shirt on that side—"

"It's an old shirt. What if it tears?" Camwyn could not believe their voices were so calm.

"I'll feel it; I'll grab for you. But I need both hands."

It took much longer than either wanted to get back up to the chimney and its ladder—where the roof was now dry—and then they were in the dark, with the trapdoor secured overhead and a long climb down a vertical ladder to the passage below. Their bare feet made no sound on the rungs, but the rungs started a cramp in Camwyn's left foot. He tried to use only his right foot, but he missed the rung and slid, banging Aris on top of the head and setting off another panic.

Then they had light. Camwyn stared at his hand, wondering what else could possibly go wrong. Light and heat glowed from it, and when he looked down, he saw the light reflected in Aris's eyes.

"You—" Aris began.

"Just don't say anything," Camwyn said. "My foot's cramping, and I can't get it to stop while I'm on this ladder."

Aris went on down the ladder; Camwyn followed, hanging by his arms most of the way. It was easier in the light; he could see the rungs before reaching for them. Aris waited at the bottom, shoulders hunched. When Camwyn touched the level surface and was able to force his feet to uncramp, the light in his hand went out like a snuffed candle. Dim light from the door they'd left open remained, enough to see Aris's expression.

"Did you know?" Aris said.

"Hush," Camwyn said. "We *are* late now, just as you warned, and we don't want to be caught around here."

"You—that was *magery*!"

"I don't think so," Camwyn said. "I hope not."

"But did you *know*?"

"Not exactly," Camwyn said. "I'll talk to you later about this, but we have to get back to my rooms and clean up before they find us looking like street thieves." Their clothes bore the stains of everything that had been on that roof.

"But magery—that's—"

"That's illegal. I know. Beclan was banned for it. I know. Later, Aris, *please*. Just don't spread it around right now."

Aris nodded, his mouth pinched tight. Cautiously, they eased into the branch passage and made their way down from the top floor of the north wing to the next and then the next, where they were immediately collared by palace staff before they could reach the passage that led to Camwyn's room.

"Where have you been? We've been looking everywhere for you—the king is most displeased. And you're filthy, both of you!"

"It's my fault," Camwyn said. "Mik—the king had given me permission to go up on the roof if I had a friend along, so I asked Aris, and—"

"What were you doing? Rolling about like puppies in a dunghill? Because that's what it looks like."

They were near enough to Mikeli's rooms that he might hear. "I'm sorry," Camwyn said. "We'll clean up, we'll change—"

"No. The king said bring you straight to him when we found you."

Mikeli looked all king this morning, none of the caring older brother about him at all. He looked them up and down and said to one of the servants, "Take young Marrakai off to bathe and change. Camwyn will breakfast with me."

Aris left; Camwyn hoped he would not reveal anything.

"Sit down, Camwyn," Mikeli said. "You look like someone who had an unfortunate adventure. Care to tell me about it?"

As much as he could without . . . Camwyn sorted his memory of events and began. Finding himself suspended in the air for a few moments and the light that showed him the ladder's rungs never made it past his teeth.

"So . . . as I'm trying to organize and prepare for the first royal progress to be made in the kingdom since you were born, you chose to lark about up on the roof and nearly get yourself and your friend— who just happens to be my best friend's little brother—killed?" The temper Mikeli rarely let himself show was an almost visible flame on that side of the table.

"I thought . . . you said we had no lessons . . ."

"That doesn't mean you had no *duties*! Cam, if I weren't determined to take you along, I'd have you locked in a closet for the duration. Where was your *thinking*?"

Camwyn looked up and saw both the anger and the fear behind the anger. Tears stung his eyes; he fought them. He was too old to cry. "I know it's my fault, sir king. I know I was wrong. I just can't—one day I can think like you and my tutors—or some of it—and another day I think I'm thinking, but at the end of the day—I wasn't." His voice broke in the middle of that, a jagged switch of high to low that made it sound as if he were crying. "I try," Camwyn said, in the harsh new voice.

Mikeli leaned across the table, the angry flame dying down, the concern returning. "Camwyn . . . sometimes trying isn't enough. I'm sorry; I wish it were not so; I wish I could protect you forever, but Cam—dear brother—you must try harder to think first, not once you're in a pickle."

"Did you ever get in trouble?"

That brought a snort of amusement. "Yes, Brother, I did, but I was the heir, and I had more watchers. And possibly—likely—you are bolder than I ever was or would have been even if I'd not been in leading strings so long. So my troubles were different ones. I was not overfond of protocol." He shook his head. "But you're the heir now, and I'm afraid I'm going to have to insist you restrain your adventurous nature. Whatever possessed you to climb onto the north roof, anyway?"

Camwyn felt the heat rising in his face. "We hadn't been there yet," he said.

"Well, sate your desire for new experiences by making yourself useful to the officer organizing the order of march and the precautions to be taken for the safety of the king's majesty. One of the staff will escort you to him. After you bathe and dress, of course. I will expect you to report to me at luncheon. I have a different errand for Aris Marrakai, but he may have the same duties in the afternoon as you do. There'll be no more escapades on the roof before we leave; there's too much to do."

Camwyn found himself paired with a Royal Guard officer for the rest of the morning, watching as the man made list after list of what must be carried along with them, handing each to Camwyn. Camwyn asked questions at first, but clearly the officer—who preferred to be addressed as Captain Rassen though he wore the Bells on his collar and must be a knight—thought princes should listen and not interrupt. He was left to figure out for himself why Captain Rassen inspected a stack of wagon wheels and rejected two and then demanded three to replace them. Why the rations carried for the horses and mules included much less hay than he'd expected. Why it mattered which wagon was where in the supply train.

He brought his conclusions to Mikeli at lunch, where he found Aris serving the table for them both, looking a little wary as he did so. "You're mostly right, Cam," the king said. Then, to Aris, "Thank you, Aris; you may eat now. Sit there." And back to Camwyn. "This afternoon, I want you and Aris to go to the library and see that the maps are ready, correctly labeled, and that the carrying tubes are long enough for them. If any of the buckles or straps are worn, make a note and let one of the servants take it to the saddler for repair. I have a list of the maps I'll need—I had them copied onto smaller sheets."

By the time they set out two days later, Camwyn felt stuffed with new knowledge. His hands had not lit up again, and Aris had not asked any more questions, as they had not been alone long enough to discuss anything serious.

To his delight, his own clothes for the journey included the mail Mikeli had worn some years before—not a perfect fit, but—as Mikeli said—it was no use changing the fit while he was growing so fast. By midday, however, he felt much less gleeful about wearing real mail. It was both heavy and hot, and as the morning heated up, he wished he'd followed Mikeli's advice to wear it around camp in the evenings for a while.

He told himself to ignore it, and that proved easier than he'd thought as they neared the edge of Mahieran lands and ventured into unknown—for Mikeli at least—territory. Ordinary-looking fields and orchards and pastures and patches of woodland . . . but ones he'd paid little attention to, riding in a carriage with Lady Verrakai and Egan, then his new best friend on that long-ago trip to Verrakai. Now, riding his own horse, he tried to notice everything. On their left the Honnorgat rolled on, sometimes near enough to see long-necked wading birds prowling the shallows fishing, sometimes screened by a field, a hedge, a fringe of trees. On their right, the land rose to distant hills, clearly arranged in some kind of pattern.

They made little progress that first day, as people lined the road on either side, waving flowers, branches, kerchiefs. Riding behind the king, Camwyn remembered his instructions: smile, nod, or bow as rank suggested and maintain suitable demeanor—something the palace master of ceremonies had gone over repeatedly. He tried not to sneeze or cough as the king's spirited stallion, impatient with the slow pace, fretted, jigged, and even pitched a few times, tossing dust in Camwyn's face. As a result, Camwyn's mount did the same, and he needed both hands on the reins until lunchtime.

Those first few days were all delight, with new sights at every turn of the glass. The first evening they camped, Camwyn was thrilled to see the royal pavilion rise on the chosen meadow. He and Aris watched and even lent their weight on the ropes as it went up. They ate at the king's table outdoors, food that tasted much better for having been cooked over a fire-pit. Camwyn had wondered if the curtains that divided room from room and moved slightly in the breeze would keep him awake, but he fell asleep quickly and woke only when the camp commander blew the morning signal.

The third night under canvas changed everything.

CHAPTER TWENTY

C amwyn woke before the turn of night to the unwelcome reality of his magery: his hand was brightening from a soft glow
already. He stuffed his hand back under the blanket. Light
leaked out through the weave, brighter every moment. Bright enough
to see that Aris, on the other cot, was sound asleep on his back like a
tiny child, mouth open, one arm flung out as if it had no weight and
just rested on the air.

Please, he begged a deity who so far had not cooperated. *Don't let
this happen. Please.*

The light stuttered like a candle in a breath of air, like a cool draft
blowing through the tent, when someone . . . lifted a curtain. He
turned toward the draft, dread chilling his body more than the air.
Mikeli's face in that haunted light looked monstrous, terrifying. The
face of someone who might kill him now, this moment.

"You're not asleep," Mikeli said quietly.

The light in his hand went out, plunging them both into darkness. Now he could see beyond Mikeli, through the two opened curtains between his chamber and Mikeli's, the faint glow of a candle,
fainter by far than his hand had been, lighting nothing.

"Come," Mikeli said. "Now." He stood there, outlined from behind by that distant candle, while Camwyn struggled out of the tan-

gle his bedclothes usually made, trying to keep quiet so Aris wouldn't wake.

Excuses tumbled through his mind, but he knew it was too late for excuses. He stubbed his toe on the leg of the camp bed and managed not to make a noise. Mikeli stood aside to let him out and then dropped the curtain behind him. Then he felt Mikeli's hand—a man's hand, larger than his own, harder-callused, stronger—on his arm, moving him into Mikeli's side of the tent.

As his eyes adjusted to the fainter light of the real candle, he could see Mikeli's camp bed, the camp chair with its leather seat and back, the table with folding legs, the footstool.

"Sit there," Mikeli said, pushing him toward the stool.

Camwyn folded himself onto it. The candle flame fluttered as Mikeli dropped the curtain to the passage and then sat in the chair. It should have been ludicrous, Camwyn thought, a king in his nightshirt, bare legged and barefoot . . . but there was nothing amusing about Mikeli's expression.

Mikeli leaned forward, putting his face a mere handspan from Camwyn's. "And just *when*, Brother, were you planning to tell me about *that*?"

No use to pretend he didn't know what "that" was.

"And do not try to tell me this was the first time."

Camwyn had already rejected that excuse. "I hoped it would go away," he said instead. "I asked Gird to stop it. I knew it was wrong—"

"You weren't trying to make it happen? Wanting to know if you had magery like Beclan?"

"No! I wasn't . . . but . . . I dreamed."

"Dreamed?"

"Voices. And—maybe it was my fault."

"How?"

Camwyn's voice seemed stuck in his throat, but he got it out bit by bit.

"The *crown* called you?" Mikeli's face, in the dimmer light of the flickering candle, had seemed slightly less frightening, but now it hardened again. "Was that why you asked to see the treasury? Were you lying to your tutors and the steward as well as me?"

"I wanted to see if I could . . . find it. I never saw the chest before;

I didn't know what it looked like. If I could find it, then . . . then maybe I could open it. It wants to be free, Mikeli—sir king." He knew he was crying only when the tears dripped down his face.

"And you blame the crown?"

"No—not that—it's my fault. I could have—could have stopped—"

"Did you break into the treasury?"

"No!"

"Softly. Were you *thinking* about breaking into the treasury? Was that why you went up on the roof?"

"Yes, sir king."

"Does anyone else know about this? Aris?"

He saw now, when he knew he should have seen earlier, that truth was the only road open. "Yes, sir king. When we went out on the north roof—"

"The time you fell."

"I . . . caught Aris. And I couldn't have."

"What do you mean?"

"I was sitting on the ridge, kind of scooting along, and he slipped, behind me. It was my fault—he thought I was teasing him about being afraid, but really I told him to stay because I thought I'd be faster alone and I wouldn't have to worry about him. So he stood up fast and he slipped, and I was facing the wrong way and all bent up, and when I tried to move—" His voice failed then; a sob wanted to burst out. He fought it back.

"What happened?"

"I—I caught him. And he said 'You're flying,' and I saw I must have—none of me was touching the roof. Then I fell down onto it, but we didn't slide off." Camwyn swallowed and told the rest. "And then on the ladder my feet cramped and I nearly fell, and . . . my hand lit up so I could see where the rungs were."

"And Aris saw."

"Yes, and I asked him not to tell anyone about it, even you, because I would. But I was afraid—I know I'm supposed to be willing to die in your service, but . . . but I don't want to. Yet. But I'm your brother, and if I have magery, you have to kill me—"

"No, I don't," Mikeli said. He sat back a little, elbows on his knees. "Cam, think: I didn't kill Beclan Mahieran, and he's only my cousin. Even though many men—many good men—died because of him and his magery, I did not condemn him. You're my brother. You're right; your having magery is a problem—and it couldn't happen at a worse time, with High Marshal Seklis in the next tent—but you're my brother, and I'm not going to kill you. Not for that, anyway. I'd sooner kill you for lying. For that you *will* be punished."

Camwyn wanted to ask how but did not dare. "You sent Beclan away; you made him change his name."

"Yes. And I cannot do that to you without risking my own rule. Enough tongues wag already." Mikeli heaved a sigh that seemed to rise from his bare feet. "I thought you'd lit a candle—a dozen candles—in there and were up to some mischief. That's why I came to see. Tell me, does it happen more than once a night?"

"Not . . . usually," Camwyn said. "But I never know when or for how long."

"Can you light candles with it?"

"Yes, and that helps it go away. Sometimes I light one over and over."

"Try." Mikeli handed him an unlit candle.

Camwyn put out his hand to the wick. One finger burst into brilliant light; a flame rose from the wick. His finger hardly dimmed.

"I don't suppose you can use it up by some other magery," Mikeli said. "Flying, perhaps?"

Camwyn hesitated before answering and realized he was now on a level with Mikeli, whose mouth dropped open. "I don't know—" he began, and then he fell, bare feet thudding on the rug first, followed almost at once by the rest of him crumpling in a heap with a loud thump. His hand held no light now, and ached as if he'd plunged it into the winter river. He lay, too tired to move. The candle he'd lit went on burning.

"Sorry," Mikeli said. "I didn't really think—"

"Is everything all right, sir king?" came a soft voice from the passage, along with approaching footsteps.

"Yes," Mikeli said. "Prince Camwyn and I are just talking; I knocked over the stool. We were both restless. Don't be surprised if I light another candle."

"Something to drink? Eat?"

"No need," Mikeli said. "Thank you."

The footsteps receded. Camwyn felt himself sinking into sleep; as the darkness closed over him, he felt his brother's strong arms lifting him, settling him in a bed.

When he woke, he was in Mikeli's bed and Mikeli was nowhere in sight. His head ached. He rolled over. A pillow and blanket were on the rug . . . but across the passage, he heard a man's snore and a boy's lighter one in the chamber that had been his. Outside, he heard a horse neigh, and then another one. The camp was waking. Soon the horn would blow, and servants would come.

Camwyn rolled out of the bed, tossed the blanket and pillow back atop it, and eased the curtain back. No one in the passage. Across to the other chamber . . . he moved the curtain back and forth. Mikeli's snores stopped.

"Cam?"

"Yes. It's morning."

"It feels like the middle of the night." Now more noise from outside, muffled sounds from men and completely unmuffled sounds from the mules. "Let me get back to my side," Mikeli said. "We'll talk later."

Outside the sky was already light, the grass heavy with dew. Camwyn and Aris had their assigned chores, readying the tent's contents for the wagons. Shaking out the bedclothes, folding them; folding up the beds, the tables, the stools and chairs; carrying the lighter things out to the assigned wagon.

At breakfast in the open air—deliciously fresh and smelling of spring—Mikeli said, "You will not ride with me today, either of you. I believe you know why."

"Yes, sir king," Camwyn said. Was he being sent back? He stuffed a bite of sausage and bread into his mouth to keep from pleading.

"You will ride in the last supply wagon today, the next to last tomorrow, and so on. I expect a complete tally of everything in the wagon you're in each night. You may use tally sticks, but you will write the tally neatly for me to read when we stop for the night. If you do this faithfully, you may ride with me again when we come to Harway."

Camwyn's heart sank. Day after day in the hot wagons at the

dusty end of the procession? And not even free to sit and watch the countryside pass by, but digging about in the wagon to note what was in it? And yet . . . at least he wasn't being sent back to Vérella in disgrace.

"Yes, sir king," he said.

"Go on, then," Mikeli said as his own squires approached. "I see you've finished your breakfast."

On the way to the wagon, Aris said, "He knows?"

"Yes. Last night. My hand again."

"Did you tell him all?"

"Yes. But he's more angry with me than with you. You but did what I told you."

"Well," Aris said, "at least we'll learn something about supplying a company of this size traveling this distance."

It was not what Camwyn had wanted to learn, but he knew he must make the best of it. Sulking would only make things harder— and on Aris, too, who had not deserved it.

The teamster for the last wagon had already heard he was transporting the prince and his attendant and what they were to do. He handed over a scroll with a set of tally marks, one for each type of cargo, and a sackful of blank tallies. "I won't have you making a mess back there," he said. "There's naught in the bottom compartment, so don't you be shoving things out of order to get to it." Camwyn stared at him, wondering if it was some trick, but the man's gaze was steady. "The load's balanced as it is; things is labeled with the tally mark."

Camwyn scrambled into the back of the wagon, Aris right behind him. Far ahead, someone yelled; Camwyn thought it was the command to start. Nothing happened at first.

"If we start at the back, maybe we can see out the front before day's end," Aris said.

Camwyn nodded and looked at the first box with its mark. "Dried fruit," he said. "It doesn't say what kind. Or how many." The box's latch was firmly tied with an intricate knot. "I don't think we're supposed to open things, but . . . they do in the palace inventory."

"Then we should," Aris said. "We can compare that knot to the ones on other boxes to get it right."

Inside the box were sacks, each labeled with the kind of fruit. Camwyn sniffed at them, then began cutting notches on the tally stick. Aris worked on the box beside him. "I got thirty-eight sacks," Camwyn said. "Fourteen apple, sixteen peach, six cherry, and two plum."

"Mine had thirty-eight as well," Aris said. "But twenty-two peach, five apple, and eleven plum. No cherry."

"We'll have to check every box," Camwyn said. "And without upsetting the teamster." He retied the latchstring—at least all the knots looked the same—and counted down as far as he could reach. The boxes were stacked four high.

The rest of that day was as miserable as he'd feared. Once the wagon was in motion and the troops at the rear of the procession moved out, dust rose in clouds, drifting in under the wagon cover. Moving the boxes one by one to open them and count through their contents took much longer than he'd hoped. Camwyn and Aris emerged at the noon break, covered with dust and thirsty, to find that they were supposed to eat with the supply train, not at the king's table. "You'uns is too dirty, and it take too long to clean you up," their teamster said. "Here's water and bread and cheese and a hunk of hard sausage."

Nobody laughed at them or scolded them, but still . . . it was hot beside the road, and they had not finished half the wagon's contents yet.

By the time they halted for the day, they were still not finished, and the teamster pored over the interior of the wagon to be sure they left it neat. "No, you'uns can't stay here by you'sefs. Gird only knows what mischief you'd get up to. What's done is done; what's not done there's another day for. Get you gone."

Servants halted them at the entrance to the king's campsite, brushed them down thoroughly, and then sent them to bathe and change. Camwyn felt bruised all over—the wagon's ride had been rough, for all that this was the best road in the kingdom, and he and Aris had lurched into the hard-edged provisions boxes more than once. They bathed from the same bucket, changed, and Camwyn took the tallies they'd filled. He had the report to write before supper.

Mikeli at supper seemed calm and pleasant, greeting them both and continuing his own conversation with Juris Marrakai while they ate. As the servants removed plates and offered dessert, he turned to Camwyn. "Your report, please."

Camwyn handed it over and eyed the dessert tray. Mikeli read, brows slightly furrowed. Camwyn took a pastry; Aris had already eaten two.

"You didn't finish even one wagon?" Mikeli said.

"No, sir king." Better to be completely formal. "We had to open every box—"

"Why?" Mikeli asked.

"Because, sir king, I remembered that when the palace cooks were doing inventory, they opened everything and counted it—"

"The palace cooks . . . you were in the kitchens?"

"Yes, sir king."

"For what reason?"

Beside him, the crunch of pastry as Aris ate stopped.

"I was snitching treats," Camwyn said. "It was a dare."

"I see." Mikeli turned over the scroll and read the back. "And I see you did a thorough job as far as you got. What about the bottom compartment?"

"Sarnthol told us not to dig into it," Camwyn said. "He wasn't really happy we were moving boxes; he said it affected the load's balance and the bottom compartment was empty."

"And you believed him?"

Camwyn frowned. "He's . . . he's . . ." "Adult" would not be a good choice. Some adults did lie. "He's your servant, sir king. He wears palace livery. I trusted him. Should I not?"

"You should append to this report a note to the effect that he told you not to open the lower compartment. It is true that a teamster is in charge of his load, responsible for it. He has a right to say so, and you have a right to follow his orders, but it is something I need to know. Do you see that?"

"I . . . I do now."

"Good. I trust you can finish the rest of this wagon by midday tomorrow and move to the next wagon for the afternoon."

The next several days passed in the same way: all day inside one swaying, jolting wagon after another, taking inventory in each. By the third day, the teamsters were friendlier, though it was clear that some form of "Prince Camwyn is in disgrace and this is punishment" had passed through the whole entourage. They did not ask what he had done, and their guesses were wide of the mark. To his surprise, his roof exploration back at the palace was widely known, along with earlier adventures.

"Hangin' about the kitchens takin' treats—I don't see as that's so bad. There's food enough; it's not like you was takin' from others."

"The Marshal said it was stealing," Camwyn said, and bit off another hunk of the hard sausage. He liked it now.

"So it was, and a good wallop is what it deserves, not diggin' through wagons makin' lists." Tamnis, teamster from the first wagon in the train, drank deeply from a jug they hadn't been offered and wiped his mouth with the back of his hand. "Here's what I think— it's not fair to hide the prince away from those who want to see him— aye, lad, there's folk who thought they'd see you and the king both."

"It's not our business," Sarnthol said. "They'll see the prince later, and whatever the king says is fine enough for me. You'd best watch your tongue, Tam."

"What, you're going to complain of me to the king, Sarn? You know better than that!"

"Royal Guard's not that far away, and if I can smell your jug, so might they. You know the rules."

"Pfaugh!" Tamnis said, and spat. But he put a plug in the jug, took up a waterskin, and drank heavily from that. Then he grinned at the boys and turned back to the others. "We've the pleasure of the prince's company all to ourselves, I suppose. Nothing to complain of there. Was only thinkin' of others."

By the time they had worked their way to the front wagon, Camwyn no longer thought the job quite as boring, or midday meals with the teamsters worse than lunch at the royal table. From the fourth day on, he and Aris had been allowed to exercise their mounts in the evening, riding up and down the road with four Royal Guards blocking either end. At night, Mikeli and Aris watched as Camwyn tried to bring his magery under some control. It was not hard to make his hand give light; Mikeli provided candle after candle for him to light and Aris to snuff. Sometimes he could rise off the stool or rug as high as the seat of Mikeli's chair. And this exercise kept him from waking to an unexpected light later on.

On the evening before they expected to make Harway, Mikeli relented. "Tomorrow you will ride with me. I am pleased, both of you, with the way you accepted your punishment and performed your duties. But mark it well: there will be no more secrets from your king, Camwyn and Aris. Camwyn, your duty to me is as both brother and subject. Aris, your duty to me outweighs your duty of friendship to Camwyn. Do you understand?"

"Yes, sir king," Camwyn said. Aris followed.

"And neither of you will speak of this without my command. Clear?"

"Yes, sir king."

"Well, then. Tonight we will do our best to exhaust Camwyn and prevent any untoward displays of that power he must not have. Once we get to Duke Verrakai's domain, we will consult her . . . that part of your plan, Cam, showed sense."

Once more a-horse, once more able to see everything they passed, Camwyn saw his position differently, as no doubt Mikeli had intended. The wagons were not merely a hindrance slowing them down, raising clouds of dust, but a necessity—the assurance that the entire party would have food, shelter, supplies for any emergency. The teamsters and servants were no longer faceless and nameless; he did not know all of them, but he knew enough to know the difference between the man willing to drink too much at midday and snore through the afternoon pretending to drive and the man who sat upright and alert the entire time. He knew he must not protect the drunk, because that risked everyone. The drunk drove the wagon with weapons and other supplies for the Royal Guard. He had told Mikeli, and the Royal Guard captain had "noticed" the jug and taken it away from Tamnis. Now one of the Royal Guard who had twisted a knee drove that wagon, and Tamnis was at the back of the train.

The occasional farm family or shepherd running toward the road to wave and shout as the king rode by were now closer together. Closer yet. Now a continuous line—men, women, children, waving anything they could, throwing flowers at the king. A few landed on

Camwyn; he remembered to smile to both sides and wave now and then. The horses, settled by days on the road, did not even jig.

Harway, though smaller than Vérella, was the next largest town Camwyn had seen. It had a grange, a Field of Falk, a town hall several stories high, large inns, and cobbled streets lined with shops. The wagons peeled away to the south somewhere, and Mikeli rode with his guard to the Lyonyan border. There both his own border guard and the Lyonyans in russet and green saluted him. He gave a package—Camwyn had no idea what was in it—to one of the Lyonyans, who bowed and handed it to someone in a green tunic with a ruby in her ear. She mounted a horse at once and rode away. Then the Lyonyan guard handed a green velvet pouch to Mikeli.

"Lyonyan King's Squire," Mikeli said to Camwyn as they rode back through the town toward the inn where they would stay that night. "King Kieri uses them as couriers."

Camwyn had his own room in the inn, solid wooden walls between him and any watching eyes. As if such a place were no challenge, his hand did not light up all night.

The next morning they started early for Verrakai Domain.

CHAPTER TWENTY-ONE

Verrakai Steading

Dorrin could not help considering the irony that although girls were considered more vulnerable, and thus rarely had a chance to serve as squires, her one female squire had caused no problems at all, while both Beclan and Daryan had—well, it wasn't fair to say that Daryan had gotten himself in trouble—but say rather both had fallen into trouble. Gwenno Marrakai appeared to have no problems other than those any lively girl would generate at her age. Gwenno, who had grown up with a houseful of other younglings, including a full suite of brothers, handled the attention she received with ease.

Dorrin could have envied her—did envy her, she admitted—the kind of family life Gwenno had as a child. The girl seemed highly intelligent, energetic, good-natured, and uncomplicated, which made it easy to spend her time and thought on Daryan and Beclan, especially Beclan. And yet—even if Gwenno could learn by herself—that wasn't what her family had intended when they asked Dorrin to accept her as a squire.

She had planned this afternoon's meeting for that reason, and when she heard Gwenno's cheery greeting to the cooks on her way through the kitchen, she could not help smiling. Gwenno appeared in the office door with a plate of pastries, one already in her mouth.

"Sorry, my lord," she said after setting the plate on Dorrin's desk and removing the pastry from her mouth. "I just couldn't resist the smell."

The pastries did smell good. Farin had reported ample supplies of butter and honey for the king's visit to come. Dorrin picked one up and left Gwenno to pour the sib, then gestured for her to sit down. "When you're through with that one," Dorrin said, "tell me about your patrol." She bit into the pastry. A warm soft-cheese filling, lightly spiced.

Gwenno ate quickly, took two swallows of sib, and plunged in. She had noticed everything, it seemed: the land, the woods, the crops, the livestock. Though Daryan had been better at patrol reports early on, with his more methodical way of approaching things, Gwenno had learned. Now Dorrin got a vivid picture of conditions along her patrol route—conditions that continued to improve with time.

"And I met Marshal Daltor in Nin's Well—that's near Lower Hedgy; we both talked to the people, and I think they're not so afraid of Gird now." She picked up another pastry.

"Excellent," Dorrin said. "Now—the courier came with word that the king would soon leave Vérella. You will stay here through the visit, as will Daryan. By the king's command, Beclan will remain until the king arrives. We will have a day's warning; I'm sending someone to Harway to ride here at speed."

"I could do that," Gwenno said, as energetic as if she were not just in from patrol.

"No, I need you here," Dorrin said. "One of the militia will do well enough. How are you coming with your weapons training when on patrol?"

"First thing every morning," Gwenno said promptly. "Well— those assigned to camp chores do that first, but the rest of us have a half-glass of exercises. And then again in the afternoon after making camp." She looked at the last pastry on the platter, and Dorrin nodded permission.

Beclan knocked at the door. "My lord?"

"Yes, Beclan."

"Looks like there's a storm moving up the river—big enough to reach us, maybe. Should I send to have the home herds brought up?"

"Is there much rain in it?"

"I think so, my lord."

"I'll look. Come along, Gwenno."

Out the front entrance, Dorrin could see the great cloud, dark beneath and snow-white on top—and not just one cloud but a mountain range of them. In the strange light such storms produced, the household cattle, down in the water meadow, glowed as if carved from colored wax. If all that rain fell, the river would rise fast.

"Yes, Beclan. Get some men and bring them up behind the house."

He saluted and jogged off. Gwenno made a move to follow, but Dorrin stopped her. "Do you know where the children are? I don't hear them—"

"I passed them coming in," Gwenno said. "They're berrying in the woods—" She gestured.

"Well, find them and start them home."

"At once, my lord."

With Gwenno off to find the children and Beclan after the cattle, Dorrin thought of Daryan—out on patrol to the northwest—and hoped he'd find shelter in the woods. He was due back the next day or the day after. She met her steward coming briskly down the main passage.

"Laundry's in, my lord. There's a storm—"

"Yes, I saw it." She ducked into her office, picked up the empty platter the pastries had been on, and went into the kitchen. "Storm coming," she said to Farin.

"I thought so," Farin said. "The fire's not drawing well. Thank you for bringing the dish back, my lord."

A crash of thunder startled Dorrin even as she sat down at her desk, shaking the house and then rumbling away into the distance as if giants were rolling barrels on stone across the sky. Dorrin looked out the office window in time to see the first drops of rain. Then a curtain of water smashed down onto the courtyard. A dank current of air ran through the house.

Shrill squeals came from the back entrance, and the sound of feet running and high excited voices meant the children were back—but probably wet. "Wait!" cried an adult voice, but as Dorrin reached the door of her office, several children pelted past her and ran into the kitchen. Down the passage she saw Gwenno leap over another child and bar the passage, arms and legs outspread.

"You don't run like that in the house," she said to the children as Dorrin came nearer. "And you don't dirty up the floor with muddy feet. There's a scullery passage back here for a reason."

Now Dorrin could see the whole bedraggled group, nursery-maids in the rear and excited children jumping up and down. "Thank you, Gwenno," she said. "If you get the mud off their feet, they may walk upstairs to change."

"Yes, my lord," Gwenno said. "It's my fault, really. I saw the curtain of rain coming and said we should go through the garden to beat it, but we weren't fast enough. If we'd gone through the stables, they could have shed all the dirt there."

"No matter," Dorrin said. "While you younglings get your feet cleaned, I'll fetch the runaways."

Farin was already dragging them back down the passage when Dorrin turned.

Once the children were upstairs, Gwenno came padding back down the passage in her sock feet, holding her boots in one hand. "We almost made it," she said.

"So you did—and a good job, too." The rain still pounded on the roof, falling so hard it made a mist on the stable court. "This will bring the river up . . ."

"And make the grass grow, my da always says. Never mind the rain; it's the dry you have to fear."

"The dry . . ." The words caught Dorrin's mind, and she had a sudden vision of barren rocks and waves of sand as vast as the sea. Old Aare . . . Ibbirun's curse, the Sandlord's domain now and forever.

No. Not forever. Come to us. Take us . . .

She shivered.

"Are you all right, my lord? Are you taking a chill?"

"No," Dorrin said. "I just thought of Old Aare, and the thought of that desert here, in this green land . . . horrible."

"It wouldn't happen here," Gwenno said with the confidence of youth. "Tsaia has always been forest and field. The Honnorgat has flowed from the memory of men."

"There are older beings than men," Dorrin said, and wondered where that thought had come from. "And it's said Old Aare was green once."

"But not as green as this, I would wager," Gwenno said. "And besides—if Ibbirun's curse has not gone beyond Old Aare in all this time, why would it now?"

"You know the legends," Dorrin said. "Some great evil was done that set Ibbirun free. Are we so free of evil these days and in this place? Consider my relatives, who cursed trees and wells. Could such as they not have invited Ibbirun here?"

Now Gwenno shuddered. "My lord—that's horrible. How could anyone—"

"How could anyone torment and cripple a lad like Daryan, or kill children to take over their bodies? Evil lives, Gwenno Marrakai, whether we see its reasons or not. The iynisin who killed the Lady of the Ladysforest . . . I do not understand them, but I cannot deny they exist."

"But you killed one. And you healed the well and brought water again—"

As you should. As you must. Come, free us!

Dorrin tried to calm the voice in her head, the voice that could be only the crown in Vérella. To Gwenno she said, "I know my magery cleared the well, Gwenno, but the water—that, I truly believe, was the gods' grace."

No. Your own magery. Take your gift. Use your gift.

"My lord, I have heard . . . that the crown speaks to you. The one you gave the king."

"How did you hear that?"

"It's . . . it's talked of, at court. The crown talks to you, and it cannot be moved unless you move it. Even the box it was in . . ."

"So much for keeping secrets," Dorrin said. She wondered which of them had told it and to whom—the king, the Marshal-Judicar, Duke Mahieran? Did *all* the peerage know by now? It was almost laughable that she had kept the secret so close and they—who bade her keep it close—had blabbed.

"Your people here know about the well," Gwenno said. "Kindle people told the neighboring vills—of course they did. And everyone noticed the change in the water of the stable well and the one down in the meadow after you spoke to the *merin* for them. Everyone thinks you have the water magery like the Sier of Grahlin in Gird's time."

The Sier of Grahlin, who had driven a river's water underground and then forced it all out a well to break the fort Gird's forces held in besieging his city.

"The water lifting you up in that well in Kindle was just like the water in Sier Grahlin's well . . ."

"I hope not," Dorrin said. "I certainly don't aspire to be Sier Grahlin. He used that power to kill—"

"And you used it to bring clear water to people who had none. I know, my lord, you don't like to talk about your magery, and you are teaching Beclan in secret, but—but I cannot help seeing what I see and thinking what I think."

She couldn't, Dorrin knew. Gwenno Marrakai was Marrakaien through and through, and for all her good traits of sanity, generosity, intelligence . . . she was also, still, enthusiastic and impulsive, traits with as much tendency to trouble as to peace. Best not to encourage that . . . or squash it, either. A difficult balance, given all the other elements in the current situation.

"Independence of vision is a good thing," Dorrin said. "So is thinking. But speaking and acting well require reflection—consideration."

"Yes, my lord." Gwenno looked worried now.

Dorrin relented, hoping that was the right choice. "Squires learn by doing, just like the rest of us," she said. "You can tell me what you see and what you think. I'm not angry. Only we still have a lot of work to do before the king comes."

"Yes, my lord! What should I start on?"

What could she start the girl on in the midst of a rainstorm? "Your house has hosted important guests," Dorrin said. "Come with me to the rooms where the king and other nobles will stay; I depend on you to tell me what furnishings may need to be moved." They started for the stairs. "And you can talk while we work."

Gwenno's suggestions sent housemaids scurrying to the attics for items Dorrin had thought useless fripperies. "Pillows," Gwenno said. "And my mother always put a tapestry screen in front of fireplaces in summer."

Dorrin nodded, privately thinking that a well-cleaned fireplace with polished hardware was adequate. But now she thought of it, the palace in Vérella had screens over its fireplaces. By supper, all the fireplaces had been blocked by screens and dozens of decorative vases, pots, and boxes awaited cleaning in the upper hall. Meanwhile, Gwenno had proposed a double handful of ideas about the regalia, its origin, the motives of previous Verrakaien dukes, and what she would do if she were Dorrin. Dorrin struggled not to show that the crown answered some of those ideas with enthusiasm. The supper bell came as a welcome reprieve.

Conversation at the meal stayed firmly on weather, crops, livestock, and other estate-related matters, and Dorrin sent her squires off after Gwenno had cleared the table. "I have other work to do," she said. Once in her office, Dorrin leaned back in her chair and looked down the length of the room, now free of all its magical protections.

Anyone—even the king—could sit safely in any of the chairs. The books on the shelves were just books, not traps. No evil spirits emerged from walls or floors except her own bitter memories, and she did not let them command her. Her people did not live in constant fear, in the certainty of hunger, suffering, punishment, that had held them down so long. She had not done so badly.

Though—she could not let herself rest in that moment of self-praise—she had managed to alienate a large portion of the peerage and get one of her squires cast out of the royal family. "I still make mistakes," she said to the steady beat of the rain outside.

You are still my Knight.

That was clear enough. Cheered, she went all the way up to the children's rooms to check the nursery. Three of the younglings were still awake when she peeked in.

"Auntie Dorrin?"

"Sleep in peace," she said, and stepped back. Tears blinded her for a moment. Peace. Here. In this place. While out in the orchard, under the last row of trees, the ones she herself had killed lay buried. And yet it *was* peace for these. Maybe someday for all.

CHAPTER TWENTY-TWO

The king's progress

Mikeli rode through the forest that lay between Harway and Duke Verrakai's residence, glad of the cool shade and the lack of crowds along the way. The discovery of Camwyn's magery had ended all hope that this royal progress would be a pleasant break from his duties in Vérella and a chance to know his realm better. With another mage in the family—his own brother—nothing would ever be simple again. So far, High Marshal Seklis had not seemed to notice anything, but the older man was not a fool. He would have to be told, and soon. Mikeli hoped to talk to Dorrin first; perhaps she could reassure him that he had none of his younger brother's magery.

Here, with no reason to insist on the king's precedence, he called Camwyn up to ride beside him, stirrup to stirrup. Lost in his thoughts, he rode on. When he glanced toward his brother again, Cam was sitting facing backward like some farmer's brat on a plough horse headed home. Anger swelled.

"What do you think you're doing?" Mikeli said in the exact tone he remembered from his father. He reached over, took the reins Cam had dropped, and moved his leg away from his own mount.

"It's easier to talk to Aris this way, and the horses haven't spooked for—" At the touch of Mikeli's spur, Camwyn's horse shied, rump swinging wide; Cam grabbed for the cantle of his saddle and then looked at Mikeli. "You did that!" he said.

"Yes. Because if there is anyone in these woods with evil intent, a foolish prince sitting backward with the reins loose would be too tempting to miss. Turn around."

Cam turned around again; Mikeli handed him the reins. Camwyn said nothing, but the flush on his cheeks wasn't from the sun. Good. Maybe Cam wouldn't do anything else dangerous or annoying until they reached Verrakai House. He hoped the duke had allowed Beclan to stay for the official arrival.

C amwyn ignored the grins passed between the nearest Royal Guard troopers at Mikeli's scolding. At least he hadn't fallen off, and so far Mikeli hadn't told High Marshal Seklis about his magery. He looked ahead, catching a glimpse of open meadow and a great stone house in the distance; then the forest ended at the edge of a water meadow where the Duke was waiting for them.

Camwyn glanced at Duke Verrakai, then looked at her squires. The girl must be Aris's sister Gwennothlin, her face browned by sun; she grinned past him at Aris. The other was Daryan Serrostin. Camwyn looked at his hand, hoping to see the twig-thumb of rumor, but Daryan wore gloves.

After the greeting, they rode on toward the house, set on a low rise beyond the stream that trickled through stones of the ford. Camwyn saw rows of children holding flowers and repressed a grin with an effort. He, prince of Tsaia, was going to ride through another rain of flower petals. A perfect day!

CHAPTER TWENTY-THREE

D orrin Verrakai waited with her escort at the forest edge. She
heard the king's party already—the thud of hooves, the jin-
gle of tack and harness, the voices.

The king's party appeared shortly: his standard-bearers in front,
great banners drooping in the still air, then the king and the prince,
flanked by Royal Guard troops, including two trumpeters. Behind
them High Marshal Seklis in Girdish blue and white, Duke Marrakai
in red and green, Count Konhalt in yellow with blue trim, and Baron
Nunaver, one of Konhalt's vassals. At a little distance, Dorrin heard
the noise of the royal baggage train. They stopped; the trumpeters
blew a fanfare, and the standard-bearers hailed Dorrin.

"Behold the king of Tsaia, Mikeli of the house of Mahieran."

Dorrin bowed in the saddle, as did her squires and escort.

"Be welcome, lord king, to Verrakai lands and Verrakai House."

"Thank you, Duke Verrakai," the king said. "Ride with me if you
will."

Dorrin edged her horse nearer the king's as the standard-bearers
once more led the way and her squires spread to either side.

"Lord king, if I may—my kirgan—"

"Is he here?" the king asked.

"Lord king, he awaits at the house, but I have an urgent errand
for him elsewhere if it please you—"

"I'm glad he's here; I will greet him, and then he must leave. I must meet all heirs, and . . . I want to see and judge him for myself. I will explain later."

"As you will, lord king. He is ready to leave on my signal."

"I will tell you."

"Your command, lord king." She bowed again, then faced forward. Verrakai House looked well—the broad meadows spangled with wildflowers in all colors, the cattle at a distance, the house itself with the royal colors draping the entrance and windows, the children, backed by servants in Verrakai livery, flanking the way up to the steps, flowers in hand. She glanced at the king.

He looked as handsome as ever, erect in the saddle, his skin touched more by the sun than she'd seen before. Perhaps the days of riding in the fresh summer air, away from the city and the confines of court, had relaxed him. He smiled as he caught sight of the children. "You have outdone yourself, my lord Duke."

"They've never had a chance to see a king," Dorrin said. "They're so excited—I hope they remember to toss the flowers softly and not jump up and down and squeal. They did practice."

He chuckled. "They won't spook my mount, not after the days on the road. My father used to tell me nothing settled a horse like days of riding. He was right; we've had no jigging about since the third day."

They came up to the waiting children and servants; his trumpeters blew another fanfare. Beclan waited to one side of the entrance. At Dorrin's hand signal, he moved another step to the side. Now the king rode forward; the children tossed their flowers to form a gold and white carpet on the grass—only a few forgot and squealed—and the royal party rode up to the foot of the steps. Dorrin's grooms waited to hold the horses.

Up the steps; the king gave Beclan a quick nod, then turned to face the little crowd below the steps. Dorrin had stopped a step below him with her squires a step below that.

"It has been many generations since a Verrakai duke welcomed a king of Tsaia here," he began. "And I for one am glad it is this duke, Dorrin Verrakai, who has welcomed me. May Gird's grace and Falk's honor rest here, and as long as my standard is planted here, any who wish the king's justice may apply." He looked down at Dorrin. "My lord Duke, present your kirgan and the others."

Beclan looked startled; Dorrin signaled him to take a step forward. He went to one knee. "Sir king," she said. "I present my kirgan, Beclan Verrakai."

"Kirgan Verrakai," the king said, and nodded; Beclan stood again and bowed. "I understand your duke has an urgent errand that only you can accomplish. I give you leave, therefore, to go upon your Duke's command."

"Sir king," Beclan said, bowing again. He looked at Dorrin.

"Beclan, you have my seal of authority in this matter; you may go now," Dorrin said.

Beclan bowed to her, again to the king, then entered the house. Dorrin knew horse and escort awaited him outside the stableyard walls in back. He would not return until Dorrin sent word that the king had gone.

The king's party was even smaller than she had expected, and only he and Duke Marrakai, the High Marshal, and the peers would stay in the house itself. Everyone else, he said, would camp in the meadow.

"Sir king, would you prefer to refresh yourself before a meal or eat now?"

"A bath would be a delight," the king said. "Your way shelter is adequate, but I have ridden several days, and it's warmer than I expected."

"This way, then." Dorrin led him upstairs to her own apartment, now set aside for his use; she had had a bath prepared, and it lacked only another can of hot water should he desire it. She left him with his squires to attend him and showed the others to the chambers prepared for guests.

The king came down in lighter clothes, only a short rose-colored cape around his shoulders with the deeper red rose of Mahieran embroidered on the back. "Now I'm hungry," he said, rubbing his hands.

The long table was laid in the front hall for the midday meal:

platters of sliced meats, loaves of bread, fresh greens from the garden, the earliest fruits of the year. They set to eagerly, their talk initially all of the journey.

"I cannot believe," the king said finally, "that I've never been so far from Vérella before. I understand why my guardians did not want me traveling around. Some of them did not trust the former duke here, and that was, as it turned out, wise. I don't imagine that had I visited here as a prince, I would ever have come out alive. But being away from the city and the palace—not just on Mahieran estates or the royal hunting preserve—has already taught me a great deal."

"You came to Marrakai once as a small boy," Duke Marrakai said. "You might not remember—"

"I don't . . . not for certain—"

"And that's west of Vérella, not east. I have never been here either, my lord. I see you have worked on the track from Harway."

"I had to," Dorrin said with a laugh. "When I first came, it was nearly impassable near the border—intentionally. It is not yet as smooth for wagons as I could wish. But the old Middle Trade Road—that I spoke of, sir king—will be the main road someday. My kirgan and I have been alternating in the supervision of that construction."

"Is the purpose trade?" Duke Marrakai asked.

"Yes, primarily, though the king's forces need an interior route to move troops as well. There was no way to get our products to market or resupply here but by pack train. Isolation suited the former duke, but it does not suit me."

"That old road is on the oldest maps in our library," High Marshal Seklis said. "What do the Lyonyans think about it?"

"King Kieri favors it," Dorrin said. "I believe he expects to start work on it from Chaya next year. This year he wants to work on the River Road. The middle road would be shorter and serviceable in seasons the River Road is a morass from floods. If my neighbors to the west agree."

"I will make that case to the count involved," the king said. "Will you want to found a town on its way through Verrakai lands, or will it come near this house?"

"The straightest way—the old way—would pass south of here," Dorrin said. "I had not thought of founding a town, though I had in mind suggesting another new road connecting Harway to some southern town east of Fiveway——"

"Brewersbridge, for instance," said High Marshal Seklis.

"Yes. That would allow movement of both trade and troops if necessary."

"Do you really think we need to garrison our border with Lyonya?" the king asked, brows raised.

"From danger in Lyonya? No, sir king. But at the moment Lyonya bears almost all the burden of border watch. They have had incursions of brigands from here. They would be glad if we kept our criminals from crossing the border."

"I see. That would involve you and Konhalt—and those south of Konhalt as well. Perhaps we could remit some of the Crown levy this year for those contributing to the construction of such a road." The king looked at Count Konhalt. "Do you have any sort of track along the border?"

"There are forest tracks but nothing like a wagon road," the count said. "But like Duke Verrakai, we have few outlets for our goods—we formerly traded only through the Verrakaien, who took a toll—" His look at Dorrin was not entirely friendly.

"I'm sure my uncle did," Dorrin said.

"If you build this middle road," High Marshal Seklis said, "will it be a toll road?"

"It must be," Duke Marrakai said. "No one can afford to build a road for nothing. Even maintenance—"

"I haven't decided," Dorrin said. "Considering what my family did . . . I would prefer rather to serve than take. But you're right, my lord: my family left fewer resources than I really need."

"Other roads are tolled—even the Valdaire road is tolled in some stretches," High Marshal Seklis said.

"Indeed," Dorrin said. "One thing the Crown should insist on is free passage for Crown business—royal couriers or troops moving at royal command."

The king nodded. By this time they had quit eating; Dorrin nodded to the servants, who cleared the table.

"High Marshal," she said, "the Marshals sent here have asked if you will have time to visit them while you're here. We have three granges—or will have when the buildings are finished. Darkon Edge was here when I came, though the Marshal who fought bravely was assassinated later—probably at my uncle's command. Marshal Nemis is building a grange along what will be the middle road from Tsaia to Chaya; Marshal Fenold has a circuit of villages, including Kindle, a little west of here. Marshal Istan took over Darkon Edge. Marshal Daltor isn't founding a grange yet; he says the population in my southern half is too thin, but he's traveling about meeting people."

"An excellent idea," the king said before Seklis could answer. "You can report to the Marshal-General, Seklis. I'll be here a few days; we can spare you the time."

Seklis nodded. "Sir king, that is what I'd hoped to do. If Duke Verrakai could provide an escort who knows the ways—"

"Of course," Dorrin said. "And a pack mule, as well, for supplies."

"I'll leave tomorrow, then," Seklis said. "A night in a real bed will do me no harm."

Later, Dorrin took the king, Duke Marrakai, and Count Konhalt into her study to show them the maps she had and her plans for the roads.

"What is the best route from here to Konhalt?" the king asked, running his finger along a thin dotted line.

"I'm not sure," Dorrin said. "There's an area of damaged trees— trees both Queen Arian and the Kuakgan Ashwind said had been damaged by evil magery, though whether by Verrakaien or by kuaknomi they aren't sure. My squires have patrolled there without difficulty, barring the ugliness. It's more open than the deep forest, but there's no actual road. It extends down to the Konhalt border."

"Count?"

"I have always gone in from the west," Count Konhalt said. "Though it's but a crooked, narrow track."

"Perhaps the Verrakaien damaged the trees to make travel easier without the work of building a road," High Marshal Seklis said.

"Perhaps. Do you think it's safe to travel that way, my lord?" the Count asked Dorrin.

"I would think so," she said. "The Kuakgan Ashwind came from the south; he said he cleared the evil ahead of him. And the king's escort is amply large enough to deter any small brigand band."

"But I'm not going on," the king said. "That was the plan, but Queen Arian's visit was delayed—and I'm delighted she came, late or no—and then our progress here was slower than I expected. I must be back in Vérella by Midsummer Court, and my escort will go with me. Do you have no one who could guide the Count to his domain?"

"Only to the border," Dorrin said. She turned to Count Konhalt. "I'm sorry, Count Konhalt, but I have found none who have traveled into your lands. I would gladly lend you one of my militia, but he would know no more than you."

Konhalt nodded and turned to the king. "Then, sir king, if you will excuse me from Midsummer Court, I will travel back west and south and enter Konhalt by the only way I know."

"If you have nothing to bring before me, I excuse you," Mikeli said. "But you must then attend Autumn Court without fail."

"Of course, sir king. Thank you." He turned to Dorrin. "I agree that it would be better to have more access, Duke Verrakai, and I would participate in road building from here south, if it please you."

"It would indeed please me. We need more communication, not less," Dorrin said.

"I would like to see some of your vills," the king said to Dorrin. "Especially the one where you healed the well. Since I'm not going farther, I thought I might spend a hand of days here; we have things to discuss."

"Of course, sir king," Dorrin said. "Kindle, in fact, is near enough to reach this afternoon if you like."

The king shook his head. "To be honest, I would rather spend the rest of this day on something softer than a saddle."

"Of course, sir king. Whenever you wish."

The next morning, High Marshal Seklis rode away with a small party to make a round of the new Marshals. Scarcely a turn of the glass later, the king came in from the garden, where he had been walking with the others after breakfast, and found Dorrin.

"Do you have a secure place to confer, Duke Verrakai?"

That sounded ominous. Had he changed his mind about Beclan? Dorrin nodded. "Yes, sir king. My office. Down this passage."

"Come along, Camwyn, Aris," the king said. Dorrin glanced back, surprised. Prince Camwyn might need to be privy to the king's concerns about Beclan, but Aris Marrakai, she'd heard from Gwenno, was the veriest mischief. Why include him?

"In here, sir king," Dorrin said. The king entered and looked around. Dorrin shut the door; whatever this was about, the king would want no eavesdroppers.

"Was it in here you found the regalia?" he asked, pointing to the niche on the far wall.

"Yes, sir king. That niche was covered by the portrait I told you of, now burned."

The king gave the niche another long look, then sat down at the table and gestured to a chair for Dorrin and the two boys. "We have grave matters to discuss," he said. "I must have your word you will not reveal what I say to anyone—anyone at all—without my leave."

"Of course, sir king. On Falk's honor, I will not."

"First you must know that the crown you gave me now speaks to me as well as to you." Dorrin said nothing; he went on. "It bids me set it free—it wants you, Dorrin Verrakai, despite your oath of fealty." Another pause. Dorrin could think of nothing to say. "I ask you, on that oath: have you told it what to say?"

"No," Dorrin said. "On my oath of fealty, I have not. All I have said—thought—in return to what it tells me is that it should bide where it is and be still." She shook her head. "But I cannot rule it; it continues to speak to me—and now to you."

Two seats down from the king, the prince stirred. The king turned his head. "Camwyn? You have something to say?"

"By your leave, sir king," the prince said.

"Not yet," the king said. He turned again to Dorrin. "The second thing we must discuss I learned about only on my way from Vérella and is a graver matter yet."

"What is that, sir king?"

"Camwyn is a mage."

Dorrin stared. The myriad implications of that tangled in her mind. She looked at the prince. "You? Have magery?"

The boy nodded. He looked frightened and embarrassed, as well he might.

"Show her, Cam," the king said.

The prince pushed back his chair and lifted his hands above the table. One was glowing, bright enough to cast shadows.

Dorrin glanced at the windows, murmured "By your leave," and went to close the curtains. The stableyard outside was full of activity, but for a mercy no one was staring at the windows. In the dimmer light, the prince's hand showed brighter.

"Show her the rest, Cam," the king said.

The light in the prince's hand faded, but as Dorrin watched, he lifted from the chair, face taut with effort. One handspan, then another. Floating. He slid sideways in the air about an armspan, then landed hard on the floor.

"*That* is my problem," the king said. "My brother the magelord. The very *illegal* magelord. Can Beclan do that?"

"No," Dorrin said. "He can light all the candles on the dinner table at once and shift a few papers or a tossed ball to one side. He can't lift it off the table by magery, let alone lift himself."

"You know what this means," the king said. "I will have to give up the throne. The law—"

"Sir king." Dorrin's tone, more commanding than she intended, stopped him. "Sir king, as your Constable, I advise that you *not* give up the throne while the realm faces possible invasion. Who could take the crown instead? Not the prince—leaving aside his magery, he's not of age nor trained. Not Duke Mahieran, as the father of another mage. Not his son Rothlin, as the brother of a mage. And in what other family will you find a king? *You* are our king; you are the one person born to and chosen for this duty. You must not shirk it."

"But the law—when people know, they will demand my abdication. The High Marshal—"

"Yes, the law . . . and the Fellowship of Gird." Dorrin held up a hand again when the king opened his mouth. "You should send a courier to the Marshal-General at once, explaining what has happened. Ask her advice—"

"After I talk to the High Marshal?"

"No, sir king. You should have her ruling on this *before* you tell him—or at the very least tell him you have applied to her. This is a matter of command. She heads the entire Fellowship of Gird. Whatever comes out of Fin Panir will have authority; Marshals in Tsaia will align themselves with her, including High Marshal Seklis. When you have a command problem—when you need a decision—go to the top."

"But the High Marshal will feel I did not respect him. And the Marshal-Judicar—"

"No, sir king. When they think about it, they will realize that any decisions about magery appearing in the Tsaian peerage cannot be made in Tsaia . . . not without bending the Code of Gird to breaking point. The Marshal-General will have a broader view. Because if magery can appear in a family where it has not been known for generations, who is to say it cannot appear in Fintha as well? In any family, anywhere?"

"That thought terrifies me," the king said. "What if—what if *my* hand suddenly gives light? What if a trooper in the Royal Guard? A merchant? Or—though surely Gird would prevent it—a Marshal?"

"Exactly," Dorrin said. "Did not the magelords sire children on their peasants in the old days?"

The king nodded. "But nothing has happened until now," he said. "Why now?"

"I don't know," Dorrin said. "But there will be a reason."

"I wondered if it was you," the king said. "I wondered if you had awakened magery in Beclan—but you haven't been near Camwyn."

"I have awakened no magery in my other squires," Dorrin said. "Nor in my soldiers, in all those years, nor in my household here."

"Could it be the regalia?" the king asked. "But no—it has talked to me, but nothing has happened to me as it has to Camwyn."

"I thought maybe it was the dragon," the prince said.

"The dragon?" Dorrin looked from one to the other.

The king sighed and put his head in his hands. "A dragon came, in the guise of a man—"

"And said his name was Camwyn," the prince said.

"Yes. Sir Camwyn. He came from Count Arcolin's domain with Sergeant Stammel because of the gnomes—do you know about that?"

"A little," Dorrin said. "The dragon who stopped the scathefire in

Lyonya visited Arcolin and went off with Stammel, who was blinded in the south. Arcolin gave the gnomes rock-right, according to Girdish law."

"Yes. That dragon. Camwyn—" He looked at his brother. "Cam's always been fascinated by his namesake, and begged the dragon for a ride."

"Did you touch tongues?" Dorrin asked the prince.

"We both did," the king said. "I, to seal the bargain: I agreed to the gnomes having rock-right and would not dispute the land the dragon took from Tsaia. Camwyn, so he could ride in the dragon's mouth."

"So I thought," the prince said, "because dragons have fire and can fly, that maybe my magery was from the dragon."

"That would not explain Beclan's magery," Dorrin said. "I suppose there might be many causes, but you and Beclan are cousins— they often share family traits."

"Then it was my grandfather," the king said. "He sired both my father and Duke Mahieran's." He looked bleak.

"Or your mother and your aunt . . . or your grandmother . . . or anyone with any mageborn blood, on either side, as far back as you can look. Sir king, I return to your thought of the regalia. Granted, Beclan had no direct contact with it. But if its effect is to waken magery, then . . . we have no idea how far its influence reaches. He was in Vérella when it was."

"Why would it do that?"

"I don't know," Dorrin said. "But . . . is it possible that the diminishing of the magelords' power that preceded the Girdish revolt was due in part to my ancestors using blood magery to lock the regalia away? Now that it's free again, its influence has returned."

"So it's your fault after all?" The king smiled as he said it, then shook his head. "I applaud your honesty, Duke Verrakai, but I cannot think it true." He was silent awhile. Dorrin held her peace, but the boys fidgeted. Finally the king said, "Your recommendation has merit. I will write to the Marshal-General first—but when Seklis returns, I must tell him."

"Yes, sir king—but tell him only what he needs to know, not every detail. The more he hears, the more he will want to take charge. He is an honorable man, but was it not he who approved the plan to first isolate Beclan in that hunting lodge and then use him as bait? That plan led to deaths for many and near disaster for Beclan and Duke Mahieran."

"But he's trained in war—"

"Sir king, I do not doubt his loyalty to you, or to Gird, or his personal fighting ability. But he has never seen real combat. It was— with all due respect—a fool's plan, discounting the enemy's intelligence, ability, and will." Dorrin waited; the king finally nodded.

The next day, they rode out to Kindle vill, where the king saw the well and drank water from it. The people there were less impressed with the king than Dorrin could have wished, but they were respectful. They plaited him a crown of spring flowers, which he put on. From there they rode on to the next vill and on again, stopping for a picnic lunch in the shade of woods.

"You have considerable woodland," the king said. "And the cultivated fields seem small."

"Indeed," Dorrin said. "That is what I meant when I said I wanted to accept new settlers, good farmers if I can get them. Verrakai produces almost nothing to trade, barely enough to feed its own people. I did not realize, when I left home those years ago, how poor it was. The losses in the attack on Kieri reduced the workforce even more. There is only one mill, for instance. Many homes still use handmills."

"Yet the lords Verrakai always appeared wealthy when at court," Duke Marrakai said.

"From other business perhaps," Dorrin said. Business she preferred not to contemplate. "But I have enough to do here. Roads are but the first step on the path I hope this domain will take. We must have towns as well, crafters and merchants in addition to farmers."

"Some of the smaller domains have complained there's not enough land for their population," Marrakai commented. "I don't know if their people would want to move here, but some might."

"I would welcome younger families, people with energy and the will to work," Dorrin said. "It's easy enough to find malcontents—I've had some of those show up—but I want to settle good people on the land. If they're also active in a grange, that's an advantage."

"Can you feed them the first year?"

"Depends how many," Dorrin said. "That's always the difficulty—Kieri had the same in the north when we were starting there. He had the advantage of starting with retiring soldiers who knew him, but he needed specialists, too. The miller, for instance. Cost at least half the profit that year to set up the mill and hire the miller, who wasn't at all sure he wanted to move to the wasteland, as he thought it."

"Well," Marrakai said, "wasn't that count in the south . . . Lordal, wasn't it? . . . saying he was overcrowded?"

"Yes," the king said. "You might speak to him at Midsummer Court, my lord, and offer for some of his farmers."

"That's an excellent idea," Dorrin said. "Thank you."

After the royal procession left, Beclan came back to the main house. "Why did he let me stay to greet him, then send me away?" he asked.

"He says he must know everyone's heir," Dorrin said. "In fact, he does trust you and care for you, but it's the way things are—he must be seen to distance himself from you. He asked how you were coming in your study of magery. He wants you to continue."

"He does? But then—after you—I mean—not that I want it—" He had turned deep red with embarrassment.

"When you succeed me," Dorrin said, emphasizing each word, "he will have a known magelord as duke here, yes. He knows that; he seems to have accepted it. He'd rather have you than any of Verrakai blood, Beclan. Whatever your name, you're his cousin."

"I see."

"Not completely, I fear. But I'm glad he gave permission—nay, encouragement—for you to continue learning about your magery." She would not tell him now about the king's presentiment that she herself would leave with the crown that spoke to her, and her oath bound her not to tell him about Camwyn.

"What about Gwenno and Daryan? You did not want me attempting any magery in their presence except the dinner candles."

"I still think that's wise, and not so much for secrecy as for their protection. Your magery appeared without warning, with no indication at all that you might have it. If they have the same potential, we do not want to waken that by accident."

"You think——? But they couldn't. Their families never married into Verrakai."

"I think no one knows where the old strains of magery went or how they might rejoin. No one knows who might have had buried magery two or three or more generations back. So we will not shake the box to find out if its contents are breakable."

Beclan nodded. "I see the wisdom in that, my lord."

"All Gwenno and Daryan need to know is what they already know: you're studying with me. But beyond that, it is our business. Family business, if you will." She paused. "Have they been asking you about magery?"

"No, my lord. Gwenno said you'd asked them not to, and they haven't. It's—it's really strange to see Dar's thumb growing out, though."

"It is indeed," Dorrin said. "And I think the other one's going to bud, as he hopes."

"He feels better about his family after his father's visit. I'm glad for him; it's hard to be separated." Beclan's voice sounded husky on that last.

"Well," Dorrin said. "You had that time in Chaya. Another may come. Now: let's get to work."

Beclan had been practicing, she found, but despite his increasing strength, Prince Camwyn's magery was much stronger.

"Have you thought more about Falk?" she asked, when he could do no more.

He looked worried. "My lord—must I change allegiance to Falk?"

"To become a Knight of Falk, Beclan, yes. Right now you are barred from study with the Knights of the Bells, as you know, and I had thought the Knights of Falk—"

"But they were enemies, weren't they? Falk was a magelord, and Gird hated magelords."

"Falk was not in Gird's time," Dorrin said. "Nor here in the north. Falkians and Girdish have been allies before, you know."

"I know, but . . . I grew up Girdish." That in a low voice.

"Beclan, you're not asked to abandon Gird—whom we both believe saved your life by awakening your magery. If you find you cannot follow Falk without feeling a traitor to Gird, then you must stay Girdish, though it may mean you cannot gain a knighthood." Even as she said it, she remembered that a company of Girdish knights had a training hall in Fin Panir. Would the Marshal-General allow a young magelord to train with them? Unlikely, though she could ask. Still— neither Arcolin nor Paks had been knighted.

"I understand," Beclan said. "I suppose I can learn fighting skills with you, can't I?"

"You can, though both of us have other duties. I may have to import an armsmaster specifically for you squires." As she said it, she realized how sensible that would be—relieving her of the need to supervise their practices.

Marshal Fenold, when she called him in to talk with her and with Beclan, nodded. "You explained about your squire's difficulty when you brought him back, my lord; I have no problem with the king's command that he learn more magery, or with his taking instruction at Falk's Hall. We learn about Falk's Oath of Gold; we honor Falk." He turned to Beclan. "I honor your thinking on this, too, Beclan. You're loyal to Gird for the right reasons, not just that you grew up Girdish. But you have need of guidance in the use of your powers—powers Gird did not have. I don't think Gird will mind if you study with Falkians."

Beclan moved his hands restlessly. "I don't know if I can pledge to Falk."

"No need to decide that now, Beclan," the Marshal said. "But I advise you to consider Falk when you are practicing magery, just as I advise you to consider Gird when you pick up a hauk. It doesn't hurt a man to have more than one friend, down here or up there."

"I hadn't thought of it that way," Beclan said. "I wouldn't have to give up believing in Gird?"

"Of course not. I've been known to call on Falk myself in some circumstances, and I was born and brought up in Fintha. That should tell you something."

"I see." Now he looked more cheerful. "My lord Duke tells me they're much alike in their rules."

"So they are. When I studied in Fin Panir, we read all we could about all the great saints and the gods too, what little is known. I met Knights of Falk before ever I met your duke; they were welcome at our table. If you become one someday, Beclan, I will welcome you to the grange just the same as I do now."

"Thank you, Marshal."

CHAPTER TWENTY-FOUR

Valdaire, Aarenis

Count Arcolin, commander of Fox Company, led a column into the outskirts of Valdaire as he had many times before. Cracolnya rode beside him; Versin had dropped back to the rear with Cracolnya's cohort. The recruit cohort was first, as always on arrival.

Arcolin halted the column at the gate, and the familiar game played out—the troops in the compound snapping into formation with unnatural speed. The recruits looked as stunned as always. Arcolin took Selfer's and Burek's salutes, nodded, and for the first time since Kieri's departure, the three cohorts of the Company were together, in the South, with a contract. It felt like the old days, though without Kieri and Stammel it could never be the same.

Within a turn of the glass, the recruits had been given their final assignments, filling in the two southern cohorts and bringing them all slightly overstrength. Arcolin, in the Company office, listened to Selfer's report of his cohort's journey and the winter's events.

"You did exactly the right thing about the oaths," Arcolin said. "We'll have a formal ceremony day after tomorrow, just to make it clear, but that was very well done. And I approve your releasing those who wanted to stay with Dorrin." Selfer looked relieved; Arcolin remembered his own first time away from Kieri, his worry that Kieri might not approve decisions he'd made. "Harnik—yes, a mistake, but how could you have known? Even Kieri hired bad officers at times. I don't blame you for that. How did the next substitutes do?"

"Captain Ivats is back with Clart Company, my lord." Selfer was still very formal. "But he was a great help over the winter—made a solid training schedule possible. M'dierra's nephew will make a decent squire in time; he's just young and still dazzled by the big city and all."

"Is he still here?"

"Not today, no," Selfer said. "Because of his youth, M'dierra asked that he be given one day in ten off to visit Golden Company. Today was his day. He'll be back in the morning."

"And you, Burek—how have things been with you?"

Burek grinned. "It seems I'm no longer in bad odor with Andressat, sir. It's a long tale, but the short of it is that the Count has acknowledged me his grandson and offered me a name and place. I chose to stay with the Company, and he accepted that choice."

Arcolin felt his brows rising. "The Count of Andressat? I heard from the king he'd been through Vérella after going the long way around—I thought he was going to Lyonya."

"Indeed, and he did."

"And you came back to us . . . why? Not that I'm not pleased."

"I belong here," Burek said. "It is a place I have made for myself—with your help, of course—and I am happier here than I have ever been."

"Good."

"How is Sergeant Stammel?" Burek asked. "Did he—can he see?"

Arcolin shook his head. "No, he's still blind. And there is another long tale. I have several. Have you heard of the war in the north?"

"War!"

"Over now. Pargun attacked Lyonya in the winter, following some dispute between their king and his brother. It's a long story, but Achrya helped the traitors find and hatch dragon eggs—"

"Dragon eggs! But—but that's just a legend," Selfer said. "Dragons haven't been seen since—well—Camwyn Dragonmaster drove them all into exile."

Arcolin almost laughed. "That's what we thought. But I've now

seen a dragon myself, talked to one. Dragonspawn burned out an entire town in Lyonya before they were stopped, and the dragon—" He
shook his head. "You will not believe this, but Burek, you remember
Stammel as the Blind Archer."

"Yes . . ." Burek let his voice trail away.

"Stammel could see the dragon as a shape of fire. And he could
see dragonspawn." Arcolin told the rest as briefly as he could. "He
asked me to release him from his oath of fealty," he said finally.

"You couldn't talk him out of it?" Burek asked. "Surely he'll
grieve—"

"He was already grieving," Arcolin said. "He sent his uniform
and a letter, written by a scribe to his dictation. The letter made some
sense of his decision, and the dragon's report made more. I could not
do other than release him. He deserved that."

"Well," Selfer said, "I lost Vossik to Dorrin."

"And he died," Arcolin said, "saving Dorrin's squire, the Mahieran boy."

"Vossik dead!"

"Yes. And that's another long story for an afternoon on the march.
For now   what's this about your arrangement with Arvid Semminson . . . or Burin? I've heard a lot about that fellow."

Selfer and Burek told of their meeting with Arvid and why they'd
commissioned him to make some purchases on the Company's behalf.
"It's not so bad now," Selfer said. "What with the longer days and
milder weather, the Thieves' Guild master having been killed, and
the city watch waking up, there've been fewer attacks."

"I'm not sure I like having a Thieves' Guild enforcer practically
on our payroll," Arcolin said. "At the least I'll need to meet him."

They had eaten supper sent in from the mess hall when finally
Burek said, "Excuse me, sir, but it's time for my watch."

"Of course," Arcolin said. "And I'm for bed. I can hear the rest of
your winter in the morning, Selfer."

The next morning Arcolin rode into the city to visit his banker,
his factor, and Clart Company. Ser Kavarthin greeted him as an

honored customer; it took two turns of the glass to complete both the required courtesies and the business they needed to transact. The first payment of his contract with Foss Council had indeed been deposited, Kavarthin told him, and Paltis had been submitting accurate accounts since being audited by Kavarthin's son.

On his way to Clart's headquarters, Arcolin spotted Aesil M'dierra in the central market and hailed her.

"I heard you'd arrived," she said. "You know I've foisted my scamp of a nephew on your Captain Selfer—"

"Only until the campaigns start, I understood," Arcolin said. "Unless you want to sign him squire to one of us."

"Not yet," she said, grinning. "He needs a year under his aunt's wing, his mother says. I think he'd rather be with you."

They rode together up the street leading north from the market. Arcolin surprised himself by feeling nothing more than comradeship— here was an old friend, no more.

"Captain Arcolin!" That came from a side street; Arcolin turned and saw a man in Marshal's blue and white.

"Yes?" he said. M'dierra waved and rode on.

"If you have time, I need to speak with you about a matter of concern to the Fellowship."

Arcolin looked at the shadows on the street. Past midday but not long past, and he could see Clart another day. "Certainly," he said. He dismounted and followed the Marshal to his grange.

"I remember that you are Girdish," the Marshal said.

"Yes," Arcolin said.

"What do you know of a man called Arvid Semminson, a thief from the north?" The Marshal kept going toward the platform at the end of the grange.

"Only what Paksenarrion told," Arcolin said, and repeated what Paks had said.

"Did she say much about him as a person?"

"Not really. I haven't talked to her myself for over a year, but I heard from Dorrin Verrakai that Paks suggested Gird might have plans for him and the Guild. Nothing more than that." Arcolin wondered where this was leading. "I know my junior captains made some sort of agreement with him over the winter, but have not yet sorted that out—or even met the man. I know he was using a false name."

"Here is our relic," the Marshal said, and reached into the niche. "It has been effective before in testing liars and scoundrels. Take it."

Arcolin lifted his brows. Did the Marshal think he was a liar or scoundrel? But he took the hand-polished length of wood. It felt as it looked: an old stick or branch, smoothed by use, and nothing more. He remembered the relic in the grange where he had first joined the Fellowship and the way that one had warmed under his hand.

The Marshal took the relic and put it back in the niche. "As we both expected, the relic did nothing when you held it. But here is the extraordinary thing: when Arvid Semminson first set foot into this grange, the relic came alight—brighter than I have ever seen it. When he held it in his own hand, it did so again, so bright that we could see his bones through his flesh."

"Why did he come here?" Arcolin asked.

"We saw a man dressed like a thief dragging along a boy who had obviously been abused; we challenged him. He showed a pass supposedly from the Marshal-General, and that made him my responsibility. I have never been so surprised, Captain Arcolin, as I was that day. A thief and murderer fresh from a kill—he admitted he had just killed the Valdaire Guildmaster—and yet the relic did not strike him down. None of us could believe his story at first, but the relic does not lie. *Cannot* lie."

"What do you want from me?" Arcolin asked.

"You're a northerner born and bred—" the Marshal began.

Arcolin shook his head. "No, Marshal. I was born in the South, far from Valdaire, though I now have a home in the north."

"Good enough," the Marshal said. "And you came through Vérella, I'll warrant. Is it true, as Arvid has told me, that he was Guildmaster there this past year?"

"I don't know. I do know the Marshal-General called him to Fin Panir to give his account of Paksenarrion. The latest rumor at court had him missing. Run away or been killed, no one knew for certain."

"He nearly *was* killed by the Guild here in Valdaire, he told me." The Marshal kicked at the floor. "My dilemma, as you can imagine, being a commander yourself, is that I am caught between what seems to be Gird's clear interest in this man and the equally clear duty I have to this grange—to the Fellowship here in Valdaire—to protect Girdsmen from the kind of influence this man represents. A Guild enforcer: a killer by trade. I cannot but see him as a poisoned blade aimed at the heart of the Fellowship—and yet Gird's relic says nay. And then there's the boy he was dragging along."

Arcolin raised his brows. "Surely just an incidental to the Guildmaster's murder?"

"He may be Arvid's son of the body," the Marshal said. He sighed. "The boy tells the same tale as Arvid about the day Arvid rescued him from the Guildmaster. The boy says his mother named him Arvid for his father. That wouldn't mean much, but his mother was a serving wench at an inn years back. The man Arvid admits to being in Valdaire at the right time, but didn't know about a child. When the woman died, leaving the boy an orphan on the street, the Guild picked him up."

"And you have him now," Arcolin said.

"Yes. Fostered away from the city, but he's in danger from the Guild. The boy is sure Arvid is his father and wants to live with him—natural enough for an orphan, but impossible. Arvid is in danger himself; besides, his . . . background." The Marshal looked at Arcolin with an expression that begged for help without actually asking.

Arcolin had no idea what he could say or do, but found words coming out of his mouth before he could think to stop them. "I need to talk with Arvid anyway, because of that agreement with my junior captains. I will—" What could he promise? "I will talk with you when I have."

"Thank you," the Marshal said. "And—if you have no urgent errand—we might trade blows."

"Of course," Arcolin said. In a moment they were on the platform, and Arcolin discovered that the Marshal had better skills than most of the Marshals he'd met in the north.

"It's having so many soldiers about," the Marshal said when they were done. "At least a few Girdish in every decent Company, even

M'dierra's, and sparring with men who fight for a living forced me to improve past training peasants with hauks."

Arcolin put his offering in the basin and then pulled out two Guild League natas. "For the boy's care, Marshal. I know your grange will do its part, but—I was orphaned myself, though not so young."

"Thank you," the Marshal said. "I know you're busy, but you'd be welcome at the grange any night. Any of your troops, too."

Arcolin rode back to the northeastern quarter of the city. As he neared the Dragon, he saw Selfer walking toward it and waved. He dismounted, gave his horse to one of the boys employed by the inn, and he and Selfer entered the common room together.

At this hour, few customers were about. Selfer said, "Is he in his rooms?" to the barkeep, and the man nodded. Arcolin followed Selfer along a passage and down that to an open door. Inside, a lean, dark-haired, dark-eyed man put aside sharpening stone and rag and slid the sword he'd been sharpening into its scabbard.

"My lord, this is Ser Burin, as he's known here, whom I told you of. And this is Count Arcolin, Ser Burin."

Burin bowed, his eyes never leaving Arcolin's face, as if confused. "I greet you, my lord." He turned to Selfer. "Captain, Dattur has another three dozens of gloves ready; he has gone to fetch more glove leather."

"I brought payment," Selfer said. To Arcolin he said, "Dattur is Ser Burin's gnomish partner in business and an excellent glovier."

"You have just come from the north, my lord," the man said. "Perhaps you have news from Vérella."

"Indeed," Arcolin said. "But it is not for all ears. Selfer, shut the door . . ."

Selfer complied; the man gestured at the chair and stool by the table, and himself sat on the nearest bed. Arcolin took the chair.

"Selfer tells me your real name is Arvid Semminson, and you're the thief enforcer who got Paks out of that mess alive," Arcolin said.

"Yes," the man said. His expression changed; he no longer looked slightly befuddled. "And you were her cohort commander."

Arcolin nodded. "So what news from the north do you want?"

"All of it," the man said. Arcolin looked at him. Ser Burin? Arvid?

Merchant or thief? Spy? Or—as the Marshal had suggested—a man in spiritual torment?

"That's a long tale," he said. "Do you have a specific interest?"

Arvid—Arcolin settled on that, as it was how Paks had known the man—grimaced. "Indeed. I believe the man now heading the Thieves' Guild in Vérella is of the Horned Chain. I was fool enough to believe he would change. He was my second when I headed the Guild; in my absence he spread word I was a traitor."

"Most Girdish in Vérella think you ran off with the Marshal-General's gold."

Arvid slammed his fist into the bedding. "There's no chance, is there?" he asked. "Both think I'm a traitor, then, and I might as well have died there in the wild."

Arcolin recognized desperation in Arvid's voice and expression. "Surely not," he said. "I heard you have a gnome companion whom you helped escape."

"If not for me, he would not have been in that peril," Arvid said.

"And the Marshal here in Valdaire tells me you saved a child from torment."

"A child whose very existence may be my fault," Arvid said. "Again—if I did not exist—"

"But you do," Arcolin said. "And like all of us, your existence changes the world. For your acts in saving Paksenarrion, you have *my* thanks and admiration. Was that so wrong?"

Arvid looked up, tears streaking his face. "I don't . . . I can't . . . she's a . . . a *paladin*."

"And yet her life cost others," Arcolin said. "Not just the scouring of the Thieves' Guild in Vérella, but among my troops." Should he tell? No, he decided; Arvid wasn't ready for that. "A paladin is not harmless," he said. "And neither are we."

Arvid said nothing, but his expression eased a little.

"No one is," Arcolin continued. "But equally, no one is incapable of doing good. You have done good, Arvid, in your life. At least once that I know of. Probably more times than that."

"Thieves are not known for doing good," Arvid said. He twisted the polishing rag in his hands.

"But do you think them all evil, you who have been one?"

"No. Not all. And not all the time." Though his voice was thick with tears, Arvid sounded less on the edge of some mental precipice.

"So," Arcolin said. "The people who said they thought you had stolen the Marshal-General's money were wrong. I suppose, if you went back to Vérella and committed yourself to the Guild, you could manage to kill your rival and regain your power. If that is what you truly want."

"At first I did," Arvid said. "Now—I am not sure. How could I trust any of them?"

"Did you ever?"

"Yes. Or thought I did." Arvid sighed. "I am a shadow of myself here, a false person, and—"

A knock came at the door. "Dattur?" Arvid said.

"Yes," came the answer.

"We have men from Fox Company," Arvid said. "Come in if you will."

Arcolin looked at the gnome who entered: dressed in colors, not a gnomish uniform, and thus *kteknik*. He summoned the gnomish he'd learned and greeted the gnome in that language. "Welcome, rockbrother, and forgive my errors in your tongue."

Bright black eyes looked back at him. "It is that you speak the words of Law?"

"It is that those rockbrothers I know taught me it was more courteous to greet you in your language."

"No obligation," the gnome said. Then, cocking his head to one side, he asked in Common, "What gnomes? What princedom?"

"Their princedom fell," Arcolin said, "and they are *kteknik* by the Law."

"They? But princes do not exile whole princedoms—" The gnome walked up to Arcolin and stared straight in his face.

"I have the word of a dragon," Arcolin said, "and the word of the estvin of the rockbrethren. The dragon thinks their prince betrayed a trust—"

"A *dragon's* trust?" the gnome said; his voice had weakened, and his skin paled. "They *dared*?"

"Their estvin thinks the prince was captured, perhaps tortured . . . The princedom, he said, had been weakened by many attacks, and no one came to aid. When the final attacks came, those remaining were too weak to prevent what happened."

"You know what happened!"

"Yes. The dragon's—"

"No! Do not say it. It is not to say, never. It is not Law for you to know, and you must not say!"

"Dattur, what is it?" Arvid asked.

Dattur glanced back at him and then stared again at Arcolin. His accent thickened as he spoke. "It is that a pact, a binding, made between dragon and rockfolk in old age. It is not to speak. It is not to fail. Hakken failed, being not of Law. Bad . . . bad came. Dragon gave task to us—to rockfolk of Law. Each princedom made binding." His eyes closed; Arcolin felt the stones of the floor trembling against his boots.

"Dattur, *no!*" Arvid said. Dattur's eyes opened, but he did not look at Arvid.

"It is must."

"No! As your *master,* Dattur, I command you. Do no rock magery here!"

The stones quieted. Arcolin felt cold chills, a reaction to a threat he had not recognized. What had the gnome thought to do? And why had the gnome obeyed Arvid?

"What happened to those?" Dattur asked Arcolin.

"They were cast out of their stone-right by a dragon," Arcolin said. "In winter. I took them in; by now they will have moved into new stone in my domain."

"You . . . you saved them?"

"I was not," Arcolin said, his voice roughening as it did every time he thought of those exiles, "going to see women and children starve and freeze in the snow."

"You are their prince," Dattur said, as if he announced that apples grew on apple trees: simple fact.

Arcolin stared. "Prince? No, I'm no prince. A peer of Tsaia, yes, but not a prince."

"Prince of new place," Dattur said. "Who gives stone is prince."

"But—"

"Is no question. It is that you are prince of . . . of Arcolinfulk."

The gnome appeared perfectly serious; gnomes always did.

"But I'm not a gnome. And I don't know your Law, only Girdish law."

"Is no question. It is that a princedom falls, a prince fails, the fulk *kteknik* . . . and if new stone-right, then new prince. Law."

"Oh," Arcolin said. It was all he could think to say. Then, "I thought the estvin would become the new prince."

"No. Law. You."

"They didn't tell me," Arcolin said. Dattur's expression made it clear that he thought Arcolin should have known, and probably the gnomes in the north thought the same.

"I wish you luck," Arvid said. He had a glint in his eye that suggested secret amusement. Dattur rounded on him.

"Is no luck. Is *Law*." He turned back to Arcolin. "It is necessary that the prince learn Law, to speak Law to the people."

"I cannot go north now," Arcolin said. "I have duties here. Contracts."

Dattur considered for a moment, then nodded. "Contract is law under Law. Promise given must be kept. And you have king, is it not? Oath to king?"

"Yes," Arcolin said.

"Oath is law under Law. Is right; you cannot go until fulfilled."

CHAPTER TWENTY-FIVE

I don't know how I'm going to explain to the king that I'm now a gnome prince," Arcolin said to Selfer after they were back in quarters. "It's ridiculous. I can't be a gnome; I don't know their Law . . ."

"I don't see that you have a choice, my lord," Selfer said. He wasn't grinning, which was a mercy.

"And defining a uniform for them—I gave them the cloth we had, not gray. It's all wrong. They didn't tell me."

"You could order gray cloth, have it sent up."

"I could, but—I know it's the details, and I don't know anything about that."

"Dattur probably does."

"I suppose. But it's one more thing . . ." He shook his head. "And that Arvid fellow: Marshal Steralt wants my opinion of him. What's yours?"

"He's been honest with us, my lord. He's passed on useful information. Fought off thieves at the inn, too, one night. Killed 'em. Jostin at the Dragon has only praise for him. He's in danger now; I know that."

The next morning, Arcolin confirmed the proxy oaths, then rode across town to find Nasimir Clart. Clart was in the common room of his company's lodgings, eating an early lunch.

"Thank you for helping out," Arcolin said. He waved a waiter over and ordered sib and the cheese crisps this inn was known for.

"Ivats enjoyed his time with you, but you can't have him. I hold his contract for another two years," Clart said, grinning.

"I'm not trying to poach," Arcolin said. "Thought you might like the latest news from the north, firsthand."

"You're prospering, I can see that," Clart said. "Count, isn't it? Should I bend the knee?"

"Hardly," Arcolin said, grinning. "You've heard about the war up there?"

"Business?" Clart leaned forward.

"No. War's over. Pargun attacked Lyonya; they were repelled. Halveric won't be coming south again for a long time, though—Phelan's hired them as the core of a standing army. And they're short—they lost nearly a cohort in the war."

"Tsaia?"

"Worried about unrest in the South, but with Pargun out of contention, things are much calmer. I've told my king about Alured the Black." Arcolin took a bite of the little triangular cheese pastries. "My king let me bring the whole Company south; last year he wouldn't. I'm hoping to recruit more this year."

"Some strange rumors going around," Clart said. "A mysterious treasure in the north—or treasure *from* the north." He raised one eyebrow as he reached for his mug.

"From the north maybe," Arcolin said, treading carefully around his king's prohibitions. "There was a necklace stolen from Fin Panir—from the Girdish treasury."

"Necklace . . . doesn't sound like what I was hearing." Clart wiped his mouth.

"Someone was killed for the necklace," Arcolin said.

"That bastard Alured's after it, whatever it is. Can't see him so interested in just a necklace. It's a crown he wants, clear enough. And if he gets control of the Guild League, he can afford whatever crown he wants."

"Think he'd really move on the north?" Arcolin asked. Clart raised his brows but said nothing. "I'm a peer of Tsaia now; I owe my king fealty. He's worried."

"He should be," Clart said after a cautious glance around. "The man's mad, I think. Surely Immer's a big enough prize for anyone . . . but he wants it all. You know; you were here last year and ran into more than you expected over in Vonja, isn't that right?"

"Indeed," Arcolin said.

"He's stirring up trouble between the cities; I'm sure he's behind the counterfeiting. There've been disappearances—even murders— over the winter, more than usual. Guildmasters, traders and city-bound both. Lot of suspicion all around. Your contract's with Foss, I hear—"

"Yes."

"We're with Sorellin, mobile patrols. We expect trouble. If he can wear us all out with one little war after another—"

"Yes," Arcolin said, cutting him off with a flick of one finger. He had seen another mercenary captain approaching.

Clart looked up and scowled. "Blues," he said under his breath. The commander of Blue Company gave them both a bleak glance and walked past without a word. Clart watched him; Arcolin didn't turn around. "He's gone into the back," he said. "He's still angry with you. More about your hiring his former captain than about winter quarters, I hear."

"Arneson's a good man," Arcolin said. "He's taken over as recruit captain up north."

"It was a bad business," Clart said. "I'm glad you took him on." He sipped from his mug of sib, then said, "I hear the Blues have con-tracted east this year."

"How far east?"

"East of Cilwan. One of his soldiers told one of mine they're not coming back to Valdaire next winter, either. Nothing definite, but I'd guess hiring to the pirate lord."

Arcolin thought back to Siniava's War and the long pursuit . . . the marches, the battles, the ambushes. "Alured tried to bully An-dressat, you know."

Clart snorted. "Andressat? Nobody bullies him. He might as well be a king, for his pride." He stretched and pushed back from the table. "You'll pardon me, Arcolin, but we've got a long exercise today and new mounts to train. I must go."

"Of course," Arcolin said. He laid his hand on the meal-tag an instant before Clart touched it. "Mine, this time," he said. "For your kindness."

"Least I could do," Clart said. He paused. "If I learn anything that doesn't breach contract—I'll send word."

"And I the same." On his way out, Arcolin thought of others who might be willing to share news of Immer. M'dierra of Golden Company. Other commanders he'd known over the years. Perhaps a visit to the Mercenaries' Hall.

The next time Arcolin met with Dattur and Arvid, he asked Dattur about uniforms for the gnomes in the north. "I did not realize I had that responsibility," he said. "I gave them cloth, but it was not gray."

"They were *kteknik;* that was appropriate," Dattur said. His accent had softened, Arcolin noticed, with familiarity.

"But now, if I am their prince, are they still *kteknik*?"

"No, my lord."

"Then I need to supply them with gray cloth, do I not?"

"It is own weave."

"But . . . they did not ask for sheep." Arcolin considered the number of sheep on his northern lands and the wool production, all of it presently used by his human vassals. How would he afford more sheep? Did gnomes ever have sheep, or would he need to provide more sheep herders?

Dattur's face contorted in what Arcolin now recognized as a stifled grin. "It is not needed, sheep."

"But the design," Arcolin said. "I know there's a difference, from princedom to princedom—"

"It is prince's name, in gnomish. What was name before?"

"My name?"

"Their clan name."

"Karginfulk," Arcolin said.

"Karginfulk!" Dattur jerked as if he'd been stabbed, and a long jabber of gnomish, too fast for Arcolin to follow, came out. Just as Dattur threw himself on the floor and kissed Arcolin's boot, Arvid opened the door.

"What's this?" Arvid said, in a drawl that sounded faintly dangerous.

"I'm not sure," Arcolin said. "Is he—Dattur, are you Karginfulk?"

"*Kteknik* . . . but before, yes. It is—" Another jabber of incomprehensible gnomish followed. Then Dattur took a long breath and shifted back into Common. "Prince made *kteknik* for—for not having respect. Said Lawbreaker. Said go and learn Law among the Lawless; return only when make Lawless Lawful." He glanced at Arvid.

"You were supposed to make *him* lawful?" Arcolin asked.

"Is not my master Arvid, to start," Dattur said. "Prince meant all—it is that impossible. He knew. He knew . . . meant . . . forever. But now—it is prince's word. It is prince must know of life debt owed to my master Arvid, for my blade in another's hand drew his blood, and he also saved my life, twice. It is prince's word: this one *kteknik*, not *kteknik*."

"You saved my life, too, Dattur," Arvid said. "I told you—"

"It is what *prince* says," Dattur said. "Prince is Lawspeaker." He bowed to Arcolin again.

Arcolin felt the responsibility on his shoulders like an iron bar. "I would hear exactly what you did, that the former prince called you Lawbreaker," he said. What he really wanted to know was whether that gnome prince had been under Achrya's influence at the time.

Dattur's tale made it clear that his crime—his Lawlessness—came from challenging the prince and that alone. "Prince said messengers went for help. No help came. Prince said messengers failed. But would not say who was sent. I found body in the rock, dead, broken."

Chills ran down Arcolin's back. "So you asked him about that?"

"Yes. He said, '*Kteknik*: silence him,' and they bound me and put me in wagon that went a long distance. I could not see; I could not talk. Then blow to head. Then day, another day, tracks on ground beside me, no one."

The rest of the story covered Dattur's journey to the center of Tsaia and his meeting a dwarf—the one Arvid had killed—in Vérella. Arcolin listened attentively, though some of it he still did not understand—why, for instance, Dattur's blade, even wielded by another while he was unconscious, could create an obligation for him.

Girdish law, with its emphasis on generosity as well as fairness, laid no formal obligation on the recipient of a gift, even of life. Certainly Dattur's actions—helping Arvid out of the cellar and saving them both from the thief-enforcers with his rock magery—would more than balance the other, to any human.

But Dattur wasn't human. And when he finished his story, he stood perfectly still, looking at Arcolin's face, awaiting his fate.

"Dattur is no longer *kteknik*," Arcolin said. "But until return to the clan, Dattur is not obliged to wear the clan's pattern."

"May wear?"

"May wear, but may choose not to, if proper cloth not available." Arcolin shook his head; he was beginning to sound gnomish. "However: Dattur owes Arvid life-debt. Dattur will serve Arvid until Midsummer, when life-debt will be paid in full. After that, Dattur may choose to take wages or return to the north alone." He hoped that was close to something a real gnome prince might have said.

"I stay with my prince," Dattur said.

"You can't," Arcolin said, appalled at the thought. "I am a soldier. I will be in the field, with troops. It is not the place for a rockbrother."

Dattur made a sound in his throat that Arcolin knew he himself could never make. "Gnomes know war," he said then in Common. "Gnomes train Gird."

That story was well known. "Yes, but—that's different." Dattur in the Company would cause comment. Questions. Bad enough that he would have to tell King Mikeli by letter, not in person, that the gnomes in the north now considered Arcolin their prince. What would his employers think, when word got out that the man they'd hired as a minor peer and mercenary captain was also prince of a tribe of gnomes?

Yet as one of the former Karginfulk, accepted by Arcolin as such, Dattur was legitimately his problem, as much as any of his other oathbound vassals. Which meant that Arvid Semminson was also his problem, even as Marshal Steralt had suggested, but for a different reason. He himself had just told Dattur to serve Arvid until Midsummer, but Dattur said his Law—honored by the Code of Gird— required him to be with his prince.

Asking himself "What would Kieri Phelan do?" wouldn't help at all. Kieri had never faced this, and he could not imagine Kieri being any less dumbfounded than he was himself. A thief—or former thief in the throes of spiritual crisis—and a gnome traveling with the Company?

He thought in silence for a few moments; neither Dattur nor Arvid spoke as he felt his way toward some decision that might work. He looked at Arvid first. "Marshal Steralt—and you—think you should become Girdish. But if you stay here, you are in danger from the Guild. You've been doing work for Fox Company. If you came with us—" Arvid opened his mouth, but Arcolin shook his head and went on talking. "Do you know what a sutler is?" Arvid shook his head. "A merchant who buys supplies for a military unit," Arcolin said. "It would take work off my staff to have someone we could send to buy supplies."

"But I'm—you know my background—"

"And both Captain Selfer and the innkeeper here say you've been honest the whole winter. I don't expect you'll cheat me. Every Foss Council city has at least one grange; you could start your Girdish training there. That way Dattur—" He looked at the gnome. "—could serve you until Midsummer and not have to make a solitary journey to find me thereafter, since Dattur wishes to stay with his . . . prince. You will live in the camp, both of you. I will stand sponsor for you to the grange." He looked hard at Arvid, who nodded.

"I will come, then. I can see no better alternative."

Dattur nodded when Arcolin looked at him. "It is that it is a good plan. Worthy of prince. Is prince willing to learn Law?"

"Yes," Arcolin said. "Though I will have little time to study, I will study Law and language both, with your aid."

"When do we leave?" Arvid asked.

"Day after tomorrow," Arcolin said. "You can ride in one of the supply wagons."

Arcolin wrote a long letter to King Mikeli that night and next morning sent it off with the fastest courier he could hire. "All I meant to do was save them from starvation and freezing," he concluded. "My liege, when I come to Autumn Court, I will bring with me the gnome Dattur, who can testify to my surprise when he told me that to these gnomes I am accounted their prince because of the gift of stone-right."

Marshal Steralt nodded when Arcolin told him what he had done about Arvid. "Good. It gets him out of the city. I will give you a letter of reference to any Marshal in Foss Council."

W hen the column came past the Dragon in the dim predawn light, on its way at last, Arcolin paused; Arvid and Dattur were waiting there, little encumbered by their bundles. "First wagon," he said. "Teamster's let the tailboard step down for you. Once you're in, pull up the tailboard and stay under the canvas." Spies lurked everywhere, and no company marched without rousing them, but the Dragon's windows were shuttered tight, and the street empty. He did not wait to see if the two made it into the wagon, but rode on at the head of the column as usual.

Once through the city's east gates, the Guild League road stretched out, ever more visible in the growing light. To either side, scouts paralleled the column of three full cohorts and the supply wagons. Two rode well ahead, and two more came behind. Arcolin and two of the five captains took the lead. The other three captains stayed with their cohorts; they would change positions at midday.

Farmers coming in with loaded carts gaped at them; children waved. By the time the sun hit them, they were well out of sight of Valdaire's walls and the outlying buildings, and Arcolin's eager chestnut had given up jigging, with only an occasional toss of the head to indicate a need to run. To his right Cracolnya rode the dun he favored, half-nomad bred to look at, and on the left Selfer's new junior captain, Garralt, rode a leggy bald-faced black.

"Ah, the wonderful South," Cracolnya said. "Hot already. Fruit almost ripe."

"Missed it, did you?" Arcolin asked.

"This much," Cracolnya said, his fingers a hazelnut's width apart. "But for the profit in it. Which I hope, my lord Count, we still see. You've heard the rumors, I'm sure."

"Indeed. And told you what I knew back north."

"Well, we knew that lad was trouble when we worked with him before. What bothered me—" He glanced around and then, satisfied, went on. "What bothered me was not finding Sobanai or Vladi—or at least their agents—in Valdaire."

"Or Sofi?" Arcolin asked.

"Or Sofi, yes, but since he's said to be married into Fallo, not as much. But if the Blues have gone to the pirate, and Vladi's still sheep-dogging Sofi—"

"Which we never knew for certain," Arcolin said. "Though I grant it made sense."

"And Sofi's in Fallo, then they're both in reach of the pirate. I can't see Vladi, at least, going that way—"

"No. Nor Sofi Ganarrion either, really. Maybe Fallo got sense and hired them both . . . even Sobanai."

Garralt spoke up. "My lord—there was rumor of the winter that Sobanai's troop disbanded. A fever, I heard."

"Sobanai was always careful of his camps," Arcolin said. "Did you hear where?"

"They'd been at Lûn, downriver, and never made it back to Valdaire in the fall. Others said they'd decided it was too far to come."

"I think we can take it that the pirate's planning to take Lûn," Cracolnya said.

Up ahead, Arcolin saw the forward scouts signal: caravan coming. He glanced back. The cohorts had spread a little as the morning warmed. Now he waved twice, and the command passed down; the files closed up, and supply wagons moved to the edge of the road.

One of the forward scouts rode back to report. The caravan was out of Sorellin, traveling under its pennant and bound for Tsaia. The caravan master wanted to speak with "the commander" and would halt his caravan when they were closer.

"Tell him yes," Arcolin said; the scout wheeled his mount and rode away. He turned to Cracolnya. "The man might have news out of Immer. Lead them on; I'll catch up."

"Yes, my lord." Then Cracolnya grinned. "And I would suggest— your helmet."

Arcolin laughed, shaking his head. "Old joke, Captain. If you had eyes, you'd know it was on my head."

He turned aside when they met the other caravan, greeting the caravan master. They both backed their horses almost to the ditch, watching as Fox Company marched by.

"There's trouble ahead," the caravan master said. He wore a broad sash in Sorellin's colors. "You've heard of this new Duke of Immer?"

"Yes. We knew him as Alured the Black in Siniava's War."

"You remember Rotengre, then: brigands' city it was then, preying on trade and causing trouble all around. Full of evil magicks." The caravan master chewed his lip a moment. "It's gone bad again. We've had refugees coming in from there, starting last autumn, and the tales they tell—well, it's clear to us it's Immer. We hired Clart this year."

Arcolin nodded. "I met Nasimir in Valdaire; he told me."

"We'd have hired Sobanai as well, if we could have got them— sent word downriver to Lûn last summer we wanted to talk contract. Word came back they were interested, but in autumn we had a courier from Koury not to let anyone from Lûn into the city for fear of the black fever. Koury shut the gates to anyone from downriver. Never heard more from Sobanai until early spring, this time from Cilwan, saying half the city had died, and Sobanai Company lost its commander and more than half the soldiers."

"Bad business," Arcolin said.

"Filthy business," the caravan master said. "They're calling him the Black Duke now all over the east, from Cilwan on. Worse than Siniava. It's said he has the old magery and can kill with a glance. That he has fever demons in his service—though I expect it's as like to be jugs of foulness poured into wells. We know he has assassins;

we've lost two of our Council to assassins this past year. One admitted he was pressured to speak with Immer's voice and was killed within the same day's round. The brigands on the road between Koury and us are grown bolder."

"The trouble we had in Vonja's outbounds," Arcolin said, "I lay to Immer's account. Did Vonja tell the other cities?"

"Not us."

Arcolin quickly recounted the evidence for some outside power.

"And you found counterfeiters' dies—just for Vonja?"

"Yes. But I'm sure the same exist for every city in the League, a way to create distrust among you."

The caravan master nodded. "Distrust there is, for certain. Koury has spoken of leaving the League, since it cannot keep the road between us free of brigands; Merinath the same, and blames Sorellin for dangers. We lack the means to patrol all that. We found counterfeit among our own coins, summer before last. Cost us a contract renewal with Golden Company. I am not even sure I trust everyone in my caravan, though I spoke to each, even the least." He shook his head, his expression gloomy, as he stared at the Fox Company wagons now trundling past. "It's good you're here; the Foss Council Speaker told me they'd hired you. I'm sure they'll tell you what I reported, but I thought you'd rather have it from me."

"Indeed so," Arcolin said. "Thank you." He had noticed that his first wagon had the tailboard neatly fastened up, and no one could have told that it carried two passengers, a former thief and a gnome.

"I don't know what gods we've offended to get another Siniava, or worse. And if he can dispose of one city at a time—"

No need to answer that. They both sat, silent on their horses, as the last Fox Company wagon passed. Then the caravan master reached out; Arcolin clasped arms with him, turned his horse back across the road, crossed the ditch on the far side, and cantered along the grass way until he reached the head of the line again, where he rejoined Cracolnya and Garralt. He told them what the caravan master had said.

By the time Fox Company reached their destination, just outside Ifoss, Arcolin had heard more rumors from both traders and Foss Council officials. Fear of fever had cut off all travel from downriver through Cortes Cilwan, though rumor had it some traders knew back roads, both north and south of the Guild Road. Travel was up on the difficult western route north from the Immerhoft Sea, starting at the port of Confaer, then upriver to Cha and Sibili and overland to Pliuni. Foss Council, sure Ifoss was their weakest city, the most likely to be infiltrated by spies, asked Arcolin to camp there.

Ifoss lacked a fortified encampment for them to use, so laying out the camp for a full season's occupation by three cohorts in a flat space outside the city's east gate meant making a secure perimeter and then arranging everything within it. Nothing new to Arcolin, but Arvid—released now from hiding under canvas in a supply wagon—seemed fascinated by the process. Arcolin had no time to explain everything to him and advised him to stay out of the way.

"You'll have your own tent, you and Dattur, near mine. We all use the same jacks—that's over there, where you see them digging a trench. There'll be two more jacks trenches outside the perimeter."

"Yes, my lord," Arvid said.

"You can have a jug in your tent at night, if you need it, but you'll have to empty it."

"Do you want me to get anything from the city today?" Arvid asked.

"No. I want to introduce you to the Marshal first. Once the Marshal's got you on the rolls, you'll be safer."

Arvid looked dubious but nodded. Arcolin waved over a sergeant, who led Arvid to one of the tents, and watched as Arvid set his bundle of clothes inside it and came back out.

Once the camp was organized, Arcolin led Arvid through the city to the local grange. Marshal Porfur of Ifoss Grange was a lifelong Fossian who had been to Valdaire only three times in his life. "Too big, too noisy," he said, looking out the grange door to the drill field and the wooded hills rising beyond. "We had enough noise in Siniava's War. So, your friend wants to become Girdish?"

Arcolin glanced at Arvid, who wore his merchant's garb and a glum expression. "Yes," Arvid said.

Porfur smiled at him. "Come, man, it's not as bad as all that. The Count tells me you have a letter from the Marshal-General herself. And from a Marshal in Valdaire. If you're worried about the exchange of blows—"

"Oh, no," Arvid said. "It's not that. It's the Ten Fingers. I get mixed up."

"As long as you mean to follow them," Porfur said. "Let me see your letters, please." When Arvid handed them over, Porfur moved to the light at the door and read them carefully. "Did *you* see that relic come alight?" he asked, looking at Arcolin.

"No, Marshal. I wasn't in Valdaire then. But I talked to Marshal Steralt about him, and will stand as his sponsor."

"And you told Marshal Steralt in Valdaire that you had been a thief . . . even a Guildmaster?" Now Porfur looked at Arvid.

"Yes, Marshal," Arvid said.

"And you now foreswear that allegiance?"

Arvid took a long breath, then let it out sharply. "Yes, Marshal."

"Do you have tokens of identity with the Guild?"

"Yes, Marshal." Arvid fished out the familiar medal and held it out. "I would not advise any person unfamiliar with thieves' ways to use it."

"I don't want to use it!" Marshal Porfur sounded so shocked that Arcolin almost laughed.

"Marshal, sometimes one wants to . . . to infiltrate another . . . um . . . operation."

Porfur scowled. "You think the Marshal-General wants you to do that?"

"She did ask me to trace stolen property," Arvid said. "I suppose she has others who might be asked to do other things."

"Then you keep it. I trust the gods will punish you if you revert to thievery."

"Perhaps Count Arcolin would keep it for me," Arvid said.

"*Me?* Not likely," Arcolin said. "I have a mercenary company to take care of. The Marshal-General's not going to ask me to run her errands."

"Put it away," Porfur said. "Now, Arvid: you will stand on the platform and recite the Ten Fingers."

Arvid stepped up onto the platform, and—for a man who claimed he found them confusing—recited the Ten Fingers with only a few mistakes. Arcolin suspected those were deliberate, but Arvid seemed to take the subsequent oath with due seriousness.

The exchange of blows almost went very wrong indeed, but Arvid was able to pull his thrust at the last moment; Porfur was not that good.

"I need not worry about your fighting skills, I see," Porfur said. "But that does not excuse you from grange duties, Arvid. All newly sworn yeomen must come to drill night every hand of days for a year, barring illness or an excused absence. When the campaign season is over, I will send a letter for you to give to a grange in Valdaire, if you stay there with Count Arcolin, or wherever you go after that. Should Count Arcolin need to move the troops, he will tell me, and I will arrange something for you."

"Thank you, Marshal," Arcolin said. "If I have other troops with no duties, I presume they're welcome to come along to drill night?"

"Of course. We go a year and more here without visitors, so they're always welcome."

On the way back to the camp, Arvid said, "Drill? Every five days? With . . ."

"Your fellow Girdsmen," Arcolin said. "You're not some over-privileged noble, Arvid. You've been among common folk all your life."

"Not this kind of common folk."

"True. You may find you like them better than you think."

"Gird has a truly wicked sense of humor," Arvid said.

"I expect you're right," Arcolin said. His own relationship with a gnome clan—finding out he was considered a prince in their terms—must be some deity's jest. Gird's? He didn't know.

Arcolin's duties as commander kept him busy for the next hand of days, but despite having more than three hundred troops, it felt easier than the year before. Foss Council had always been the most organized and reliable of the Guild League city-states. He also now had the other captains and more support staff along, as well as Arvid to take some of the work of supply off himself and his staff. But on drill night, he went along with Arvid and three hands of off-duty soldiers from the Company.

Porfur and the grange members stared for a long moment, and then Porfur said, "Welcome! Welcome to you all, yeomen of Gird."

By the end of that evening, all were sweaty and some were bruised. Arvid, walking back to camp with Arcolin, had a spring in his step.

"Not so bad as you thought, eh?" Arcolin asked.

"No," Arvid said. He rubbed the back of his head. "No . . . not bad at all."

A hand of days before Midsummer, Arcolin received a letter from King Mikeli, who seemed more amused than upset at Arcolin's new status as a gnome prince. He quit worrying about Mikeli's reaction and instead practiced his gnomish daily with Dattur.

At dawn on Midsummer, he found Dattur waiting outside his tent, having been there—he learned—since the turn of night. "The prince named my debt to Arvid Semminson paid in full," Dattur said. "Is true?"

"It is so," Arcolin said.

"Now it is my duty to the prince," Dattur said.

"Would you like to go north and rejoin your rockbrethren in the stonehold?" Arcolin asked.

"Is not my wish, but my prince's command," Dattur said.

"Without practice, I might not learn and remember more of kaprist-islik," Arcolin said.

"Humans forget," Dattur said.

Arcolin already knew that gnomes thought they themselves did not forget anything, ever. "Yes," he said. "We do. To learn kaprist-islik, I need someone to practice with. And I do not know enough Law." He paused. Dattur said nothing, standing attentively before him. "But kapristi in the north, in the new halls, have no prince with them, and no word from me. Perhaps they need to . . . to communicate. Someone to carry my words to them and their words to me."

"If need, estvin send," Dattur said.

"You stay, then," Arcolin said. "Teach me kaprist-islik; teach me Law." Dattur bowed. He did not smile, but Arcolin sensed approval of his decision. He was not sure whether Dattur really wanted to stay in Aarenis with him—if this represented some power play on the part of that gnome—or if he wanted to be sure his new prince learned how to be a gnome. Dattur continued to wear human clothes in his size, shifting to darker colors but not into gray, though Arcolin offered again to supply cloth.

"When in halls," Dattur said. "When prince tells estvin Dattur is not *kteknik*, then clothes . . . but others will have made cloth by then."

In the meantime, Dattur took over duties somewhere between personal servant and squire. He even joined in Company weapons practice. Arcolin had done his best to explain to the troops what Dattur's position was, so no one laughed outright when he lined up in formation that first time with hauk and shield . . . and no one thought of laughing again after that first bruising practice.

"I had no idea," Burek said, after watching Dattur demolish an opposing line. "I thought he'd be trampled."

"Rock strength," Arcolin said, though he, too, was surprised. "In the north, we're told that the gnomes taught Father Gird warfare, but nobody's seen them fight for lifetimes." Just as well, he thought, that no humans had provoked them to it.

CHAPTER TWENTY-SIX

Andressat

Filis Andressat rode eastward out of Cortes Andres before dawn, across the gently rolling hills below the escarpment. On this familiar journey—for he visited Cortes Cilwan on Andressat's business at least twice a year—he had refused his father's offer of an escort. He would spend Midsummer at Cortes Cilwan without having to endure insinuations from the regent that quartering his escort and their horses was a drain on the boy count's resources.

By the time he got back, maybe his father and brothers would have given over their harping on his attitude toward that bastard. At least the man had had the sense to know he could not fit in and had taken himself back to Fox Company. This half-year later, Filis recognized that Burek was—though a bastard—the kind of man he himself would have liked as a brother or nephew if only Burek had not been Ferran's get on a servant. By all accounts, he was a fine young officer. But the public scolding the Count had given Filis for that earlier outburst still rankled, and the constant comments by his brothers did nothing to make Cortes Andres comfortable.

The cool morning mist burned away quickly, summer's steamy heat replacing it. Filis stayed to the shadier forest tracks as long as he could and by evening had come to his own command, the easternmost Andressat fort. He gave his captain the latest news from Cortes Andres and left his usual orders, as he did before every absence.

The next morning, he set off again. He passed the cluster of stones marking the Andressat–Cilwan boundary just as the sun rose. Toward noon, he came out of the woods on a bare hillside with sheep spread out on its slope. He reined in and glanced around for any sign of people. He spotted two typical sheepdogs and then the shepherd, sprawled facedown on the short grass. Taking a midday nap, no doubt. Below the pasture, Filis saw the deserted farmstead he remembered, relic of Siniava's War: several roofless huts and a barn mostly whole. Sometimes he stopped for lunch there; once, in a storm, he had spent the night. The old well held good water.

To the north, a thunderstorm towered high, rumbling steadily as growing storms did. Already wispy veils of rain fell across the valley, thickening even as he watched, moving nearer. That shepherd was due a drenching, if he didn't wake up.

Thunder rumbled louder; a breeze lifted his hair. Filis grinned. Race or wet, that was the choice. He sent his horse down the slope at a hand gallop, certain the hoofbeats would wake the shepherd if the thunder didn't.

Chill air met him ahead of the rain, and rain lashed his face in the last few strides to the barn. Inside, most of the roof remained; he led his mount to the driest corner, loosened the girth, and opened a saddlebag for the sausage, cheese, and bread he would eat for lunch.

Not long after, he heard the clatter of hooves and baaing of sheep outside. Then they poured in, a wet, gray, sheep-smelling mass of woolly backs, black ears and faces. His mount whinnied and stamped; the sheep scuttered back, only to be chivvied in by the dogs. The dogs shook themselves, then growled at him. Filis kept a firm hand on his mount's bridle. Finally the shepherd came in, a boy now wrapped in a ragged cloak. He called the dogs to heel.

"Sorry, surr," the boy said, in the accent of the region. "I see you go in, but t'dogs don't." He stared at Filis in the gloom of the storm-darkened barn. "Who yurr be? Where be goin'?"

Filis had come this way before but had not seen this boy; it spoke well of the child that he asked, given the times. "I'm from Andressat," he said. "On my way to Cortes Cilwan to visit relatives there."

The boy nodded. "It come rain," he said. "Won't clear afore dark, maybe. Share bread?"

"Yes," Filis said, though he had no desire for the coarse hard bread the boy would have. "I have cheese."

The boy smelled of wet sheep, wet dog, and dirty boy, but the ritual of sharing food meant Filis must take a hunk of the boy's bread, as the boy took a hunk of Filis's cheese. That close, Filis was a little surprised to see that the boy was a redhead whose pale skin had freckled heavily. Red hair was rare in this area; he tried to remember the nearest vill with a redheaded adult who might be this boy's parent. The boy ate rapidly, almost gulping the cheese, looking past Filis at the horse, then at Filis's hands, at the rings he wore.

"Yurr from Andressat," the boy said, after wiping his mouth. "Yuh know t' count?"

"All in Andressat know the count," Filis said. Of course the boy would notice his horse, his rings. He wished he'd left his gloves on, but too late for that now. For an instant he felt a twinge of anxiety, but he had his sword and he could take the boy and the dogs as well if he had to.

"Jus' wonder," the boy said. "Yurr rich, though." His gaze flicked to the horse, back to Filis's hands, and then to the hilt of his sword.

"Not very," Filis said. "Only one horse." The boy just stared. The back of Filis's neck tickled. Well. He could ride through rain if need be. He stood up, eased his way through the sheep, and looked out into the storm. The branch laid across the opening was no barrier for his mount—an easy hop, even onto wet ground. Rain still fell, though less heavily, and it looked lighter to the east. He turned back to see the boy edging toward his horse. "Storm's breaking up," he said, and the boy jerked to a halt. "I'd best be on my way."

"Still rainin'," the boy said. He stood oddly, feet a little wide.

Filis dropped his hand to his sword hilt, casually, as if checking its readiness. The boy's eyes narrowed, then he moved away from Filis and the horse. "Not that hard," Filis said. He was in no real danger, he was sure; probably the boy had only wanted to filch more food from his saddlebags. But the two dogs, now standing alert, ruffs bristling, were worrisome.

He turned his mount so he could see the boy and the dogs while he tightened the girth he'd loosened, then mounted and rode at the sheep; they scattered from his path, leaving an opening. A touch of his spur, and the chestnut rose on his haunches and hopped over the branch into the rain outside. The rain had lessened enough that he had no need to stop and unroll his cloak from his pack.

Filis rode on through the afternoon, wondering about that boy. The sheep—ordinary sheep for this region. The dogs—sheepdogs for certain. The boy, though . . . all the past year he'd seen no sheep on those hills. People might be moving back into the old vills, but . . . easy for brigands to buy some sheep and set them and a boy out to watch for travelers.

For himself in particular? Unlikely. But not many travelers went from Andressat to Cortes Cilwan by this route, not since Siniava's War. There'd been talk at home about the brigands the year before, in Vonja outlands. Burek had fought them, his father told him, with what was now Fox Company. Brigands who might be in the pay of the Duke of Immer.

As the storm moved up the Immer lowlands to the west, blocking the sun, the afternoon stayed gloomy. At first he saw no hoofprints on the muddy track he rode. The track forked at a well; there had been a vill here once, but only tumbled stone walls remained. Filis watered his horse and pressed on. Here he found tracks: someone else had ridden, driving cattle. A small flock of sheep or goats had crossed the tracks of cattle and horse. He passed farmsteads, men and women at work in the fields, a child perched on a rock watching geese. A familiar vill, women on wooden pattens taking water from the well, their skirts splashed with mud. Bare-legged children, mud to the knees, chased one holding a leafy twig: some game. They all watched him pass; he smiled and nodded, and so did they. All the same as usual.

As he came to another fork, he paused. A faint trail led right, to the hump of ground where he usually camped in an old stone shelter. If someone had set a watch on him, it would be wise to avoid his usual campsite. He could reach a vill he knew, not until well after dark, but a place he was sure would be safe. He'd stayed there before, and even when he passed through, he gifted the headman with a coin. He turned his horse left to the wider track.

It was full dark indeed, the muddy track having slowed him more than he expected, when he reached the vill. If not for the mud, he'd have ridden on to the outskirts of Cortes Cilwan—on a dry track only a half-day or -night's ride—but he and the horse were both tired.

The village headman opened to his knock and lit the way to the barn with a clay lamp that he set on a ledge inside. He helped Filis untack and rub down his horse. "My lord, I'm sorry, but my two youngest are down with fever. You should not stay in the house."

"The barn's fine," Filis said. "I'm sorry to come so late, but the storm—"

"Of course, my lord. I'll bring you something hot in just a little."

Filis made a bed of his blankets and a pile of hay, and by then the headman had reappeared with a basket: a bowl of good-smelling stew, a half loaf of bread, a small jar of fruit jam, and a large jug of ale.

"It's m'own wife's brewing," the headman said. "Last time you came, we was short—"

"This is bounty indeed," Filis said. He fished coins from his belt pouch. "After the day I've had, this is luxury."

"Nay, my lord, you needn't—" Polite refusal preceded grateful acceptance.

"I must," Filis said. "For your kindness—and if it is too much, pray help the next stranger who needs a meal."

"Thank you, my lord," the headman said. "And sleep sound."

"I'm sure I will," Filis said. "And I'll be off in the morning."

He ate the stew, hot with the spice mix preferred in Cilwan; smeared the fruit jam—plum and peach mixed, he thought—on the bread; and drank deep of the ale. Yes, the goodwife here had a gift for brewing. He drifted easily into sleep, deep and dreamless.

Filis woke to a nightmare that lasted days—cramped in a box in what he presumed was a trader's wagon, jouncing on the road somewhere. He guessed east to Lûn or even Cortes Immer, but he had no way of knowing. He was allowed out once a night for necessities, which did not include a full meal or a full draft of water but plenty of knocking about by those who surrounded him. He had no chance to attempt escape—they had stripped him, bound him, and even as he squatted beside a tree, his arms were bound and his captors stood over him.

He cursed himself for the stupid decisions that had led to this. If he had brought an escort, if he had camped apart, if he had not drunk that ale . . . He wondered if the regent in Cortes Cilwan would search for him—if anyone would recognize his horse, any of his things— but reason told him his captors would have found ways to dispose of them. His father—he did not want to think what his father would imagine. The family hothead running off in anger to turn traitor, sell his father's secrets to his father's enemy? Surely not. Surely his father knew him better than that.

But every day took him farther from home, closer to the man even his father feared. He saw no chance to escape, no hope in any of the hard faces around him that one might be bribed to help him.

Cortes Immer's broken walls had been repaired, its towers rebuilt. Filis had only a glimpse of this before he was dragged inside, then down level after level to the old dungeon. His belly clenched with more than hunger. He would die here, and die in some horrible way, he was sure. He tried to set himself to accept that and save what little honor he could. Whatever the threat, he would not betray his family.

When Alured the Black—the Duke of Immer, his guards announced—finally appeared, he looked Filis up and down with obvious contempt. "I could wish it had been any of the others," he said. "I know about you. The troublemaker. Quarrelsome, gambler, drinker. Your father may count himself lucky you ran off, though he may worry about what secrets you brought." He stood silent a long moment, while Filis tried to hold himself with dignity. Alured was much as his father and brothers had described: tall, well made, black hair in a braid now decorated with ribbons in his colors rather than the green feathers he'd worn in Siniava's War. He wore gold armlets, a wide collar set with jewels, and over that a necklace that flashed in the dimness like sunlit water, blue and white.

The necklace . . . he looked away, hoping his face showed nothing. Alured smiled. "You recognize this?"

Best not to answer. But pressure built in his head, as if to burst his skull, and he heard himself say the truth: "I never saw that before."

"But you heard of it."

"Yes."

"And you know what it is part of?"

"I have not seen it."

"But you have heard . . . no, do not answer. You must have heard; I know the gossip in Valdaire and Foss Council and Vonja, all the way downriver." He shook his head. "If only you were more valued by your father, Filis, I would use you. But though we shall wait to see, I think he will not waste much to trace you. If that should be true, you will have no value to me. Think on that." He turned away, said a few words Filis could not hear to the guards, and went back up the stairs.

What came next was a black hole into which he was shoved and a heavy lid slamming down over the opening. He had no way of knowing how long he huddled in the dark; it was too small to lie down in comfortably, the stone walls and floor rough, chill, and damp. Though he could stand, his outstretched arms touched the sides. Hunger and thirst tormented him; when he was finally pulled out, he was too weak to walk and fainted.

Cold water splashed on him, wetting cracked lips and dry tongue. He opened his eyes. Men stood around him, wearing Immer's colors. He lay on a platform; beyond the men he saw only dimness. They soused him again, rubbed him down with ungentle hands, yanked his head up by the hair. One got a hand behind his shoulders and shoved him upright so that his legs dangled over the edge. One offered a mug. "Drink this."

Thirst rode him; he drank in gulps as the man held the mug to his mouth. Sour wine, certainly not of Andressat's vintage; he recognized the grape as a wilding that grew across southern Aarenis. He shouldn't drink it—he needed water, not wine—but he was too thirsty to resist the second mug offered.

The same hand took the mug away and shoved a piece of coarse bread at his mouth. "Eat."

Maybe the bread would help. He ate. His stomach, roiling from the wine, settled. A small chunk of cheese followed the bread. He managed not to spew, and shortly after that found himself strapped upright to a wooden chair. Muzzy-headed as the wine made him, he was still trying to understand what might happen when Alured—Immer—came in.

"How much?" Immer asked without looking at Filis.

"Two mugs, m'lord."

"Excellent." Immer swung around, and the men brought forward a padded stool; Immer sat, facing Filis. He smiled—a smile that seemed all good humor for a moment before it vanished. "Now, then, Filis Andressat. You have had time to consider your position. I have had time to consider you." He paused, put out his hand, and one of the men handed him a mug. He sipped, without taking his gaze from Filis, then held his hand out without looking, and the man took the mug, setting it on the table where Filis had been laid. "You stink less," he said then. "I told them to clean you up. You've had drink and food. Let's see if you're worth your keep. Tell me, Filis, what value you have for me."

The pressure he had felt before squeezed Filis's head; he fought the compulsion to say . . . to say whatever Immer wanted to hear. How could the man do this? It must be some kind of magery, but no one had said Alured—Immer—was a mage. Filis shut his eyes, trying to think clearly through the wine fumes and the pressure.

"Come now," Immer said. "Open your eyes." His voice was gentle, coaxing. Filis's eyes opened as if on springs. "You see, Filis, you will yield. Thirsty men drink whatever they can find, eh? You wished it were not wine. You feel the wine now, I see in your eyes, but it was not merely wine."

Filis looked around the room, desperate for something other than Immer's face, Immer's peculiar eyes, to focus on.

"We're alone now," Immer said, in the same gentle tone. "You need not fear witnesses to your weakness, your treachery." In an instant, his expression shifted; the deep black eyes seemed flat as shiny river stones. "Any other witnesses, that is. You should fear me." Then Immer's eyes gained their depth again, and the man's mouth curved in what could pass for a friendly smile. "But not yet. Now . . . *are* you worth your keep?"

Filis's lips parted against his will, and he heard himself say, "Yes . . . lord."

"Good," Immer said, his smile wider. "Very good. Tell me . . . did your father find my ancestry in his archives?"

Filis tried again to stay silent, but as Immer's expression shifted again and his eyes took on the fixed, flat stare . . . once more Filis heard his voice saying, "No, lord."

"No Vaskronin in his archives?"

"No, lord."

"And what of his own ancestry? Is it as high as he claims?"

"I . . ." His father had once claimed higher. Now he did not. Filis felt the wine, the drugs, and Immer's power compelling him to speak, but this time he did not know which truth Immer wanted. "When?" he finally said.

"When? That's not an answer. I ask the questions here." Then Immer's expression softened. "Your father traveled north . . . I have word he went to Lyonya and Tsaia and spoke to Kieri Phelan and King Mikeli of Tsaia. Is that so?"

"Yes, lord."

"Why did he go?"

"I . . . do not know. I was not there when he left."

"But he told you when he returned, I'm certain. What did he tell you, Filis?" A pause, then, "I heard a story that he found something in the archives, something that upset him, and he told those in the north . . . and he would have told you later. The story I heard was he found his ancestry was tainted. Is that true?"

Filis almost choked, but the words escaped in spite of his resistance. "Yes, lord."

"You see, it is no use resisting, Filis. The wine, the truth potion, my own powers—you are helpless. And yet you do have something I want and need." Immer stood abruptly and walked around the chair,

still talking, running his fingers lightly along Filis's bare shoulders.
"Your father . . . has contempt for me. I will not tolerate that. He has
refused my requests—my polite requests. He must be made to submit
to my rule. If courtesy will not serve, then I must try something else.
This scar here, on your shoulder—how long have you had that?"

"Since I was nine winters," Filis said. He shivered; Immer's presence at his back was like a cold wind.

"Ah. So your family knows that scar. But one is not enough. Let's
see . . . this looks like a blade-cut, here on your upper arm. You
weren't holding your shield high enough."

Filis felt a yank on his hair and Immer's fingers running over
his scalp. "No scars here, that I can feel. But—how interesting. Your
ears—"

His brothers had teased him about his ears when he was a boy.

"Very distinctive shape. So. Enough easy marks for your father to
recognize."

Filis did not flinch. He'd known from the first he was going to die
in this place. His father probably knew it, too. If they sent his father
his body, that would be no worse.

Immer sat down again in front of him, smiling pleasantly at first,
as he had before, as a host might smile at a welcome guest. He said
nothing, merely looked at Filis. The black eyes shifted again from the
lively sparkle to flat opacity—first one then the other, several times,
as Filis struggled to make sense of it. With that change came another;
Immer's expression changed with the eyes. Why? What was happening? Then, past the hunger, the fear, the wine, and whatever had
been in it, he remembered the story his father had told them, of the
Fox Company sergeant blinded by a demon trying to invade him.

Something was *inside* Immer. Something . . . some*one*? Another
memory struggled up through the thickening haze of wine and magery: stories from the north, of the Verrakaien who could move from
body to body, taking over . . .

"No," he said, his voice shaking with sudden terror. "No!"

The flat cold gaze lay on him now like snow. "No," Immer said—
or the being in Immer said. The voice had changed along with the
eyes. "You do realize what I am . . . but no, I have no desire to move
from this body to you. He is stronger even without me than you are.

You will be spared that . . . but not the knowledge that you will never be able to tell your father—or anyone else—what you know." Immer's hand touched his knee, almost a caress. "Your father will have proof of my power, but not that knowledge, when he unwraps the present I will send him." Immer's expression changed again to the more lively one. "You know you want to ask, Filis. Every man wants to know at such times."

He did not want to know; he knew already it would be more than he could bear, but pressure filled his head again, forcing his mouth to say the words Immer wanted to hear. "What present?" he asked.

"A work of art," Immer said. "Leatherwork."

Cold sweat broke out on Filis's body. He could imagine his father's face . . . his father's reaction . . . his brothers' faces. He told himself it was no worse than any other death. But he could not believe it, not with Immer's satisfied smile in front of him.

CHAPTER TWENTY-SEVEN

Chaya, Lyonya

Midsummer. A year ago, Kieri had waited here for his grand-mother, for the ancient rites that the human and elven rulers of Lyonya performed, singing the sun up. Now . . . he had no idea what to do. The Lady was dead; Orlith was dead; Am-rothlin swore he did not know of equivalent rites. The old human rites would do for humans, but for elves? And besides, under that flower-strewn mound lay the remains of a mysterious settlement he still knew nothing about.

He started up the hill in the King's Grove two days before the ceremony, leaving Arian below with the Squires. Though the path marked with small white stones still led straight up, he stepped aside at an urge he could not have explained and began walking around the hill instead, climbing slowly in a spiral . . . but not a spiral ex-actly, for sometimes he turned back and sometimes paused, baffled. It felt almost familiar, and yet not familiar. It was midday when he finally reached the flattened summit where the Oathstone stood, where he had been crowned, where he and the Lady had pledged their commitment to the land and taig.

"And now what?" he asked aloud. "What am I supposed to do now, with no elf to sing the song with me, no way to repair the elven-home?" He put his hand lightly on the Oathstone.

You came.

Was that the voice of the skull he had found at Midwinter?

"I am here," he said.

They are gone.

"If you mean the Lady and the elvenhome, yes, they have gone. That is not a good thing, I deem."

It is almost Midsummer. Come, then, and sing your own song, and see.

Kieri shivered despite the warm sun. "I will be here at the rising of the sun," he said. "And I will sing."

You will see. The King's Justice will restore us.

"This king wants justice for all," Kieri said. "Not just for a few."

Fair deeds must match fair words.

That was clear enough. Kieri bent and kissed the stone, then walked back down the mound, once more in a spiraling pattern.

On Midsummer itself—had it been only one year before that he had first sung the sun up with the Lady, and first encountered the elf-maid who wanted to marry him?—Kieri followed all the rituals he had learned then. Dressed in the same white robe, he led the procession into the King's Grove and went up the mound alone, his followers forming a circle at its foot. He watched the stars move across the sky, waiting until the moment the Summerstar touched the oldest blackoak's crown.

At that moment, he began his song. To his surprise, Arian— below in the circle—sang the responses. The sky lightened, color returned to the trees; he felt the taig's response as well as his own. Relief: he was doing the right thing; all would be well.

Then—as the sun cleared the treetops and the first ray of light struck the Oathstone—the ground shivered. The Oathstone itself sank slowly, finger by finger, into the green grass. Kieri struggled to keep his voice steady. As the Oathstone sank below ground level, leaving a smooth shaft behind, the ground heaved up, then down, as if it were an ocean wave. Kieri staggered as it subsided beneath him, around him and the Oathstone's shaft, spreading as it lowered until he stood below a circular dyke.

The Oathstone, once more almost waist-high, stood in front of him. An old skull, the earth still clinging to it, poised delicately on top, its ancient grin challenging. Though he had not seen the skull in the dark at Midwinter, he knew this was the same one.

Kieri looked around. His court lay scattered in disarray on the dyke; most had fallen as the ground rose, but Arian stood, arms outstretched for balance. He looked at them, then at the skull and the level circle around it. On two sides, sunrising and sunsetting, gaps in the dyke led away into the King's Grove.

He bowed to the skull. "Elder," he said. "Be at peace."

Justice is worth more than peace.

"True, but you have earned your rest." He picked up the skull and once more kissed its forehead. "There will be green leaves for you, or a place in the royal ossuary, as you wish."

My people were here, and here their bones remain, but scattered. Build them a house, O king, and you will have my blessing.

"It shall be done," Kieri said, laying one hand on the skull and one on the Oathstone. "My word on it." A song of thanksgiving seemed appropriate; he began the one he knew best, and his court—somewhat raggedly—joined in. As they sang, bones rose from the soil, through the grass, and the grass grew together again beneath them. Soon the ground within the dyke was covered with bones—bones that slid clicking against one another to form assemblages—one skeleton after another.

Kieri felt the hairs standing up all over his body, prickling, but he sang on even as other voices faltered, welcoming the bones back to the light in words he had never heard before. Was it even his voice singing? He was not sure.

Finally all the bones lay still. Their arrangement resembled the layout of the royal ossuary, with aisles between the rows of skeletons. Kieri walked among them. They had been long in the earth, but under the dirt he could see some trace of color here and there, less crude than he had expected.

With a bow to the skull on the Oathstone, he called his court down. "We must find the sacred boughs to lay on them now," he said. "And build them a bone-house as they once had, that some of the Sinyi—or iynisin, I do not know which—destroyed. For these are the ancient peoples who lived in this holy place before the elves did, and they require honor."

The Seneschal advised which leaves were best to place and how; Kieri felt the gratitude of the bones as one and then another had eye-holes and earholes touched with green under the sun. Then with a bow to the skull once more, Kieri led the procession back to the palace.

The procession was silent until they were within the palace walls; then Sier Halveric said, "So . . . the Oathstone is not from the elves?"

"Apparently not," Kieri said.

"Did you know about this?"

"What happened to me at Midwinter suggested that something lay beneath the mound. I had thought to have it excavated, but with Arian's miscarriage and the Lady's death, I had not done that yet. The Kuakkgani said there was something very old and the answer would come at Midsummer."

"Were those people murdered?"

"Not all of them, surely. They had a settlement of some sort and a bone-house. I am sure people lived here before elves came, and their sacred place was taken over."

"By the Lady."

"I am not sure of that," Kieri said. "She said no . . . and we know she had traitors within her company."

Sier Halveric nodded. "I would like to hold her blameless, sir king, in spite of all we know."

"So would I, as she was my grandmother. But unless we find proof . . . what can we think but that she is at least tainted with suspicion?"

Construction of the bone-house began immediately after the end of the Midsummer festivities. Kieri insisted it must be completed by the Autumn Evener, but the simple structure stood ready to receive its guests well before that. The Seneschal spent time with each skeleton, then told Kieri where it should go. The oldest skull, the one Kieri had found at Midwinter, rested on the Oathstone.

"I wonder what other secrets the elves left us," Sier Davonin said after the dedication of the bone-house. "Patterns that let enemies into the palace, a pretty hill to cover an ugly crime . . ."

"We are not likely to learn them all," Kieri said. "And some, I hope, were not so dire."

CHAPTER TWENTY-EIGHT

Vérella, Tsaia

The atmosphere among the peerage at Midsummer Court was less strained, Dorrin thought. She still caught sharp glances from some of the women and a few of the peerage, but Dukes Mahieran and Serrostin were back to being friendly, and Duke Marrakai had never been less. Daryan Serrostin attended Dorrin at court and also visited his family's house. Gwenno Marrakai did the same. Beclan, who could not attend court or meet his family, had been allowed to come to Vérella "for his safety" but stayed in Verrakai House. He did not complain and set himself to study the estate rolls Dorrin had brought along and write up her notes from the meetings every evening.

"We have a situation," High Marshal Seklis said to Dorrin on the second day. "The king and I must speak to you privily."

Dorrin sighed. She suspected there would always be a situation where she was concerned. "At the king's pleasure," she said. She was not surprised when, at the conclusion of the morning session of Council, the king nodded to her and Seklis. She followed him away from the other peers and the table set out with food and drink.

"First—as you know already—Prince Camwyn has shown mage ability," Seklis said when they and Marshal-Judicar Oktar were closeted in his office. Mikeli had waved Dorrin to a chair, but himself wandered the office restlessly. "He is not the only one." Dorrin looked at the king, who was staring out a window. "I had . . . um . . . not told the king," Seklis went on, "that I first heard of someone outside the royal family having magery near the Spring Evener. Marshal-Judicar Oktar and I considered it a matter of Girdish law and sent word to the Marshal-General, as you told him to do, quite correctly."

"If I had known," Mikeli said, still looking out the window, "I would have spoken with Seklis at once about Camwyn. It was . . . unfortunate." His voice was quiet, but Dorrin realized it masked anger.

"I agree," Marshal-Judicar Oktar said. "I was wrong to instruct Seklis to withhold that information. We wished to have the Marshal-General's opinion to give the king the best advice, but still—"

"Well." Mikeli turned back to them, meeting Dorrin's gaze. "So it was done, and so I found when I told Seklis about Camwyn's magery. Go on, Seklis." He turned away again.

"The Marshal-General has convened a special conclave to consider the issue, to which I am bidden," Seklis went on, looking at Dorrin. "She informs us that magery has appeared in Fintha, as well as in Tsaia. In children as young as five winters, though most are over twelve, and a few adults, all bred of families with no record of it."

"Where?" Dorrin asked. "In cities or—"

"Scattered across the land, including Fin Panir itself. In remote villages where—unfortunately—some were killed out of hand by zealous Marshals. The Marshal-General has ordered no more killings, but there is . . . unrest . . . in some areas."

Dorrin repressed a shudder. A crisis in the succession of Tsaia—even in the Crown itself—was nothing to the chaos that could result from the entire Fellowship of Gird losing its cohesion.

"In the meantime," Seklis said, "she bade me inform the Marshals under my eye that they are to report any signs of magery to Oktar, but take no action. She forbade killing suspected mages here, as well as in Fintha. She would like Prince Camwyn to come to Fin Panir with me—"

"And I forbade that," Mikeli said, without turning to face them. "I have but one brother, and he is dear to me. Let him be as wrong in the Code as he is, and I will still protect him."

"How many know about him?" Dorrin asked.

"We and Aris Marrakai," Mikeli said. "For a wonder, given their ages, they have not said aught to anyone else, and a combination of physical exertion and the daily exercise of his power in secrecy has kept it from displaying publicly. So far."

"Has the Marshal-General any idea why magery is suddenly appearing?" Dorrin asked.

"Several, and none proven," Seklis said. "The Marshals and paladins she has called to study this may find out."

"The dragon destroyed Achrya before Midwinter," Dorrin said. "And is that not when gnomes came to Lord Arcolin? Could it be connected?"

"*Anything* could be connected," Mikeli said. "Kieri—King Kieri—used to say everything was. But we do not know, and without knowing we cannot act—"

"Good deeds as well as bad have consequences," Dorrin said. "It may not be a threat."

Mikeli finally looked away and sat down abruptly in the remaining chair.

Seklis cleared his throat. "There is more, Duke Verrakai. When we returned from the king's progress, messages from the Marshal-General also told us of elves come to Fin Panir. Did you know that magelords were in some sort of enchantment in the far west, in that stronghold discovered a few years ago?"

Dorrin frowned. "Paksenarrion said something about that, one night up at the stronghold. I don't remember any details."

"Well, there *are* magelords—clearly magelords from the ancient days—in both the records of the place and by the look of them. They're just . . . there. Silent, motionless, unresponsive. The elves now demand that all humans leave—the Girdish and the magelords both. The Marshal-General has ordered the Girdish expeditions home, but has no idea how to remove the magelords—they cannot, it seems, be picked up and carried off. The elves claim they cannot remove them, either, but insist they must be removed. It will take a magelord, they told the Marshal-General, to break the spell that binds them."

Dorrin's brows went up. "They cannot mean for *me* to do it!"

"The elves did not know of you," Seklis said. "The Marshal-

General, however, did. She regrets that she mentioned you to them. I was told to ask if you had any idea how. Despite the outbreak of magery here and there, you are the only adult trained magelord we know of. I certainly have no skills in breaking enchantments."

"Prayers to Gird?" Dorrin suggested. "The High Lord?"

"Will be tried, of course. The Marshal-General sent a paladin by the mage-road to Kolobia for that reason. We have not heard back, which suggests that so far the gods have not granted it."

"Do you even know what kind of enchantment it is?" She thought of the reading she had done in the Verrakai library: nothing suggested a way to hold someone enchanted for all those lifetimes.

"No. But if the elves say it is not theirs—"

"If they are telling the truth," Dorrin said.

"You would doubt them?"

"Kieri's grandmother, the Lady," Dorrin said. "She was not always truthful. Elves love harmony, as you know, and will avoid conflict if they can. Including by subterfuge."

"Do you then think it is an elven enchantment?"

"I don't know," Dorrin said. "I have not seen the enchantment . . . I have not seen *any* enchantment of that kind. It is like a bard's song or a fireside tale . . . and the only tales I heard spoke of enchantment from eating something enchanted."

"I have spoken to witnesses who have seen the stronghold and its contents," Seklis said, "so I know the enchantment is real. Do you think you'd recognize the magery used if you went there?"

"Went to Kolobia? I doubt it. And anyway, I can't go." She glanced at Mikeli. "Not without your command, sir king, and with the messages from Arcolin on the situation in the south, I should stay in Tsaia."

"I agree," Mikeli said. "Unless you thought you could quickly deal with the enchantment and return. We also want to know whether you can open the box that shut itself when Paksenarrion was here."

"I don't know," Dorrin said. "I can try—if you truly want me to."

"I think it best. Among other things, we need to know if the pattern on the box is the same as the pattern the elves use to move about. Queen Arian found such a pattern; we have chiseled out the stones where it was and put them outside the city. I would rather not have a sudden arrival of elves in *my* palace."

Dorrin could understand that. They all went to the treasury, and she looked at the plain wooden chest.

"As you see, the wood grew together—there's no longer a way to open the chest."

"Nor can we move the chest," High Marshal Seklis said. "Several strong men cannot move it a finger's width."

He and the king looked at her as if she could move it with a touch. Dorrin almost laughed but laid her hand on the chest.

"Is it talking to you?" they asked.

"No." *I am here,* she thought at it. The chest trembled beneath her hand; her hand tingled. She took her hand away; the chest lurched a little toward her.

"I saw that," Seklis said. "I can hardly believe it, but—ask it to open, Duke Verrakai."

"Please open," Dorrin said, laying her hand on the top of the chest. With a sound like ripping cloth, a crack appeared around the chest where the opening had been before. Dorrin said, "Thank you," and reached forward; the top lifted without her assistance.

Inside, the contents appeared as they had before, wrapped in clean white linen, the oblong shape of the box that held the rings and bracelets, the shape of the cup, and the irregular shape that held the crown.

I am yours. Take me—put me on. The crown in its wrappings lifted in the chest. Dorrin put out her hand to hold it gently in place, and the light of its jewels blazed through the cloth.

"It's—doing that again," Mikeli said. He sounded more interested than angry.

"It is not yet the time," Dorrin said to the crown. "But as I promised I would return, so I have returned. I would see you again, and the others."

A sense of sadness, of yearning.

"I wish I knew where you came from," Dorrin said. The colors shimmered through the cloth. *Take me. See me clearly.* "I cannot wear you now," Dorrin said, "in courtesy to the king of this land. But I will unwrap you and look."

She took the crown in her hands and set it in her lap, unwrapping it. The jewels blazed. *See us all.* To Mikeli she said, "It wants me to unwrap them all."

"Go ahead," Mikeli said. "We must learn what the mystery means, and at the moment no assassins are with us."

One by one she lifted the other items out. She ran her thumb along the pattern on the box of regalia and lifted out the rings, the bracelets. She set the cup atop the chest and laid the other things to either side.

"You are beautiful," she said to the array. "But I do not understand you. I do not know where you come from, or who made you, or what you truly are."

The light from the jewels brightened even more, shimmering on the walls and ceilings of the treasury like reflections of sunlight dancing on moving water. Dorrin looked at them more closely than she ever had. Blue of deep water . . . clear as water, as well. The jewels of other colors on the goblet and on the top of the velvet-lined box seemed garish in combination with the blue and clear.

What could it be? Fire and water? Air and water?

"There is a necklace," Dorrin said to the jewels. "It is not here; it was stolen long ago and stolen again last year. One who saw you and that necklace both thought it belonged with you. Do you know?"

Yes.

"Who made you?"

Ask the right questions in the right order.

"I do not know the right order," Dorrin said. "Let me tell you what I do know. Long and long ago, men came to the south from farther south, from over the sea. Once that land was green, but then it became sand, so men sailed a sea and came north."

Silence as heavy as gold filled the room.

"I believe you came with those men," Dorrin said. "And I believe you remember."

Into her mind a flood of images: men, ships, women, children, waves of green water edged with foam and waves of sand edged with . . . blood. Dorrin shuddered. "Ibbirun," she said. "The Sandlord? And . . . invasion? Blood?"

No.

"Is that the old story about the Sandlord having sent waves of sand into Aarenis, making it a desert?" the king asked.

"That's what I always heard," Dorrin said with a sigh. "The fall of Aare was caused by the Sandlord, Ibbirun, a servant of the Unmaker. But that's not what I'm getting here."

"Perhaps they did not know how to care for farmland," High Marshal Seklis said. "Perhaps they—" He paused suddenly, scowling. "In the west, in Kolobia, the former magelords turned farmer. And while that settlement prospered, they turned rock and sand into farmland. According to the records we found there, they brought in soil from Fintha and multiplied it by magery."

"Multiplied it?"

"So it was written."

"I have no idea how they did that," Dorrin said.

"What I'm thinking is . . . good farmers make the land better. Bad farmers make the land worse. What if there were bad farmers in Aare who ruined the land? Then they might have blamed the Sandlord rather than themselves."

"But if that's so, how could they be good farmers here in the north?"

"They learned from the old humans, those who were already here," Seklis said.

"I suppose." Dorrin looked down at the crown she held, its jewels no longer flashing brightly, though they still shone. "Did they ruin the land?" she asked the crown.

No. Light filled the room again, shimmering once more as if under water. *Not land. Water.*

"They did something to the water," Dorrin said, looking up to meet the king's eyes. "That's what it told me."

"Something to the water?" Mikeli frowned. "What could they do to water? Foul a spring, I suppose, but—water as element—it's too much."

"In Gird's war we have the tale of a magelord named Grahlin," Seklis said. "He could make water disappear or reappear; he took a river's water and diverted it to a well, making the well burst. Gird's friend Cob was lamed for life by that."

"I remember now," Mikeli said. He turned to Dorrin. "And you," he said, "you brought water back to a cursed well."

Dorrin stared at him. "I . . . removed the curse and took the bodies out . . ."

"According to the Marshal-General," Seklis said, "you did more than that. You moved stones by magery, you removed the curse—it must have been by magery or Falk's power or both, and magic in any case—and you told her that water returned to the well when you prayed over it and your tears fell."

"It was Falk," Dorrin said.

"If it was Beclan's own magery mixed with Gird's power that saved him," the king said, "it could have been your own magery mixed with Falk's power that brought water back. It could have been your magery alone, for that matter, like Grahlin's. It was your magery alone that killed the traitor."

"What I don't understand is what the regalia have to do with it all," Seklis said. "Are they calling you simply to tell you that your ancestors—or someone's ancestors—stole the water from Aare and you're supposed to put it back? The first is unprovable, and the second impossible."

"I don't know, High Marshal," the king said, leaning back in his chair. "Unless we learn to travel in time, you are correct that we cannot know exactly what happened in Aare. But as for impossible . . . what is not possible for me is possible for a Marshal, and what is not possible for a Marshal may be possible for a paladin."

"But I'm not a paladin," Dorrin said.

"Does anyone know ahead of time if they're a paladin?" the king asked, looking at Seklis.

"Paksenarrion did not, by all accounts," Seklis said. "But there's much we don't know about magelords . . . Have you done any other magery with water, Duke Verrakai?"

"No," Dorrin said. "Although . . ."

"What?"

"Well . . . my people have told me that in the year since I became Duke, the wells and springs have all become cleaner." They started to speak, and she held up her hand. "But understand—the people had been forbidden to follow any of the old customs: dressing the wells for the *merin* in spring, performing the usual ceremonies of cleansing. I did nothing myself but make it clear that they were free to do so."

"And did you yourself dress the wells?"

"Not except putting herbs on the two wells nearest the house. But more importantly, I had my people clean them out in the same way you'd clean a cellar. One of them, in the stableyard, had trash in it when I arrived. Stands to reason if you take rubbish out of a well, the water is cleaner."

"And do you feel any particular . . . affinity for water?"

"Affinity?"

"When you were in the Duke's Company, were you in charge of water, or anything like that?"

"All the captains were," Dorrin said. "Dirty water makes troops sick." She thought back, trying to remember if she'd ever done any-thing, however minor, to indicate any power over water. Nothing came to mind. "I do not remember that I knew more, or was more careful, than the other captains. Besides, at that time my magery had been blocked by the Knight-Commander of Falk."

"And was your cohort healthier than the others?"

"No less healthy, I would say," Dorrin said. "Duke Phelan—King Kieri—was strict about cleanliness, and ours was healthier than most mercenary companies." Then she laughed. "One thing, though—I like to swim. Arcolin can swim but does not much like it, and Cracolnya cannot." She glanced from one to the other and then went on. "I do not think the answer to our puzzle lies in my past. It lies in these—" She touched the regalia.

That night, Dorrin dreamed of water . . . waves rising up, so clear she could see the fish swimming in them, stretching into the distance. She could smell the wet sand and rocks, feel wavelets lap-ping at her feet . . . and in that dream she walked out into the water until the waves lifted her feet from the sand below. She rode the waves the way a fallen leaf rides the current of a stream. She rose from the water in a fog, looking down on a land with streams and rivers that ran into a blue sea . . . and fell from the cloud as rain, to wake with rain spattering the windows of Verrakai House.

She listened to the rain and thought about the regalia. When she'd put the regalia back into the chest, the chest's lid and body grew together again as soon as she took her hand from it. Whatever mind inhabited the regalia, it was determined to protect itself from anyone but her. Thieves could not steal it. Could another magelord? If Alured the Black had mage powers, would he be able to open the chest? Would the necklace function like a key?

The next day, a courier rode in from the south. Dorrin paid little attention; she had conferences scheduled with her bankers and several men of business. In late afternoon, she returned to Verrakai House to find that the courier had dropped off a letter from Arcolin, and the king wanted another private conference after dinner. He would, his message said, send an escort.

Arcolin's letter occupied her for the next turn of the glass; she accepted the cup of sib Beclan brought her but did not speak until she had finished it. When she put it down, her squires were all three back in the house.

"I thought you were staying overnight with your family," she said to Daryan.

"Lady Mahieran is there with the two—with Beclan's sisters," Daryan said. "The girls backed me into a passage and wanted to know all about him. I didn't know what I could say, so I said I had to leave."

"How are they?" Beclan asked.

Daryan looked at Dorrin.

"Of course you can tell him," Dorrin said. "It's not a state secret. You can't pass messages—especially not notes—but you can tell Beclan how his sisters looked, and you can tell his sisters how Beclan is doing. Which is very well," she said with a glance at Beclan.

"I do miss them," he said. "Especially Vili. She's a pest, but—but she's sweet."

"You would not think her sweet if you saw her and *my* sister together," Daryan said. "My mother said they'd been a trial all the afternoon. Is that your aunt, Maris Verrakai, who was with them?"

"Great-aunt. The family bitter apple. She's a widow; her husband died in one of the old wars. But my father said she was sharp-tongued before that." Beclan turned to Dorrin. "My lord, supper is ready. Would you rather we brought you a tray?"

She shook her head. "No, I'll eat in the kitchen. I'm ready now."

As they ate, she thought whether to tell them of the threats Arcolin had mentioned. Beclan would need to know, as her heir. The others— their fathers would know soon enough.

"I'm meeting with the king after dinner," she said. "I'm sure it's about what Count Arcolin wrote, threats from the south. But as usual, squires, this is not to be talked of anywhere else—though if your fathers mention it, you may tell them what I'm telling you. Clear?"

"Yes, my lord," they all said.

"You have probably heard about the necklace stolen from Fin Panir—"

"Yes—and it wasn't taken by that thief the Marshal-General invited—"

"Correct, Gwenno," Dorrin said. "In fact, the Marshal-General sent him to find the thief and get it back, if he could. He followed the trail to Aarenis, where the local Guild captured him and nearly killed him. Arcolin believes the necklace is in the hands of the man I knew as Alured the Black." She finished the cutlet on her plate before going on. "He's the one I think may try to invade the north if he can gain control of the Guild League cities. He's using counterfeiting to disable their economic organization."

From their blank looks, she realized they had no idea what that meant. She had expected them—all from wealthy families—to know more about money. She pulled three silver pieces from her belt pouch. "What do you think these are worth?" she asked.

Beclan answered in terms of the fraction of a gold crown, Gwenno in terms of how much bread a silver would buy in the market. Daryan answered last. "It's supposed to have a certain amount of silver— weigh a certain amount, but I don't know how much."

"You're all correct," Dorrin said. "And you're all incomplete. I'm supposed to meet with the king again this evening; I don't have time to explain now. But as you'll all be part of Tsaia's rulers someday, you must learn about both true and counterfeit money." Dorrin finished her supper quickly.

As she pushed back from the table, Daryan said, "Which of us do you want as escort tonight?"

"The king's sending an escort," Dorrin said. "I suspect he'd rather not have you roaming about the palace waiting for me."

"Could we go for a walk in the city?" Daryan asked.

"No," Dorrin said. "A night here will do you no harm, and Be-clan's had to be on guard these days you and Gwenno were home with your families. It's Beclan's choice whether he wants to sleep early or stay up and talk with you. Daryan, you're on until the turn of night, and Gwenno, you'll have the late watch. And before you ask, I don't yet know what day we're leaving. It depends on the king's wishes."

They nodded. Beclan, who had been up the previous night, yawned and said he'd like to sleep.

ow urgent do you think the danger is?" the king asked Dorrin. "This man has the necklace, and he's undermining the Guild League agreements. And there's this secret passage to the north. Count Arcolin thinks he may have captured one city—" He glanced at the scroll. "—Lûn, already, by spreading fever."

"Lûn and Immervale have outbreaks of fever every year," Dorrin said, remembering that part of Aarenis all too well. "Low, sometimes marshy land. But to hear that Sobanai Company's disbanded—that's serious. They were allies in Siniava's War; if they were Lûn's troops, then Lûn will certainly fall. If Vaskronin spread fever—or another disease—and it killed enough, he could take Lûn and Immervale both. This seems what Arcolin's suggesting. Do you have maps of Aarenis?"

"Somewhere," the king said. "I don't know how accurate they are."

Dorrin repressed a sigh. She wanted—they needed—the accu-rate, annotated maps Kieri Phelan had used. They belonged to Arco-lin now. "Sir king, your librarian must find them—I can look at them and add what information I remember. Arcolin has good maps; ask him to have a current one copied and sent to you. The point is that there are two routes from eastern to western Aarenis." She began to trace them out on the table. "The southern route, along the west-leading branch, is the main trade route and a Guild League road that will take heavy traffic in any weather: stone-flagged, drains to either side. The northern route is not as traveled nor as well built. It connects the east coast, then Sorkill on the west of the Copper Hills, and on through Merinath to Sorellin and Ambela. Most trade turns south from Ambela to Pler Vonja, but there's a usable track along the foothills all the way west to Valdaire."

The others stared at the tabletop as if trying to make it a map. "So—you are saying Vaskronin could move west by either route?"

"Exactly. Or both, if he has enough troops. If he has Lûn and Immervale, he can ignore the eastern branch of the Immer, take Koury, and then strike Sorellin or Ambela, cutting off any reinforcements from the east—if any are left—to command the north road. Once past Ambela and on the lesser-used track, no cities impede him and he could bypass opposition. Up the main trade road, he needs to take Cortes Cilwan—" She paused. The Count of Cilwan was still Andressat's ward, his father having been killed in Siniava's War and his elder sister married to one of Andressat's sons, who had taken over as regent. How solid was his support in the city?

"Then surely he will take the northern route," High Marshal Seklis said. "It is much to his advantage."

"What about supply?" the king asked.

Dorrin nodded. "Yes. If he moves on the northern track, he must take all his supplies with him; the foothill farms aren't rich, though he can eat mutton until it comes out his nose. If he takes Cilwan and Vonja, he will have food, arms, treasure in plenty."

"Which do you think he'll do?"

"I don't know. He is clever; he learned from us that last year in Siniava's War. He will try for surprise, and he will do something we do not expect. Without knowing his resources—how many troops he has, what supplies he has stocked—and whatever powers of magery he has, with or without the necklace, I cannot hazard a guess. That Pargunese commander used Achrya's powers to ensorcel his troops and push them past what men will do on their own. If Vaskronin has that ability, he could do more with a smaller army."

"Arcolin promises us frequent reports," the king said. "As soon as he hears anything—"

"You can be sure he will do his best," Dorrin said. "If it please you, sir king, let us go to the library and see what maps you have—

I have none—and I will share all I know of the lands of Aarenis as it was when I last saw it."

"I met the Count of Andressat," the king said. "He did warn us."

"And he is a staunch friend," Dorrin said. "But his land does not lie on either of those roads. He will do well if he can defend his own land."

The royal library's maps of Aarenis were as old and faulty as Dorrin had feared, but she was able to show the others where the roads were and make clear the dangers ahead.

CHAPTER TWENTY-NINE

Fossnir Outbounds, Aarenis

Three hands of days after Midsummer, Arcolin was leading his cohort alongside the Guild Road—a patrol that had proven very successful in deterring not only bands of robbers, but quarrels among caravans at this busy season—when he was hailed by a caravan master.

"You're the new Duke's Company commander, aren't you?" the man said when Arcolin rode closer. "I remember that horse from last year—when those foot travelers were attacked."

"That's right," Arcolin said.

"Have you heard one of old Andressat's sons is missing?"

"No. When? Which one?"

"Whichever one had their eastern fort. He was due at Cortes Cilwan for Midsummer Feast—visiting his sister or some such—and never arrived. Gossip along the road is he'd been riding out alone in Vonja and Cilwan lands, to and from Cortes Cilwan. Andressat patrols haven't found him yet. There was a courier left Cortes Cilwan Midsummer night for Valdaire, they say, looking for word of him along the road." The man hawked and spat. "What's your contract this year, may I ask?"

"Foss Council, Guild League security. Road patrols and other duties."

"Good to know," the man said. "We had a bit of bother coming across Vonja. Do you know if that bad place in the Valdaire outbounds is clear?"

"So I hear from Valdaire's patrols," Arcolin said. "I haven't been by there since we marched here." He turned his mount and rode back to his cohort.

Arcolin remembered what Burek had told him about Andressat's sons. Was this the difficult one who had disappeared? Had he defected to Alured? Not a topic to discuss here by the road.

The rest of the day's patrol passed without anything but the usual—the cohort intervened in a stoppage when one trader's third wagon dropped a wheel and others tried to swerve around it. Teamsters yelled at one another about precedence, traffic stacked up behind . . . until the hundred and three armed men, plus two very determined captains, got everyone back in line and moving again—albeit more slowly. Burek had a tensquad unload the wagon and guard its contents while the trader's own people mounted the spare wheel Guild League law required each trader to carry. Arcolin ordered all pedestrians and riders to the side paths and then alternated the traffic flow—two northbound, two southbound. He sent another tensquad back down the road in each direction to slow oncoming traffic and tell them to maintain their intervals and a courier to Fossnir. Anyone whose vehicle broke down on the road was assumed to be overloaded or lacking maintenance and due a fine; Fossnir would send out an official to assess it.

In camp that evening, Arcolin told Burek what he'd heard.

"That would be Filis," Burek said. "The one who was angry about the Count offering me the family name."

"Angry enough to turn traitor to his family?"

"I don't know," Burek said. "They told me he was the family hothead, but hothead doesn't mean cold heart. And if it's true that he was riding alone back and forth to Cortes Cilwan, it's just as likely that Alured's agents captured him."

"But he's bound to know important family secrets."

"Yes. And Alured would want them. We can hope he's just lying out somewhere with a broken leg, unable to get to help, and they find him quickly."

"Dead would be better than Alured's captive," Arcolin said, remembering what he'd seen in the Immer port cities after Siniava's defeat. Burek stared at him. "I am serious," Arcolin said. "I know what he does to prisoners."

CHAPTER THIRTY

Lyonya

As time passed and no more obvious dangers threatened, Kieri decided to visit Tolmaric's domain and see for himself how the work on the roads and the port was progressing. Arian stayed behind, for the summer heat tired her more than usual, though her pregnancy scarcely showed. "But are you well enough I can leave?" Kieri asked.

"I am well," she said. "It is, I'm informed by every Sier's wife in Chaya and your uncle Amrothlin, a predictable effect of half-elven pregnancy at this stage, and I am advised to be very glad it is so early, and to eat the proper foods. Though not all agree on what those are." She laughed then. "Go, and do not worry."

"I cannot help worrying, but couriers will keep the dust in the air between us. Do not fail to send word daily."

"Of course," Arian said.

Kieri rode off with his Squires. How different from the previous summer, when he had been beset with visiting princesses and their difficult guardians and had sensed impending war. Now every ten-day, Torfinn of Pargun sent a message reporting on the progress of rebuilding or offering advice on the design of a "proper port." Torfinn wrote as he spoke, and even in writing had a tongue like a rasp, but all that old animosity had burned away. And the king of Kostandan seemed downright friendly, crediting Kieri with Ganlin's chance of marrying royalty in Tsaia.

But the Lady's death made a difference, though not in Kieri's sense of the taig. While she was alive, the elves—when not absent with her—seemed full of purpose, vividly alive. Now, when he saw elves at all, they seemed uncertain, vague, and almost too cooperative. No elves had come to the Midsummer ceremonies.

Still, they had not left the kingdom, and that was to his credit. He had asked their advice on the road west toward Dorrin's domain—which trees might be cut, which must be left—and they had answered sensibly enough. They had been alarmed at the thought of a river port, but mollified somewhat by his intention to use the scathe-fire tracks as the road to it.

"'Tis a pity, in that case, the scathefire did not burn along the river from Riverwash to where you want the port," one said. He was younger, Kieri had been told, scarcely five hundreds old. The others were horrified, he could tell.

He shook those thoughts from his mind. Today, riding down the scathefire track with fresh green showing at its margins, he need not deal with elves. Today was for today's problems.

Not far ahead, he saw Lady Tolmaric waiting for him beside the road at a new clearing in the forest. Here on her own land, with the time between to get past the worst horrors of Sier Tolmaric's death, Lady Tolmaric seemed like any solid, competent countrywoman. Now she smiled at him less shyly than before.

"We have something to show you, sir king," she said.

"I can see already you have made progress," he said, looking around the clearing. He followed her down a lane, expecting to see a farmstead under construction—perhaps even a barn and house completed. Instead, he saw a building as large as a barn but laid out very differently. Stone below, timber above, it looked like . . . like an inn. Stone steps up to the entrance with a wider door than any farmhouse. Windows to either side. The width, he judged, would allow for a sizable downstairs common room and kitchen. Several chimneys poked out of the tall roof; a streamer of pale smoke drifted from one. A wall of upright timbers to either side, with a gate to the right. The farmer and his family stood before it, bowing.

"We are partway from Chaya to the new port," Lady Tolmaric said. "I thought—I thought travelers would want somewhere to stop on the way. Some, anyway. It isn't finished . . ." She looked at him again, clearly worried that he might disapprove. "And right now, Jermys's cows are in what will be the stableyard . . ."

"It's—it's remarkable," Kieri said. Most remarkable that she had thought of it and had gained confidence to do it without asking permission. "You're absolutely right: when the ships come, and merchants are busy on this road, they will need a place to stop overnight. An excellent idea."

"Then . . . would the king consider . . . staying here this night instead of at the old place? No one has slept inside yet, and it would be an honor . . ." She bowed; the farmer and his family all bowed.

"Of course I will," Kieri said. "But you must also come inside and rest there as well. How did you manage to clear the land and build all this in so short a time?"

"I brought both families here," Lady Tolmaric said, following Kieri into the building. The flush of embarrassment faded from her face, and her voice steadied. "They had been neighbors before; they did not mind settling together."

"So . . . this will be the common room," Kieri said, looking at the large room. It was bare, just a big empty space, but well lit with its large windows. Doors opened from it—one, no doubt, to the kitchen; something there smelled delicious.

"Yes, sir king," Lady Tolmaric said. "The kitchen is in use already . . . the two families together number three full hands. The rest of the furniture will be made by the time there's traffic on the road. Will you come upstairs to see the chamber we prepared for you?"

"Gladly," Kieri said. He wondered who had designed this building. He had not suspected Lady Tolmaric of such talent—nor the Tolmaric farmers, either.

"You may remember," Lady Tolmaric said, "that while we were in Chaya, before . . . before my husband died, we were living in a house we rented. But my husband bade me visit several inns, just to see how they were made. He had already thought of building an inn along the road in case of travelers, if you granted him the right to take new forest land. 'See what they've got,' he told me. 'Especially the kitchen and suchlike, and the stabling, too.' So I did." She was breathless, climbing the stairs. "And then we built it."

The stairs were broad, well pitched; the rooms on the first floor above opened off a passage that ran the depth of the building, where another stair led upward. Most doors were open, the rooms bare as the common room below. The room she led Kieri to was at the back, with windows open to the yard below. It had a well-made bed with an obviously new-woven blanket and pillows, a table, several chairs, rows of pegs on one wall, and a cabinet with doors and drawers both on the other. It smelled of herbs and beeswax. On the table was a somewhat battered tray with a pitcher and three mugs and a vase with a bouquet of wildflowers.

"It's lovely," Kieri said. "What a pleasant place! I will rest well here, Lady Tolmaric. Thank you."

She flushed again. "There's plenty of room for your Squires and all . . . but we only have the one bed made up."

"That's fine. This is so much better than what we expected to sleep in." He moved to the window and looked out. The yard was a long rectangle, amply wide enough for wagons to enter and turn around. At present, posts marked out what would eventually be all the accouterments of a successful inn: the smithy, the stable, storage for fodder, and so on. Already stone walls supported a bracken thatch in one corner, where a gate led out the far end.

"Cow byre," Lady Tolmaric said, pointing. "Smith's still working outside, but we'll have a roof on by winter. Set all the posts now—they're mostly set—and we can enclose more of the outbuildings."

"You need a mill," Kieri said. "Both for grain and for lumber. Is there a swift stream nearby?"

"Yes, sir king. And we've a plan but no time yet to build it."

"I don't think you need my advice, but I'd make the mill next after you get a roof—even a simple one—on those outbuildings."

"We want to, sir king, but right now they're building mills near the port. I couldn't find someone who knew how to set up the mill to turn a stone or move a saw."

"Perhaps I can help with that," Kieri said. "Do you have a name for your inn yet?"

She flushed again, and tears rose in her eyes. "I wanted to name it for Salvon, but it didn't sound right: Salvon's Inn. Travelers won't know who he is."

"Your innkeeper could tell them," Kieri said. "But why not Salvon's Hope? He wanted to build an inn, didn't he?"

"Yes . . . yes, that's right. Thank you, sir king!"

At the next meal, Kieri met the whole group of them—Lady Tolmaric, the eldest Tolmaric son and daughter, the two farm families. The kitchen was big enough to cook for a small army; they ate around the worktables, silently at first and then talking more freely as they became used to Kieri and his Squires. Only Lady Tolmaric and her daughter had been as far from home as a river town; her account of city life was the only one they knew. Kieri told them of Vérella and Valdaire and Fin Panir—legends to them.

"This will seem a poor place, then," Lady Tolmaric said, waving her hand at the room.

"Not at all," Kieri said. "It's going to be a very successful inn, I'm sure, and you will make improvements as you have time and income. Your plan is excellent; right now you lack materials and workers to do more than the good start you've given it."

"We're thinkin' we can provision it from the farm, sir king," said one of the men.

"You probably can," Kieri said.

"How many people will we need to run the inn?" Lady Tolmaric asked. "The inns in Chaya were so full, they said they had extra staff, and they didn't really have time to talk to me."

"Minimum," Kieri said, thinking of the little inn far away in Duke's East, "you need cooking staff: a good cook and at least two helpers. You need common room staff—if it's not busy, cook's helpers can serve customers food there, but if it gets busy, you'll need some just for that. Someone at the bar—you'll have drunks to deal with, so that one must be strong and steady. You'll need a guard or two, as well, once you start filling up. Upstairs—someone to clean the rooms, light fires in those rooms with fireplaces. Someone to wash linens.

Stable staff to care for your animals and those of travelers and keep them from stealing all the fodder."

"They would?" Lady Tolmaric asked.

"They do," Kieri said. "Most travelers are honest enough, but every inn attracts thieves as well. They'll make off with whatever they can carry, and without paying if they can. Collect the money first, and guard it closely. Make sure the blankets are still on the beds, the mugs—" He gestured at the table. "—still in the rooms. Better yet, let them use their own in the rooms or come down to eat and drink. Travelers often carry their own."

"We don't want thieves and such," one of the men said.

"Of course not, but you can't have an inn and not have some of them. Be firm and fair from the very first and you'll have less trouble." He fished in his belt pouch and laid a gold coin on the table. "Even the king should pay his way: I will set the example. You have stated no price, but this would cover the room and board for me and my Squires and our horses overnight. Will that suit?"

"You mustn't," Lady Tolmaric said, going red and teary-eyed again. "You've done so much—"

"The inn must pay its way," Kieri said. "Let it start now, with the king's gold Tree." He smiled at them all. "I am pleased with all of you for your initiative and your work; I want this inn to succeed. So I will pay, and you will allow it."

Mutters of "Yes, sir king" and "As the king wills" went around the table. Two fat tears ran down Lady Tolmaric's red cheeks; she wiped them away with her sleeve and nodded. "I cannot thank you enough—"

"Except by thriving," Kieri said.

He slept well that night, and the next day they rode on, taking Lady Tolmaric with them, to see what progress had been made at the port.

It looked, in fact, like a huge muddy mess. A great swathe of forest cut down, a broad ditch of muddy water leading out to the river, and rows of tree trunks sticking out of the muck that remained.

"But those aren't trees," a foreman explained to Kieri. He was a Pargunese Kieri had hired with Torfinn's help, a man who had helped maintain the Pargunese port and sailed around to Aarenis on Pargunese ships. He spoke Common with a strong accent but was understandable. "They're sections of tree, pounded in as deep as we can make 'em. That's to put the buildings above the spring floods. Might be better if we had stones enough, but we don't. Wood quays will do for now. Had to make it wide enough for ships to pass, and we'd really like a turning basin—but if we want any kind of port by next trade season, that'll have to wait."

"How's the port over on your side?" Kieri asked.

"They're working on it." The man spat into the mud. "Fire didn't hurt the structure itself but took ships and buildings. We had stone, y' see." He looked out at the construction site. "Two ports won't hurt trade at all, my lord. It doesn't at the Immer mouth, does it? More room for ships, more ships come. We don't have the ships now, so it'll be waiting for others to come to us."

"Are you also a shipwright?"

"No. I've a straight eye, not one for wave-shapes." He looked around. "This won't look such a mess by freeze-up, sir king. And come spring break-up, you'll have a place for ships."

When he left the port site, Kieri traveled on to the Honnorgat and then up it, along the rough track that ran from river village to river village. Riverwash, upstream, had grown again, with trade coming in from Tsaia. It looked raw and unfinished, but the stone foundations of some buildings had survived the scathefire, and those already bore new structures atop. Here he intercepted a Royal Courier from Tsaia with a letter from Arcolin and another from the Marshal-General, as well as a long one from Mikeli.

Arcolin's letter was much as he'd expected: Alured the Black almost certainly had the missing necklace and was believed to have captured one of Andressat's sons. Unrest was growing in the south, and Arcolin thought a move might be made along the north road.

The Marshal-General's came as a surprise. Elves in Fin Panir? Demanding that enchanted magelords in the far west be removed? He recalled something about them, but not any details. The appearance of magery in the peasantry was not as surprising. He had half expected news of this sort since Beclan had shown magery. The Marshal-

General had convened a special council to discuss this—well, that made sense.

Mikeli revealed that his brother was now showing magery—he had waited to tell his neighbor king only, he said, because he had awaited the Marshal-General's ruling on it—but he had not yet told his Council. He wrote at length about the steps he'd taken to keep Camwyn's magery secret and why, and without actually asking for advice, he hinted that he would be glad of it.

Kieri determined to find Amrothlin and ask him about the western elves—perhaps he knew something about the magelords in their cave or whatever it was.

CHAPTER THIRTY-ONE

If that pirate could sail up the river," Arian said, "could he not march inland across Prealíth or even come over the mountains here—you said there were other passes—instead of at Valdaire? Without the Lady—without the elvenhome—who will watch the borders east and south?"

Kieri scratched his head, sweaty from an extra session in the salle. "He could indeed. I've been thinking about that, too. We need more rangers; I can take some from the north and west, since Pargun and Tsaia aren't a problem now, but not all of them."

"I've always wondered what it was like, the deep elvenhome we couldn't enter. The elves claimed it was the most beautiful, but the forest near here is beautiful."

"We should go look," Kieri said. "I don't even know where the border with Fintha is or what kind of border watch the Sea-Prince keeps. I wish I'd had more time to talk with him when he came for the wedding."

"He didn't seem eager for that," Arian said. "He left the very next day after the wedding, you recall."

"Yes, but I thought that was because his elven escort wanted to get him back through the Ladysforest." He sighed. "I just can't believe it's gone, after all the ages the elves lived there and nourished it. The taig here feels no different. We should go look, Arian. I want to preserve as much as possible, and I can't do that if I don't know what it is."

"I agree," she said. "But we can't both leave; if trouble comes to Tsaia, one of us must be here. You should go; I had my long trip earlier, and I'd just as soon stay here." She set her hands over the bulge of her pregnancy, now clear to see.

T he transition from the forest open to humans to the formerly closed Ladysforest was immediately obvious as Kieri crossed that line. Though Kieri had thought the Lyonyan forest astonishing when he first saw it, the Ladysforest, even without the Lady, had a magical quality. The taig here had additional layers of complexity, a rich confidence, that he had not felt before.

As he rode on, the enchantment grew. Here was beauty such as he had never imagined let alone seen. Nothing at all like the clipped and tended gardens of men . . . no obvious design . . . except that everywhere he looked the forest seemed both completely natural and artfully designed, every detail perfect. The trees rose around him, boles as heavy as the inner ring of the King's Grove but even taller. Sunlight pierced the canopy in flickering shafts, each picking out a detail: a leaf here, a flower there, a tiny perfect mushroom growing from the bole of a great tree, a frond of fern poised gracefully at the verge of a tiny waterfall. He felt the immensity of its age and the freshness of each leaf and flower. Everything made a pattern . . . patterns in patterns, and all the patterns made beauty. Yet he saw no sign of artifice. Nothing needed trimming; there was never too much of this or too little of that.

It came to him that this had been achieved not by the tools of men, by steel or stone . . . but by song alone. This was the work of the Sinyi, their proper work. Every living thing here throve, fully healthy; every living thing achieved its full beauty. Surely this was still the elvenhome as it had been. He wondered why the elves didn't recognize it.

Ahead, through the trees, he could see more light and rode toward it, noticing as he did how the trees formed a colonnade and framed a view as he came near enough to see it. A glade, open to the sky, spangled with flowers, the air alive with wings—butterflies, orange and red and gold and white. In the center, a small pool reflected the sky, fed—he saw as he neared it—by a spring below. A single flowering tree arched over it, fragrant white blossoms glowing in the sun. One petal, then another drifted down to the water and sailed slowly across and then along the rivulet that ran out the other side.

Kieri's throat felt tight. The beauty was overwhelming, as the Lady's had been when he first saw her. Beyond mortal . . . and yet surely the trees died, and the ferns . . . or had the elves sung them into immortality? He did not know . . . He felt he wanted to breathe in forever, taking the beauty into himself, and then exhale a song to sustain it.

He rode on across the glade and into the forest again . . . the forest ever changing with the rise and fall of the ground, the different trees, the variation in the lower growth. He came upon streams gurgling gently over gravel or rushing loudly down rapids. Sorrow came upon him after a time, that his mother and grandmother were not there so he could thank them for this beauty.

When the light faded, he stopped; his Squires, respecting his mood, made their simple camp in silence. When they would have lit a fire, he shook his head. They ate cold rations. He dreaded the need to dig . . . but found that the ground opened a little of itself to receive their waste and then closed over again. He wondered at that—if the elvenhome was truly gone, how could that happen?

They were several days into the journey when he stopped suddenly. His throat closed; his sight dimmed; pain tightened his chest. He struggled to see past the darkness . . . The way here descended gently through trees more widely spaced. Ahead was another glade. He dragged a breath in, and as his sight cleared, he knew.

"It was here," he said aloud, startling himself with his voice.

"Sir king?"

He could not answer. He could not move. Memory rushed over him, powerful as a river. As if in a dream, he was that child again, delighted in the beauty they rode through, unaware of danger—until his mother cried out. He had turned in the saddle to look at her—she had snatched him from his mount to hers. That instant's delay in drawing her sword . . . his adult self saw what his child self could not, that he had hindered her even after she dragged him over the saddle bow.

But she had drawn her sword—only the attackers were many. As a child, he had not seen them all before he was yanked away, before he fell . . . He did not remember striking his head, but he remembered the waking. Rough hands, harsh voices, cords binding him, too tight.

He had never thought to be here again, in this dire place—he looked again at the peaceful trees, the empty dell with the little outcrop of rock to one side, as beautiful as the rest, except for his memories. He knew tears were running down his face.

"Sir king—is there aught—"

"It happened here," he was able to say after a few moments. "We were riding, just down there. They rose up from the ground, men in dull clothes. She cried out—I did not know why. She grabbed me from my mount, but that hindered her—"

"Sir king—" Their faces around him now were as strained as those he remembered, but not in cruelty or anger. He saw love and compassion instead, mingled with amazement that he remembered.

"I must . . . stop here awhile," he said. He dismounted. His knees nearly failed him, but he stiffened his legs and managed to walk down the gentle slope. Walking helped: he was not a terrified child on a horse now. He was aware of the Squires behind him, but he ignored them; they did not press closer, leaving him space. His memory called up details he had long forgotten—the sound of his mother's breathing, her horse's squeals as swords struck, the smell of her blood as she took wound after wound. He had been facedown over her saddle bow, clinging with his hands to the horse's harness, unable to help. He could not have helped by being upright; he knew that, but . . .

It was as if he could see the course of the fight still marked on the ground. Here exactly she had cried out and snatched at him, tried to wheel her mount away . . . but more had risen from concealment, hemming the horse in, grabbing its reins, striking at it, finally slicing deep into its legs, crippling it. He had a last remembered glimpse of her—a memory that had lain deep-buried all these years—her face turning to him as he fell and then . . . nothing.

Mother . . . I lived. I am here. She had been full elf; he could not hope that in some afterlife she knew that. Elves died, when they died, without any spirit to survive. But he said it again anyway, this time aloud. "Mother, I lived. In spite of all. And I am trying to be what you and my father wanted, a good king for all in this realm."

He heard nothing, felt nothing, but when his tears ceased, he felt easier. He still did not know who had plotted against his mother and against him, but he was alive. He breathed in the fragrance of the violets that now carpeted the ground, rose from his knees to walk the circuit of the glade, touching trees, rocks, bending to touch the violets.

"We will camp here tonight," he said.

"Here?" asked Berne. "Is this not a cursed place?"

"No," Kieri said. "These trees, these flowers, even these rocks had no part in the evil done here. I know elves make no memorials to their dead, but I am only half-elf, and I would make one for my mother. Pitch the tent up there—" He pointed back up the slope. Unbidden, a wisp of melody came to mind, and he found himself humming it as he walked across the glade to the rock outcrop. He picked a few violets and laid them there.

After a few moments, the silence deepened; he felt enclosed in a space apart, though when he glanced back, he could see his Squires setting up camp. Was this leftover elven enchantment . . . or something else?

He waited, resting in that bubble of silence, of peace, until it slowly faded. Whatever it had been, he felt it was proof that the glade was not cursed, that he was right to be here.

Nothing disturbed them that night. Kieri woke a little before dawn, as usual, and as the first rays of sun filtered into the glade, he saw what he first thought was a vision. Where only violets had been the day before, a royal purple carpet, now a scatter of objects lay, glinting in the early light. And the rough rock on which he had laid his bouquet was now smoothed and shaped into the very shape he'd thought of having carved. The violets he had placed, still unwilted, lay on a polished shelf under an arch.

He walked over to the objects. He'd thought any jewels had been stripped from his mother's body, but here lay a ring and a twist of ruddy gold. He'd been told her body had been laid straight in the way of elves; nothing had been said of these things the earth had now returned to him, baubles less precious than herself.

Or you. Kieri shivered. It was his own mind, he was sure . . . and yet he had heard the voices of the bones, of his father and sister and the others. He picked up the ring, the gold torc he now recalled his mother wearing around her neck, the enameled fitting with the leaping hound and stag entwined that he recalled from her belt. They were all bright and clean as if they had just come from a jewel case. A little enameled box that rattled softly as he picked it up . . . His fingers found the catch easily, and there were the tiles he remembered, blue and green and red, with the runes on them in gold and silver. It had been a selani set, a game he had just been learning . . . and what had he been told about it? A game we play? He'd not seen it anywhere since. He'd played with the tiles, stacking them, arranging them in patterns, and then his mother had put them back in the box and said, "Your grandmother will teach you." Teach him what? Was it an elven game?

He looked at the tiles more closely, sighed, and poured them back into the box, latching it again. Selani . . . how could he have forgotten that name? But in the years of slavery, he hadn't known his own name for a long time.

What should he do with these things? Did they belong here or . . . *Not here.* He shivered again. It must be Falk . . . he touched his ruby and murmured a prayer. When he had gathered all that lay in the grass, he took them back to the camp and showed his Squires.

"I didn't see those yesterday," Berne said.

"Nor I," Kieri said. "They were here when the sun came . . . and did you see the rock?"

They looked at the rock, then at him. "Did you carve that last night, sir king?"

"No. Yestereve, I thought of having it carved, exactly like that— a marker of my mother's death, a place to remember her—but I'm not a stonecarver. I could not have done it."

"Save by magery," Berne said.

"I'm not rockfolk," Kieri said. "And elves have no power over stone, do they? Even the Lady had rockfolk carve out her underground stronghold. Besides, I would know if I were doing magery; I would feel the power leave me. I felt nothing; I slept the night."

"What's in this?" asked Panin, another of the Squires, pointing to the box.

"Selani tiles," Kieri said. "Do you know that game?"

"Selani? I don't know the word."

"They were my mother's—she was starting to teach me to play the game. You don't know it?"

"I never heard of it. How do you play it?"

"I don't know . . . I hadn't learned yet. I do remember she said my grandmother would teach me. Perhaps it is an elven game." He opened the box and showed them the tiles. "I don't know what these symbols are, either."

"That one's truth," Linne said, one of the half-elf Squires.

"Truth?"

"Yes . . . and look, this one here. This is untruth." She flicked the tiles around. "Honor . . . dishonor. Reward . . . disgrace . . . danger . . ."

"And this was a game?" asked Panin.

"So I was told," Kieri said. He could not now remember anything of the game. He had liked the colors, he did recall, and the glitter of the silver and gold. "What kind of game . . . ?" He picked up the tile marked with "Truth" and ran his finger over the rune.

"Would it be like dice?" one asked. "Shake them in the box and pour them out? Toss them?"

"We could see," Berne said. "Sir king?"

"I am not sure." Kieri picked up Untruth and held the two in one hand. What question could such answer? He shook them in his hand, and thought, *This was the place,* and released them.

On the cloth Truth lay upright; Untruth had landed blank side up. Both were red; both had gold runes. It could be chance, after all. But the chill that ran down his back suggested something more than chance.

"I heard once," one of the new Squires, Ceilar, said, "that the elves had ways of telling what would come and of divining the inner aims of other elves. These might be such, might they not?"

A game, his mother had said. But was it? Adults might say that to a child when the truth was more complicated, even dangerous. He picked up Untruth again and looked more closely. Was that gold, or . . . he picked up Truth again . . . no. Not gold, but fool's gold. He shivered . . . this, like all the rest, had come to him for a reason, a reason that had survived his mother's death, and by a power he did not know or understand.

"The gods may reveal it," Kieri said. He was not sure which of the gods. His mother had been full elf, so her god would have been the Singer, for whom the only name he knew was Adyan, Namer. He touched his ruby again. Falk had a name for truth and mercy, for keeping oaths and releasing prisoners. Here, in this place, he had to wonder if Falk had had anything to do with releasing him . . . and why, if so, Falk had let him suffer so long. The old sorrow rose again, though this time he could breathe through it. Here, in this place, he had changed from the child he had been and started on the road to the man he now was. None of this had been his choice, but since then he had made many choices, and they had led back here, to the place of no-choice.

"Is there a tile with a rune for choice?" he asked, looking back down at the dell below with its carpet of violets.

He heard the gentle clatter of the tiles as Linne turned them all. "Yes, sir king. One for choice, and one for coercion. That one can also be read 'necessity.'"

"I am not surprised," he said. He took a breath and let it out slowly, reaching for calm. "You know what happened here, but . . . you may not know all that grew from this seed."

"We were robbed of our queen, your mother, and you . . . the heir," Panin said. "And you suffered . . ."

"Yes. And as you would expect, that changed me—would have changed any child. But what I see now is a pattern. It started here, for me, though for my mother perhaps it must have started somewhere else, some other time—this was her pattern's end. I had no choice then, or for years after, being young and unable to choose anything— my master chose for me, chose pain and humiliation. When I was freed . . . the only choice I had was to take the chance or not take it. And I took it. But I did not feel it as a choice . . . I felt it as inevitable. I long thought that the man who saved me had laid a geas on me . . .

that it was his will that I escape, more even than my own desire to flee."

"And was it?"

"I do not know. I do not know if it matters. But the choices I made later mattered. I am not the man my father wanted—though his bones are satisfied, they tell me now. I am not the man my mother hoped for, to whom she had given—" He stopped abruptly. He had told no one what Amrothlin had told him, that his mother had transferred her power to create an elfane taig to him. "To whom she had given her elven heritage," he said. "I am the man my choices made me. And here is where I learned that choices could be unmade. Here, in what should have been a safe place for her and for me."

"What of the robbers?" Jostin asked.

"Dead men were found here, weren't they?" Kieri asked. "I remember being told that. Robbers, they said. What did those who found them do with the bodies?"

"I don't know . . . Would they have buried them? Burned them?"

"And risk harm to the land? And ugliness?" He looked again at the scene . . . the violets, the stone now a graceful little shrine with its offering of flowers. "I think they would have taken the bodies away, somewhere beyond the bounds of the elvenhome."

"If they didn't find the . . . your body, sir king, why didn't they search for you?"

"I have heard two tales—one that they did but did not find me because they did not cross the sea, and one that they assumed I was dead and the body simply not found, scattered by animals, perhaps." He shook his head. "It doesn't matter now. What matters is . . . coming here, these things that rose to meet me, and that stone. It is meant to complete something, this pattern, and to begin another pattern. Each of these things means something, not merely the tiles of the game—if it was a game, and not my child's misunderstanding." He turned to the other objects: the ring, the torc, the fitting for the belt. "I think I am meant to learn why these were given me and to consider my choices, past and future. And to do it here."

"How long, sir king?," Panin asked. "We will need provisions if we stay long."

"I do not know," Kieri said. He sighed. "Until it is done. I have had little leisure in my life to stay in one place and think. I trust it will not be too long, for I would not want to worry the queen and my Council. Only two of you need stay with me. The others—Berne and Varne, continue to the east and let the Sea-Prince know of the changes since he left. He met you both at the wedding. Jostin and Ceilar, return to Chaya and tell the queen of what I found. Send back two other Squires with provisions enough to reach Prealíth—we will need a courier service to and from the Sea-Prince if he agrees, the sooner the better. If I do not return betimes, start back here with more provisions. I will write the letters now."

He saw protest in their expressions, but they left him to write the letters and set to dividing provisions and other supplies. The Sea-Prince—he hardly knew the man and nothing of his attitude toward elves, though he had been escorted through this forest by them. By the same way? Perhaps, or perhaps not. Perhaps wrapt in elven magery and allowed to see nothing. A land looking to the sea would value ship timber: mastwood and sparwood. Did Prealíth have forests, or was it mostly farmland or scrubland? He could not remember that from either journey.

Change has come, he wrote. *The Lady of the Ladysforest was murdered by one of the iynisin, and you and I, lord prince, must see to our borders that she long guarded.* Would the Sea-Prince even know what iynisin were? If he did, would he be insulted to have it explained? *You may know iynisin by another name: these are those who rebelled against the Singer when the First Tree sang with the first Kuakgan. Some call them kuaknomi or blackcloaks. Pray send your envoy, that we may discuss how best to accomplish what profits us both. These my envoys are King's Squires such as you met on your recent visit, and will return your messages to me, or guide your envoy, as you desire.*

To Arian he wrote of what he'd found, what had happened, and what he thought he was supposed to do—a much longer letter—and begged her to share any thoughts she had about it. He asked if she'd ever heard of the game selani, and did his best to draw the runes on all the tiles. *Ask the elders,* he concluded, *if they ever saw such things or heard my mother use the term. Especially the Seneschal.*

Then he handed the letters to the two groups of Squires and bade them take provisions for their own journeys. "I have no positive warning that the Sea-Prince would do you harm, but he remains a stranger, so stay together, rather than one return to me, unless there is great need."

They bowed. "Yes, sir king."

When the four had ridden away, the glade's silence seemed once more to close in; Kieri walked down to the little shrine and knelt there. He laid the ring on the shrine's shelf. The stone was pale green, nothing as dark and rich as emerald but like clear water in a deep pool over white stone. The design incised on its rounded top showed a fern frond, the setting heavy gold. His mother had worn it on her heart-thumb, he recalled. Now, as he watched, a flicker of light rose from within the stone. He glanced aside a moment. No ray of sun was near: this was the stone itself. Under the fern frond, another design showed, etched in light: a dragon shape, tiny but perfect in detail. Then it faded again.

His heart thundered in his ears. Was this a dragonspawn, somehow captured or about to break free in scathefire? But the ring suggested no menace. He looked at his hands. He wore his father's ring on his sword hand, a peculiar stone that flashed red-in-green. He'd been told it was the symbol of the power shared by human and elven.

He picked up the ring, kissed it, and slid it onto his heart-hand thumb; it fit as if made for him. The light returned again; the tiny dragon seemed to writhe, his hand and arm tingled, and then the stone showed clear pale green again and the sensation vanished.

When he put the gold torc on the shrine, the twisted strands brightened, then slowly untwisted to show something gleaming between them . . . the strand on which they were wound. White, glowing like polished ivory, itself twisted . . . he reached out, and the gold tightened, closing over it again. He laid his hand on it. He felt it was something magical, but he had never seen anything like it. No vision or word came to him, but the conviction that he should wear it. He ran his hand over the thing . . . His mother's neck, as he remembered it, was smaller than his own. But when he set it about his, it also fit precisely, comfortable . . . even comforting.

Well. The belt clasp next. The bright enamel shone as if lit from within, which did not by this time surprise him. Tiny letters appeared like those on his father's and sisters' bones; he could read those, though the words made little sense at first, jumbled together as they were. They faded before he could read them clearly.

Finally, the only object left was the box of selani tiles. He set that on the shrine. The clasp opened of itself, and the lid lifted. The box inverted itself, pouring the tiles out on the shelf. Two rolled off the shelf; Kieri caught them in his hands. Both were green, their runes in silver. He didn't recognize them, but the meaning seeped into his mind as he held them. Loyalty. Regard. Not opposites, this time.

He considered loyalty: to whom had he been loyal, and who had been loyal to him? To Aliam Halveric . . . to his oaths, to his kings, to his soldiers . . . and he had known loyalty from them. Regard? Yes, that, too.

He laid those two on the shelf, and another two stirred. He picked them up. Pair by pair, the same thing happened—runes he could not read revealed themselves and sometimes gave him alternatives and sometimes merely examples. He did not understand the colors . . . why loyalty and regard were green, and courtesy and kindness were red and blue, respectively, but all of that kind—virtues or valued qualities—had their runes in silver. The ones with opposites had their runes in gold and false gold.

By day's end, he had worked through perhaps half the tiles. When his Squires called that they had prepared a meal, he stood up—finding himself less stiff than he expected—bowed to the shrine, and poured the tiles back into the box.

The next day he began again. At times the pairings did seem playful—like a game—but at other times he found himself thrust deep into his own history and heart. He kept on, but for a rest in midday, and by evening had worked his way through all the tiles. The meanings of all were now clear to him, as was his past life. Choices he had made and where they had led. What lay behind those choices. He saw the choices before him more clearly than he had before. He looked at the tiles, took them into his hands, and put them into the box again.

"We will return to Chaya tomorrow," he said to his Squires. Their eyes held curiosity, but they did not ask.

CHAPTER THIRTY-TWO

Kieri woke at the turn of night; the ring on his heart-thumb glowed faintly. He had no idea what had wakened him—he felt no alarm—but he was too alert to return to sleep. Quietly, without waking his Squires, he dressed himself, belted on his sword, and eased out of the tent.

Stars burned in the clear sky, giving more light than he expected in a forested place. Every leaf was edged in silver. Dew frosted the grass, the violets. The scents of violet and fern, rich damp earth, and mossy bark came to him. The same melody he had heard before ran through his mind, and he hummed it. He walked down to the shrine, knelt as usual, and waited. In spite of all he had been told—had even experienced with the Lady's death—he was sure he felt a presence that must, he thought, be his mother's.

Silence and peace held the glade, deepening as he knelt there. No breeze stirred the leaves, no creature made the slightest noise. The sense of presence, of someone somewhere near, increased. He looked around, expecting nothing but layer upon layer of silver and darkness.

Deep among the trees, something moved—pale—a glow of silvery light. He stared, his body prickling suddenly as if dipped in snow. What—surely it could not be a wraith of his mother? Elves vanished utterly at death, leaving nothing . . . but the shape was tall, slender, comely—a woman in raiment of the purest white, bathed in the silvery glow of elf-light, her face indistinct as she wandered nearer, turning here and there among the trees as if searching. And who else—

"I am here," he said, scarcely louder than a breath.

For an instant the shape turned toward him, enough to show the elven bones, the gleam of eyes, but not close enough, in that light, to reveal the face he had long struggled to recall. Then she beckoned, and turned to one side, passing behind another tree, emerging just a little farther away.

"Mother?" he said. His voice caught in his throat; he rose to his feet and stepped away from the shrine. The glowing figure did not turn toward him but held still for a moment.

He had to know. He took a step, another . . . carefully, almost as if the figure were a wild thing that might take flight. It moved, but languidly now, circling around the glade away from the side where his tent stood. Deeper into the trees, deeper. Slowly, its glow spread, lighting his way through the denser trees, but more like a mist than the light the Lady had shed with the elvenhome or Paksenarrion's clear and brilliant light. It blurred the details of the figure, but his certainty that it was elven in origin—alive or not—drew him on.

"Who are you?" he asked, pitching his voice to reach the figure.

"Who do you want me to be?" came the answer.

Kieri shut his mouth but felt the wish pour out of him as if the figure had opened a door in his heart. *Mother.*

A soft sigh reached him and then a gentle chuckle and an indistinct murmur. For an instant he felt it as soothing, as her hand on his brow, but then a chill ran down his back. He looked around, startled. He had come farther into the trees than he'd realized, out of sight of the shrine, the clearing, the tent where his Squires slept. His mother's ring glowed brighter on his heart-thumb; the tiny dragon figure writhed. Around his neck, his mother's torc warmed. Did it move a little? He wasn't sure. He realized he had stopped walking; he stood half-mazed, feeling coils of power wrap him round.

White mist swirled toward him, faster than the figure had ever moved. "She's dead," a voice said, its sweetness cloying. He had heard that voice before. He struggled to remember, though it seemed fog filled his mind as well as the forest. "Poor little boy . . . you still miss her . . ."

Kieri's hand found his sword hilt before he thought of moving; the green jewel in it blazed. His mind cleared; the power clinging to him lessened. As he drew it a few fingerwidths, his own light rose, holding back the other's misty tendrils. Now he could see, within the mist, the figure running toward him. For the first time he recognized—

"*You,*" he said. The elf-maid who had sought him out, who claimed to be his mother's friend, whose proposal had chilled his loins. Understanding came in a rush, before she said a word: here was the traitor. He had only a moment to thank Falk that Arian had not drunk the potion she'd brought, before he saw that she wore elven mail and carried a sword of her own. On her head she wore jewels he remembered on the Lady's head.

Her smile was colder than the ossuary at Midwinter as she paused out of his reach, full of confidence in her power. "I thought it would work," she said. "You are a mere child, after all. And now, boy, you will die, but not until I have had my full revenge."

Kieri waited. Elves liked to talk; she would likely spend time taunting him; he could attack any time, but better she thought he was held by her power. She would relax; she would come close.

Sure enough, she paced back and forth, admitting what he already surmised. "I hate you. I hated you from before your conception." She turned back. "I hated you when you lay in your mother's arms . . ."

It was not hard to make his voice sound strained. "Why? You were her friend—"

"*Friend?*" Her laugh rang out jaggedly; she flung out her arms as gracelessly as he had ever seen an elf move. "She was no friend to me. I hated *her* long before you. She had everything—the Lady's daughter, the elvenhome gift. She would have ruled us later . . . *I* wanted to be queen of something, and my one chance was your father . . . but she charmed him. I begged her—she had so much—but she would not relent. He would have married *me,* but she stole him! And swore she would not use the elvenhome gift, but pass it to you—"

"But if you were not given it, you could not benefit by killing her—or me."

"Oh, but I shall," she said, taking a step toward him. "Those things you wear, that you saw rise from the ground—when I take them off your living body, they will be mine, and with these—" Her heart-hand touched the jewels in her hair. "—I can command the rest: the sword, the dagger, and most of all that spark deep in your heart no mortal should have. My will is strong; in the old days, that is how elvenhomes were made, not only by gift. I shall rule and rule alone. Humankind will be gone from here, forever."

Kieri felt the pressure of her power again. It must be the jewels she had taken—surely not been given—from the Lady's body. He flexed his fingers; nothing held him but his curiosity. He wanted to know more—most of all, he wanted to know if other traitors existed, if they were allied with her.

"I lured her here in the first place, you know," she said, her voice languid again. "And you as well."

"How?" Kieri said, making his voice harsh.

She shook her head; her hair swirled. "I will not tell you," she said. "But I will tell you that when I am done with you, I will kill your Squires . . . and then your lady and those unborn children you're so proud of." She looked down the length of her sword. "Ah . . . I think I have lingered enough." She opened her heart-hand again and showed the bright silver curve of a small knife. "This, to start."

She walked toward him, utterly unafraid. Kieri judged the distance, drew the great sword and his dagger just as she came in reach, and struck. He missed her; she danced back, laughing now. "Foolish boy; I have elven mail and sword, and I am far more experienced than you. I wondered were you truly snared."

Kieri had heard that elven mail could not be broken by humans, but his was an elven sword. Perhaps . . . He began a turn to the right; she matched him on the circle, perfectly aligned. She was, like all the elves, tall and lithe, in her first youth, perfectly fit. He reversed; she did the same.

"You dance well," she said. "But you cannot dance forever." She moved in then, quick and sure with the correct move for her position; he blocked her thrust easily, and she parried his. As parry followed thrust again and again, Kieri tested her skills. He soon knew her for a novice—fast, strong, schooled in all the standard moves, but she had learned swordplay as recreation, as a dance, as anything but what it really was. Had she been other than his mother's murderer, Orlith's murderer, and the murderer of all those unborn babes, he would have warned her. Instead, he played on, testing which of her moves gave him the best openings given the mail she wore.

She pushed harder with her magery, trying to slow him, but it had no effect. He pressed his own attack, forcing her to respond faster than she had. Suddenly her heart-hand flashed, and the curved knife sped toward his face. He jerked his head aside without dropping his guard; he'd seen such tricks before. But she rushed in anyway, not waiting, counting on a gap that wasn't there.

His response came automatically: the block with his dagger, the practiced thrust any soldier would have made to kill a novice crazy enough to make such a naive attack. To his astonishment, his blade slid through the elven mail as if it were not there and pierced her through.

"For my mother," he said, as her eyes widened in disbelief. Her knees buckled, though she still breathed, as strength left her and life ebbed. Her weight dragged his blade down; he stepped back, pulling it free. "And for my father, and my sister, and for me. For Orlith and the children unborn."

"You . . . will . . . never . . . know . . . who . . ."

"I know enough," Kieri said. She lay now on the ground, the silvery glitter in her elven blood dying away. He could not pity her, who had brought so much sorrow to so many. She struggled, trying to push herself up; he regretted the pain in her face and the undying enmity. But she was neither enemy soldier nor one of his, to whom he could give the death-stroke and end it.

Her light was gone now. His own brightened, reflecting from her eyes. They widened. "You . . . cannot . . . have . . ."

"What?"

"Elfane . . ." Then a rush of blood from her mouth, and she sank back, unmoving, her sightless eyes staring upward.

Kieri had no feeling of a spirit freed from its husk, as he'd often experienced when humans died . . . She died as an animal died, all at once, with nothing left. Her body looked dead, the white gown now dabbled with her blood, all luster gone from her skin. The elven mail crumbled to grit as he watched.

Kieri took a deep breath, then another. He looked around. The last of the mist had gone; he could see every tree trunk, every fern and herb, each leaf and petal. The light—the light was his own, he realized. It spread, more silvery than sunlight, true elf-light. Silence held him, but the feel of the taig was stronger than he'd ever experienced. What it conveyed was . . . joy. It seemed to nestle into him as his first children had nestled in his arms. Within its bubble was peace, silence, joy, health . . . and a dead elf.

He sighed. A dead elf must be laid straight with the sacred boughs upon her, whether evil or no. But . . . his mother's murderer? Here, so close to the shrine he had built? She should be laid straight, yes, but . . . not here.

Here. The word resonated in his head and seemed to shimmer in the margins of his light.

Here? Why here? Was it not an insult to his mother . . . to the pain this elf had caused his father and his sister . . . and himself?

Light flashed from his mother's ring, from his father's, from the pommel of his sword . . . warmth from the torc around his neck. Dazzled, he blinked against the light and saw—for an instant that lasted the rest of his life—his mother's face, the face that once seen he could not believe he had ever forgotten, and felt the true embrace of her love.

Here, closing the circle, completing the pattern, but in joy, not hatred. Tears sprang to his eyes, and now pity rose in him for the dead. His mother, beloved in memory by those who had lost her. And this elf, who had given up all hope of love and joy to seek lasting vengeance. He wept for them both, for the friendship they could have had, and finally for himself.

Here it would be, then. The boughs he needed were outlined by light more green than silver and fell into his hands when he reached for them. He wondered, without pausing in the task, why this was so. When he had them all, he moved the dead elf as gently as he might to straighten her limbs—arms at her side, legs together, her spattered robe arranged neatly—and laid the branches in order. He looked at the jewels in her hair: they had been the Lady's. Should he take them back to Amrothlin? Or as the dead elf had hinted, did they have some connection to his mother's ring and torc? He hesitated. Robbing bodies was wrong. The jewels flashed at him. He put out his hand and touched one; it clung to his fingers; the others moved to join it. He held them a moment, still a little reluctant to rob the dead, then slipped them into a pocket. She had robbed others; he intended restoration.

"Once you were the song the Singer sang," he said to the dead face. "Once you were born of love and beauty and loved beauty. Let that be your memory."

When he looked around, he saw he was not even a hundred paces from the clearing where the shrine to his mother stood. As he neared it, radiance moved with him, spilled across the clearing, spreading to the tent where his Squires slept . . . and then beyond. He stood still, awestruck. This was unlike the first time light had come to him, when Torfinn was wounded. He felt no exhaustion, no sense of power leaving him. The light moved but had a definite edge, like . . . like the Lady's elvenhome.

He heard noise within the tent, his Squires rousing, muttering, then crying out, "The king! The king! He's gone!" and they came out, half asleep, shading their eyes from the light. "Sir king!" they called, as if they could not see him.

"I'm here," he said, and, through the waning hours of night, told them all that had happened.

Kieri rode in silence most of the way back to Chaya. He tried to imagine what he would tell Arian, what he would tell the Council, what questions he would ask of whom, in what order, but the wonder and horror of what he had seen, what he had done, dominated his thoughts. The light that now, as he rode, moved with him, barely perceptible in sunlight but clearly seen before dawn and after dusk, was a constant reminder that he was, at least in some measure, what the Lady had been and what his mother had hoped for.

Impossible, Amrothlin had said, but what would his uncle say now? What would the other elves say? Or—given his Squires' response—what would his human subjects say? He was not even sure how it had come to him. Was it all the elvenhome gift from his mother, or were the jewels the Lady had worn, the ring and torc that had been his mother's, part of what created it?

Around him the forest acknowledged his new power, the trees singing their slow songs he could now hear, the birds and animals calling to him, naming him their lord. As the power upheld him, he felt the weight of responsibility.

All the beauty he had admired on his way into the old forest he must now take as his duty. As limbs had dropped into his hands after he killed the elf, limbs would drop or burgeon at his request. He shivered again. No mortal could possibly . . . and yet . . . he was. As with the unasked kingship, he must find a way to be what he had never imagined. *Change nothing now,* he thought at the forest. *There is time.* He hoped there would be time. Surely the Lady had not done something every day, every minute. Elves cautioned against haste. He would not be hasty.

He tried focusing on the objects he had received. The torc, the ring, the belt clasp, the jewels from the dead elf's hair . . . and the tiles. What was that white core of the torc? A sea-beast's tusk? He had never seen anything like it, and he was not, he suspected, likely to see it again. The belt clasp, he thought, was of human origin; he had seen enameling like that—discounting the tiny letters that appeared when he touched it and disappeared shortly after—in Aarenis. The dragon in his ring, appearing and disappearing under the fern carved above it—what was that? An elf and dragon symbol, as the stone in his father's ring was an elf and human symbol? That these were magical he knew, but not what the magic was, except that the traitor elf had said they had something to do with the elvenhome power.

Halfway to Chaya, they met his Squires Ceilar and Jostin returning with supplies, and halted early.

"Sir king . . . ?" Ceilar looked shocked. Jostin shook his head, and Ceilar fell silent.

"I will tell you," Kieri said, "when we have eaten." They both nodded, and all the Squires set about making camp. Kieri bespoke the trees for firewood and then with a gesture opened the carpet of moss that here covered the soil, making a bare space safe for fire.

"It will close again when we have put the fire out," Kieri said to the Squires. He left them to light it. That first hot meal in days seemed unduly rich to him; they all ate without speaking, but as soon as it was done, he spoke again.

"What did you see, as you came near?" Kieri asked Ceilar and Jostin, with a glance for each.

"That light, sir king," Jostin said.

"You looked like the Lady," Ceilar said. "Because of the light. But like yourself—more than yourself."

"I will tell you what happened," Kieri said. When he finished, he asked for news of Chaya. "Are many elves in the city now?"

"Not many, sir king," Jostin said. "Though they come and go. Amrothlin is there, staying in that inn they favor, according to Queen Arian. What do you think they will do when they see you with . . . what you have?"

"I don't know," Kieri said. "Amrothlin told me repeatedly that it was impossible I should have this power . . . but I am sure he will recognize it. I hope he will help me learn to use it."

"With branches falling into your hands and the moss opening at your hand to make a fire-pit, I would think you already know," Ceilar said.

Kieri chuckled. "I know a little, true, but the whole . . . As I understood Amrothlin, an elvenhome binds elves within it to the vision of the one who generates the elvenhome."

"And humans?" asked Panin.

"I don't know. Do you feel bound by anything other than your oath as Squire?" Kieri looked around the circle. Four Squires looked back, serious, thoughtful.

"I am not sure," Linne said after a moment. "I—I feel strange. Like you, sir king, I am half-elven; I feel . . . something . . . when I am inside the glow . . . that I do not feel outside, and it is new. It is as if the two parts of my heritage are more . . . are aware of each other. As if I had two persons inside me."

"Does that trouble you?" Kieri asked.

"Not . . . now," Linne said.

"I feel nothing different than I did before," Jostin said. "Aside from the wonder of it. I admired you from the first. That's what made me want to be a King's Squire. But I have little elven heritage, if any."

"What is your vision for this land?" Panin asked.

"What it was before," Kieri said. "For this beautiful land and those who live in it to be healthy, to prosper, to flower into greater beauty as the gods give grace."

"It does not take elven magery for me to want the same," Panin said.

The next morning, as the Squires packed the horses, Kieri fetched a bucket of water to quench the last coals. As the first drops hissed, water rose from below, faster even than the water pouring from the bucket. The soil opened; the burnt sticks and ash swirled downward with the water. Soil closed back over it all, and moss flowed across the soil as swiftly as a carpet unrolled, leaving no trace. Kieri stared; he had not consciously asked such a thing. "Thank you," he murmured, but whether to the taig or the gods he did not know.

O n the last day of travel, Kieri discussed with the Squires what might happen when they reached the city. "Though I can contract the elvenhome almost to myself alone or expand it to cover us all—and more—it will be obvious to any elves and, I suspect, to most Lyonyan humans."

Jostin nodded. "It will be seen, and it will surprise people. Frighten some but please others."

"Questions," Kieri said. "I'm sure there'll be many questions, and to some I have no answer. For others I have answers, but I must speak first to Arian, my uncle Amrothlin, and the Seneschal."

"The ring and torc will be noticed as well, sir king," Linne said.

"It is likely," Panin said, "that this new power will help you silence questions you are not yet ready to hear."

"A dangerous precedent," Kieri said, shaking his head. "I do not want to evade questions, merely delay answers, and only briefly."

"Do you still believe that elf was the only traitor in the Lady's domain?" Jostin asked.

"I do," Kieri said. "But not the only danger. The iynisin—we may have blocked them from entering the palace, but we do not know where all such patterns are."

In the long summer afternoon, they rode into Chaya itself. The bubble of light that had been scarcely visible in the sun now brightened and expanded as they neared the inn the elves favored. Even as Kieri glanced at the inn, elves hurried out the door, Amrothlin in the lead, and stared at him. The elvenhome transmitted their reaction— the mix of hope, disbelief, fear, with touches of anger . . . and more longing.

"You . . . I cannot believe it, and yet I must—" Amrothlin had tears in his eyes and took a step forward, one hand out as if to touch something fragile. "It is . . . real," he said. "*Real.* How?"

"It can't be!" another elf said. He pushed past Amrothlin, drawing his blade, and the light blazed . . . He cried out and staggered back. "It's not the elvenhome—it's some evil—"

"Put down your blade," Kieri said. "And then see. You cannot come within, intending to harm me." He wasn't sure that was true, but it made sense. "Amrothlin, come within and tell them."

Amrothlin came without hesitation, his eyes shining. The change in his expression once he was within astounded Kieri, for he had not witnessed an elf moving from without to within the elvenhome before. A relaxation, a joy, lit Amrothlin's face with his own light. "It *is*," he said. "It is real." Two more elves pressed nearer, then another. As they did so, the light expanded again, as if enfolding elves enlarged it without Kieri's intent.

The elf who had drawn his blade sheathed it and edged forward, still wary. Kieri smiled at him. "Come," he said. "I intend you no harm."

"If indeed you have done this without harm to the Sinyi, I honor you," the elf said. "If not—"

"See for yourself," Kieri said. As quick as his thought, the elvenhome light engulfed the doubter, and his face, too, relaxed.

"How did this happen?" Amrothlin asked.

"I do not know," Kieri said. "But I have much to tell, and more questions for you, Uncle."

"Will you restore the elvenhome and keep it apart, my lord?" asked one.

"Not the way it was," Kieri said. "But there will be an elvenhome, do not fear."

With a half dozen elves walking beside the riders, and the elvenhome glow shimmering over them all, people in the streets stopped and stared. Some shrank back; some pushed forward. One ran pell-mell toward the palace. Kieri smiled and waved at them, but did not stop to explain, riding on at a foot pace. The elvenhome enlarged his elven senses; he understood the elves around him better than he ever had.

At the palace he met the same astonishment mixed with concern and joy. Only Arian, who had known the secret of his heritage, showed unalloyed joy, a joy he felt directly when the elvenhome welcomed her in.

As soon as he could, using the excuse of his travel, he escaped to his own suite to bathe and change.

"What was the Ladysforest like?" Arian asked.

"More beautiful than I can say," Kieri said. "I thought Lyonya's forest was beautiful the moment I arrived, but this . . . this was more. You must see it for yourself."

"I want to."

"I found the place where we—" His voice broke for a moment. "Where my mother was killed and I was taken."

"Kieri, how horrible."

"It was . . . but it wasn't, in the end. Let me tell you." He told it all—the memories the place brought back, the treasures restored to him, the traitor elf, the revelation of his new powers. "I feel whole in a way I never have before." He leaned closer to where she lay on the pillows. Her eyes widened.

"Kieri—where did you get that neck ring?"

"This is one of the treasures that appeared. It was my mother's. So was this ring." He held it up. He was not surprised when the light in it flared and the tiny dragon shape flickered, all fire.

"That's . . . Dragon."

"Yes, but I don't know how or what it means. I remember my mother wearing this ring on her thumb, and this on her neck, and this—" He stood and pointed to the belt clasp he now wore.

"They're beautiful, but . . . I've never seen a torc like that."

"Nor I. I need to talk to those who knew my mother, see if there's any record of it. And even more mysterious than that . . . are these." He pulled out the enameled box and spilled the tiles onto her bed. "I remember the name, selani. She told me it was a game, but they have another use. Divination."

Arian stirred the tiles, then laid all of one color together. "My father had a set of these. He let me play with them, but did not teach me anything like a game. He would say, 'Which do you feel calling you?' and I would hold my hand over them and one would feel right."

"Do you know the meanings of the runes?"

"Not all of them. He would only tell me the ones that I said called me. Do you know them?"

"Linne knew the runes but not how to use them. I began to learn, I think."

"A king to wake the mountains, Amrothlin told me once you might have been. I think waking the taig is enough." Her smile was luminous.

"And so do I," Kieri said. "But how to use it well . . . I am still uncertain."

"You will learn," Arian said. "Because that is what you do. And now our enemy is dead, our children are safe."

"*One* enemy is dead," Kieri said. "I would not say all are; we know one iynisin escaped alive."

"True," Arian said. "But for this night, I will feel safe, for you are here and the elvenhome is with us again."

CHAPTER THIRTY-THREE

Ifoss, Aarenis

Arvid Semminson found the soldiers far more willing to learn tricks of swordplay from him than the Ifoss Girdish, distrustful as they were of "thief tricks." For his part, he watched the Company weapons practice with interest. He had not paid attention to soldiers before meeting Paks other than to consider how they might be vulnerable to thieves. Her command of that little group in Brewersbridge impressed him more than he had admitted. Now he saw where she learned the skills—and skills they were. When the weaponsmaster offered to let him drill with them, he did so, taking his lumps without complaint. As Midsummer neared, he felt more and more at home with the soldiers.

It was different at the grange.

"We don't need such," one of the senior yeomen said. He was a master mason with his own yard, Arvid's height but more heavily built, his shoulders thick with muscle. "We fight honest, as Girdish should." Beyond the man, Arvid could see one of the soldiers roll his eyes.

Arvid said nothing, and when Marshal Porfur asked him to trade blows, he picked up the staff, not a sword. "Are you giving up the sword, then?" the same yeoman asked.

"Regar," the Marshal said. "A man's entitled to choose his weapon."

"I just thought—" Regar began, but subsided at the Marshal's glare.

Arvid held the staff and stepped up on the platform. As a new yeoman, trading blows was a regular part of his drill night attendance, and the Marshal had begun to assign others to the ceremony with him. Tonight, the Marshal called on Regar. Though the exchange of blows was supposed to be only a test of willingness, Arvid suspected Regar had something else in mind.

As the Marshal gave the starting signal, Regar lunged forward, aiming a swing at Arvid's head that would have knocked him flat if he'd been in its way. Arvid sidestepped and rammed the end of his staff into Regar's gut. Regar turned an unlovely color and collapsed, gasping.

"You . . . thief . . ." he managed.

"A fair blow," the Marshal said. "You moved first, Regar."

"He's a thief!" Regar said.

"He's a yeoman of Gird now, and that's that," the Marshal said. He looked at Arvid next; Arvid was careful not to smirk. "You don't have to like each other, but you will not start trouble, either of you. Is that clear?"

"Yes, Marshal," Arvid said. Regar was a beat behind him; Arvid figured he had a sore belly.

After drill, the Marshal called them both to stay behind. Regar glared at Arvid; Arvid looked past him. This could end very badly, he realized, and he hoped the Marshal understood that. Regar was a bully, but a popular bully, and local. Arvid was the stranger—the handsome stranger. Always before he'd used that to his advantage, and this time, trying to be honest . . .

"I fault you both," the Marshal said, looking from one to the other. "Regar, you're local, and everyone knows you. Knows the quality of wall you build and the strength of your arm. You've taken advantage of that, gathering that little gang around you. As a local leader, welcoming visitors is part of your job—"

"You didn't appoint me yeoman-marshal," Regar said.

"No, and if you want to know why, come ask me and I'll tell you. But your way with strangers is part of it, I'll say that. A yeoman-marshal's job includes recruiting new yeomen."

"I could've gotten you a dozen—"

"If I'd asked and promised something in return. That's not how it goes."

"You'll take a stranger, a thief born and bred—"

"I'll take any man who learns and follows the Code, recites the Ten Fingers, and shows respect to every other yeoman in the grange. People change. Gird changed; that's the heart of the story. He was a farmer who became something else."

"A farmer, yes. But a thief? Gird was never a thief!"

"Regar, your head's harder than granite—"

"Excuse me," Arvid said. "Marshal—Regar's right. Not that I'm a thief now, but that I was one—as you know—and that he cannot trust a former thief. We all have something impossible to us."

Regar turned on him, glowering. "Don't you play the judicar with me, thief. I don't want your help."

"And yet someday you may need it," Arvid said. "There's trouble coming—everyone knows that—and if yeomen cannot stand to gether, things will be worse."

"That was *my* speech," the Marshal said. "And you are not a Marshal, Arvid. Yet, and most likely never. Be silent and listen. I have a proposition for you both." He looked from face to face and then went on. "There's an old way of breaking in a young ox or dray horse, you know. Hitch it together with an older trained one and give the pair a load to pull. I can't have the two of you dividing the grange's loyalties. So if you want to remain here, either of you, you're going to work together. And it starts tonight." He turned and took the relic out of its niche.

Arvid shot a glance at Regar, whose glance was equally brief and alarmed.

"You will be hitched—under an oath sworn on this relic—as if by a rope to work side by side at your trades—"

"How can we do that?" Regar said. "I have a commission to build—"

"One day the two of you will work at your trade, Regar, and then the next at Arvid's. He is not a mason, and you are not a merchant: you will each serve the other as assistant. You will eat together from the same dish and sleep together—"

"No!" they both said.

"—in the same room," the Marshal went on, unperturbed. "I expect you both snore and neither wants to admit it. You will do this for the next tenday, and after that we will see."

"What about my wife?" Regar asked. "My children?"

"You can stay at the soldiers' camp with Arvid, or your wife can put up with the two of you. Take your pick. On the night before your day's work, the one whose work it is will choose where to sleep. Since tomorrow will be Arvid's day and you will assist him, he will decide where you sleep this night."

Regar glared, but Marshal Porfur simply looked at him. Regar's shoulders finally slumped. Arvid bowed slightly to the Marshal.

"As you command, Marshal," he said.

"I have to tell my wife," Regar said.

"Go with him, Arvid," the Marshal said. And as they turned away, "And don't make me actually shackle you together—if any sees you more than an armslength apart, I surely will."

In silence they left the grange and in silence headed for the main street of Ifoss, trailed at a little distance by the soldiers who had come with Arvid to drill night. He assumed they'd listened at the door.

"I suppose you're happy about this," Regar said. "Seein' as old Porfur thinks I'm worse than you."

"I don't think he does," Arvid said. "And it's no joy to me to be linked to you."

"It won't be on my day to choose your work," Regar said. "You'll learn what work is, and you'll be howling for mercy before the noontide." He walked on a few strides. "Which you won't get, any more than I did when I was a 'prentice." A few more strides. "I'm not having you in my house, let alone my bedroom. You'll have to find me a bed."

"Suits me," Arvid said.

"Ten days," Regar said. "Lia will kill me."

Regar lived down a twisty lane, a house on the north margin of Ifoss, adjacent to a walled yard. A tall, stout woman stood in the door, watching them come.

"You're late," she said. "Been to the tavern again?"

"No, Lia," Regar said. His tone with her was almost pleading. "Marshal bade me stay behind. On account of this fellow."

Her gaze went over Arvid like a scrystone. "You're the thief he talks about, aren't you?"

"I'm the new yeoman of Gird, yes," Arvid said.

Her lips thinned, and she looked at Regar. "Why did you bring this man here?"

"Marshal said. There was a quarrel—"

"Who started it?"

A long pause during which Regar slowly turned red. The woman nodded before he said anything. "You did, then. And you with a good contract at last, and children who need food on the table, and something tells me the Marshal's solution is going to leave them hungry. Am I right?"

Silence from Regar. Arvid said, "He bade us stay no more than an armslength from each other for the next tenday."

"Day *and* night?" Her brows were up, but she sounded more resigned than surprised.

"Yes. And each day we must work together, alternating days. He assigned tomorrow to my work as a merchant."

"Much good you'll be as a mason's assistant," the woman said, lip curling. She looked at Regar again. "If you lose this contract, Regar, I swear I'm going back to my family. It's the best you've had in a hand of years."

"I won't," he said. "I swear—"

"And you," she said to Arvid. "*You* don't have a wife or children, I'll wager."

"I have a son," he said. "In Valdaire. His mother died of fever, years back."

Her brows went up. "Well, then. You know children must eat." A noise in the house behind her; she turned her head just as two children tried to squeeze past her in the doorway. One escaped and launched himself at Regar; the other, the woman caught by the arm and held fast.

"Da! Supper's ready. I'm hungry!" The boy wasn't even hip high on Regar and skinny as Arvid's own son. He wore a ragged shirt that hung to his knees. The girl the woman held back wore the same, but with a patched vest and skirt as well.

"We've not enough for the both of you," the woman said, eyeing Arvid. "If you must eat together, let him feed you. And what are you going to tell Invarr, when he comes in the morning to see your progress?"

"I'll go there now and tell him," Regar said.

"Do, then. Come, Carn, don't be making a scene in the street." She turned away; the boy hugged Regar and ran after her into the house.

"There's an inn—" Arvid began.

Regar shook his head. "I must find Invarr; she's right. He comes once a hand of days, and tomorrow's his day. I must not lose this contract."

"How many children do you have?" Arvid asked.

"Seven," Regar said. "Two from my first wife, one of them 'prenticed out. Five of Lia's."

They had crossed back to the main street and now came to a much larger house in the area Arvid recognized as wealthy. Regar tapped on a door; a servant opened it. "What do you want?"

"I need to speak to Invarr," Regar said. His hand moved toward his waist, where his purse hung.

The servant wrinkled his nose. "About what?"

"About a matter concerning Invarr," Arvid said. "Pray inform him."

"Who are you?"

Arvid said, "Arvid Burin, a merchant associated with Fox Company and with Mason Regar."

The servant withdrew, shutting the door.

"Why'd you interfere?" Regar said.

"Because he's playing you," Arvid said. "You were going to bribe him, weren't you? Just to do what he's hired for: tell this Invarr you need to speak to him."

"It's not a bribe," Regar said. "Exactly . . ."

"It *is* a bribe exactly. You're a master craftsman in good standing, right? And a Girdish yeoman? You deserve respect; you don't have to bribe another man's servants."

Regar chewed that over for a moment. "You think I deserve respect?"

"Yes," Arvid said firmly. "He's coming back."

"How do you know?"

"I have very good hearing."

The door opened again. The servant glared at them. "Master Invarr will see you when he has finished eating. You—"

"We will come in and wait," Arvid said. He stepped forward; the servant gave way, sputtering.

"But you're—and he's—"

"It's honest sweat," Arvid said, having more fun than he'd had since he'd left Valdaire. "We've been to drill at the grange. Aren't you Girdish?"

"Me? Uh . . . no."

"Well, we are, and it's because of events at the grange that we must speak with Master Invarr."

"Both of you . . ."

"Yes." Arvid looked around the entrance hall of the house, which was lit by oil lamps carved of alabaster, and spotted a padded bench a few strides on. "We will wait here," he said, moving past the servant and waving at Regar. The look on the faces of both Regar and the servant was, he decided, delicious. His conviction that the Marshal would not have approved of all this made it even better.

Regar sat on the edge of the seat. "You'll lose me the contract," he said in a hoarse whisper when the servant had left again.

"No, I won't," Arvid said. "We're here on legitimate business. You will assure him the work will not suffer."

"But it—"

"It will not suffer," Arvid said. "Hate me if you will, but I do not break my word."

Far down the passage a door opened. The servant, hovering outside it, bowed; the man who came through it turned, saw them, and came forward. Neither lean nor fat, neither old nor young, he wore a merchant's robe open over a thin white pleated garment belted at the waist with links of silvery metal.

Arvid rose, and beside him Regar lunged upright.

"I have seen you," Invarr said to Arvid. "You're that merchant attached to Fox Company. You were at the grange, my servant said. Are you Girdish?"

Arvid bowed slightly. "Indeed I am, sir, and my name is Arvid Burin—a northern name, as you will recognize, from Tsaia come last fall."

"Ser Burin." Invarr bowed in return, equal to equal. "And you, Master Regar," he said to Regar. "You both have business with me? I hope you have not been hired away by this man because he is a Girdish comrade."

"Not at all," Regar said.

"It is a grange matter," Arvid said. "Marshal Porfur, whom I'm sure you know—"

"Indeed I do. He has more than once urged me to join his grange."

"Well, tonight at drill he bade Regar and me to spend ten days no farther from each other than an armslength and to alternate the days of work—both of us on each man's task, day by day, so that neither's work would suffer."

"Why would he do that?"

"It is a long tale," Arvid said. "And more my fault than Regar's, but in short—we quarreled, and as Regar has such distinction in the grange—which he of his modesty would not tell you—the Marshal chose to make an example of us to the others."

"You quarreled . . . and I see no marks on you," Invarr said. "Regar is—you will pardon me—a man more strongly built than you."

Arvid smiled. "I am perhaps quicker. Of tongue as well as body, and therein lies my fault. It is a northern thing; I do not know customs here as I ought."

"It is not all your fault," Regar said. "Marshal knows I have a temper."

Invarr chuckled. "Everyone knows you have a temper, Regar. But I know you to be an excellent mason. So long as my warehouse is built and you do not strike me, I am content. Will you need more time, then?"

Regar's "Maybe" overlaid Arvid's "No."

Invarr nodded at Regar. "As your contract is with me, I thank you for your honesty in coming this evening and admitting the building may be delayed. If you must spend every other day learning merchanting—for how many days?"

"Ten, if we satisfy the Marshal that our quarrel has ended," Arvid said.

"Not much delay, then, even if Ser Burin proves an inept pupil," Invarr said. "It is well. Shall I come tomorrow or the following day? Or wait until the end of ten?"

"The following day, ser, if you could," Regar said. "Tomorrow the Marshal declared I must assist Arvid."

"Fine, then." Invarr had an expression Arvid feared was pure mischief, and his next words proved it. "Perhaps tomorrow I will see what commodities Ser Burin might have to trade with me: two merchants should know each other."

"Thank you, ser," Arvid said, bowing again. "You are most gracious, and I would welcome the chance to learn local customs. You should know I am contracted as sutler to Fox Company."

"We'll see," Invarr said. He opened the door for them himself and bade them a pleasant evening.

They had hardly walked past the end of the house before Regar stopped. "That was . . . that was not entirely honest."

"No? But we are not cheating Invarr. I will work honestly for you, and his warehouse will be built, will it not? Do you think his concerns really run to every detail of our quarrel?"

"No, but—"

"His servant will hate me and not you," Arvid said. "Clearly I am the one to blame for your resistance this day, though frankly I think you might refuse to give another bribe. Especially since his master clearly does respect you."

"He does?"

"He called you Master Regar and hired you to build a warehouse," Arvid said. "That's not a small commission; he would not hire someone he did not respect. Not a bad man, Invarr."

"He's rich."

"If you think rich is bad, you will never be rich, Regar, and with all those children you should not despise money. Come—I need to let Count Arcolin know you'll be staying with me in camp."

At the end of that street the four soldiers waited, propped against a wall. "You all right, sir?" asked one.

"Fine," Arvid said. "Making sure we get to camp or that we follow the Marshal's orders?"

"Might be a bit of both."

"Is Cela's still open?"

"Nah—only the Blue Mule."

Arvid fumbled in his belt pouch. "Will one of you go to the Mule and bring back two meals to the camp? I need to speak to the Count."

"'Course," one of them said. He took the coins and set off; the other three walked with Arvid and Regar to the camp and gave the countersign at the sentry for them.

"You live in the camp?" Regar murmured.

"It's easier," Arvid said. "I have a tent. We go this way, to Count Arcolin—he's the commander. He has the big tent."

Arcolin was not best pleased to find his protégé in trouble at the grange, but after a glance at Regar he gave permission for the two of them to share Arvid's tent. "I'll have Dattur bring you a pallet for him," he said. "And what about mess? Will you need something—?"

"One of yours went to the Mule and will bring back food for tonight," Arvid said.

"Good. Tomorrow you'll need to take a wagon over to Garmead and fetch those hogs we ordered."

Regar ate his meal in silence; Arvid could not tell from the way he ate whether it was better or worse than the food his wife prepared at home. For himself, he found the Mule's cooking merely acceptable. After the meal, Arvid showed him where the jacks was and then took him back to the tent they would now share, leaving Regar there while he fetched a yoke and buckets of water for bathing.

Regar did indeed snore, great snorting, gurgling snores. Arvid was sure he himself did not, and he finally stopped his ears with wads of the wool he kept for oiling his blades.

The camp was up by dawn, as usual, and Arvid woke reluctantly. Regar still snored. Arvid stared across the still-dark tent at the vague shape on what had been his bed and wondered how he was going to survive the next ten days.

After breakfast, he hitched a team to one of the Company supply wagons and put coils of rope in the wagon bed. Regar helped, his expression showing he hadn't expected Arvid to know how. He and Regar climbed to the seat. Regar said nothing during the trip. By midmorning, they arrived at Garmead, where Arcolin had contracted for the future delivery of four hands of young hogs and two of cattle.

Arvid knew at once something was wrong. He saw no animals penned in the village square, only a group of men, all looking tense and unfriendly. The village headman, glowering, said, "What do you want?"

Arvid showed him the paper with Arcolin's seal on it, countersigned by someone in this village. "You're holding livestock for Count Arcolin of Fox Company; I've come to take them and make final payment."

"No."

"No?"

The man spat too close to Arvid's boots for courtesy. "No stock for sale here. Sold 'em all. And anyway, you're not Fox Company. No uniform."

"You sold them to Count Arcolin," Arvid said. "And yes, I'm a civilian. He hired me to come here. I'm his agent. This is his wagon." He pointed to the foxhead insignia painted on the side of the wagon.

"Fox Company no good," the man said. "He pay too little. Got better price."

"You signed this contract," Arvid said.

"Not me. Looks like my cousin Vili's mark, when he's drunk." He guffawed; the men behind him did the same. "And he's not here," he added. "No pigs here. No cows here. You go."

The Thieves' Guild knew how to handle situations like this. In Arvid's enforcer days, he could have turned the village upside down for such insolence. But now he was Girdish, and Girdish yeomen did not, he was assured, take out their swords and beat sullen peasants into submission. Exactly why he'd thought less of Girdish all these years. And he had Regar with him, so reverting to his former self, even on such good grounds, would not be good strategy.

"Count Arcolin paid you to hold those animals for him," Arvid said. "You owe the money now. Give it back."

"He didn't come soon enough," the man said. "He's not getting a niti back. They kept eating."

Arvid glanced at Regar. He looked angry, but was he willing to help?

"You are in Foss Council jurisdiction," Arvid said. "A complaint will be filed with the nearest judicar, and you will be hailed to court. We have the proof that this vill contracted to supply animals, that a deposit was put down. Do you really want to be hailed to court and end up paying a fine?"

The men looked at one another but said nothing. Arvid could feel the tension rising. Six men there before him, and how many others nearby? They didn't have swords, at least not these six, but what about those he couldn't see? As he was thinking what best to do, Regar said, "Look out!" and pushed Arvid off the wagon seat. The men on the ground let out a nervous laugh, but the unmistakable sound of an arrow hitting the seat back caught Arvid's attention. He had rolled off the wagon with the push; Regar was on the wagon floor, behind the dashboard.

"This side, Regar," he said, hoping the other archers weren't all around them. Before the villagers had quite recovered—they had not expected that arrow either, he could tell—he had reached the headman, yanked him around, and held him between himself and the direction from which the arrow had come, one of his knives at the man's throat.

"Call them off," he said in the man's ear.

"Got another one," Regar said. "Can't lead the horses while holding 'im, though."

Arvid and Regar dragged their captives back toward the wagon; the other men broke and fled to the huts around the small square. Regar threw his to the ground and sat on him. Arvid forced his to his knees, keeping the knife pressure on him.

"Both hands on your head," he said. "If you move, I'll stick you." The man complied. Keeping the point of the knife at the man's neck, Arvid fished a thong out of his pocket with the other hand. No more arrows came while he and Regar finished with their captives—one hand tied behind to a choke-thong at the neck. That worried Arvid. Where was the archer? Creeping around to take them in the flank?

"Who's shooting?" he asked the headman.

The man paled even more. "I can't tell!"

"You'd rather die?" Even as he said it, the man's answer suggested a more serious problem. "Someone's here—not your people. Did they take the animals?"

The man nodded, lips pressed tight.

"How many?"

"I can't—"

"They'll kill us all if you don't. I can save us if you do."

"They left two," the man said. Tears streaked his face now. "I can't—"

"Say more. Fine." Arvid looked around. Two archers could shoot them where they crouched now, beside the wagon, one to either flank. Or they could be waiting to see if the villagers revealed anything about them. Two archers—only part of "they"—and the stories about last year's campaigns in Vonja . . . It didn't take a soldier to put that together. The town was an ambush, and an ambush aimed at Fox Company. They'd be lucky to get out alive.

Unless he could convince the watchers he had nothing to do with Arcolin but as a hireling and not one valuable to Fox Company.

"So you're telling me I wasted a whole day on a fool's errand? That Fox Company sent me here as some kind of joke? Damn them all, I say!" Loud enough to be heard through the vill. "They promised me a nis when I brought the animals back, and now I'll get nothing!"

He stood up, skin prickling with awareness of danger. "Come on, Sim," he said to Regar, giving him the first name he could think of. "Those bastards in Fox Company set us up, and for all we know it's them shot the arrow. They can go hungry until winter for all I care. This is what we get for trying to make an honest day's wage with mercenary scum."

Regar, for a wonder, followed his lead. "I told you yesterday—"

"So you did, and I should've listened. Last time I'll take a job like that, but I thought it'd be easier than hauling freight to Valdaire." To the headman, Arvid said, "Help us turn the team, will you? Do you think your friend will stick an arrow in us?" He unfastened the choke-cord as he spoke.

"N-no," the man said.

Nothing happened while the team was being turned, convincing Arvid that the enemy didn't have the manpower to attack, just enough to scare the villagers. Someone's wife or child was probably a hostage.

"Get in, but stay low," he said to Regar. "Down in front of the seat. It's going to be rough." Instead of mounting the wagon, he took the reins, as if inspecting the harness, then stepped on the trace and threw himself on the wheeler's back, yelling and laying a whip on the lead pair. They squealed and bolted, as did the wheelers.

Nobody followed, somewhat to his surprise, but back at the Fox Company camp, he found four arrows in the tailboard and the back of the driver's seat. He had slowed the team once he was sure they weren't being followed but continued to ride the wheeler until they were in sight of the camp. Then he dismounted, climbed up onto the driving seat with Regar, and proceeded at a walk. Arcolin wasn't going to like what he had to say.

"We could have died," Regar said when the team had moved on.

"Yes. It was close," Arvid said.

"You knew what to do."

"I knew some things to try. I didn't know they'd work. We were lucky." He sighed. "Regar, I'm sorry you got dragged into this. You have family—"

"You said you had a son—"

"I do. But he's in Valdaire—well, actually not in Valdaire but near it—being cared for by a grange. Your family's here, vulnerable, and there are more of them."

Regar scowled at him. "You're worried about *me*?"

"It's not an insult, dammit," Arvid said. "It's just a fact. Marshal Porfur didn't know working with me on something as simple as hauling supplies to Fox Company could put you in such danger, nor did I."

"I'm not dead," Regar said. "Or injured. And I did grab that man—"

"So you did, and I'm grateful. Let's not quarrel now. We're supposed to be learning not to quarrel, aren't we?"

Regar snorted, half annoyance and half amusement. "Marshal's been at me about that for years. It's my nature."

Arvid raised his brows. "If Gird's making me quit being a thief, don't you think Gird might make you quit being quarrelsome?"

Silence from Regar. Arvid sneaked a look at him. Regar actually looked thoughtful. At the camp entrance, Arvid reined in. "Where's Count Arcolin?" he asked the sentry.

"Off with a cohort checking a report of bandits," the man said. "Where's our pigs?"

"Trouble," Arvid said. "It was an ambush. Headman claimed he'd sold for a better price, refused to give the advance back, and then someone started shooting at us." He showed the arrow that had been stuck in the seat back. "There are more of these on the tailgate and back of the seat." The sentry craned to look, then nodded. "If you want my guess, this is some of the same sort you had in Vonja last year. Can I send someone to let the Count know?"

"Captain Garralt is in camp. Tell him."

"Thank you," Arvid said. He drove into the camp, turned the team over to the supply sergeant, and went looking for Captain Garralt, taking with him the arrows yanked from the wagon.

"Damn," the captain said when Arvid told what happened. "Cooks were asking when you'd get back with the critters. They have the poles up and ready. Market open today?"

"Not for live meat," Regar said. "Day after tomorrow."

"Should I bring back a carcass?" Arvid asked.

"Probably best," the captain said. "Any idea of the price?"

Arvid didn't know, but Regar did; the captain whistled, but handed Arvid the money. The team hadn't been unharnessed yet, so they took the same wagon into the city. The only large carcasses left were not worth the price; Arvid managed to haggle them down but not, he thought, enough. Arcolin was not going to be happy, and neither were the troops.

"How many is this for?" Regar asked as they started for the camp again, three rather scrawny beef halves in the back of the wagon.

"Over three hundred," Arvid said. "Safer to figure three hundred fifty."

"That's . . . a town."

"Yes. And they eat a lot."

At the camp, the cooks scowled at the quality of the meat—and no wonder, Arvid thought—but Garralt had told them what had happened, and they did not complain to him. When they'd pulled the halves out of the wagon, he and Regar drove down to the stream and spent a half-glass cleaning the wagon bed.

"I don't see why," Regar said.

"Because the Count insists on it," Arvid said. "For a man engaged in the business of killing and wounding, he has a surprising dislike of bad smells."

CHAPTER THIRTY-FOUR

As Regar had insisted he did not want Arvid in his house, Arvid expected they would spend the night in the camp, and so it proved. Before full dawn, they walked back to the city and Regar's home and stoneyard. Regar banged on his house door, and his wife passed him a leather bag of tools, then shut the door again. By daylight, they were hard at work. Four other men showed up and began work under Regar's direction.

Arvid had never worked with building stone or brick in his life. Regar handed him a chisel and hammer and showed him a rough block. "This needs to be square. I've made a chalk line for you. Knock off anything outside the line; don't knock off anything inside it."

"What if it breaks?"

Regar snorted. "It won't, not with that chisel."

Arvid put the chisel to the stone and hit it with the hammer. *Ting*. He couldn't see that any stone had gone. Again. *Ting*. And again. *Ting. Ting. Ting*. He lifted the chisel and saw a pale line in the rock, no more.

"Slant the chisel more. Like this." Regar had come up beside him; he put his own chisel on the mark Arvid's had made, slanted it toward the bulge, and hit it four times quickly. *Ting-ting-ting-tonk*. Three little chips and a larger one flew up. "Like that," Regar said. "A little bit at a time." He moved off to the other men, more than an armslength away, but Arvid didn't remind him of the Marshal's words.

Arvid tried again. At a slant, the chisel hopped when hit, and he banged his knuckles on the stone. He kept going. His hands cramped, and his shoulders hurt.

"Good day to you," someone said at the yard entrance. Arvid glanced aside. Invarr stood waiting, and Regar walked toward him, brushing the stone dust off his hands. The other men did not stop their work. "How is your apprentice, Regar?"

"Making a start," Regar said. "Never used a chisel in his life, but he's learning. I've had worse."

"Good, good."

Arvid went back to work. Now and again he had to stop and flex his hands, but the next time Regar came to see, he had a row of grooves, a total of a handspan wide, and the bulge was noticeably less. "That's it," Regar said. "Keep at it. After lunch we'll take some stones to the building site and do the finish shaping there."

By midday, Arvid had bruises and scrapes and an ache in his back to go with the ache in his shoulders, arms, and hands. Regar's wife appeared with a large pot of beans. She went back to the house and returned with a platter piled with flat round loaves of bread. One of Regar's workmen brought back a large pitcher of ale from the nearest inn.

They broke the loaves open and scooped up beans and shreds of goat meat. To Arvid's surprise, the beans were tasty. A half-glass later, a wagon and team showed up—Regar must have ordered them, he realized—and Arvid helped load stone onto the wagon. The stones were just as uncooperative that way, unrelenting in their weight and bulk. Then it was off to the building site, walking alongside the wagon.

Invarr's new warehouse was on the east side of the city, within sight of the Fox Company camp, and Arvid wondered that he had never noticed it. "The important thing is that the stones are all laid level and set square—no leaning or it'll fall," Regar said.

Arvid had never paid attention to building construction. Now he asked what "square" meant, and for the rest of the afternoon, as he worked until he thought he would fall over, Regar explained far more than he really wanted to know. Arvid didn't hear all of it, as out of breath as he often was, but Regar seemed tireless . . . and very happy to have a new ear to bend.

Arvid hoped tomorrow's assignments from Arcolin would be something easy, but he suspected he'd have to make another trip out to get meat or livestock. At least tonight wasn't a drill night.

Arcolin called him in when he got to the camp, and Regar came along. "Garralt told me about yesterday. I think you're right that this is related to what happened in Vonja. I've reported it to the Foss Council judiciary, and they're taking it up. You'll be needed as a witness. In the meantime, I'm sending a patrol with you to pick up livestock west of town tomorrow. It's a vill called Sweetcreek."

"I know them," Regar said. "I have an uncle there."

"Good," Arcolin said. "Then maybe we won't have any more problems." He looked more closely at Arvid. "Are you all right? You look—"

"Tired," Arvid said. "I'm just tired. I'm finding out how heavy stone is."

Dattur, who had been sitting silent across the tent, head bent over some sewing, looked up with a grin. "Good stone?"

Regar turned and stared. "It's a . . . a dwarf boy?"

Dattur scowled. "Not dwarf. Kapristi. What you call gnome."

"But—"

"Dattur is helping me," Arcolin said. "He is of the same tribe as those who live near me in the north."

"Is that why he's wearing . . . colors?"

"Yes," Arcolin said before Dattur could answer. And to Dattur he said, "Regar is a mason here, building a warehouse for a merchant in town."

"Arvid helps him?" Dattur said, brow furrowed.

"The Marshal commanded it," Arvid said. "Every other day."

"You displeased Marshal?"

"Er . . . yes," Arvid said.

"If you'll take my advice," Arcolin said, "ask our surgeon to clean out those gashes for you."

All Arvid wanted was to fall into bed, but he made his way to the surgeon's tent, empty but for one pallet at the end where someone, the surgeon muttered, had been stupid enough to drink water from a ditch instead of a running stream and now suffered the consequences. He looked at Arvid's hands, prodded his back muscles, and by the time he was finished, Arvid felt slightly better, though the interim had been unpleasant.

Next morning, he was stiff but able to move around, and he chose to walk beside the wagon to loosen up while Regar drove. Two ten-squads went with them, back through the city and out the west road, which soon turned to a rutted lane between hedges. The trip went smoothly. The village had the required animals neatly penned, and Arvid felt better for the walk.

The rest of the ten days passed without incident. Regar went with Arvid to market in the city and out in various villages; Arvid chipped stone and hefted rocks in and out of the wagon and onto the wall. He learned to use string and chalk, bob and level, and made no complaint about the scrapes and bruises and broken nails he got from the unforgiving stones. He heard a lot about Regar's wife, her family, the children, the problems Regar had running his own business.

At the end of ten days, Marshal Porfur called them into the grange and looked from one to the other. "I hear from the other yeomen in town that you have indeed stayed close to one another as I bade you, day and night, for this ten days. I hope you've both learned something."

"I have," Arvid said. Regar nodded.

"And what is that?" the Marshal asked.

"Regar is a hard worker, a good man, and a good father," Arvid said. "I respect him."

"Regar?"

"Arvid's not a thief anymore," Regar said. "I know that now. He works hard."

"Very well. And do you think, yeomen of Gird, that you could stand shoulder to shoulder to defend the people against evil?"

"Yes." They both spoke.

"I am glad to hear it. I release you from this task but expect that you will remain in fellowship with one another—and with others. Let me see a *proper* exchange of blows before you go."

This time it was wooden practice blades the Marshal handed

them. Each made a touch—Arvid could have made four to Regar's one, but he finally understood this was ritual, not a reason to show off. They walked back through the city.

"Stand you a mug at the inn," Arvid said.

"If you'll let me stand you one," Regar said.

They drank their mugs in silence and parted with an arm grip.

The next time the grange met for drill, Marshal Porfur announced that Count Andressat's youngest son was missing. "You all know there have been brigands in our area," he said. "We are fortunate to be in a well-managed region like Foss Council that hired an additional force to protect us. And now we know the Count of Andressat's son is missing, believed taken, and a reward has been offered for information about him. I tell you this to make it clear that even a rich man with his own army is not perfectly safe. Even here in Ifoss, with Fox Company patrolling the roads, you know that a few villages have lost livestock and some have been injured. So every yeoman must be alert and ready to respond if there is danger. Some of you are old enough to remember Siniava's War—and other wars before—and we must pray to be spared another. Yet we must prepare. When winter comes, Fox Company will be gone; we must defend ourselves if trouble comes."

"Who's the enemy this time?" someone asked. "Is it Vonja?"

"Why do you think Vonja?" Marshal Porfur asked. "They're in the Guild League, same as Foss Council."

"Doesn't mean they can't be up to something," the man said, standing forward. "My da said, in one of the battles in Siniava's War, they ran like rabbits."

"That's as may be," Porfur said. "But running away isn't the same thing as stealing someone's son. What I want you to do is tell the yeomen who aren't here—who've been skipping drill night—that this is no time to slack off. I think there's trouble coming."

Arvid could feel the reluctance of these hardworking men to believe that skipping a drill night could put them at real risk. He said nothing, nor did any of the Fox Company soldiers attending that night. Drill went well, though the night was overwarm and even the walk back through the city did not dry all the sweat from working out.

"They don't know a thing," one of the soldiers said.

"You didn't tell them anything," Arvid said.

"Not my place to go telling what the Company knows to the locals," the soldier said. "You should know that much."

"I do, but . . . well, maybe they've heard Alured's name in the taverns. Or that new name . . . Vaskronin. I wonder where he got that. It doesn't sound like anything I've heard before."

"Made it up, like as not," the soldier said.

When they arrived back in camp, Arcolin called Arvid to his tent. "I need your expertise," he said.

"My expertise?"

"You're surely aware that soldiers are offered stolen goods from time to time. We warn them, but they see something gaudy and think of a brother or sister back home—"

"You want me to stop them buying from thieves?"

"Not . . . exactly. We're being plagued by counterfeit coinage, and they get counterfeit coins in change—and then are accused of passing them when they try to buy something else. You knew this was a growing problem in the south, I assume."

"No . . . no, I didn't."

"Well, it is. The Guild League coins have been respected for generations; the Guild League has had a system of testing that eliminated most counterfeits. The only difference between the Guild League mints was the design on the obverse, the seal for each city. That testing still does eliminate counterfeits of the types seen before . . . if the counterfeit is light in weight or the wrong density to be a genuine coin."

"It must be one or the other to be worth making," Arvid said.

"Yes, you would think so. But the Guild League is now seeing counterfeits—we found some last year—that have too much silver or gold. Mostly silver."

"That's . . . ridiculous."

"Not if someone's trying to trust in the coinage. It doesn't matter which way it's wrong—unpredictably wrong is even worse than predictably wrong. It slows down the transfer of funds."

"And what do you think I can do about that?"

"As a merchant you have a reason to express concern, and as a former thief you may have ways of finding out who's passing the counterfeits here in Ifoss. In Vonja last year it was a Guild trader who claimed he'd been coerced by a gang . . . He thought Alured was involved, and a family member had been taken."

"I can try," Arvid said. "But I don't know—the yeomen here know I was a thief—"

"Porfur told them? He shouldn't have."

"Somebody did," Arvid said. "I thought it was Porfur and was surprised, but maybe his yeoman-marshal, Gan. At any rate, I think it's likely others in the market will know. Makes it hard to ask questions without being noticed."

Arcolin looked thoughtful and worried both. "If the yeomen know . . . some of them trade all the way to Valdaire—could the Thieves' Guild there find you here?"

"It's possible," Arvid said. "There's only a small Guild presence here—most of 'em in Foss Council are in Foss itself. More traffic on the road, more . . . targets."

"Have they shown any interest in you?"

"No. And I would know if they were," Arvid said. "I'm keeping my oath, but I still have eyes and ears."

"Still . . . they could hear from the yeomen if they're halfway competent."

"They could. At least the Marshal didn't make me use my full name." Porfur had insisted on knowing that full name but allowed him to keep using Burin as his surname.

"Perhaps I shouldn't ask you to do this . . ."

"I don't mind. It'll be a challenge." Arvid grinned. He relished the thought of getting back into that familiar world, even on the opposite side.

"But it may be more dangerous than I thought—"

"Danger," Arvid said, "is my delight."

Arcolin looked at him a long time. "I hope you're joking," he said finally. "That's the kind of thing I expect from boys who want to be squires."

"I was never a squire," Arvid said in a more serious tone. "And

I am good with danger. I will find counterfeiters before they find me."

"I hope so," Arcolin said.

Despite what Arvid had said publicly, he knew that it was only a matter of time before the Valdaire branch of the Thieves' Guild penetrated his disguise and sent someone to assassinate him. As he had been on the other end of such assignments, he knew what precautions to take—and how little use they were if the assassin was truly skilled.

Yet Ifoss seemed remarkably clear of Thieves' Guild activity. His search for counterfeiters made no headway, and his activities in the market on Arcolin's behalf did not lure so much as a pickpocket. Perhaps the penalties dealt to the vill harboring brigands had scared them away, or perhaps the Guild had ordered a pause in their activities—which could mean assassins were about to arrive.

Despite the summer heat, Arvid never went out without his cloak and its useful pockets. He paid the Company armorer, with Arcolin's permission, to make him a lightweight mail shirt, though it was miserable to wear in that season. He ate and drank only in company with others, and only what they ate and drank, never taking his eyes from his own mug and plate until he was through.

He was in the market, buying fresh fruit for the camp, when the first attack came. He caught sight of someone in an alley smoking a pipe . . . no, a short blow-pipe. It would use darts. Arvid snatched a bullwhip from an astonished teamster and snapped it in the man's face; the man screamed and dropped the pipe. It shattered on the ground; a second man grabbed the first by the shoulders and pushed him down the alley.

Arvid looked at the broken pieces of pipe and the dark poison-tipped darts that lay beside it.

"That's my whip, you thief," came an angry voice from behind him. The teamster and two other men had charged after him.

"It is indeed," Arvid said, handing it back despite the man's red face and furious expression. "That fellow was trying to kill me. Look—" He pointed at the broken pipe and the darts.

"What's that?"

Arvid explained. One of the other men bent to pick up a dart.

"Don't!" Arvid said. "They're tipped with poison." The man jerked his hand back.

"How do you know that?" the teamster asked. He had coiled the whip and looped it to his belt. "What are you?"

"Oh, he's that merchant with Fox Company," one of the others said. "I've seen him with the captain and at the grange, too."

Arvid nodded. "That's right. I'm Ser Burin. I came from Valdaire with Fox Company."

The teamster still looked suspicious. "But how did you know those were poison darts? And where did you learn to use a whip like that?"

"I did not start as a merchant," Arvid said. "For a time I drove a team—freight—for a merchant." He had, though only briefly. Mixing experiences, he went on. "Brigands use poisoned darts. Lost a guard to one once."

"And where was that?" the teamster said.

Arvid shrugged. "Over the mountains, in Tsaia. Up there they use blow-pipes a lot."

"Oh." The teamster relaxed. "Never seen anyone but a teamster or a cattle drover so fast with a whip."

"It's not a skill you forget," Arvid said.

"Was he trying to kill you or someone else?"

"I'm not sure," Arvid said. "I'll take these things to Marshal Porfur."

"You should report this to a judicar," one of the other men said.

"I'll find one," another man said.

Soon Arvid found himself explaining to a judicar what the broken pieces of clay were.

"You're the one was attacked in that village, weren't you? You spoke at the trial of the villagers who broke contract with Count Arcolin."

"Yes," Arvid said.

"This was probably revenge for that testimony," the judicar said. "Brigands, I expect—I don't think those villagers would risk another judgment." Arvid had not thought of that possibility and accepted it gratefully as an alternative to explaining why the Thieves' Guild would be targeting him. "Would you recognize the men again?" the judicar asked.

"One should have a whip strike on his face," Arvid said. "Other than that—I saw the face only with a blow-pipe to it, and never saw the face of the one who guided the first one away. Both were, I would say, about my height."

The judicar took charge of the broken pieces of pipe and the darts. Arvid went to Porfur's grange, impelled by a hunch rather than a voice in his head.

"I need to talk to Marshal Porfur," he said to the yeoman-marshal who answered the door.

"He's teachin' the childer," the yeoman-marshal said.

"When will he be done?" Arvid asked.

"Another turn of the glass," the yeoman-marshal said. "Anything I can help you with?"

"No," Arvid said. "Unless . . . you know the time Regar and I were attacked?"

"Yes, of course," the yeoman-marshal said.

"Well, it seems the brigand who came to that village may want revenge. Someone nearly killed me this morning with darts from a blow-pipe."

The yeoman-marshal scowled. "Did you tell the judicars?"

"Of course," Arvid said. "But the men got away—the man with the pipe and the man helping him. I do not know if trouble might come to the grange because of that."

"Have you warned Regar?" the yeoman-marshal said.

"No, I came straight here," Arvid said. "I suppose I should have gone to him first—"

"Not necessarily." The yeoman-marshal opened the door wider. "Come on in; Marshal's in the barton, but I'll let you in the side entrance."

Marshal Porfur had a double arc of children sitting on the ground around him. As they entered the barton, one of the children stood up and recited the seventh of the Ten Fingers in a squeaky voice.

"Excuse me, Marshal," the yeoman-marshal said. "There's a problem."

Marshal Porfur looked at the sandglass beside him on the ground; most of the sand had run out.

"Short, or long?" he asked. Then, with another look at Arvid's face, he nodded and stood. "Long, I suspect. All right, juniors—that's all for the morning."

The children scrambled up and headed for the street gate.

"Just a moment," Porfur said. "You have forgotten order, I believe."

They halted, turned, looked at one another and then at him, shuffled into two lines, then recited what was obviously a rote ending to the school day. "Thank you, Marshal, for your instruction. Gird's blessing be on you, and Gird's guidance on us."

"That's better," the Marshal said. "Go with Gird."

When they had left, slamming the barton gate behind them, Porfur turned to Arvid and the yeoman-marshal and raised his brows.

Arvid told his tale again.

"I don't see that it would cause trouble here," the Marshal said, "but I agree that Regar must be warned. We will visit him together. Do you know, Arvid, whether he will be at the stoneyard or at the building site?"

Arvid shook his head. "It varied from day to day, the time I worked there," he said. "He always started the day in the yard but sometimes left for the site by midmorning and sometimes only after lunch."

"We'll start with the yard," the Marshal said.

Arvid saw nothing to alarm him as they walked back through the city. It was near noon; the smells of cooking food made his stomach growl, but he ignored that, paying attention only to the flow of traffic, the interest or indifference of those they passed. When they turned into the lane that led toward Regar's stoneyard, he felt something—as if he were being looked at with intent—but could not see anything.

Outside the stoneyard gate, they saw a wagon and team of mules. Nothing moved in the noon stillness. "They're eating lunch," the Marshal said.

"No," Arvid said. "We'd hear talking. And the muleteer never ate here or left the mules." He put off his cloak and drew his sword. The Marshal stared at him but did the same. Arvid motioned for silence, then pointed at the wall. The Marshal's brows rose, but he said nothing as Arvid hoisted himself to the wall just high enough to see over. Regar, his wife, and several workmen lay gagged and bound; one of his other workmen was dead. Five men stood over them, silent for the moment. Arvid recognized two of them from the Guild in Valdaire; one had been on guard at the entrance when he'd carried his son out of the Guildhouse. He slid back down to the ground and motioned the Marshal away—out of earshot, he hoped.

He murmured an explanation to the Marshal and told him to get help. "At least a dozen. They're very good with techniques your people don't know."

"And you?"

"I'll distract them. Be quick."

The unattended mule team was his best chance. They had brought a mule team for a purpose—probably to take their prisoners out of town unnoticed—so they would react to the team's movement. On the other hand, they might kill their prisoners before chasing after him—a chance he'd have to take. He picked up his cloak again, bundled it under one arm, and strolled down the lane and past the wagon.

Two of the mules swung an ear toward him; he saw that the first pair were hobbled. A quick slash of his dagger took care of that. Neither mules nor wagon bore a Guild mark; they'd been stolen, probably here in Ifoss. Arvid plucked the whip left coiled under the wagon seat and spoke in a whining country dialect: "What i' Gird's name ye're doin' here, y'rascals! Who took yeh? 'F it's that Regar, I'll have t'judicars on 'im!" Then he cracked the whip over the mules' backs; they squealed and lunged into motion, the wagon rattling behind them. Another crack of the whip, and they broke into a fast trot. Arvid flattened himself against the wall and shrugged quickly into his cloak, slipping his arm into the leather bracer he'd installed there. He took his serrated throwing disk into his left hand.

Curses from inside and hurrying footsteps. By now the mules and wagon were three or four wagon lengths down the lane, and the mules seemed perfectly happy to keep going. Ahead, the lane sloped gently down to a stream. They picked up speed.

Two thieves burst from the gate, focused on the departing wagon. Arvid cut one's throat before he was even seen; the other whirled—his blade already out—and opened his mouth to yell. Arvid threw the serrated disk; it severed the man's windpipe, but not before he'd let out the first sound, and as he fell, his sword, like the other man's, clattered on the stones.

Arvid retrieved the disk, snatched up the two swords—no time to collect the other weapons or any place to stash them—and darted back to the scant cover of the low wall. He stuffed one sword, naked as it was, into his belt, held the other between his knees while replacing the disk in its pocket, then took the sword in hand.

Down the street he saw a couple of men staring, but nothing of the Marshal and a posse. The men stood as if nailed to the ground; then one of them turned to run away, and one walked toward Arvid.

People who watched someone kill two men and then approached were not necessarily allies.

"Look out!" the man yelled, flinging up an arm.

Or maybe they were. Arvid jumped sideways, and the man on the wall, already jumping down where he'd been, stumbled on landing, off balance. Arvid made use of the sword, running it between the man's ribs before he could get up. Another man was on the wall now; Arvid backed away from it. The man who had yelled to warn him was now calling for help, and others appeared from doorways. The man on the wall snatched a small crossbow from under his cloak; the bolt, Arvid knew, would be poisoned, and this close the bow had power to penetrate.

Arvid threw the sword—a bad throwing weapon but a visual distraction—and then his wrist knife.

The thief got off one shot, badly aimed, and the knife slashed the side of his neck. He dropped the bow to stanch the rush of blood, then jumped back off the wall on the inside. Someone else, Arvid knew, would pick it up and use it better.

"They've got Regar!" Arvid yelled down the street. "They've killed Gorlin! Call the Guard!"

Now the street had come alive—more men came out of doorways, some armed. Far down the street Arvid could hear the rhythmic thud of boots that he hoped meant either the city guard or Marshal Porfur.

He'd killed three and wounded one. He'd seen five. But on a mission to a distant city, after a known thief enforcer, would they send only five? Not likely. A minimum of two triads: six. So three were still alive, only one wounded. Where was the one he'd not yet seen? Where were Regar's children? His heart contracted at the thought of the thieves taking those children.

As the other citizens approached, Arvid looked up at the house roof. Nothing. Back along the wall. Nothing . . . Wait . . . a crossbow's prod, just above the wall, swiveling to bear on him; he leapt aside as a bolt zipped past and shattered on the building behind him.

Now the others were near, yelling; the bow disappeared. He charged the gate, saw the man with the crossbow running toward Regar and two more holding struggling children, dragging them toward the back of the stoneyard. Regar's son was doing his best to kick the thief where it would hurt.

Arvid leaped for the wall to one side of the gap, pulled himself up, and jumped down onto the stacked blocks of stone. He took a moment to throw the serrated disk at the man with the crossbow; the man jerked aside and then ran to help the other two. Arvid followed, just as Regar's son landed a hard heel in a soft and vulnerable spot. That thief yelped and loosened his grip. The boy wriggled free, grabbed a stone fragment from the ground, and tried to attack the thief.

Now the others were in the entrance, tangling with one another in their hurry. Arvid ignored that but for a quick glance to be sure no one was attacking his back. Could he save the children?

Call on me.

Not now!

NOW.

Something blurred his sight, a flat peasant face, broad and lined, yellowed gray hair. He wanted to argue with the voice—surely it knew about the children—but the face was there, in his way.

"Gird," he muttered. "DO something!"

The face disappeared. Regar's son's rock connected solidly with one thief's eye; the man yowled, dropped his dagger, and put both hands to his face. The boy hit him again, with a larger rock, and he went down. Meanwhile the third thief had taken one of the girls from the man who had struggled with both.

Arvid reached one of them, applied the necessary grip and force, and peeled the girl out of his grip. "Run," he said to the girl, as he evaded a knife slash with the man's other arm and tried to position himself to force the man down. But they knew the same tricks; they had the same training, the same weapons.

"I'll kill her!" the last man warned, holding a knife to the throat of his captive. Arvid, fully engaged with his opponent, could do nothing. *DO something,* he thought at Gird. He heard more people coming—the thud and scrape of boots, the sound of blows, cries of anger and pain. Then a cudgel as thick as his upper arm came down past his nose on the thief's head, and the man sagged. Before Arvid could shift his own blade, someone else had cut the man's throat.

"Here—" A meaty hand reached down, and Arvid took it, pulling himself up. He'd seen the man who helped him up in the grange but had never talked to him. He looked around. Regar and his wife were both unbound, alive, though bruised and scraped; Regar had a broken nose and a black eye. The bound workmen, freed, were only bruised. Regar's oldest daughter had run out the back with the two youngest; they were safe. Of the other three, the middle girl had a knife gash on the side of her neck, but she would live—the Marshal was already healing her.

All the thieves were dead. Their disappearance would hamper the Guildhouse at Valdaire, Arvid knew. With help—but the account would be laid to him—he had reft the Valdaire house of almost two hands now: the Guildmaster, the two who had taken him and Dattur away, and now these six. The Guild would want revenge, and they would take it where they could. *Gird, guard my son!*

"Thanks to Gird," Marshal Porfur said, and the other men echoed. Arvid joined in, as he must; only a few of the men looked sideways at him as he retrieved the bloody throwing disk and tucked it away.

Regar, his broken nose healed by Gird's grace and the Marshal's skill, came to give him a brother's hug. "I thought we was all dead, and the children, too. Thanks to you—"

"To Gird," Arvid said. It came more easily from his mouth now.

"Yes, but you were the cudgel in Gird's hand this time," Regar said. "And if you'd not been a thief before, you'd not have known how to fight 'em. What can I do—?"

"Be wary," Arvid said. "I've brought trouble on you, and more might come, though not for a while. They'll need to hire from other houses. I'll talk to the Marshal, get his consent to leave. If I'm not here, you'll be safer."

"But Arvid, man—"

"I'll talk to the Marshal," he said, and with a last squeeze set Regar aside, bowed to Lia, and went to the Marshal, now organizing the men to carry the bodies away.

"Six," the Marshal said, puffing out his lips. "They sent *six* after you?"

"They knew my abilities," Arvid said.

"Evidently not. They should have sent twice six."

"They didn't have twice six. Not like these." He felt cold suddenly and shaky as the battle fever left him.

"You should eat and drink," the Marshal said. "Come with me." He gave a few more orders, putting one of the yeomen in charge, and led Arvid down the street to the first tavern.

CHAPTER THIRTY-FIVE

I need to leave," Arvid said, as they crossed the threshold.

"You think you can outrun them?" the Marshal said.

"No. But I think I can lead them away from here—from Regar and his family, from you and this grange."

"Sit down, lad." The Marshal settled into a chair at one of the tables and waved to the man at the bar. "You've not completed your year."

"I know," Arvid said. He leaned forward. "But I'm a danger to you, Marshal, and to the people here, the grange. The longer I'm away from here before they come again to find me, the better for you."

"You still don't understand," the Marshal said. "Gird did not create this Fellowship to seek safety, but to provide protection to one another in danger. You say you're bringing trouble, but your captain says it's coming from the east, with that new Duke of Immer. There's always trouble somewhere." To the man who approached the table, he said, "Ale, bread, and honey."

"I am not impugning your courage," Arvid said, when the man had left. "I just don't want—"

"To make trouble. I understand that, Arvid, and I respect it. You've come a long way from what I judge you were. Tell me: did you call on Gird in this fight?"

Arvid nodded.

"Good enough. And thanked him after. I heard. That was well done. But you should not leave without a plan, and I must know that plan."

If the Marshal knew, he could be made to tell it. Arvid hoped that did not show on his face. Ale arrived, and a platter of warm bread and a bowl of honey. He poured ale for both of them and buried his face in his mug.

"The thing is," the Marshal said after a long swallow of ale, "you're a grown man and an expert in your own way. So it is not easy for you to take direction, and you have worked hard to learn to work with other yeomen. But what you cannot see, that is clear to me or any Marshal, is how thin a layer of Girdishness is laid over what you were."

"Gird seems deep enough in my head for me," Arvid said, around a mouthful of bread dipped in honey.

"Gird needs to be here—" The Marshal pointed at his midsection. "Not just here." He tapped his head.

True.

Arvid shivered. Not here; not now.

"You are in more danger than I am," the Marshal went on. "In danger of more than a knife in the ribs from your former friends. Gird has chosen you for something; we do not yet know what. But when Gird or a god has chosen you for a task, then you must do it. Such tasks are not given lightly, for the gods' amusement, you know."

"I never thought about it," Arvid said. He was suddenly hungry; the bread and honey suited him exactly. He swallowed a large lump and washed it down with ale. "What, exactly, is more dangerous than a knife in the ribs?"

Marshal Porfur sighed. "There, you see, is your problem and that of most novice yeomen. Think back, Arvid: did you not see worse than death in what happened to Paksenarrion?"

His jaw seized; he blinked and felt hot tears on his cheeks. He could not answer.

"Yes—you did. I see that you know it. But you don't hold it in mind—"

Who could hold that in mind? Arvid glared at the Marshal, who gazed peacefully back at him and sipped from his mug.

"Gird has some plan for you," Marshal Porfur said.

"Paks said maybe he had a plan for the Thieves' Guild, not for me," Arvid muttered, when he could speak.

"Or maybe both," Marshal Porfur said. "Paladins don't know all. You might be Gird's instrument to reform the Guild, or those might be two different things. But right now, you need to learn how to listen to Gird—"

As if Gird himself weren't already talking to him. Arvid hunched his shoulders, hiding his expression in his mug.

"And for that, my lad, you need an experienced Marshal to guide you. You can't expect Gird to speak as clearly as a man, inside your head."

"He does," Arvid muttered, even more softly, into the ale. He reached for another hunk of bread without looking up, only to have Marshal Porfur clamp his hand to the table.

"*What* did you say?"

"Umm . . ." Lying to the Marshal was against the Code.

"You hear voices in your head? How long?"

"I don't remember," Arvid said. He tried to laugh, but Marshal Porfur's expression stopped it behind his teeth.

"Before you met Paksenarrion?"

"No." He was sure of that.

"Before her trials?"

"No . . . I don't think so . . ."

"You hear Gird?"

"I . . ."

The face: a challenging expression. The voice: *Well?*

"Sometimes," Arvid said, staring at the grain of the table. He could feel the heat in his face and ears; he could not look the Marshal in the eye.

Marshal Porfur let go of his hand and sighed gustily. Arvid dipped a piece of bread in honey and stuffed it in his mouth.

"That changes things," Marshal Porfur said.

Arvid chewed, swallowed, nearly choked, then got it all down.

"How? If it . . . if he . . . if there's something I'm supposed to do, I could still be wrong. Hearing it wrong."

The snort of contempt in his head should have been audible to Marshal Porfur, but Porfur's expression didn't change.

"You're not stupid, Arvid," Marshal Porfur said. "That's one of the things that's worried me, how smart you are. Intelligent men think up ways to get themselves in tangles a stupid man would never imagine. But if you're hearing voices—and more, if you're really hearing Gird . . ." He shook his head. "You said you called on Gird today: tell me about that."

"He told me to," Arvid said. He told the rest, including his impatient reaction. "But I knew I wouldn't get to the children in time. So I asked—"

Told.

"I guess it was more like . . . *told* him . . . to do something."

"You would," Marshal Porfur said. He was not laughing. "Arvid . . . if indeed Gird speaks so to you, then you are beyond my guidance. No—" He held up his hand as if Arvid had spoken. "You are not yet ready to make all your own interpretations, but you are beyond my guidance. You need to be instructed by a High Marshal, at least. Perhaps the Marshal-General. I think you should go to Fin Panir."

"Go—but—" *You just told me to stay,* he almost said, but managed to shut it off.

"The difficulty will be getting you past Valdaire, I'm sure—"

"But—go now—?"

"You wanted to leave now anyway, didn't you?"

"There's . . . there's my . . . he may be my . . . son."

Marshal Porfur nodded. "You'll want him safe with you. Where is he now?"

"Marshal Steralt in Valdaire found him a place."

"I'll send word to him for you. I'll need to talk to your—to Count Arcolin. I should think the trouble's done for today, don't you?"

"Yes, Marshal."

"Then come along to the grange; we'll have our service of thanks. I'll go with you to see the Count afterward."

It seemed everyone involved and their families were packed into the grange that hot midafternoon: Regar and his whole family, the other men, even the mule team's owner, who had stopped grumbling about the damage to his wagon when the Marshal pulled him aside on the way to the grange. Someone must have run to the camp, because a squad of Fox Company soldiers and Count Arcolin were there, too, at the last moment.

He would have scoffed at Marshal Porfur's words a season ago. Porfur pounded his points home with repetition: this was the Fellowship's duty, to respond to threats to the community, and they should remember this day whenever trouble came. By standing together . . . and so on. Now it seemed much less fussy and overblown. Now he had seen for himself what it meant, and he stood silent and sweating with the others, listening to Porfur, feeling a kinship with those he'd despised.

When it was over and the crowd had edged out of the crowded grange, dispersing into clumps and obviously reliving their actions, Marshal Porfur called Arcolin and Arvid into his private office and shut the door. It was stuffy, and Arvid wondered why he didn't at least open the separate outside door.

"What is it, Marshal?" Arcolin asked. "Do you want to ask Ifoss Council to authorize a squad of my men to help the city militia?"

"No," Marshal Porfur said. "It's Arvid. He's told me he hears the voice of Gird in his head."

"Um." Arcolin looked at Arvid and back at the Marshal. "And why are you telling me?"

"I'm not telling everyone, you notice. You, because you brought him here and stood sponsor for him. Has he acted strangely since you met him in Valdaire?"

"Other than being a thief trying to turn honest? No, I wouldn't say so."

"I think the same," Marshal Porfur said. "But—you do not hear Gird's voice in *your* head, do you?"

"Not commonly," Arcolin said. "I mean—there's a sense, sometimes a strong one, of what I should do, but it's not . . . not someone else."

"So. Madmen hear voices—you've seen those poor souls, I expect, convinced that some god told them to eat pebbles or go about naked or stand on one foot until they fell over—"

"Or pick up a sword and stab the next person wearing green—yes, Marshal. Pitiable, mostly; dangerous, sometimes. Arvid, as I've said, is nothing like that. I knew back in Valdaire that he was distressed—that he felt he'd changed in some way since he rescued Paks, but I thought of that as her influence, perhaps, turning him away from evil and toward the good."

"From Paksenarrion to Gird is a short stride," Marshal Porfur said. "Arvid tells me Paks said Gird might have a use for the Thieves' Guild—but Gird might also have a use for Arvid himself—and be guiding him directly."

"And you do not want others to know," Arcolin said. He glanced at Arvid again, then turned back to the Marshal. "Madmen generally tell everyone about the voices they hear—they are eager for others to know. Arvid has not."

"Yes. I am not saying he is mad, Count Arcolin. I think he does hear Gird's voice. I could wish for that—"

"No, you don't," Arvid said. "It's not what you think—"

"I think nothing," said Marshal Porfur, "because I have never heard it."

"It's not . . . comfortable," Arvid said.

"I wouldn't expect it to be for someone with a great change to make," Marshal Porfur said. Arvid said nothing, and after waiting, Porfur nodded. "Well, then," he went on. "You're willing to listen to Gird; you even began listening to me after a while. You can be taught. And the place for you to learn is not here."

"Surely, Marshal—" Arcolin began.

Marshal Porfur shook his head. "I'm a competent Marshal for the grange of a small city that's not more than one-quarter Girdish," he said. "Arvid's been good for me—good for the grange—but I'm not what he needs now. I know that. We're taught, we Marshals, to recognize someone who needs special training and send them to get it. That's what I'm doing, same as you'd send a promising squire to take training for knighthood."

"But I don't know if I—" Arvid began. He stopped as both the others stared at him.

"If you're not a madman," Arcolin said, "then you really hear

Gird's voice. And if you really hear Gird's voice, then there's a reason. And the reason is that Gird needs you to do Gird's work somewhere."

"But I'm not . . ." Arvid felt tears stinging his eyes again and blinked them back. He would not cry, not again. What good did the tears do? "I was a *thief*," he said, his voice hoarse with the unshed tears. "I was an enforcer for the Guild. I—I threatened people, scared people, hurt people. *Killed* people. I was . . . bad. Why would Gird want *me*?"

"I don't know," Marshal Porfur said. "But the word sent from Valdaire was that Gird's relic lighted the moment you came into the grange there . . . lighted in your hand without burning you. You hear his voice. I cannot answer your question, but I can send you to those who will help you answer it."

"You have been of service to me," Arcolin said. "I have found you to be sensible, honest, and hardworking—and a good dinner companion those times we've shared a meal. But for all you make a reasonable minor merchant, I don't think that's why Gird is talking to you. There are plenty of Girdish merchants already. Possibly only one former Guild enforcer."

"I knew I had to change," Arvid said in a more normal voice as his throat relaxed. "But not to know where the change ends—"

"Nobody knows where change ends," Arcolin said. Arvid looked at him, remembering the look on Arcolin's face when Dattur prostrated himself and called Arcolin "prince."

"Indeed," Marshal Porfur said. "Count, can you do anything to get Arvid safely through Valdaire?"

"Possibly. I send my people to Valdaire on errands; he could go with them. Beyond—I am not sure; I would have to ask."

"If you say I must go that way," Arvid said, "then if I can buy a couple of good horses in Valdaire, I will be fine on the road—"

"Or not," Arcolin said. "I will be sending a letter to the king in a few days—I am still compiling the information he should have—and beyond Valdaire you could ride with the courier."

Entering Tsaia again as Ser Burin, in colorful clothes and riding with Fox Company, he should go unrecognized if he stayed away from Vérella. "Thank you," he said. "And my son?"

"I will send word today," Marshal Porfur said. "If you're leaving a few days from now, Marshal Steralt will have time to bring him to the grange."

T he journey to Valdaire went smoothly: a tensquad of Fox Company soldiers, several pack animals, Arvid, and two small traders who had begged to travel with them. Arcolin checked their references, especially the one claiming to be from Cilwan, and thought they were safe enough. They separated in Valdaire, the two traders peeling off inside the gates and Arvid heading for the grange on the far side of the city.

"Sure you don't want an escort, sir?" asked the corporal in charge of the escort.

"No, thanks. I'll be back at your quarters in the morning, if not before." He wore clothes bought in Foss's market—more southern even than the ones he'd bought in Valdaire before—and he wouldn't go near the Dragon, where someone might recognize his name and call it out.

At the grange, Marshal Steralt greeted him warmly. "I have Porfur's word—you're different, you know. And the lad is fine. Some effort was made to find him, but my yeomen don't chatter—not when I tell them nay."

"Where—should I go alone or—"

"He's here. Where are you staying? The Dragon?"

"Too obvious," Arvid said. "I can stay in the Fox Company quarters."

"Not a good idea, making an extra trip across the city. Stay overnight here, why don't you, or I'll house you with one of the yeomen in this district."

"I don't want to bring trouble . . ."

Marshal Steralt shook his head. "You won't. If anything, you'll bring an opportunity for someone to use what he's been taught. Come in, see the lad. He's grown already."

The boy turned from the table in the Marshal's room, where he'd been scratching letters on a wax tablet; his face lit up, and he launched himself at Arvid.

"You came back! You came back!"

Arvid looked over his head at Marshal Steralt.

"I didn't tell him everything in case you had trouble on the road," Marshal Steralt said. "It's for you to tell him what you will, now."

"Sit down," Arvid said to the boy. The boy had filled out, no longer scrawny-skinny though still lean, and now brown-faced from being outside somewhere. A farm, he supposed. He wore a Girdish-blue shirt embroidered with yellow stars and red circles around the neck; his trousers were too big for him but rolled up neatly at the ankle, and he wore shoes. Against the wall, Arvid saw a rolled blanket tied with thongs.

He sat down opposite the boy; Marshal Steralt left the room and closed the door, surprising Arvid. He had not been so trustful before. "How have you been?" he asked.

"Marshal sent me to a farm, a day and a half journey from the city," the boy said promptly. "It was a family. There was a girl my age and an older boy and two younger, girl and boy. They have four cows . . . well, one's only last year's calf, really. Three had calves. Chickens, too. All the eggs anyone wanted, eggs every day at breakfast. And sheep—they have sheep, and they shear them, and the lady spins the wool and they have a loom and they all know how to knit, all but the youngest. I can knit now, too. And they grow grain and vegetables, and they fed me so much, I could hardly finish it, and the lady made me this shirt and trousers to grow into, she said. And the Marshal bought me these shoes."

"Did you like being on the farm?" Arvid asked.

"Yes—it's busier some ways than the Guildhouse—everyone works at something all day—but it's not all hard work. I learned to go out with the geese first, and then the sheep, though not alone. They had dogs, too, and pigs—"

It must have been a rich farm, Arvid thought.

"And you could drink right from the stream; it was so clear you could see the bottom, and it smelled good, like herbs and mint, not like the stream here in the city."

"Would you like to stay on that farm?" Arvid asked, keeping his voice neutral. "Be part of that family, learn to be a farmer?"

The boy's face shifted expression. "I . . . I'm not ungrateful, sir, but . . . but I thought, if you came, we would be together."

Arvid leaned across the table and put his hand over the boy's hands where they were clenched together. "I do not truly know if you are the son of my body or not, young Arvid, but I care about you as if you were. If you will, you may come with me. I am going a long journey, over the pass to the north, and then west to Fintha, the land Gird came from, to Fin Panir where the Marshal-General lives. Do you want to come, or stay in this familiar land with folk you already know?"

Now joy spread across that young face. "Oh, please—I want to come with you!" he said.

"How well do you ride?" Arvid asked.

"Ride? A horse? You'll let me ride a *horse*?"

That answered one question. "I have to buy one for you first." And it would have to be that hardest to find of horses: suitable for a novice, calm in temperament, well trained, but with the soundness and endurance to handle a long season on the road.

"May I— Please, may I call you 'Da'?" the boy asked.

Arvid's heart turned over. For a moment he hesitated: how could he be ready for this? The boy's expression stiffened; Arvid smiled. "If you want," he said. "I would be glad."

"Da," the boy said, tasting it, the word he'd never been able to say. "Thank you!"

"Bide here with Marshal Steralt while I go find us horses for the trip," Arvid said.

Outside, in the main part of the grange, Marshal Steralt was talking softly with his yeoman-marshal. His brows went up.

"He's coming with me," Arvid said. "And I'm going to Fin Panir." Steralt's expression was still challenging. "He wants to call me Da."

"Then *be* that," Steralt said with emphasis. "And Gird guide your heart."

CHAPTER THIRTY-SIX

Two mornings later, Arvid, the boy, and Arcolin's courier rode out of Valdaire, headed for the pass as soon as light allowed. The Guild League ran to the boundary of the gnome princedom claiming the foothills, so the road continued a Guild League road, stone-paved, wide enough for two-way wagon traffic, with pedestrian and mounted travel to either side. A storm overnight had laid the dust, and even this early they passed a northbound caravan that must have started while it was still too dark to see. In this season, the road would have traffic all the way north. Once free of the city, the air smelled of rock and grass and something of the mountains— aromatic shrubs, the upland trees. To Arvid, it promised the north, his own country.

Arvid had searched both the city's horse markets before finding the mounts he wanted for the boy and himself. All four would ride or pack; the unridden ones carried their provisions. He led all three from his own mount. The boy clutched the saddle bow as they jogged along; Arvid had bought a fleece to throw over the saddle for him.

By midday they had caught up with and passed a caravan that had lost a wheel from one wagon the day before and camped overnight. They could see its dust behind them when they stopped to eat and rest the horses. The courier knew where a rivulet ran clear and cold not far from the road. Trees fringed it, their leaves fluttering in the breeze blowing up warm from the south, but already it was cooler than in Valdaire.

The boy came off his mount more spry than Arvid had expected for a novice rider who had been in the saddle a long half-day. He walked a bit spraddle-legged for a few paces, then shook out his legs and asked what he should do.

Arvid turned to the courier. "Will we take time to unsaddle and let them roll?"

"Might as well," the courier said. "We made a good start. Unless you want to be crowded up, we won't stay in that inn at the head of the pass. I know a little flat place we can camp. Be there before sun-setting."

"Suits me," Arvid said. To the boy, he said, "Let me show you how to undo the girths, and you can help."

He tied the horses to the line the courier strung between trees, then showed the boy how to unfasten the girths and told him to try that on the two shorter horses. He unsaddled his own, checked the back for signs of rubbing, and then unsaddled the others, handing the light packs to the boy to set down at a distance.

Explaining as he went, he showed the boy how to check the horses' hooves for stones or cuts, how to check their backs, how to lead them, one at a time, to water and then to grass, and it felt both new and familiar. The boy was as he had seemed earlier in the year: bright, willing, intensely alive. He did what he was told with a mix-ture of eagerness and solemnity that tugged at Arvid's heart, and ate a cheese-stuffed roll as they sat beneath one of the trees.

When the courier stretched and stood up, Arvid nodded at the boy. They took the horses to water a last time, saddled and packed, then mounted and were off up the trail, passing again the caravan they'd passed earlier. Now they saw caravans heading south, toward Valdaire, and the dust was thick on their side of the road. They could not move far aside, for the increasing roughness of the terrain. Arvid showed the boy how to wrap a scarf over his nose and mouth.

By the time they reached the South Trade Road in Tsaia, at Five-way, the boy rode like an expert. Arvid avoided the inn where he usually stayed—where thieves lurked—and instead found them a room in a private home, paying for stalls for their mounts in a livery stable a short walk away. He noticed that a man traveling with his son was more acceptable than a man alone. The family welcomed them without any sign of concern.

Although the South Trade Road that led west to Fintha was less busy than the Guild League road or the road to Vérella, scarcely a turn of the glass passed that they did not overtake or meet someone coming. Most were single wagons, or pedestrians, or riders, not caravans. Arvid could not help comparing this trip to the previous summer, when his companion had been a stolid gnome determined to be no more than a servant. Instead, he had the boy—wide-eyed, much of the time, seeing places he'd never seen nor heard of. Eager to talk, eager to learn . . . Arvid did not mention the little cairn of stones that covered a thief's body when they came to it. The boy, however, pointed it out and hopped off to place a stone on it for luck. "Maybe it's a hero's grave," he said. Arvid did not correct him.

Arvid chose to stay on the South Trade Road all the way to Fin Panir. They camped by the road most nights, buying food in the towns but avoiding the inns with their fleas and bedbugs. That meant avoiding granges as well; Arvid knew he should be attending drill each fiveday, but after all, these small granges probably held drill only one night in five, and it might not be the night he camped nearby. Traffic diminished the farther they went, and at last the road turned north toward Fin Panir.

Arvid recognized the well he and Dattur had reached the year before. "The city's not that far ahead," he said. "You'll see." In fact, riding at a good pace, it was less than a sun-hand before they reached the south gates.

The Marshal-General's letter wasn't needed to clear the city gates; Marshal Porfur's letter—impressed with the Marshal's seal and stating "On Gird's service for Marshal Porfur, Ifoss Grange"—was sufficient to gain entry to the city and then to the Fellowship's precincts on top of the hill.

The Marshal-General was crossing the courtyard from the High Lord's Hall when he rode in and glanced at him—then stopped short and frankly stared. "Is it you, Arvid? Did you find that necklace?"

"Marshal-General," he said, dismounting and bowing. "I fear not: I was taken by the Thieves' Guild in Valdaire and nearly killed. I am certain, however, that it went to Valdaire and on eastward from there. I suspect it is now held by the man claiming to be the Duke of Immer."

"And you were then trapped in the South by snows, I suppose," she said. She shrugged. "Well . . . if it's gone, it's gone." When he said nothing, her eyes went from him to the boy, still on his horse, and then back to Arvid. "Do you have other business with me, Arvid? My pardon, but I have a meeting now—"

"Your letter," he said, fumbling at his belt pouch. "I must return it—they took it, but I recovered it after I escaped."

"What about your gnomish friend?"

"He is with Count Arcolin . . . Marshal-General, the story is long and you are in a hurry. And I have a word from Marshal Porfur of Ifoss Grange as well. But we can wait."

"Helfran—" The Marshal-General waved to a yeoman. "See these guests have a place for their mounts and refreshment. I will see them later."

"This way," Helfran said. He led them into the stables to untack and loose the horses into a small paddock obviously made from dividing a larger one into three with a temporary fence. He brought buckets of water for the barrel. "We're full up, you see," he said. "No guest rooms in the schools, either. We've had more traffic this summer than two seasons past. Marshal-General would've told you, but she's already late for that meeting and she hates late. First it was magery, and then that elf showed up again in the High Lord's Hall and she had to talk to him . . ."

"What elf?"

"I don't rightly know. Just some elf in fancy clothes like they wear and a crown sort of thing on his head—"

"Not the Lady of the Ladysforest, then—"

"Oh, she's dead. Died in the spring; didn't you know?"

"I've been in Aarenis." It would not do to show his surprise.

Magery? Elf from somewhere other than the Ladysforest? The Lady dead? "I thought elves were immortal," he said. Everyone knew elves were immortal.

"Killed by kuaknom—the tree-haters, that turned evil after the Severance." Helfran twitched his shoulders and changed the subject. "You can leave your packs in the main court until you find a room somewhere, if you want. The inns aren't all full, just us up here, mostly. There's a nice little inn, my brother's sister-in-law runs it, just a few minutes down on your right, across from a grange, and I know they've got room because I ate breakfast there this morning. Why doesn't she send some of 'em down here? Pia asked me, meaning the Marshal-General, and I couldn't say except all them Marshals hang together like grapes on a stalk."

The hint could not have been stronger if he'd outlined it in red paint. But if there was no room here, he and the boy did need a place to sleep. "How long do you think the Marshal-General's meeting will take?"

"More'n half the afternoon, most like. Near suppertime. There's all them Marshals in for the meeting they hold every three years . . . lots of meetings, that is, really. Council on changing the Code's been at it since spring."

"Then we'll go find a room," Arvid said.

The inn he'd been told of was indeed downhill and to the right, handy to a grange where a Marshal and a yeoman-marshal stood in the open door talking to three men who looked like farmers. Good Loaf the inn was called, and the buxom woman who welcomed them into the common room was indeed named Pia. She wore a Girdish-blue shirt over a darker blue skirt. After establishing that Helfran had sent them, she grinned broadly and led the way upstairs to a large corner room with a window out to the yard behind. The rate seemed fair, the room clean. Arvid secured the room for a tenday. He was sure they would be in Fin Panir at least that long.

Downstairs, they ate lunch—slabs of cheese, that day's bread—it explained the inn's name—pickles, and a bowl of thin green soup that tasted surprisingly good. After that, Arvid took the boy with him back up the street to check on the horses. The Good Loaf had only four stalls, all filled, in its stable, but he planned to sell at least two of the horses anyway. Young Arvid no longer needed the beginner's mount on which he'd perched so warily, and it should sell for a good price here. They would need the money if they must live in an inn; he had no trade he could ply legally.

Their tack still hung in the tack room. Arvid pulled out curry-comb and brush and went into the small enclosure where their horses were. He and the boy groomed them and tossed in fresh hay. Arvid wondered what they would bring, and whether he could sell them himself or would be required to work through a horse dealer. That brought back the memory of his first time in Fin Panir, more than a year before, when he'd found his stolen horse in a market in the low end of the city.

"Will you keep them all?" the boy asked, rubbing the nose of his favorite, a bay with a narrow stripe down its face.

"I can't," Arvid said. "I don't have enough money to feed them. I must sell at least two, possibly all."

"Rowan would pull a cart, I'm certain," the boy said, as the horse butted his chest.

"If we had a cart," Arvid said. "Lad, I know you like that horse, but . . ." He thought of his favorite mount, stolen from him twice, recovered only once, and somewhere in Aarenis now with another owner who might not even know the horse had been stolen. He'd looked, in the Valdaire horse markets, on the off chance but hadn't found him.

"Maybe the Marshal-General needs horses," the boy said. "Then I could come pet him."

"You're back." It was Helfran, this time with a truss of hay. He tossed it into the enclosure. "Find the Loaf all right?"

"Yes," Arvid said. "We have a room there. I'm wondering about the horses. Now we're here, we don't need all four, and there's no stable room at the inn."

"If you're staying, they could go out on the common meadows. Rough grazing, but there's a hand of watchers to keep trouble away.

"I don't know how long we'll stay, exactly," Arvid said. "Can they bide here overnight?"

"Oh, surely. That's never a problem, one night. You've brushed 'em out, I see—any hoof problems?"

"No."

"Well, then. They'll do fine overnight, I'd think. If you come up in the morning and give a hand mucking out—do any of 'em work in harness?"

"I'm not sure," Arvid said. "We think this one might, but I bought him as a safe ride for a novice. He's been that."

Helfran nodded. "All these fancy horses about—knights and Marshals and such—we can always use another horse that works. Your four are well mannered, not like those down there." A squeal and a clatter of hooves came from the last section of the paddock.

Arvid wondered whether to wait for the Marshal-General in the courtyard or go back to the inn.

"Why not show the lad the High Lord's Hall?" Helfran asked.

A shiver ran down Arvid's back. He had avoided the High Lord's Hall on that earlier visit; he still felt uneasy nearing a holy place. And yet—he had held a relic of Gird that came alight in his hand. "Why not?" he said to Helfran, and to the boy, "Come along—let's see."

Men and women in the blue tunics of Marshals and the mail and surcoats of Knights of Gird moved about the courtyard, all clearly with a destination in mind. Some were going into the High Lord's Hall, and others coming out. Two armed men stood at the doors, like guards, but they stopped no one. Arvid and his son went in.

Light no longer flooded the eastern window, but shone through the stained glass of the south windows spreading splashes of color over the stone floor. From outside, the windows had looked dark and flat; now they glowed, even those on the north side. Arvid and the boy stood, astonished—and someone wanting to pass tapped Arvid gently on the shoulder. "First time?" the man asked.

"Yes," Arvid said. The man wore a chain with a large medallion of Gird hanging from it and had an engaging grin.

"If I were you, with the light this time of year, I'd choose a seat up there—" He pointed to some benches along the north side. "Stay as long as you like. The place will fill up when the afternoon sessions are done." He smiled a last time and strode off across the hall to the far side.

Arvid followed those directions, and soon he and the boy were resting on benches and watching the colors change as the light moved. "It's beautiful," the boy whispered once, leaning close.

"Yes," Arvid said, his throat tight. "It is." He had no idea how long they sat there. The soft colors crept from stone to stone on the floor as the voices of those who came and went echoed around them in a confusing murmur. It was still light when someone sat down near them.

"There you are," said the Marshal-General. "Have you been here since you arrived?"

"No," Arvid said, shaking himself back to awareness. "No, Marshal-General, thank you. I found us a room at an inn not far away; we ate there."

"You were supposed to have refreshment here," she said.

"You are full, I heard, and you are busy. I thought we should take care of ourselves until you had more leisure."

"Leisure is sadly lacking in my life right now," the Marshal-General said. Arvid glanced at her; the corner of her mouth quirked. "That is my own fault, you understand. I agreed to this job. You will probably be more comfortable in that inn, anyway. We are crowded right now but, I hope, not for much longer. Tell me, who is this lad?" She looked past Arvid to grin at the boy.

"My son," Arvid said. "I found him in Aarenis."

Her brows rose, but she did not ask the details. "And your name, lad?" she asked the boy.

"Arvid, Marshal-General." After the briefest pause, he asked, "Who built this place? It's so . . . so different."

"It's very old," the Marshal-General said. "We think it was built by those who came north long ago, but we are not sure. Are there buildings in the south that look like this?"

"No," Arvid said. "At least, not in Valdaire or the Foss Council cities. But it's clear some buildings were built on the ruins of older ones."

"You're wearing Gird's token," the Marshal-General said. "That's new: did you actually take the oath?"

Arvid nodded. "In Aarenis . . . things happened." He gathered his courage. "Marshal-General, when Gird talks to you, when Gird first talked to you, did you think you were crazy?"

This time her brows rose higher; he could hear the tension in her voice. "You think—you say—Gird talks to you?"

Arvid nodded.

"And what does he say?"

Arvid began with the first time, there on the cold ground, keeping his voice low with an effort. The words poured out in a torrent he could not stop even as the light faded and the great hall grew dim. He had not even reached the moment in Valdaire when the relic's light flared as he entered when the Marshal-General put a hand on his arm.

"Arvid—stop for a little. I must eat with a group of tedious High Marshals, and I cannot—I apologize—ask you to sit with us. But you and young Arvid are welcome to eat in the common hall, and I promise I will come to you after, and you may tell me more." She handed him a folded cloth.

Arvid realized that tears had wet his face. "Where—where is that?"

"The kitchens, where you were before. Come, I'll take you. There's a fountain in the small garden on the way where you can cool your face and wash your hands."

It was long after nightfall when the Marshal-General returned; young Arvid had given up yawning and now slept, slumped against Arvid and the wall behind him. "Would you rather wait until the lad's had a night's sleep?"

"It might be better," Arvid said. "We're to come in the morning and help with mucking out."

"I'll have someone light your way." She called one of the kitchen workers, who seemed quite willing to take a torch and light their way to the inn; young Arvid scarcely roused as Arvid carried him.

In the brighter light and the noise of the common room, the boy's eyes flickered open. "Time for bed," Arvid said, setting him down. "I hope you can climb the stairs on your own; I'd hate to stumble with you."

Next morning, after a hearty breakfast—Pia was a better cook than those up the hill, Arvid decided—they walked up the hill and joined Helfran in mucking out the paddocks. They had worked scarcely a half-turn of the glass when the Marshal-General appeared. "I'm sorry Helfran," she said, "but I must take Arvid away; he has information I need." She turned to young Arvid. "Are you willing to stay with Helfran?"

"Yes, Marshal-General," he said.

"Make sure he has a honey-cake at midmorning," she said to Helfran. "Lad's been on the road a long time, and he's thin."

"'Course I will," Helfran said. "Come along, lad, and I'll show you how to harness a pony to th' cart—we'll need to haul all this out to the meadow."

Arvid followed the Marshal-General back through the stables and then through a maze of passages he hadn't been in before, until they came to the kitchens and from there up the stairs to her office.

"Sit there," she said, pointing to a chair padded in leather near the window. She settled herself behind a wide table and set her elbows on it. "Start from where you were: you were taking vengeance on the Valdaire Guildmaster—"

That seemed a lifetime away. Arvid took a breath and began. Gird's light in the grange, in his hand. Gird's voice telling him to save the child. More and more often, that voice, prodding, taunting, pushing him to do what he had not ever thought of doing.

"He wouldn't let me alone," Arvid said at last. "I thought I was crazy as one of those beggars who wanders the street claiming his god tells him what will happen or that he's supposed to be king of all. Was that how it happened to you?"

"No," the Marshal-General said. "In fact, I am not sure I have ever heard Gird's voice that clear. I could envy you, Arvid."

"Don't," Arvid said. "You wouldn't if it happened to you. There's no—no privacy, in my head."

"So it's all the time?"

"No . . . but a sort of feeling that he's there, even when he's not talking."

"So . . . you hear Gird most in a crisis?"

"Yes . . . but it's *his* definition of a crisis." Arvid grinned in spite of himself. "He's . . . not what I thought he was. Nor the Fellowship, for that matter."

"I expect not." She cocked her head. "Are you miserable with the change, Arvid? Is it difficult for you?"

"It was at first, but now—not really. I missed the Guild at first—but it's different, having friends who I'm sure aren't going to stab me in the back."

She folded her hands, nodding. "Your situation's unusual, as I expect your Marshal Porfur told you. Most Girdsmen never hear Gird's voice; most do their best to follow the Code and obey the Marshal of their local grange. Marshals do their best to teach the Code and be good leaders, make good decisions. All that without hearing anything direct from Gird. It does happen; we know it's not just crazy people who hear the gods' voices. But it's rare. Which means, Arvid, you're rare, and Gird or another god has something in mind for you."

"It frightens me."

"I don't doubt it. But you were brave and—in your way—honorable before this came to you, and I believe you will do whatever it is with the same courage and honor."

"A thief's courage? A thief's honor?"

"No. Yours. Your innate qualities. A good horse can be used by an evil rider—it's not the horse that's evil. From what you tell me, something in you from childhood belonged more to good than evil." She grinned. "And now you're one of us. I'm happy for you, Arvid, and hope you aren't grieving about what you lost."

"Not much . . . though I'm not sure how I'm going to support my son. If he is my son."

"Fatherhood is more than a squirt of spunk," the Marshal-General said, shocking him out of any protest. "Whether or not you are his father by blood, you rescued him from horror and you've cared for him since. He seems a fine lad, much as you might have been."

"I want him to have a good life," Arvid said, looking out the window. On this side, the old palace had a long drop to the street below, already heading down the hill.

"So do all parents," the Marshal-General said. "If you're able, stay in Fin Panir. Let him attend the grange near the inn as a junior yeoman. He'll gain skills and friends both. When he's older, perhaps he'll qualify for the school up here if he wants, or perhaps he'll 'prentice to some craft or trade. You say he was on a farm for a while—did he seem to like that?"

"Yes, though after what he endured in the Guildhouse, he would have liked anything."

"Can he read?"

"Not much, though he's learning."

"Granges offer basic reading skills—that will be Marshal Cedlin, near the inn. What about his fighting skills?"

"None, so far as I know."

"Then the junior yeoman program will be good for him. I'll write a note to Marshal Cedlin. Do you plan to keep him with you or foster him out?"

"He wants to stay with me," Arvid said.

"That will do for now," she said. "Now as to you—you're still in your probationary year as a Girdsman, and that means you need a place to attend drill. Did you stop at any granges as you traveled?"

Arvid felt himself flushing. "No. We spent only one night in Fiveway, and I was more concerned to avoid the thieves I knew infested it. And no more than one night in any town since."

"Gird said nothing to you about that?"

"No."

"Well, now you're in Fintha—and even more, in Fin Panir—you'll need to attend drill regularly. For the time being, that's at Marshal Cedlin's grange; I'll include that in my note to him. I want you to tell me—and him—about any instance that Gird speaks to you. Now, for employment—you write a fair hand, do you not?"

"Yes," Arvid said.

"Good. I need someone to compile the notes I've made during recent meetings into a coherent report. Our scribes are overloaded. Will you accept that employment?"

"Yes," Arvid said, "though I do not want to be away from the boy all day."

"A half-day, mornings," she said. "He can go to the grange for his schooling then. Will that suit?"

"Yes," Arvid said. He did not want to ask how much, but she was already answering that.

"It will pay for your board at the inn, and we'll take care of your mounts if you'll agree to lend them—two of them, anyway—when we need them."

"Certainly. Use all of them, if you can."

"You'll start tomorrow. I'll write the note now, and you can take it as introduction to Marshal Cedlin."

Marshal Cedlin accepted both Arvid and the boy into the grange community without demur. Whatever the Marshal-General had written, she had, Arvid suspected, left out the part about his having been a Thieves' Guild enforcer.

"Certainly your son should spend his mornings here, at least until he's caught up in his schooling," Marshal Cedlin said. "He's not too old and seems a bright lad; he should make good progress." He turned to the boy. "Young Arvid, you'll be working with my yeoman-marshal Geddes for the time being. The barton's through that door; he's teaching now. Just take him this note."

"Yes, Marshal," the boy said, ducking his head, then went as he was bid.

"And polite, too," Marshal Cedlin said to Arvid. "It must have been a wrench to have him stolen away, and Gird's own grace you found him again."

"Indeed it was," Arvid said.

"Well—and you a late convert and in your first year. The Marshal-General says you read and write well—and she's hired you as a scribe, so that must be so. Then you're ready to go beyond the Ten Fingers, I'm thinking, and should start learning the Code itself. You have your evenings free, but for drill nights; you can start on the first book, and we'll see how you get on. Let's trade blows, so I can assign you to a drill group." He grinned at Arvid's expression. "Small grange, was it, there in Ifoss? Most men aren't Girdish there, I know. Here we're full every night, and we have groups according to skill."

Cedlin was indeed more skilled with staff and blade than Porfur had been, though not Arvid's equal with the long blade. "You say you practiced with the Duke's Company—or whatever they call it now?"

"Fox Company, Marshal," Arvid said. "Count Arcolin's taken the same insignia. But I did not practice with them all the time."

"You're strong, agile, excellent with a long blade, but you need more practice with the staff and in formation," Cedlin said. "I think you'll fit into Yeoman-Marshal Vallan's group, and you can meet him tonight. Your group will drill tomorrow. You'll hear the bell; Pia complains sometimes that it knocks a flask off the bar in the Loaf."

Next morning, Arvid saw the boy dash across the street and into the grange—already greeting several other children also running in—and headed up the hill. Scribes had a long room with desks in rows. He was early, as he'd meant to be; a senior scribe greeted him, showed him his desk, and then went off to stand by the door. Arvid's desk already had a stack of papers held down with a round stone, and another stack of fresh sheets, an inkstick, and a hollow stone with water already in it. He looked at the notes. They were arranged in order, the earliest on top.

By midday, his fingers were cramped, his neck hurt, and he had worked his way through the first stack and a second one the senior scribe brought him. He also knew a lot more about the workings of the Fellowship of Gird. The Marshal-General—who wrote a crabbed, squarish hand—had taken notes at every meeting she attended. Conferences, they were called, on the education of junior yeoman, the education of non-Girdish children in grange programs, the correct order of business at grange meetings, the allocation of grange relief, the standardization of burial guild practices . . . and more. Legal issues relating to the appearance of mage powers in those not known to be of magelord blood. Mage powers? Had blood magery come to Fintha?

He shook out his fingers, massaged his neck, and then approached the senior scribe. "To whom should I take the work I've finished?"

"You are working for the Marshal-General—I can take them to her office for you, but you could take them yourself."

"I will, gladly," Arvid said.

She was not in her office—at some other meeting, he supposed—and he left two stacks on her desk: the notes and the report.

Young Arvid was already in the inn and halfway through a hunk of cheese and bread when Arvid came in. Arvid paused in the door to look at him. Healthy, strong, lithe, and energetic. Happy, from the look on his face. When he caught sight of Arvid, he grinned around his mouthful of food. Arvid went to the table, and Pia immediately brought over another plate.

"I can write my name!" the boy said. "Look!" He moved his finger on the table.

"Very good," Arvid said.

"I can already say the Ten Fingers—I learned that back in Valdaire—but now I can learn to write them. And some of what we do is drill things, with hauks. They're heavy."

"For a boy your size, yes."

"Geddes says I will get stronger fast with good food. And I met a boy named Brok; he has red hair, and his father is a farrier. I told him I had a horse—well, that you did—and he said if it needed shoes to come to his father. And a girl named Piri, she's the fastest runner of all of us." He gulped down a swallow of water. "How was your morning?"

"Interesting," Arvid said. "But I'm glad not to be doing scribe's work all afternoon. Let's explore the city, shall we? I have drill tonight, and I need to walk the kinks out of my back and legs."

That walk through the streets of Fin Panir—down to the river and the gate to the River Road through which he'd ridden more than a year ago—made clear to him how he'd changed. Fin Panir was smaller than Valdaire or Vérella and tidier than both. Most people wore something blue—shirts, aprons, head scarves, belts—but other colors also. The money changers in their Guildhouse, where Arvid went to change his remaining Aarenisian coins to Finthan, wore black gowns and stiff white collars, as they did everywhere, with only a blue band around one sleeve, but most merchants in the shops he explored wore shirt and trousers like everyone else.

Those things were the same as before, but the looks people gave to a man in similar clothes, with a lad at his side, were very different from the looks he'd had when walking through the city alone, wearing thieves' black; they saw no danger in him now. Once that would have bothered him; he'd liked being seen as mysterious and dangerous. Now he enjoyed the friendly smiles, the nods, the acceptance.

It's not so bad to have friends.

He managed not to jerk. This was not a crisis . . . was it? No answer. In the next small market, fruit lay displayed in baskets: summer apples, cherries, plums, the late summer berries. Young Arvid's eyes rounded at the sight. Arvid bought a handbasket of cherries for them; young Arvid ate four to Arvid's one. Then it was time to climb back up the hill to their inn and supper.

Drill here, so near the training hall for the Knights of Gird and paladins, was more advanced than in Fossnir. As he'd been warned, the grange was almost full—and this was only part of the grange membership. They began with a recitation of the Ten Fingers—even Marshal Porfur had done that once a tenday—but then Marshal Cedlin began asking one or another to give an example of that rule in real life. After that, drill with Yeoman-Marshal Vallan began.

The yeomen were much more precise—and the drills more complicated—than those in Ifoss, more like the soldiers of Fox Company. Arvid's arms trembled when they stopped; the next drill, he discovered, was a run in formation through the streets: down the hill to the River Road gate and back up, chanting as they went. Theirs was not the only such group, he saw as they went down the hill. He had no idea how many granges were in Fin Panir, but at least a half dozen groups were in the streets, running down, up, or around a market square.

By the time his group made it back up the hill, he was winded and drenched in sweat. He wondered if he'd be able to keep up with this every few days. Vallan called him over. "You did well for your first drill," he said. "Marshal says you rode up from Aarenis, so making that run surprised me, to be sure. You're working as a scribe—if you'll take my advice, you'll spend two glasses a day, at least, in exercise."

"I . . . will . . ." Arvid said, still breathless. "We went today . . . up and down . . ."

"Very good. Geddes wanted to speak to you about your son . . . he's over there."

Geddes, his once-dark hair at least half gray, turned from the woman he'd been talking to and greeted Arvid. "That boy of yours is eager to learn and well mannered," he said. "I wouldn't waste paper on his scribbling now, but if you could manage a slate for him, he could practice."

"I'll do that," Arvid said.

That set the pattern: mornings in the Marshal-General's service as a scribe, afternoons with his son, evenings either at drill or studying the Code of Gird as Marshal Cedlin handed out one chapter after another. After he had copied out the Marshal-General's notes from the meetings, she started him copying notes brought back from Luap's Stronghold. Though he knew from the casual chat of other scribes that the conference on magery was still going on, he heard no more details. Whatever was written there did not come across his desk.

To his surprise, Arvid found both the Code and the material from Kolobia fascinating. What he was learning about the history of the Fellowship, what he saw in the Code of Gird and the papers from the distant stronghold, all showed Gird the founder to be very different from the image he'd had in his mind for years. Not, for one thing, the insufferably perfect model farmer he'd been told about and not a dull clod, either, from the increasing sophistication of the Code of Gird. He learned that Luap's version of Gird's life hadn't pleased some of his followers—including Gird's daughter. Arvid hadn't thought of Gird as having a daughter, and he wondered what she'd looked like. And Gird had had other children, who disappeared in the war that made him famous.

Luap, Arvid decided after delving into his writings, was an idiot. He took that opinion to the senior scribe, Doullan. "Why did Gird put up with him?" he asked. "Look at this letter—"

"I've seen it." Doullan rubbed a hand over his bald head. "Arvid, you write a beautiful hand, but you're young in the Fellowship. Luap was revered for years—"

"And he's so hungry for power, I can smell it all these hundreds since."

"What makes you so sure?"

What made him sure was a lifetime in the Thieves' Guild, where ambition was controlled only by force . . . as his own had been and as he had controlled others. But the Marshal-General had asked him not to discuss his background. "Experience," he said blandly. "I've run across that type before."

"You may be right," Doullan said. "I've never been out of Fin Panir, let alone Fintha. Marshal-General tells me people are different other places. It's just—growing up, we were told Luap was Gird's best friend and helper. And wrote down all the Code, when it was first made. I suppose that's why I identified with him."

Arvid blinked. The old scribe, gentle and unassuming, was nothing like the man whose hunger for renown blazed through his writings. "I understand why you admire him," he said, easing his shoulders. "If I had been born here—had become a scribe first—I'm sure I would, too."

"You know they saw him—well, some kind of figure of him—out in the west," Doullan went on. "Like a painting in smoke, is the way High Marshal described it, taller than a man . . . blue and white robes, the old-fashioned symbol on a chain, holding a sword."

"A wraith? Phantom?"

"He wasn't sure. At least, he never said more about it. But they knew it was Luap, or a . . . something meant to be like Luap. And then it blew away on the wind and never came back."

A rvid could not quite settle to the routine; he was not used to the peace. Day after day, hands of days, passed with no apparent danger. Young Arvid throve, clearly happy here and finding friends in the grange. Arvid, too, began to find friends—friends of a kind he had never known, who were not potential rivals but just . . . friends.

He knew someone might still hunt him from Vérella or Valdaire. It would not be difficult to trace a man traveling with a boy . . . but would they bother? He would have bothered, given the assignment, but did they have someone that skilled? He could not count himself or the boy entirely safe, yet . . . and yet he found himself relaxing, though he continued his habit of listening to gossip in the city, watching for anything unusual, any sign that someone might be on their trail. The undercurrent of concern about magery he shrugged off as Girdish strictness. He was no mage, nor the boy, so it had nothing to do with him. Only the occasional mention of blood magery caught his attention, but he saw no indication that it existed here.

He even left off wearing his sword when he walked up the hill to the scribes' hall in the mornings. Few people in Fin Panir wore swords in the city. It was not against the Code, but it was just another burden to carry and awkward at his desk. He felt naked the first time he went out without it, but nothing happened. He still took it to drill nights, as he was now instructing yeomen who wanted to learn that weapon. His cloak, its many pockets full of blades and tools, he folded into a box and kept under his bed; it was, he told himself, too hot to wear in the late summer heat. Only the knife in its thin sheath under his heart-hand shirtsleeve and the useful dagger everyone wore remained.

Drill with his group in the grange kept him fit; what he was learning as a scribe and as a student of Girdish law satisfied his need to learn and understand. He still found the bluntness, the lack of elegance, a bit boring. But . . . it was also comforting, as his friendship with Regar had been. To be accepted by ordinary men and women— to be admired for what he knew but not feared—was pleasant indeed.

CHAPTER THIRTY-SEVEN

Ifoss, Aarenis

Arcolin finished the day's report just as Burek came to his tent. "Captain, there's a fellow out at the gate who says he knows you and must speak with you. From Horngard, he says."

Arcolin's stomach lurched. "Horngard? Did he give a name?"

"No, Captain. That's why I made him wait outside the camp. Or I can bring him myself. He's armed, but not like us. A short thrusting spear and a short curved blade. Do you think he's one of Alured's men?"

"From Horngard? Unlikely." Not even Siniava had attacked Horngard, though he had taken Pliuni and threatened that mountain kingdom. "I'll see him," he said. "Bring him here."

"Leave his weapons outside the gate, sir, or outside the command area?"

"Let him retain them."

Burek gave him a startled glance, then turned and went back out. Arcolin grimaced, then went to the back of the tent, to his private room, and opened the little casket he had bought for his few treasures when he left Halveric Company to become Kieri Phelan's first captain. Gold gleamed in the light that came through the tent canvas: a heavy torc, a wide bracelet, earrings. He opened a small leather bag and shook a ring into his palm. Gold like the others, but with a dragon's head on one side. Arcolin put it on, just in case, but turned the dragon's head inward, also just in case. It could not be, but . . . just in case. He left the earrings, the torc, and the bracelet in the casket, then pulled out his dagger and stared at it a moment. His father's parting gift, it bore the family crest on the hilt, hidden under the thick leather wrapping he'd put over it.

Kieri had understood family troubles, estrangement, a flight in the night. He had never asked more than that. Arcolin felt sure Kieri had known there *was* more than that, but in all the years he'd never asked. "Somewhere in the Westmounts," he'd told Kieri, as he'd told Aliam Halveric, and that was true. "Some little place you've never heard of," he'd told Kieri, which was not true. His heart had twisted when he'd said that. It twisted now. It was hard to remember why he'd lied.

What to do. He must see the fellow, hear what he had to say. But he was Count of the North Marches now, a vassal of Tsaia's king, prince of a tribe of gnomes, and—not least—commander of Fox Company under contract to Foss Council.

Whatever the problem was, it could not be his problem.

He looked around his sleeping chamber again, pushing the casket a little more under his bed, and then went back to the front room of the tent.

"Captain," Burek said from outside.

Arcolin squared his shoulders and came out. A travel-stained man in a kilt, a square-necked shirt, a wide belt, and low boots stood slightly behind Burek. He had the mountain face: long and bony, a prominent nose, a wide mouth now firmly closed. His hair—dark and streaked with gray—hung in a long braid over one shoulder; his gray eyes roamed over Arcolin as if looking for a sign and paused on his hands, but the plain gold band told nothing unless he could see through the finger. The Fox Company seal on the next finger told more. Arcolin did not recognize him.

"You are Jandelir Arcolin?" the man asked. His voice, unlike his face, was instantly recognizable: Samdal, his father's Chancellor's son, who had been his companion in many a mischief those years ago. "You have some of the look of him."

"I'm Jandelir Arcolin," Arcolin said, nodding. "And you're Samdal, are you not? Veldan's son?"

"Yes. It *is* you, then. We were not sure. We had heard of you over the years, but you were with that redheaded Tsaian duke, Phelan. And now you're the commander?" He looked around. "Where is Phelan?"

"He is king of Lyonya now, in the north," Arcolin said. "I command this company, on contract to Foss Council. In the north, I'm titled Count of the North Marches, oathsworn to Mikeli, king of Tsaia." He had a place and name, that meant; he fit into the loom of society like any other length of yarn. He would not mention gnomes to Samdal. Or dragons. Least of all dragons.

Samdal bowed low. "You have been gone too long, my lord. It is time for the son of the mountains to serve the mountains and the flame." It sounded like a formula, but he had not heard it before.

"I am not a lord to you, 'Dal, and never have been. Surely you remember that." The fact of his own bastardy stood between them; Samdal had been his playmate but also ranked above him.

"Before your father and your brothers died, that was true. But now, my lord, you are. Did you not know?"

"I knew my father had died, and my eldest brother. But not the others, and Galdalir had sons. I cannot be heir." Not now, not after so many years. Not as a bastard. Surely his brothers had sired sons.

"My lord, misfortune followed your family as rain follows thunder, and washed them away. If you had not left—if you had sought word—"

"And why would I?" Arcolin asked, struggling to keep his voice even. "You know the circumstances of my leaving. I was not wanted, but as Perdal's servant." The old bitterness dried his mouth. "Should I have stayed for that? And if I had, would you now think me anything but a servant, worn out in his service as I would have been?"

"You chose northern taint and a foreign god, Jandelir. You could have busied yourself in Aarenis at least. Valdaire, perhaps—"

"I have spent most of my working life in Aarenis—every campaign season and many winters—and no one ever came to me." What he'd learned of his family had been merchants' gossip, scant enough. He had not expected better of them, but he had hoped.

"That may be true, my lord, but they thought you no longer cared. Should they seek a runaway?" In that Arcolin heard the same arrogance that had sent him away. "And besides," Samdal went on, "I can see what they could not: the man you have become. You were Camwyn's child first, fire-begotten. Your father knew that; I know he gave you marks of heritage." Another glance at the ring. "What is a northern dirt-farmer like Gird to such as you? Is not the scent of dragon on you even now?"

Arcolin tried not to shudder visibly. Samdal could not tell, he was sure, and yet Samdal was of the old blood in the Westmounts . . . and he himself certainly had touched a dragon. Legend had it that such things were possible; the dragon could have left its scent on him, and Samdal might have the Kingfinder's ability to detect it. He wondered if his gnome subjects could. "I am a mercenary and a peer in the north," he said to Samdal. "That is who I am now."

Samdal shook his head. "You do not understand, and I scarcely understand you. Please, my lord, listen to me and then answer."

Arcolin sighed inwardly. He could not imagine himself returning to Horngard, but he did want to know what had happened. "Come into my tent, then," he said. Inside, Samdal looked around at the furniture, the hangings, the rugs—all Kieri's originally. To the guard outside Arcolin said, "Ask the cook for a platter, and fetch a bottle of wine." To Samdal he said, "Sit down; we will share bread and salt and wine. But understand: after all these hands of years, I have oaths and duties elsewhere. My king, Mikeli of Tsaia, depends on me to defend the realm at need. My former commander is now the king of Lyonya, as I said; he no longer holds my oath, but he holds my respect, and my king considers him an ally. This Company—three hundred strong in Aarenis with more in the north—is my responsibility as well. So whatever it is you want, beyond my well-wishing to you and to Horngard, it is too late."

"Is that what you learned in foreign places?" Samdal glanced around once more, then sat where Arcolin had indicated, stiffly upright as a judge. "That duty long deferred is no longer duty? All this luxury, my lord, has softened you."

Arcolin felt a rush of anger. He could scarcely believe that Samdal would insult him so. "If you think me soft, then you will agree I am unfit for the task you propose."

"No. Merely in need of persuasion." Samdal set his hands on his

knees and began in the old tongue Arcolin had first learned as a
child, in the cadence of one relating a legend. "In the days of your
fathers, time and time before, Dragon granted your forefather Camwyn two boons. One was the high pass of Horngard for a stronghold,
with the dwarf-delved caverns that made it defensible. One was the
touch of Dragon to the King, tongue to tongue, that made Camwyn
the man Camwyn Dragonsfriend, founder of the House of Dragon.
This you were told: do you remember?"

Arcolin remembered, but had not thought of that legend when
meeting the dragon himself. He *had* touched the dragon tongue to
tongue—but surely that did not make him a king. Kieri and Kieri's
betrothed—now his wife, no doubt—had done the same, and so had
Stammel. And Mikeli of Tsaia and his brother the prince. "I do remember," he said aloud, "but it is now many years since a dragon
sealed that ancient bond. It is the tongue of the dragon statue in the
King's Hall that my father touched with his, and my brothers as well,
I presume."

"True. But that does not mean dragons will never return. And
you—if you told me that you had touched Dragon himself, I would
believe you."

"Why?" Arcolin asked.

"There's something. Your eyes. The scent—though I can see you
have a forge here, it's not forge fire I smell on you, but dragon-fire."

Arcolin's hand clenched on the dragonhead of the ring he'd put
on. "So . . . tell me what you must. I make no promises."

One of the men came in then with wine, pitcher, wooden cups,
and another with a platter of bread, cheese, and sliced meat. They set
them on the table and—at Arcolin's nod—poured the wine. Then
they left.

The story Samdal told surprised Arcolin except for Perdal's death:
dying by someone's blade in a quarrel over a gambling throw seemed
appropriate for what he remembered of his least favorite half-brother.

"He'd gone soft, you see," Samdal said. "Been too long a prince,
waiting . . . and he was not a man to thrive on idleness. Oh, he went
to the fighting circle now and then, but he wouldn't listen to his
brothers and he always liked his table."

And his jug, as Arcolin remembered well. Perdal had been a

heavy drinker by the time Arcolin left, though back then he had sweated out much of it in the circle and other active sports.

"And now, my lord, Dragon's come again."

"What?"

"Yes, my lord. Been seen over the mountains. And Camwyn as well: the dragonfriend with the smell of Dragon on him."

Camwyn Dragonsfriend, or that shape-shifting Dragon himself? Arcolin motioned for Samdal to go on with his tale.

"There's none of Camwyn's blood to do it but you," Samdal said. "Dragon's a sign that someone must come, must renew the bond. You'd have made a better prince than Perdal; everyone saw that, even back then. You're a man full grown now, experienced in command and in ruling a domain. And descended from Camwyn himself . . ."

"But I'm oathsworn elsewhere," Arcolin said again. "I cannot make bond with the dragon and the people if I break my oath somewhere else." He said it as if explaining it to Samdal and not to convince himself.

Samdal's expression did not alter. "None there is of the dragon's house. What does it matter?"

"It matters to me," Arcolin said. "And to the gods, I'm sure, and to Camwyn Dragonsfriend, who was no oathbreaker. If—" He clamped his teeth on the rest of that. If they had come to him while he was still Kieri's captain, hands of years ago, if he had asked Kieri's advice, as he so often did, Kieri would have freed him from that oath. Kieri might have told him to go back to Horngard, and then—he would have gone.

To return in triumph: was that not every exile's dream? It had been his once. He would show them; he would prove himself; they would be sorry . . . and now they were, but now he was not a runaway with no name. Now he carried a title, lands of his own. He had his own bond with a dragon—a different dragon, maybe, though who could tell?

He had to tell Samdal, he realized then. Only a dragon's bond would convince the man. Maybe.

"*If,*" Samdal said, picking up Arcolin's last word. "If you were not oathbound to your king?"

"And if I were not already oathbound to a dragon," Arcolin said.

Samdal's jaw dropped; he shut it with a snap and said nothing. "You were right to say I had the smell of dragon on me," Arcolin went on. "And yes, I have touched tongue to a dragon's tongue—not a statue of a dragon, but a dragon himself. I do not know if it is the same dragon, and the dragon said nothing about my past, or about Horngard."

"But then—but you *must* be—"

"The dragon came to me in my northern stronghold," Arcolin said. "It was a matter of—" What could he say, how much could he reveal without risking secrets the dragon did not want known? "A matter of land," he went on. "It demanded land which I held from the king of Tsaia."

"Why did it not come to *us*? *We* are the dragons' kin, through Camwyn—"

"I do not know," Arcolin said. "You know the legends as well as I. We do not question dragons' reasons, do we?"

"No. No, of course not."

"It came to me because those lands were granted me by my king—part of my domain." Arcolin skipped over everything about dragonspawn, gnomes, treachery. "And in return it granted me a boon. I asked its aid for one of my sergeants, who had been blinded in an attack by a—" He thought how to say it. Samdal would know nothing of Verrakaien—he hoped. "A demon," he said finally. He could see the questions clustering in Samdal's gaze and hurried on. "It was then it asked me to touch tongues with it, and I did."

"Have you seen it since?"

"Once," Arcolin said. "It came with word my sergeant wanted to retire, and it said it had found him a good place. It said nothing, either time, about my being heir to Horngard's throne, or Horngard's need of me, or that our bond related to that bond." As Samdal opened his mouth to speak, Arcolin held up his hand to forestall him. "What we know of dragons—what our legends say of dragons—whether this was the same dragon you saw or not—it would have known, it would have told me, if it had been Dragon's Will that I return to Horngard." He realized, in that moment, a vanished hope hidden deep in his heart when the dragon revealed itself, that it had indeed come with such purpose, but he had not allowed himself to be aware of it then.

And that—that alone—meant he lacked the kingliness he had once believed lay in himself. "And I know it touched tongue with others," he told Samdal. "With the king of Lyonya and his queen, with my king, Mikeli of Tsaia, and his younger brother, the prince." The prince . . . *Camwyn* . . . that thought flared in his mind. Was that just a coincidence? Or could it mean something more? Where had the Mahieran family come from when they came from the south?

"But you—my lord, *you* are heir to a throne yourself; your king will surely release you, when he knows that. Did he not release your former duke? Then he will release you. You are *our* king. You must be."

"Should one who takes oaths be one who breaks them? Can an oathbreaker hold oaths and give fealty back where it is given him? I tell you plainly, Samdal, I am not your king. There is a reason the gods placed me where they did." Samdal's hot eyes did not change expression. Arcolin went on. "This is not resentment, Samdal; this is not anger or pride. It is the truth of who I am: I am a soldier. That is all. I serve my king here, as I serve him in the north; my troops and my body will stand between any southern menace and Tsaia in the north. I will not break my oath, or ask for it to be released."

"But you must—there is no other—"

"There is always another," Arcolin said. He turned the ring on his finger so the dragon crest was outward, held it long enough for Samdal to see, then wrestled it off his finger. "You knew I had taken my father's gift, the bastard's ring he gave me in case of any need. I give it to you, to take to the Chancellor of Horngard; I have kept it from dishonor all these years. You will find a true king for Horngard; it is not my task. Though I might suggest some places to look."

"There are no more of your father's get or your grandfather's . . ."

"There were the daughters—"

"*Women* cannot be dragons' get—"

"Their sons—"

"I tell you there are none!" Samdal shook his head at the offered ring. "Only you."

"There is Andressat," Arcolin said. "He and his family follow Camwyn; he has good sons and grandsons."

"They are not of Horngard," Samdal said. "Not of the mountains."

"Perhaps Horngard is of Andressat, far back," Arcolin said. "You have the genealogies."

"Andressat will not do . . . Has a dragon come to him?"

"Not that I know of. But I know he swears by Camwyn's Claw."

"He is not a king; I have heard much of him. A fussy old man, a mere count—"

"A man of honor," Arcolin said sharply. "A man of courage and resource. But if you will not have him, if you want a prince born—" No. He must not say it. His oath to Mikeli surely forbade telling a stranger about the prince. But he could tell Mikeli about it later— and certainly Camwyn was everything Samdal would admire. Brave, rash, enthusiastic, and crazy about dragons, according to Mikeli. Almost in love with dragons, in fact . . . with one dragon, who had allowed him to fly, however briefly, in the dragon's mouth.

"What? You know of a prince born—someone else of the dragon's line?"

"No," Arcolin said. Samdal squinted at him as if trying to pierce his reticence. "No," he said again. "But I think Dragon may have touched more tongues than you know."

"Your king . . . has a son?"

"King Mikeli has no sons yet," Arcolin said.

"Then Kieri Phelan, who is now king—"

"Not yet," Arcolin said.

"But you are not telling me all you know."

"I am bound to another realm; do you not understand? I cannot tell you all I know, and I do not know all—be reasonable."

Samdal twisted the ring on his own finger; with the design upright, Arcolin saw that it was the Chancellor's ring, set with the flame-jewel, flickering reds and yellows.

"You're Chancellor now?"

"Aye. My father died two years agone."

"You could be Regent, then, until you find another to rule."

"I've been Regent since last fall," Samdal said. "I'd rather be

Chancellor alone. And I beg you: tell me what it is you are hiding from me."

"You have no right to demand it," Arcolin said. "I tell you, I am not the heir, and you and the Council—is there still a Council?" Samdal nodded; Arcolin went on. "You should consult the dragon. Since the direct line has failed, the dragon must approve whomever you choose."

"How?" Samdal said. "I said a dragon had been seen, not that I have talked to it. Am I to stand on the mountain and call?"

Only if he wanted to be scared out of his wits, Arcolin thought. He wondered then why he himself had not been more frightened—startled, yes, but not terrified.

"No," he said. "But dragons need not be present to know what you need, I've found. They are not like us—well, that is a foolish statement, but . . . we are used to dealing with beings that look like us, and that we believe think like us in some form. The other Elders—elves, dwarves, gnomes—have each their own laws and customs and languages, but we can understand them, at least mostly. Dragons are so unlike us that—"

"Excuse me, sir." That was Burek again. Arcolin scowled; it was unlike Burek to interrupt a conference. "I beg your pardon, my lord, but there is another who claims he must visit you, and immediately."

"A darkish man with yellow eyes?" Arcolin asked, as the hairs stood up on his neck.

"Yes, sir. He would not give a name."

Of course. His day needed only another encounter with the dragon . . . and he doubted the dragon had come to bring word of Stammel. Despite the obvious difficulty, a tickle of amusement rose and quirked the corner of his mouth.

"Show him in," Arcolin said. And to Samdal, "I believe this visitor may have some interest for you." Samdal stared, brows contracted, as well he might; Arcolin could hear in his own voice a tone of grim amusement that must be puzzling at best.

In the heat of a southern summer, the man who came in still wore what appeared to be dark leather garments more suited to winter in the north. With him came the faint scent of hot iron Arcolin remembered so well. "Count Arcolin," he said formally, dipping his head, though in a way that conveyed no humility. Arcolin bowed, silently. Samdal's gaze moved from one to the other; his nostrils flared, and sweat suddenly stood out on his forehead.

"Lord Samdal, Chancellor of Horngard," Arcolin said, with a wave of his hand. Samdal rose and bowed.

"Ah," the man said. "Of the House of Dragon, then, I believe?" Samdal's eyes widened. He nodded silently.

"And, Count Arcolin, I see you have in your hand a dragon ring. Where, may one ask, did you come by that? You were not wearing it when I met you in the north."

"It was given me by my father," Arcolin said. "I have not worn it since leaving him, until today, when I was told Samdal awaited me."

"And you didn't show—" Samdal began, but stopped when the dragon turned to look at him.

"I asked you once if you were wise," the dragon said to Arcolin. "And you claimed no special wisdom. Yet to be of the House of Dragon and not claim that connection . . . that was wisdom indeed. As, I perceive, was your choice today to bring that ring from hiding."

"Sir . . . Camwyn," Arcolin said, using the name the dragon had used in Vérella. His heart pounded. What if the dragon insisted he accept the throne? Could he gainsay a dragon? This dragon? He searched for a distracting topic. "If I may ask—what of the sergeant?"

"He is well," the dragon said. "I do not visit often, you understand, but he seems content and is well liked. He would not wish you to know—"

"I do not ask," Arcolin said. "Only of his welfare, not his location."

The dragon bowed, this time. "Such care is worthy of you, Count. But now—this ring—"

No help for it, then. "My father was a king, as I believe you know. The Lord Chancellor here tells me other heirs have died, and so he sought me out. But as you know, I am oathsworn to Mikeli of Tsaia and also have responsibilities to . . ." His voice trailed away; that lay too near what the dragon might wish kept secret. "I told the Lord Chancellor: I cannot accept this honor."

"And so the ring is no longer on your finger, and you would give it to this Chancellor to be returned to the treasury of Horngard?"

"Yes," Arcolin said. He stared into the flame-golden eyes, hoping the dragon could not see the division in his heart—still that yearning for recognition, still that plea he must not hear, from the boy's heart eager for a throne for the wrong reasons—and the older, harder determination to do his duty without seeking for what could not be his. That side of him had long given up resentment that he would not be king.

The dragon nodded. "I see honor and wisdom in that, but not the whole of wisdom. Let me ask this: have you considered the fate of those you disclaim?"

Arcolin felt his brow furrow. "I am not sure I understand," he said.

"If you will not have them, whom will they have?" the dragon asked. He turned to Samdal. "Lord Chancellor, he names you. What is your lineage?"

Samdal gaped a moment, then said, "My lord, I am the son of Veldan, Chancellor before me, and he the younger brother of Selmar, Chancellor before him. The lineage goes back to Vaskarin, at the founding of Horngard."

"A notable heritage," the dragon said. "Tell me, Samdal Chancellor of Horngard, are you wise?"

"Wise? I . . . am accounted wise in Horngard."

Arcolin heard that with astonishment; could Samdal really be such a fool? And yet, nothing Samdal had said in their conversation would be considered wise.

"Are you?" the dragon asked, mildly enough, but his voice sharpened. "And yet you left Horngard, Regent though you be, to wander about in search of the last heir of the Dragon Throne . . . and I do not see with you couriers who might keep you informed of what happens there, or by whom you could send your counsel back."

"The Council—"

"Of which you are the head. Why did you leave, Samdal Veldan's son, instead of sending someone else?"

Samdal was trembling now; Arcolin could see his hands clenched at his sides. "I—I—they wouldn't—they didn't think—and I—I'd known him—"

"We were friends as boys," Arcolin said, to spare him.

"So your Council ignores you?" the dragon said, still looking at Samdal.

Samdal looked down. The dragon cocked his head on one side, as Arcolin had seen lizards do, focusing on prey. Arcolin watched . . . and out came that impossible tongue, far too long to fit into the human-shaped head, shimmering from its own heat.

"See me clearly, Chancellor," the dragon said, without moving tongue or lips.

Samdal looked up, panic in every line of his face.

"What am I, Sssamdal?"

"I—I—not a—not a—a dragon?"

"Yesss." The tongue withdrew. "I am Dragon, Samdal. You claim descent from Horngard's first Chancellor. What is your duty to dragonkind?"

Samdal dropped to the carpet and bowed his head to touch it.

"I . . . am Dragon's servant, no more."

"No." The dragon's voice was low but uncompromising. "Your duty to dragonkind is to keep the faith in Horngard should the king be absent or die. You are not my servant only, but Horngard's. Your duty lies elsewhere, and yet you are here."

"I—I thought—"

"Wrongly." The dragon sighed, a long breath of hot air. "Your duty is wisdom, Chancellor, but a fool cannot advise a king. Count Arcolin learned his wisdom in war, and not all war-wisdom is of fighting. What I see is order in his company's camp, as I saw it in his domain; he governs well what he has, and he shows wisdom in understanding that he no longer belongs to Horngard. He has other oaths to keep. You, on the other hand—you have left your duty, apparently without knowing." He turned to Arcolin. "Count, I will myself take that ring you hold, for this man should not be in authority. Will you yield it to me?"

"Certainly," Arcolin said, his mind whirling. Samdal not fit to be Chancellor? When a boy, he had seemed as apt as any other in the skills they learned and the tasks they were given. But he had been surprised that a Chancellor would come himself rather than send a messenger. He opened his hand with the ring, and the dragon extended his tongue, curled it around the ring, and took it in. "I have a few other things from Horngard—" The torc, bracelet, and earrings, the dagger.

"They are not necessary," the dragon said. "The ring, however, should return." Then it nodded to him. "I also commend your responsibility in the matter of the kapristi. We must talk more of this later, but for now—" He glanced at Samdal, then back at Arcolin. "For now it is clear that dragonkind must once more take note of events in the House of Dragon. This is your personal quarters, I perceive; I cannot in courtesy ask you to leave, but I must speak with this Samdal alone." Turning to Samdal, the dragon said, "You will accompany me?"

"I—I—" Samdal looked at Arcolin as if hoping for rescue.

Arcolin could think of nothing to say. He did not believe the dragon would actually kill Samdal, but he expected the encounter would be unpleasant, and if the dragon said Samdal was unfit to be Chancellor, he would lose that post.

"Samdal, you have my answer," he said as the silence lengthened. "I am not the right person for this task. I wish you—and all Horngard—good fortune in finding someone suitable." To the dragon he said, "Sir, as this man has been my guest and we were friends as boys, I would hope no harm comes to him."

The dragon's stare was daunting, but Arcolin did not drop his gaze. "Those without wisdom often come to harm," the dragon said at last, "but I would wish harm on no one who does no ill."

With that Arcolin had to be content; he bowed, and the dragon gestured. Samdal moved as if he were led by strings like a puppet in a fair stall, and the dragon followed him out. Arcolin sat down again and picked up one of the pastries on the tray, then put it down again. Later. The dragon would talk to him later about . . . about the kapristi? About Horngard? Both? He put his hands to his face and rubbed his eyes. Well . . . the ring was gone, and with it all temptation and also the old ache and resentment.

He called Burek in and told him the whole story.

"Horngard! So . . . that's why you did not mind that I was a bastard who had left home under a cloud?"

"Exactly. I'm glad you've reconciled with your grandfather, but equally glad you've not tried to go back into that . . . that . . ."

"Whirlpool," Burek said with a grin. "Like the ones in the Chaloquay—suck you in, and you go 'round and 'round, hitting the rocks and never getting anywhere." He poured more water for them both.

"It's odd, now I think of it," Arcolin said. "I didn't before. But the three of us, Kieri and Dorrin and I, were all the same in that way. None of us had a happy situation growing up. Kieri's was the worst, those years of slavery, but Dorrin's was bad enough. Mine was easiest, until that final split. More like yours in that, I think." He shook his head to clear it. "The dragon's coming back to talk to me sometime, he said. You were right to bring him in, and I'll tell the others that if they see him, he's to be guided to me. Though I expect he could find me by himself."

"Yes, sir."

"Any new gossip about Vaskronin or Andressat's missing son?"

"No, sir. Just the speculation we heard before. Gone over to Vaskronin, or captured by Vaskronin, or dead." .

Arcolin set himself to write the letter to his king he felt he must write, this time revealing who he really was and what he had been offered and refused. Would the dragon make the connection between Prince Camwyn and Horngard's need? Almost certainly, but with dragon wisdom, not a human's. He phrased very carefully his own thoughts about that.

CHAPTER THIRTY-EIGHT

Vérella, Tsaia

When will she give an answer?" Mikeli, king of Tsaia, glared at Marshal-Judicar Oktar. "We're almost to Autumn Court. I cannot hide this from the peers forever."

"Sir king, the Marshal-General is doing her best—she cannot force the Council to come to an answer any faster."

"If she were more forceful—"

"If she were more forceful, she would have a revolt—and there would be blood in the streets. Is that what you want, sir king?"

"No. But we will have one here, where I would like it even less, if we do not have an answer, a way of reconciling the Girdish—"

"Do you really think a mere change of the Code would solve the problem?" Oktar asked.

Mikeli stared at him. "It's the Code. The law. Why wouldn't it?"

"Because the people most opposing a change may not obey a change. If they believe it's against Gird's will—" Oktar drew his finger across his throat.

"Then how do we convince them?" Mikeli asked. "Or do you think we should let matters take their course?"

"No, sir king, I do not." Oktar frowned. "In anticipation of a ruling from the Council along the lines of the Marshal-General's first communication here, I have been telling Marshals in Tsaia to hold all cases for review until we have that ruling. But—as you know—the number is growing. Besides those you yourself heard of on your progresses, I've had reports of more than four hands . . . five hands and three, to be exact. Word has already spread; several Marshals have reported panic in their granges."

"And we don't know why," Mikeli said. "Something must have happened to start this—"

"The eldest so far is Kirgan Beclan . . . so if it was something that happened, it must have been that far back—"

"Except that all signs of magery have emerged in the past year."

"One possibility no one has mentioned," Oktar said, tenting his fingers, "is that the gods have granted magery again because we will need it."

"*Need* magery? Why?"

Oktar shook his head. "Sir king, consider beyond this single problem. Magery was here all along, let us say, like water under the ground. Its one outlet we know of in this kingdom was the Verrakai family. Perhaps they . . . they drew out so much, for their own use, that little was left for others. They are dead; only one Verrakaien remains, and she—I will say firmly, of my own judgment—has not been seeking others' power. So whatever magery is, there could be more of it, rising like springs."

"I never thought of magery that way," Mikeli said.

"Nor did I, sir king, until now. But if this reappearance is not caused by some evil power with some evil intent, then it could be as natural as the return of seasons, or be the deliberate intervention of good powers for our benefit."

"Have you suggested that to your fellow Marshals?"

"No, having just thought of it. But I will, with those here in Vé-rella, and see if that can ease their minds." He cocked his head. "How long, sir king, do you plan to keep your brother's magery secret? How long do you think you can?"

Mikeli shook his head. "I don't know. I live in fear that it will out. That haunts my sleep, like the dreams that damned crown forces on me."

"Better to come from you than be found out," Oktar said. He had counseled that before without success.

Mikeli nodded slowly. "I am coming to that belief myself,

Marshal-Judicar. But how, without condemning my brother—without plunging the realm into chaos?"

"Tell your dukes first. You trust them, do you not? And Duke Verrakai already knows. Duke Marrakai's holdings border Fintha; he must have heard about the problems there. Tell him. Your uncle—he already knows the problem. And Duke Serrostin has a son who's had contact with magery."

"I suppose we should be grateful we don't have an outbreak of Kuakkgani," Mikeli said.

"Perhaps." Oktar looked thoughtful. "If we knew what was coming, we would know . . . but we don't."

"Do you really think it could be within Gird's will?"

"Within the High Lord's will, I would say, sir king, or perhaps Alyanya's, or both. Gird is my patron; I am trained in Gird's way, but what we have learned from these explorations in Kolobia suggests what we know of Gird Strongarm is still very far from all the man was or thought."

Mikeli sighed, then nodded. "Well, then. Marrakai and Serrostin are off at their estates, so I will send word to my uncle that I need to talk to him."

He wrote that note, handed it to a courier, then went to find his brother. Camwyn and Aris were reading, he discovered, a most unusual activity for the pair of them, explained only by the slightly cooler breeze coming from the shaded north windows.

"What's that?" he asked, as they scrambled up from their seats.

"Marshal Oktar suggested I study the different versions of the Code," Camwyn said. He looked pale, Mikeli thought, not nearly as brown as he'd been earlier in the summer. Yet he was both taller and more muscular.

"Relating to magery in particular?" Mikeli asked.

"Not just magery," Camwyn said. "He asked me to compare the versions across time and between the Finthan Code and ours."

"Going to make you a judicar, is he?" Mikeli said. "I wouldn't think you'd like that much, would you, Cam?"

"I don't know." Camwyn scratched his head, then shook it. "Not if it means always staying indoors—but this is more interesting than I thought."

Mikeli closed the door to the room and sat down on the remaining chair. "I need to talk to both of you. You've been careful; no one's found out yet—but that won't go on forever—"

"I'm trying—"

"I know. But what I haven't told you before is how many other people are showing up with some sign of active magery—and not just here in Tsaia. In Fintha as well. The Marshal-Judicar tells me that's why we've not heard anything definite from the Marshal-General. She's dealing with outbreaks of magery there, and there's growing fear in the population. As there is here."

"There are others?" Aris said, sitting up straight.

"Yes. All of them younger than Beclan, so far, that we know of. No one knows why it's happening, what caused it—"

"Or *who* caused it," Aris said. Then, belatedly, "Sir king. Pardon."

"Or who, you're right."

"I think it's the regalia," Camwyn said. "Or the dragon. Or maybe both."

"However," Mikeli said, in a tone that silenced both of them, "since it's important that the announcement come from me, I'm going to tell the peers, starting with the dukes. So you, Aris, won't have to keep secrets from your father any longer." He saw the relief on Aris's face and nodded. "And you, Cam, won't have to keep it secret from our uncle." Camwyn nodded, a slight frown creasing his forehead. Mikeli anticipated his next question. "Before you ask, this will not reverse Beclan's position. I did what I did to save him—his life, as I was sure it would be—and he has settled in well with Duke Verrakai as her kirgan. Restrictions on his access to his family will change, but not the adoption."

"When will you send word, sir king?" Aris asked.

"Immediately. Your brother Juris is leaving tomorrow to visit your family; I'll send a letter with him. I've already sent a courier to Duke Mahieran, asking him to come to the city tomorrow."

"What will happen to me?" Camwyn asked.

"I hope, nothing," Mikeli said. "I'm reasonably certain the dukes will listen to me and to the Marshal-Judicar. That others have shown magery, including merchants' and farmers' children, means condemning you would mean condemning many. My hope is for a peaceful settlement, with the agreement that those who are not using magery for evil are no different than wizards."

"But it's still a secret for now?" Aris asked. "I can't—I can't tell Juris?"

"No. Neither of you can tell anyone anything until I've talked to the dukes and probably the whole Council."

<hr/>

What's this?" Duke Mahieran paused in the doorway, looking from Mikeli to the Marshal-Judicar. "Am I in trouble, sir king?"

"Not at all," Mikeli said. "But what I have to tell you concerns the Marshal-Judicar as well." He waved at the chairs. "Sit down, do."

Mahieran sat, a little stiffly. Mikeli noticed with a pang that his uncle seemed aged more than a year since the previous summer. No wonder, with all that had happened.

"Have you heard any of the rumors from Fintha of magery?" he asked.

"Magery in Fintha? No," Mahieran said. "Nothing of that. What is it?"

Oktar leaned forward. "There's a Council convened in Fin Panir by the Marshal-General, to deal with it. Magery in children, mostly— some older, near-grown, with no known mageborn ancestry."

"But then—" Mahieran turned to Mikeli, hope in his eyes. "Beclan—"

Mikeli held up his hand. "Uncle, I must tell you that magery has also appeared in Tsaia. I was waiting for a ruling from the Marshal-General, but it's taken too long. We must—I must—act for Tsaia."

"You're not going to—" Mahieran turned pale.

"I'm going to ask you and the other dukes to look for magery on your estates and protect those you find from retribution—and make it known that only evil deeds make magery evil."

Mahieran let out his breath. "Well. And what about Beclan?"

"There's more," Mikeli said. "There's another mage in the royal family—"

"Celbrin? One of the girls?"

"Camwyn," Mikeli said. Mahieran stared, obviously shocked. "And, Uncle, I have kept this a secret from you and the Council, hoping as I said for word from the Marshal-General."

"You—but you know what it means! Your brother—"

"Cannot be my heir. Yes. He knows that; I know that. But I'm not going to kill him or the others. Nor let this realm fall into chaos, not when we have enemies who might invade next year."

"What about Beclan?"

"I won't reverse the adoption, Uncle. But I will allow him contact with the family. He is a better heir for Duke Verrakai than her kinsman was, in my opinion, and his being of Mahieran and not Verrakai descent ensures no taint of their kind of magery."

"And my wife?"

Mikeli looked at the aging face, the man who had been like a father to him after his father died, and felt pity for him. "It's not just about whether she has magery. She tried to kill a peer. She is still angry with me; she still—she says—hates Duke Verrakai and blames her for everything. As such, she is a danger to my policies. Uncle, I know she was a good wife to you, and cared for you and your children. But consider carefully. Can you keep her from causing any more trouble—any kind of trouble—either directly or through talk with her friends?"

Mahieran bowed his head. "I . . . am not sure. I never thought she would act as she did that night."

"Your daughters, my cousins, have shown no signs of magery, and are no more confined than their aunt would have them. I have not received them here, but I will. Your wife . . . we must be certain, Uncle. There are other evils than magery, and if Celbrin's mind has turned that way—"

"I am loath to believe it of her," Mahieran said. "But she had always great pride and temper. Oktar?"

"I tried to persuade her, my lord, that Beclan's magery did not come from Duke Verrakai or any act of hers. But the friends who used to visit her—those you allowed, my lord—no longer go, saying she is too bitter."

"May I go, sir king?"

"Yes," Mikeli said. "But be careful. I do not think she has magery—it would surely have shown by now—but if her mind has failed she might do you a hurt. And I cannot afford to lose any of my dukes—or my only uncle."

"And if she swears to me she will be sensible?"

"Then take her home and see that she stays there."

"I will do so, sir king. Thank you. Now—what am I to say of this, and to whom?"

"First to your Marshals on Mahieran lands: report any who show magery to the Marshal-Judicar, but do not punish them for magery."

"Tell them," Oktar said, "that we are awaiting word from the Marshal-General, but that I am certain this new appearance of magery, in common folk and nobles alike, is a gift of the gods, to be used for good."

"I'm assuming you've sent couriers to the other dukes."

"Yes. Next it will be counts and then barons—"

Mahieran shook his head. "Sir king—Marshal-Judicar—forgive me, but I must disagree. With this present Council—and this present generation of peers—you will do better to inform all at once. They all need to know what the Crown thinks of this new thing; they may all have it breaking out on their estates. They will resent being left out."

"Are you sure, Uncle?" Mikeli asked. "I thought the dukes would be able to bring their influence—"

"Less than you think, sir king," Mahieran said. "Since the lower ranks of peers know that commoners have been elevated to duke, they have less natural respect for all of us. It was an argument made at the time the first commoner was chosen, and the Elorran family— valuable as they were at that time—did nothing to make the commoner-duke more palatable to those whose titles were older. Gerstad's ancestor had saved a king, yes, but he annoyed almost everyone else. In all seriousness, I beg you consider the advantages of sharing this knowledge widely and at once."

Mikeli looked at Oktar for his response. The Marshal-Judicar sat silent for a long moment, brow furrowed in thought, before speaking. Then he looked up at Duke Mahieran. "You are right, my lord. I was in error in my advice to the king, and that shames me. Tell them all, and quickly."

Mikeli sat back in his chair. "Very well. I will have the same message I sent the dukes yesterday copied and sent, and will speak to those members of Council here in the city today. Will that do?"

Mahieran nodded. "I believe that is best, sir king."

Most of the peers were out of the city, as usual between Midsummer and Autumn Courts, but a few had come to the city on other business, and on Oktar's recommendation, Mikeli summoned the masters of the guilds, though only two were formally on the Council. Baron Brenvor and Count Kostvan were found lunching together at the Count's city quarters, and soon they and a round dozen of the guildmasters were seated around the long table with Mikeli, Oktar, and Duke Mahieran.

Mikeli laid out the problem, with Oktar giving his report on what he knew of the situation in Fintha.

"I was wondering, sir king," Master Lurton said, after a quick look at the other craft masters present. He was already formally on the Council, so the others had held back. "Yes, we do know about this magery—and in fact, some of us were thinking of coming to you or the Marshal-Judicar there, since our own Marshals couldn't tell us aught but wait for word from Fin Panir. Our people are worried. The children are all at odds, not sure if they might have it and it might come out."

"But if it's magery released because the evil's gone, that's got to be good," said Master Jornalt, head of the Grain Merchants' Guild.

"We hope that's what it is," Mikeli said. "But the point is, we don't want panic—it will do none of us any good—and we don't want innocent children killed. We do want a list of those who manifest magery, for their protection."

"And parents will need to know how to teach their children to use it well—difficult, since they do not have it themselves," Mahieran put in. "Had my son shown magery at five winters or so, I would have had no idea what might happen next or how to cope with it. At least, at his age, he understands danger."

The others nodded. "If no one knows how to train the children, it's like having them running around with firebrands," said Master Felnor of the Finesmiths. "It's dangerous."

"Yes," Oktar said. "But any babe just creeping about may put its

hand in the fire, or one a little older might light a spill and drop it . . .
It would be the same, to teach them not to light fires by accident,
would it not? Any child may cause harm by accident—it doesn't take
magery to start a fire or cut with a knife."

"If you put it that way, Marshal-Judicar," Felnor said.

"It's just one more thing children can cause accidents with, I'm
thinking." Master Redan of the Knitters smoothed her apron over her
skirt. "Children aren't born knowing danger; every mother knows
it's the sharp eye and training that keeps 'em as safe as they are."

Heads nodded. Mikeli relaxed a little, seeing the faces thoughtful
rather than tense.

"So are you changing the law now, sir king?" asked Baron Brenvor. "Are you making it that all magery is legal?"

"No," Mikeli said. "Blood magery is not legal. But I don't believe
children are born evil into good families like those we know have had
children show magery. And magery not used for evil ends is no more
evil than blue eyes or brown. I cannot change the Code of Gird
myself—that's for the Marshal-General and the Marshals' Council.
But I can say that in Tsaia, at least, the appearance of magery such as
we've seen is not proof of evil. Without another crime—without
using magery to injure, steal, kill—no one with magery will be con-
demned."

He looked around the table, from face to face: most were still
thoughtful and gave him a nod. A few looked worried. Duke Mahieran cleared his throat; Mikeli waved a hand, and Mahieran stood.

"Sir king, I know you plan an announcement to the rest of the
palace staff. Would you like me to gather them at this time?"

"Thank you," Mikeli said. "I'm sure we'll be through here
shortly—" He looked around again. "So yes. A half-glass, say." Then,
as Mahieran left the chamber, he said, "If you have questions about
how to proceed, Marshal-Judicar Oktar has some recommendations
for you and will be talking to the Marshals in the city as soon as possible."

All stood, and Oktar led them out. Mikeli looked up at the ceiling
for a moment and sighed. "I thought it would be fun to be king," he
said, and then chuckled. "And I dare think Camwyn is immature. I
was every bit as ignorant when I was his age."

CHAPTER THIRTY-NINE

Ifoss, Aarenis

Not long before the end of the campaign season, an Aldonfulk gnome presented itself at the camp entrance. Arcolin happened to be nearby and intervened when the sentry would not let the gnome in. He guessed what it had come about but wondered why none had come sooner. Yet he knew from Dattur it would be rude to ask.

"I'm Count Arcolin," he said. "Are you the prince's messenger?"

"It is so," said the gnome. "It is that this one enters?"

"Yes," Arcolin said. "It is better to hold talk in my tent."

The gnome hesitated but then came with Arcolin.

"It is true that our prince granted passage to humans under your command, for the value of information they brought. It is not known that humans remember such passage."

"Most don't," Arcolin said. "Two old soldiers did, however. They spoke of it where someone heard. It was not believed by one, but another may have believed. And my junior captain saw a file of creatures—rockfolk, he thought—entering a place in the mountain that no human seemed to know about. He is new in this area; he asked questions."

"And you sent word to our prince for what reason?"

"Because it could be a danger," Arcolin said. "And because my soldiers talked about it where others could hear. If an enemy locates it—"

"They will not," the gnome said. "The rock is closed except when we are using it."

"My thought was that since my soldiers might have made it possible for others to find, it was my responsibility to inform your prince."

The gnome said nothing for a moment, then nodded. "It is a reason. It is right that you tell Aldonfulk, but Aldonfulk will guard its own. Tell your soldiers who remember they must not try to pass that way; it will not be safe."

"They will not," Arcolin said.

"I will tell the prince," the gnome said.

At that moment, Dattur came into the tent carrying several packages. The Aldonfulk gnome stared at him, then back at Arcolin.

"Kteknik," said the gnome.

"No longer," Dattur said.

"It is not right dress," the gnome said in gnomish; Arcolin understood enough now.

"It is now," Dattur said, "while I am with this army."

"It is not soldier!" the gnome said. "What prince allowed?"

"My prince stands here," Dattur said. He nodded toward Arcolin. The other gnome turned to Arcolin, then back to Dattur.

"No. Not possible. That is human. It is not human to be prince. It is not human speak Law. Gnome lies is *kteknik*."

Arcolin said, in gnomish, "He does not lie. Stone-right makes a prince; my rockfolk hold my stone."

"Not! Not Law!" The Aldonfulk gnome had turned a peculiar bluish gray. "Must be lie."

"A dragon came," Arcolin said. He used what Dattur had taught him was the gnomish word, one that incorporated Eldest of Elders and Flame-Being.

The Aldonfulk gnome took a step toward him. "No dragon come human!"

"A dragon came," Arcolin repeated. "A dragon sent away gnomes from their stone. I took them in. I gave them stone-right. Dragon made contract with me; he touched my tongue."

Again the Aldonfulk gnome looked from Arcolin to Dattur and back again. "*Kteknik* . . . does he lie?"

"No," Dattur said. "He is my prince. We are his people. He has heart for Law."

"Not right dress."

"It is—had been no time," Arcolin said, struggling with gnomish. "Dragon came in winter; gnomes came to me in winter. The stone has no yielded right . . ."

"Bternos," Dattur said. "And this one was far from that stone. It is long story."

"It is strange story. It is difficult story. The prince will not like this story."

"It is true story," Arcolin said.

When Arcolin arrived in Valdaire, his banker handed him an intricately wrapped package. "A gnome gave me this," he said. "I was to give it to you the day you arrived in the city."

"It's heavy," Arcolin said. It felt heavy as stone; he realized it probably was stone.

"I know you have a gnome in the Company now—"

"Not for long; he's going north with me to join others."

"Well . . . it's unusual, isn't it?"

"The whole thing is unusual," Arcolin said. "If you're interested—"

"Indeed yes. You are of value to us. Tell on, if you will."

Arcolin told it all and finished with, "The Aldonfulk messenger said his prince would be displeased. I suspect this is some evidence of that displeasure, and I hope it does not bar me from use of the pass."

"Why would it?"

"Because the road north, from the crest of the pass on, traverses Aldonfulk territory. They made treaty long ago, but they still control travel between north and south by that route, and humans pay their toll."

"I had not realized they had the will or power to close that way," the banker said.

"It's rare, but it's happened to individuals. I hope I will not be one of them."

"Tell me, if you do not mind, what it is when you find out."

Arcolin shrugged. "I might as well open it here and see."

The gray wrapping, as thin and flexible as paper, seemed of a different texture; Arcolin did not recognize it. Several layers protected the contents: sheets of paper with writing on them in the gnomish script and a thin flat slab of stone.

"That explains the weight," the banker said. "Can you read that script?"

"Slightly," Arcolin said. He knew the first block of words was a greeting but did not recognize the rest. "Luckily I can ask Dattur—the gnome with me. I will certainly tell you, since if it is a refusal to allow me to use the pass, I must seek another way north." He knew of only two other passes, and the nearest, Hakkenarsk, north of Dwarfwatch, lay many days to the east.

"I hope it is not that," the banker said.

Dattur read the papers without difficulty; Arcolin never ceased to wonder that all gnomes could read. "The Aldonfulk prince greets you and asks your presence in his hall . . ." Dattur's voice trailed off. "My prince, he is either showing friendship or great guile. He offers the use of the gnome way through the mountain—the same given to Captain Selfer, his cohort, and the Count of Andressat. You must understand that if you accept, you will be at his mercy for those days under the mountain, and if you do not accept, it can—it probably will—be taken as an insult." He looked up at Arcolin. "And he wants an answer within a day. His messenger will come tomorrow at noon."

"I can't leave tomorrow," Arcolin said. "I have business to attend."

"It is an answer he wants, I believe, not an immediate attendance. How long do you think your business will take?"

"A hand of days at least," Arcolin said. He looked at Dattur. "Do you think it is friendship or ill intent?"

Dattur spread his hands. "I do not know. Friendship between human and kapristi . . . is very rare. Alliance is possible. Ill intent, however, is against the Law unless wrong has been done. It may be only that he wants to know and understand how you came to be a prince of kapristi. And know that he may send—may have sent—one of his own to the north to find out what he can."

Arcolin scrubbed at his head as if he could push his thoughts into order. "It is more complicated than I thought, and I already knew it was complicated. I certainly did not intend to cause trouble with other gnome princes."

"You did not . . . but the situation would be . . . bothering. Annoying, even. It does not happen before."

"You are coming with me—will it bother you to be underground in a different princedom?"

"No, my prince. It is hard if *kteknik,* but you declared me not *kteknik* and gave me cloth of your choice to clothe myself. If it was not kapristi-made, it was still the right cloth to you. So I told him, and so I will tell the prince."

"I am not sure my gnomish is good enough to follow everything a prince might say, and answer as I should."

"I will help, my prince. And should it be necessary, I will work the stone that is not my stone, though they will protest loudly."

"What is this stone, then?" Arcolin asked.

Dattur ran his fingers over it. "It's a seal-stone. It is the prince's seal, stone from his stone-mass, that certifies who he is. It may also be a key, but that we may find out from his messenger tomorrow."

The messenger arrived promptly at noon. Arcolin and Dattur were waiting at the gate when he walked up and bowed stiffly. He spoke Common fairly well. "You were able to read what my prince wrote?"

"Yes," Arcolin said. "With some help."

"And what answer do you return?"

"I cannot come at once," Arcolin said. "I have appointments made that must be kept. But I accept Aldonfulk's invitation to meet with your prince in his hall."

"It is well," the messenger said.

A few days later, Arcolin sent his escort ahead to cross the pass alone. "I am delayed here. Await me at Fiveway," he said, handing over a letter pouch for a courier. "A royal courier might be waiting; if so, hand this over."

"But sir—*we're* supposed to be your escort."

"And you will be, from Fiveway north."

"But sir, who will be your escort to Fiveway?"

"I can always find someone safe to travel with that far. After all, once over the divide, we're in gnome territory almost all the way to Fiveway. Brigands don't last long there." He grinned at them. "I don't know exactly how long my business here will be, but do not worry."

Two nights later, Arcolin and Dattur rode north out of the winter quarters and met their guide on the first ridge. By dawn, they were high on another ridge, with fog in the valley below and the flank of the great mountain in front of them.

"It will not be as with your captain," their guide said. "You travel with a gnome of your princedom, and though you are human . . . I have been told not to cloud your memory. For that reason, the prince has commanded that we enter the mountain in a different place and travel to the main passage along a new one that closes behind. Though if this frightens you, you may sleep and not know."

"I am not frightened," Arcolin said. "Or not enough to wish to be asleep."

Nonetheless, when they rode up to a vertical face of rock and it opened silently before them, Arcolin's belly tightened. The night had been dark, with rising fog dimming the stars, but the dark they rode into was darker yet. His horse balked at first, but their gnome guide laid a hand on its neck and muttered something; the horse relaxed and plodded into the dark without resistance.

All Arcolin could tell of the first part of that journey was clopping of the horse's hooves on stone and the echo of that sound off the walls of the passage. He knew the passage climbed steeply because of the horse's grunts of effort. He had the uneasy feeling that they traveled in a moving hole in the rock, but in the blackness he could not see rock opening and closing. He wasn't sure that he wanted to. Finally he saw a dim glow ahead, and they came out into a level passage wider than the one they'd been in. Arcolin looked back in time to see the rock flow together like mud and stiffen again into stone. He shuddered and did not look back again.

Light grew as they moved along the level passage; they emerged in a wider one in which it was light enough to see the expressions on faces. More gnomes waited there: a small troop Arcolin chose to consider an honor guard. From there the journey resembled what the two veterans had told him about except that they did not come out of the mountain before arriving in the great hall. Arcolin dismounted; one of the gnomes took his horse and led it away. Selfer had remembered this: the carved screen with its patterns that caught and confused the eye, the dais, the gnome prince. Arcolin bowed.

"You speak kapristi?" the prince asked.

"Poorly, as yet, but I do."

"It is not known before in all time that a man was prince of gnomes. It is not good."

"It is not good that gnomes die naked in the snow," Arcolin said.

The prince rose from his throne and came down, the dark shining eyes fixed on Arcolin's face. "It is that even mountains move," he said. He bowed stiffly. "Prince to prince: greeting."

Arcolin bowed again. "Greeting."

"You care for your kapristin."

"I do."

"It may be the Giver of Law teach you . . . it may be the Giver of Law use you to punish oathbreakers." While Arcolin puzzled his way through that, the prince closed his eyes a long moment, then opened them.

"For this my kapristin say kapristinya to your kapristin. It is prince speaking Law."

"It is prince speaking Law," all the other gnomes said.

Arcolin wondered if he should repeat the formula when Aldonfulk was already a known entity. "It is Aldonfulk prince speaking Law, and it is I learning," he said.

"This one," the prince said, looking at Dattur. "This one has not had chance to make proper clothes?"

"It is so," Arcolin said.

"Without incurring debt, as true gift to new prince, I would offer for your teacher of Law a suit of clothes."

Arcolin bowed. "It is a gift I would be honored to accept for him."

"Then let him go, and you and I will sit to refreshment and I would ask you of the men of the south, what we need to know for the safety of kapristin."

They brought a human-size chair for Arcolin, and a chair that height with a footstool for their prince. A flagon was set before them, and a measure of salt; Arcolin took out the loaf he had thought to bring for such a possibility and his own travel cup. The prince nodded at this. "Indeed, prince, you are not unacquainted with our courtesies. It speaks well of your Law-teacher." The servant—or assistant—set down a cup for the prince and poured a measure of liquid into it. In that light, Arcolin was not sure what it was, only that it was not water. With a knife the servant divided the loaf and sprinkled salt on each cut side. Arcolin pushed the piece nearer himself to the far side, and the prince did the same. Then, following the prince's lead, he picked up his portion, took a bite, and then sipped the liquid in the cup, a tart wine.

"It is good wine," Arcolin said.

"It is good bread," the prince said. "May honest salt bring savor to our tongues and fair exchange to our hearts, by the Law. And now, if you please—what news?"

Arcolin told him what he had learned in the past two summers and who he thought was behind it.

"This necklace," the prince said. "Do you have a description?"

"Yes, though I have not seen it myself. Blue and white stones, quite large. I was told that no one knows their origin—kapristi, hakken, Sinyi, and humans have all been asked, and none know."

"Has any asked Drakon?" the prince asked, using a word close enough to Common.

"Dragon! Would a dragon know?"

"Might. But where was it first seen in these days?"

"In the cellar of an old fort in southern Tsaia, near Brewersbridge," Arcolin said.

"Ah . . . and what manner of being had lived there?"

"I'm not sure. Something evil. One of my veterans was there, Paksenarrion, as well as the man I spoke to this year."

"Paksenarrion! That name is known to kapristi. She was given an oath-ring in return for her service to merchants of mine, but has never yet claimed her pay."

"She lost all to kuaknomi in the far west," Arcolin said.

"Kuaknomi . . . the elves' shame, the iynisin?" The prince sounded angry. "I thought she was now a paladin."

"Yes," Arcolin said. "But the rings she wore then were lost."

"It is a debt unpaid," the prince said. "It will be redeemed. As for the necklace you speak of—in the time of the prince before me, and that would be three or four lifetimes of men, there was a division in Tsaia, in one of the great houses, one in the east of that land. There was talk in the trade roads of something stolen, jewels of great worth and—but this was held a secret, to the limit men can hold secrets—magical as well. It was said that one fled with a part of a treasure and by so fleeing took away the power of the whole. This is not certain truth, but rumor only, and I had it from that prince, who wrote it in our remembrances. A man came here, fleeing, and asked sanctuary, but was refused, for upon him that prince smelled blood magery."

Arcolin told what he knew of the Verrakai and the Verrakai regalia; the gnome prince nodded.

"That would be the family. And the jewels would be old, from across the sea."

"Sapphires and diamonds, I was told," Arcolin said.

"Not," the gnome prince said. "For those any of the rockfolk would know. I do not know what they are, but I know what they are not."

When the prince signaled that they had finished their talk, other gnomes escorted Arcolin to a guest chamber, where he slept until wakened by a gong. Dattur reappeared in sober gray gnomish attire with braid on his jacket that did not match that on the Aldonfulk gnomes. He waited until they were once more on the road to Fiveway, the mountain behind them and their guides well behind. "Can you read this?" he asked.

"No," Arcolin said. "But you told me what it would say."

"It is a great honor. And they made this for you." Dattur handed over a folded stack of gray cloth. "It is a prince's stole, but longer, for your height. You should wear it when you greet your subjects in the north."

Arcolin started to unfold it, but Dattur stopped him. "No one must see," he said, jerking his head to a caravan slowly making its way down, two turns behind them. "Later."

Arcolin put it away, into one of his saddlebags.

CHAPTER FORTY

Fin Panir

When the first chill autumn winds blew in from the north—winterwards, as the Finthans called it—and prompted Arvid Semminson to unpack his cloak again, he realized he had not heard Gird's voice in his head for a long time. He wondered why, but when he asked Cedlin, the Marshal shrugged. "Who can know the ways of the gods and their saints? My guess would be that whatever you were called to do, you need more training, more knowledge of the Fellowship. Young lads ask what great deeds they will do later, and I tell them what I'm now telling you. Do your work faithfully, grow in strength and knowledge and wisdom, so that when trouble comes, you are ready to do those deeds."

Arvid nodded. "I understand that, Marshal, but wondered if I had missed some word—"

"From what you told me before, you hear Gird clearly enough. He had his reasons for turning you out of your old life, and you'll find them out later. Though—where would your son be, if you had not been diverted?"

Arvid shuddered. "If that was the only reason, Marshal, it was reason enough. I am content."

"Not for too long, I'll wager," the Marshal said. "I hear you're raising questions up the hill . . . called Luap an idiot, didn't you? Ambitious scoundrel?"

"Well, yes. He was."

The Marshal chuckled. "Keep that up, Arvid, and you'll find yourself rising like the bubbles in boiling water. Aiming at Marshal-General, are you?"

"No, Marshal!" Panic roiled his mind for a moment. "The Fellowship does not need a thief-enforcer for a leader."

"Only the gods know what the Fellowship needs," the Marshal said. "And someone who actually hears Gird may someday be what's needed."

Arvid shied from that thought and scrambled to find another topic. "This Council the Marshal-General's called—do they always last so long?"

"No. You know what it's about—"

"Something about magery," Arvid said. He had heard scattered comments but could not make sense of them. "Blood magery, isn't it? People using it here? Does it mean priests of Liart moved here from Tsaia when they were driven out there?"

"Not at all," the Marshal said. "Not blood magery, but innate magery, what Duke Verrakai in Tsaia has. A talent, like a talent for singing or swordplay or strength."

"But it's bad—" Even thinking of magery brought the memory of Paksenarrion's torment to mind, and everything he'd heard linked magery to evil, including the rumors now murmured in the markets here in Fin Panir.

"Is swordplay bad? Is singing? Either one can be used for bad purposes. Either one can be used for good purposes." Arvid said nothing. The Marshal reached out and tapped his hands. "You have *killed* with those hands, Arvid. And you have saved a paladin with those hands, and saved a child—your son—with those hands. Is the strength and skill of your hands bad, because you used it to steal and kill, or good because you used it to save?"

Awareness of Gird's presence settled on Arvid's shoulders like a heavy cloak. "I . . . don't . . . know. I suppose . . . it's not the strength of my hands but . . . how I use them."

"Exactly. That's what the Marshal-General is saying about magery, but many people believe it's evil no matter how it's used. That's what you learned, eh? What *we've* learned in the past few years, from

Luap's writings and other writings found in Kolobia, is different from what's in the current Code of Gird. Gird did not hate magery but cruelty. He knew—at least by the end of his life—that magery could be used for good and that cruelty wasn't confined to magelords."

"So . . . what does magelord magery look like?"

The Marshal gave him a long considering look, then nodded as if he'd seen something in Arvid's face. "Often the first sign is light—a finger or two giving off light. It's hot, like fire: a magelord could light a candle or start a fire just by touching it. A paladin's light has no heat: it gives sight only."

"Wizards make fire."

"Yes, but with spells or potions. It's not the same thing." The Marshal paused. "I do hope, Arvid, you are not becoming too interested in magery."

"If you mean do I wish to become a mage, the answer is no. But what you have been teaching me about the Code and what I have seen up the hill, copying texts old and new and listening to the talk about magery . . . I want to know more about everything."

"Everything?"

"Yes. Change is come upon all of us—perhaps I feel it more because mine was so sudden—but if someone does not see the whole whirlwind, how can any of us survive?"

"I don't know," the Marshal said. "But perhaps you will find out. Tell me, what do you think of elves?"

Arvid shook his head. "I never knew any, but to recognize them as elves. We had a few part-elf thieves in the Guild, both in Tsaia and over the mountains; no full elves. We knew about the kuaknomi, of course. No one would work with them: can't trust 'em. Other elves—I saw them on the roads sometimes, or in an inn, but had no reason to speak to them."

"But you watched them, didn't you?"

"If I had leisure."

"And you thought—?"

"Arrogant, beautiful, and terrifying."

"Terrifying?"

"The way they cast glamours . . . I hated seeing what it did to people and was afraid of being caught in it myself."

"You weren't? Are you sure?"

"Not that I know of. I could see the edge, like a faint silver line, and avoid it or . . . or shut myself up, some way, and move through quickly."

"Hmmm." Marshal Cedlin did not move for four or five breaths, then nodded sharply. "I have a task for you, Arvid, and I'm going to suggest the Marshal-General consult you as well. Look for magery in Fin Panir. I know some of the children who have shown mage ability. I want you to go about the city, just as you do now, but concentrate on magery. See what you find. Notice the reactions to it, if you find it. And tell me."

In the next several afternoons, Arvid found fourteen people—eleven children, two youths, and one older woman selling fruit in the lower market—he was sure were mages. When he told Marshal Cedlin the next drill night, the Marshal nodded. "I thought you might be good at this. How could you tell? Did you see them all make light?"

"No . . . it was more like the elves, though—I didn't feel any pressure of a glamour. But I could—almost—see something. Different but . . . something about them."

The Marshal nodded again. "I thought you might be able to tell. Anything else?"

"Yes. I didn't tell you this before, but I started hearing talk about magery shortly after I moved here. Didn't seem worth mentioning; I knew Girdish didn't like magery, and people gossip most about what they don't like. There's been much more the last few hands of days. I didn't know—I thought it might be something to do with the Evener coming, with casting-out rituals. But in the lower city especially, there's fear. Rumors that the Marshal-General wants to bring magelords back. The Marshal-General's going to die if—"

"What!"

"Marshal, everyone knows she's defending magery, especially in children, and that she's got you and the other city Marshals convinced—under her thumb is how people put it. There's a lot of 'em don't like the idea of magery at all and blame her for it coming back. They say she's afraid of magery and that's why she won't stamp it out. Or that she's a magelord herself and that's why she sent the expedition to the west. That she's too weak and too old to be Marshal-

General. They want someone else—a man who's against magery, spe-cifically." Arvid paused for breath. "I didn't realize it before you sent me out to look, but—I've been through this m'self, sir. Someone's stirring 'em up; someone wants to be where she is, just like my num-ber two in the Vérella Guild did. There's a revolt coming, Marshal. I don't think they'll wait for the Evener to cast her out. She's dead, if she doesn't take care."

"She had to kill a Marshal back in spring, before you got here," the Marshal said. "He challenged her to a trial of arms in the High Lord's Hall. That should have settled it."

"It didn't. Talk is, she murdered him in cold blood."

"What! How did you—I've been up and down the city myself, and I haven't heard this. Nor my yeoman-marshals."

"You're known to be on her side, Marshal. People don't know me as one of hers even though I work up the hill. They know I'm a new-comer who may not be in the Marshal-General's camp."

"Are you?" The Marshal's look was sharp, challenging.

"I'm telling you this." Arvid gave him the same look. "If I'd known before all I know now, I'd have told you earlier."

"Do you have any idea when something will happen?"

"As I said, before the Evener. Or as soon as a day or two, perhaps. Even this night. That's why I didn't wait until after drill to tell you. Several of the angriest people today mentioned someone coming in from outside and meeting someone up the hill, 'ready to give the sig-nal,' one of them said. Then he darted back into an alley. No names, though."

"There wouldn't be, if they're as serious as you say." The Marshal chewed his lower lip a moment. "Arvid, go up there now. You're ex-cused from drill tonight. I'll see your lad safe to the inn after his. If anyone asks on the way, it's the truth: I gave you an errand to run for me. Here's a paper—" He scrawled a few words on it, rolled it, slid it into a message tube, and handed it over. "You don't know what's in it; you were told to take it up the hill, is all. I'll come after drill."

Arvid raised his brows, but the Marshal did not explain further. As Arvid passed through the grange, someone in his drill group asked where he was going. "Up the hill," he said. "Marshal told me to carry a note."

At least he had his sword on and his cloak, bless the chill in the air. Striding along, he considered looking at the paper. Surely it was just an excuse—nothing important. But if he was carrying a real message, and it was snatched, he should know—but then, the good yeoman did not pry or sneak. But then, if he had not done a less obvious equivalent of prying and sneaking for the past days, he would not have known there was a conspiracy. As with strength, he told himself, prying and sneaking could be used for good as well as ill, and his intentions were entirely good. And it wasn't quite dark. He broke stride and turned into a convenient alley.

"Well! Looka what we got here. Fancy boy from t'grange, works for t'Marshal-General." A dark shadow moved, reaching for him; another raised an arm, holding something that would surely hurt if it hit him.

"Not exactly," Arvid said. The one trying to yank the message tube out of his heart-hand yelped and staggered back, wrist spurting; the one with the club missed Arvid's head by three fingers. Arvid spun that one around and smashed him face-first into the alley wall, kicking the other man in the knee as he turned. He slid the message tube into a pocket in his cloak, then let the knife in his sleeve fall into his hand.

The man against the wall lurched backward, trying for room and chance; Arvid thrust the short knife through clothing. The tip grated on mail. "Not so smart," the man said, turning; he had drawn a long knife or short sword.

Arvid's right hand moved with the turn, a draw cut to the neck; the man fell. The other one was squirming away down the alley, clenching his slashed wrist with his other hand and pushing with his one good leg. Arvid considered the possible advantages of gaining information—but heard boots coming up the other street, turning into the alley. He stamped hard on a sensitive area; the man curled around his pain, and Arvid sliced that throat as well.

He made it to the entrance of the palace complex without hearing any alarm raised behind him. Interesting. The few people on the street had not seemed to notice as he stuffed his bloody gloves into another of the cloak's pockets, wiped the knives on the lining, and replaced them, all with the practiced moves of someone who had killed and walked away many times before. He paused at a public fountain to clean his face and hands of the blood spatters. People noticed what they expected to notice. A man stopping for a drink, sneezing and blowing his nose—no one looked at what was on the cloth he used. Dusk was thickening, colors fading with the day.

At the gate, he found only a single sentry, who recognized him and nodded him through. "I've a message for the Marshal-General from Marshal Cedlin," he said. Along with not being noticed when it wasn't wise, being noticed when it was mattered. "Is she at supper?"

"Don't know," the sentry said. "Might be, or might have finished. The Council meeting ended a glass earlier than usual." He peered a little closer at Arvid. "Did you trip in the mud?"

"Came through a dirty alley," Arvid said. "Some people don't sweep as they should." Could he trust the sentry? Maybe—but it was more important to get his message to the Marshal-General.

"True enough," the sentry said, grinning. "Report it to the Marshal when you get back."

Arvid nodded and continued on to the familiar building. Indoors, with the lamps lit, someone might notice that the dark wetness on his cloak was red and not brown . . . and someone did.

"Arvid! You're wounded—" That was a knight he'd seen before, coming down the long lower passage, often deserted at this time.

"It's not my blood, sir," Arvid said. "But I am on an errand for Marshal Cedlin and was beset on the way—"

"Did you tell the Marshal?"

"No, sir—I was more than halfway here, and he bade me hasten. I—did them some harm, sir; they may yet be in the alley, the first below the hill."

"I'll send someone," the knight said. He looked at Arvid more closely. "The Marshal-General said you always went armed."

"Not lately, but this evening, yes. Drill night and longsword practice."

"Ah, then. She's in her office, up the stairs at the end and across the passage."

He met no one else on the lower floor and no one on the stairs, but heard voices in the upper passage as he climbed them. As he came onto the last flight, he saw brighter light above, a group around the Marshal-General's door, all the gray legs and blue shirts. Voices rose as he climbed; he could hear them clearly.

"You can't say that!"

"It's wrong; it's always been wrong. It can't ever be right—"

And then he heard the rasp of a blade being drawn and drew his own sword. He leapt up the last three steps, letting his small blade drop once more into his heart-hand.

Heads turned; eyes widened. Good: the sight of blood and a naked blade often startled people into immobility.

"Excuse me," Arvid said. "I have a message for the Marshal-General."

"You're—that's blood on your cloak."

Arvid smiled. "Indeed," he said. "But not mine. Is the Marshal-General within?"

"She's—you're not a Marshal. We have business with her."

"As have I, Marshals," Arvid said. He had sorted his memory: Marshals, all but one of whom he had seen before, usually hurrying through a passage or across the court. He did not know their names. No High Marshals, none of the resident paladins, no knights. The one who had drawn steel now let it slide back into the scabbard, as if wishing to pretend he had not. "A message from Marshal Cedlin. Your pardon, but I was told it was urgent."

"And did he tell you to draw your sword on Marshals?" asked the one who had done exactly the same.

Arvid smiled a little wider, showing teeth. With just that smile he had faced other blusterers in his past, and it had the same effect now. The man leaned back a little. "I heard angry voices and drawn steel near the Marshal-General's office as I came up the stairs," he said. "Is it not the duty of a Girdish yeoman to be alert and to defend the Fellowship?"

"And you think you are better qualified to do that than a group of Marshals?" said another, on the other side of the group.

Arvid transferred the smile to him. "I think, Marshal, that some-one who draws steel on the Marshal-General is not likely to be de-fending the Fellowship, but some private ambition of his own."

Faces reddened. Arvid stepped forward, well aware that if they rushed him, he needed room to maneuver lest he be dumped back down the stairs. Now he could see that the door to the Marshal-General's office was closed. Was she all right in there? Arming herself? Or wounded? The group in front of him moved closer together . . . So . . . they were not as intimidated as he could have wished.

"I wonder," he said, stepping sideways as if to go around them, "what you would do should I cry alarm. There are those downstairs who would come."

Hands reached to sword hilts, and Arvid prepared himself—but at that moment the door opened, and the Marshal-General, sword and buckler in hand, mail coif on her head, appeared a sword's length inside. Behind her was another, to Arvid's relief. A Knight of Gird, also armed for combat.

Arvid let his smile widen to a frank grin. "I believe, gentlemen, you are surrounded."

They broke, three rushing one way, four the other. Arvid tripped one who came near enough and thrust at another, wounding him but not stopping the man's flight.

"Hold, Arvid," the Marshal-General said. "I know their names and purposes. I am unhurt. But you?"

"Unhurt," Arvid said. He put away the knife but did not put away his sword. "I do have a message from Marshal Cedlin." He pulled the tube from his pocket and handed it to her.

She unrolled the message, read it, nodded, and gestured to the knight. "Sir Piter, come with me—and you, Arvid, as well." She started for the stairs; Piter moved quickly ahead of her; Arvid took the rear. Over her shoulder she said, "I see you are wearing another very useful cloak, if somewhat stained."

"Yes," Arvid said. "I had intended to remove that which makes it interesting, but tonight—"

She held up her hand; he fell silent. From the passage below, they heard boots and lowered voices. The knight moved silently down to the next landing. Then "Gird!" shouted several voices, and blades rang.

Arvid drew his dagger and followed the Marshal-General down. The men below—two of them the same as he'd seen above, but with new companions—now seemed determined to fight. The Marshal-General's group had the high ground, however. The clash of blades soon drew cries from somewhere down the passage to the kitchen and then from the far end of the lower passage. This time the new-comers were clearly on the Marshal-General's side.

"Once more," Arvid said, "I believe you are surrounded." The man in front of him hesitated, and Arvid thrust past the weak guard and into the belly. "Should've worn mail," he said as the man's eyes widened and his mouth gaped. He knocked the man's sword loose with his dagger.

When the brief fight ended, only two of the attackers were alive; the Marshal-General and the knight had accounted for three between them, and the newcomers had taken out four.

"Marshal-General, there's trouble in the city," one of the knights said. "We were coming to let you know—"

"Come with me," she said. And to Arvid, "Quickly. Tell me what you came for." She headed toward the forecourt.

"What you see," he said. "Conspiracy, based partly on truth and partly on lies. Someone's raising fears that you're secretly a magelord and want to return them to rule. Expedition to the west—"

"Just a moment—" They had come out into the forecourt now. It had gone full dark; people were milling about, hard to see in the flick-ering light of torches that caught the glint of a few drawn weapons. Clusters of people talking, moving uneasily. Someone said, "It's the Marshal-General—" and the groups converged, moving toward her.

"This is the Fellowship of Gird!" the Marshal-General's voice rang out; movement ceased. "Not a mob of untrained, frightened peasants. We are Gird's people today, as we have been these hundreds of years."

"But there was an alarm—" someone began.

"Yes," the Marshal-General said. "Some Marshals attacked me, to my sorrow. We are Gird's people; it is not right for us to kill each other. To pour poison in a mug . . . that is not something Gird would do. When we disagree, we argue. We bang on tables. We shout. That is how Gird's people disagree. Not secretly plotting."

The silence acquired an edge, as the listeners thought about that.

Arvid, thinking of the things he'd read in the archives, knew she'd shaded the truth there. Some Marshal-Generals in the past had come to that position by plotting.

"What if I don't think you're really Girdish? You defend magery."
A voice from the crowd; Arvid could not see who had spoken.

"You tell me so, and we argue about it," the Marshal-General said.
"I would suggest you read the entire Code of Gird and its history,
including the new material in the Scrolls of Luap beforehand, though,
because I will refer to them in my responses."

"That . . . that would take years! I have work to do!"

"It took me years," the Marshal-General said, a hint of humor in
her voice. "Much of it spent as a Marshal running a grange. But
you're welcome to argue with me, whenever you feel prepared." Silence followed that.

Arvid felt the tension leach out of the crowd. Most of these would
be people who knew the Marshal-General, who lived or worked in
the palace complex. They had reacted to an alarm. They would
now—with no immediate danger in sight—accept her words. A few
still held to another purpose; he could sense their tension. Could the
Marshal-General? He glanced at her. She looked as calm as usual,
standing poised but not tense, confident.

"People of Gird," she said, "remember what Gird stood for. Fairness, justice, protection of the defenseless. We are not a people of
fear, but a people of courage. It is time to go about our business. We
have deaths to mourn, and other deaths to prevent."

A low mutter, but no real resistance. A few turned to walk away
toward one or another of the entrances to the forecourt. A clatter of
hooves coming up the hill and the tramp of marching feet brought
them to a halt; all turned toward the gate.

Light bloomed suddenly, clear and white, a dome that covered
the forecourt and the gateway. Riding through the gates, tall on her
tall red horse, came someone Arvid had not expected to see again—
certainly not there, that night. His last memory of her, immediately
after he'd rescued her from torment, made him shudder. It seemed
she looked straight at him for a moment, and then her gaze shifted.

"Paksenarrion!" The Marshal-General's call carried no hint of
tension or relief. "Welcome back."

"Marshal-General. My thanks. I met Marshal Cedlin on the way,
and he has brought his grange; he had heard of some trouble here."

"I will speak with him." The Marshal-General walked toward the gates, trailed by the Knights of Gird. Arvid lagged behind, hoping Paks would ignore him.

Instead, she rode on into the forecourt, toward Arvid, and the red horse stopped in front of him, its head a scant armslength away. Arvid found himself pinned by its gaze while Paks dismounted. He had the distinct feeling that if he tried to turn and run, the horse would grab his cloak and hold him captive.

"Arvid," she said. He had to look at her. She was smiling as if he were her dearest friend, that open grin he had mocked for its naivete.

He bowed, with none of the grace he had once owned, and hated himself for noticing that. "Lady Paksenarrion."

"You saved my life," she said. "There is no lord or lady between us." She tilted her head, looking him up and down. "And now, I see, you are a yeoman of Gird. Will you tell me that tale someday?"

His heart skipped a beat, then raced. "I . . . cannot tell it easily."

Her expression changed. "No. Such tales are not lightly told. I will not ask . . . but I will ask what has gone forth this night. Blood on your cloak, your blade, your hands—"

"And none of it mine," Arvid said. His pulse had steadied. "Nor the Marshal-General's, which is Gird's mercy. Lady—Paksenarrion, pardon—I must ask: do you hear Gird's voice plain?"

Her eyes widened, then her expression changed again: understanding and compassion. "Yes," she said. "And that is not an easy thing to hear, is it?"

"No," he said. His throat closed for a moment. "It is not. I don't know . . . I don't know how to . . . what to . . ."

"Peace," she said.

Whatever that was, it spread through his mind, a serenity he had never felt. A glamour? A spell? Perhaps, but one he could not resist.

"You will know," she said, "when you need to know." Then she grinned again. "Or that is how it is with me, and with the other paladins I know. You, Arvid, may be given a different path."

"Paks!" Across the forecourt, another paladin, Camwynya, hurried toward them. Arvid looked around and noticed that the forecourt was almost empty now. "Where have you been?"

"I am not sure I can explain," Paks said to Camwynya. "A long way from here, in mountains I never knew about."

Camwynya laughed. "Don't tell me—you found the valley of the paladins' mounts?"

"Among other things," Paks said. "Do you know Arvid?"

Camwynya nodded to Arvid. "Indeed—he is the new scribe, making a name for himself by arguing, I've heard." She looked more closely at him. "And, I see, by fighting."

Arvid winced dramatically. "Indeed . . . for I found the Marshal-General beset. If—if I may be excused, I must go now and find my son. He will be worried."

"Your son?" Paks said. "I didn't know—"

"No. Nor I, the last time we met. He—his mother is dead."

At the gate, Arvid met Marshal Cedlin, who sent him back down to his lodgings. "You've fought well this night, Arvid, but enough: we will need you tomorrow, I'm sure, and beyond that." He turned to the yeomen. "Jori . . . Tam . . . go with Arvid back to the Loaf, see him safe home. He's had more than one fight tonight."

The others asked no questions on the way to the Loaf, for which Arvid was grateful. Once there, they said farewell and trudged back up the street. Arvid went in; the common room was empty but for Pia, wiping down tables. She stared at his bloody cloak. "You'll need to clean that before it's all dry," she said. "And before you show yourself to the lad. I've buckets of cold water in the kitchen. Come through."

He had never been in the kitchen. Like the rest of the Loaf, it was clean and workmanlike, and smelled now of soap and metal polish, with a hint of rising dough . . . a row of lumps under a cloth was on the worktable.

"Take off that and anything else with blood," Pia said, in the tone of a commander. Soon Arvid was sitting shirtless on a bench, the contents of his cloak pockets arrayed on the table. She had not seemed surprised or alarmed by any of them, but handed him cloths, a bowl of water, and a greasy lump of wool to clean them with. While he worked on the blades, she rinsed the blood out of his shirt and sponged his cloak. "I'll dry this before the fire," she said. "It'll have stains, but nothing so obvious."

Upstairs, he found young Arvid in bed, a candle burning in its stand on the table. The boy woke at the movement of the door, staring at Arvid's bare chest. "My shirt is dirty," Arvid said. "Pia's wash-ing it for me."

"I heard yelling," the boy said. "And marching, and more yelling—"

"A disturbance," Arvid said. He put on another shirt, sat down, and pulled off his boots. He wanted his bed more than anything.

"Were you hurt?"

"No. But I . . . I had to hurt others." The floor was cold under his feet as he walked over to the boy's bed. "It's all right, lad." He ruffled the boy's dark hair. "I'm here now."

The boy smiled at him, a smile that broke his heart. "Da—you won't die, will you?"

"Not if I can help it," Arvid said. He blew out the candle. "And so far, you know, I've been good at that."

Young Arvid chuckled.

Arvid lay in bed, remembering how Paksenarrion had looked at him. How she had seen—as he believed she had seen—right down inside him and had not flinched at what lay there.

Nor do I. You are not so bad as you think.

Arvid stared into the darkness, wide awake again.

Nor as good as you will be.

Now that was a terrifying thought. Did he really want to be . . . however good that was? A chuckle was his only answer. He fell into sleep without realizing it.

The next day the city felt quieter, but up on the hill, Arvid found that the Marshal-General was in no way complacent about the situation. She sent word that he was to attend a meeting with her, and he found himself with Paks, Camwynya, three High Marshals, the Marshal-Judicar of Gird, and the Knight-Commander of Gird. He told what he knew, including the incident in the alley.

"We cannot hope to get through this without conflict," High Marshal Darton said. "It's too late for that, when whole granges are declaring that you are not really Girdish."

"Do you know who started it?" the Marshal-General asked.

"To be blunt, Marshal-General," the Marshal-Judicar said, "*you* did. Not the appearance of magery—I know that, though it's one of their accusations. But you told them something so different from what they believed that they could not take it in."

"But they killed a *child*," she said. "Gird would not do that."

"No, I agree. And we know from the records that he did not demand death for all mages. Those provisions were added to the Code later, after Luap took the remaining mages away. But we have not taught that history for generations, so people did not know."

"And they aren't listening now," Darton said. "The ones who opposed you, anyway—who questioned that first expedition west, for instance—see this as a way to get rid of you. I'm afraid we face armed rebellion."

"And Tsaia?"

"Tsaia is different. I've always thought they were ridiculous to hold on to that notion of nobles and kings, but right now, their structure is working better than ours. The king and their Marshal-Judicar told them what to do, and they're doing it."

"Well, then." The Marshal-General looked around the table. "If we cannot avoid conflict, how can we cause the least harm while still coming out on top?"

No one said anything for a moment.

"Find the ringleaders and—" Arvid stopped as they all stared at him. Then he went on. "You know in any mob there are ringleaders. If you kill them—"

"Others will arise to avenge them," High Marshal Feder said.

"Not necessarily," Arvid said. "They claim to be more Girdish than the Marshal-General. What about challenging them one by one—any Marshal who incites his people to rebel?"

"That will take . . . a long time," the Marshal-Judicar said. "But it might work if the others don't take their granges to war at once."

"The Marshal-General can't do it all alone," the Knight-Commander said. "We can't risk her—"

"You can," the Marshal-General said. "And we must—"

"No," Paks said. "You met one challenger already and defeated him. Now it's the duty of others. Besides, if you tried to challenge and fight them all yourself, it would take too long."

"Arvid, what do you think?" the Marshal-General asked.

"Not you," he said. "Or, only for those who come here one by one, according to the rules for trial by combat. The others—I do not know enough. How many, who, where to send them: that is up to you." Then, feeling Gird's push, he added, "I might help. Though I'll be known here as one of your supporters, I would not in other places, and I have experience in gaining information."

"It is nearly winter," the Knight-Commander said. "That will slow them down, perhaps enough, if we act quickly."

As they talked, Arvid found himself watching Paks. She was the same . . . and yet not the same. Were those strands of gray in her yellow hair? She was so young . . . had it been the ordeal? But he had seen her afterward; he had seen no gray then. How did paladins age? How long did they live? Then she turned, caught his gaze, and grinned at him; those thoughts vanished.

That afternoon, she came down the hill with him, ostensibly to visit several granges. The meeting had ended after midday; young Arvid was waiting in the Loaf's entrance. The boy ran toward them, then hesitated, looking at Paks.

"This is my son," Arvid said. He beckoned; the boy came nearer, shy until Paks squatted down and held out her hand.

"I'm Paks," she said. "Your name is Arvid also, I'm told."

"Yes . . ." Now he flushed. "And you're—you're a—a paladin!"

"Yes," Paks said. "And a friend of your father's. Did you know he saved my life years ago?"

"Da! You never told me!"

Paks stood up and gave Arvid a look he could not interpret. "He will tell you when it's time," she said to the boy. "I must go talk to your Marshal now; we will meet again." That had the ring of prophecy. Arvid watched her cross the street to the grange, then led his son inside the inn.

CHAPTER FORTY-ONE

Vérella, Tsaia

So this is one of your gnomes," King Mikeli said. Dattur bowed; the king inclined his head. "I thought they were all in the north, in that land you granted them."

"Dattur was separated from them some time ago, sir king," Arcolin said. "But he is of the same tribe, and has helped me in learning gnomish language, customs, and their Law."

"It seems to me," the king said, "that you are holding more responsibility now than even Kieri did when he was duke. A prince of gnomes. A commander of the same size force Kieri had. Lord of one of my largest domains. And—last winter—a wise advisor in the matter of Duke Verrakai and my cousin Beclan. It has pleased me, Jandelir Arcolin, to find you as able as Kieri in the roles he held and now in this new one."

Arcolin was sure the king was leading up to something, but what?

"And," the king said, "you are both Girdish and widely experienced; you know the south as well as Tsaia; you know people of other beliefs." He leaned forward and spoke to Dattur. "Dattur, does this man please you as your prince?"

Dattur bowed again. "Lord king of men, it pleases me."

"And does it please the Aldonfulk?"

"It does, lord king of men."

Mikeli looked back at Arcolin, a spark of mischief in his eye. "It is in my mind and heart, Jandelir, that it would more suit your responsibilities if you were a duke instead of a count. At Midsummer Court, two of the other dukes told me so, and the others agreed when I asked them."

Arcolin bowed but said nothing.

"I took the liberty of contacting your steward in the north, asking for ducal court dress to be prepared for you. They said Kieri had left you his . . . so those were sent. But it is up to you . . . because I warn you, there will be even more work for a duke. As you have reported—as Duke Verrakai has warned, there is more trouble coming, and I will need you."

"Sir king," Arcolin said, "I am yours to command. If this is your will, it is my will."

"And so, at Autumn Court, you will be elevated to duke," the king said. "The ceremony is different—rare, in fact, for usually a duke's heir is confirmed in the duke's place, and not since Kieri's own elevation from count to duke have we had a count elevated." He grinned. "I was a mere babe then, not allowed to witness, so we shall hope I carry it through properly." Then he sobered. "We have much to talk about when you have your new rank, but I will not burden you with that now. You will want to confer with my master of ceremonies and prepare."

Arcolin bowed again. "Thank you, sir king—for the honor and for the courtesy of giving me time to prepare."

Later, he stared at himself in the mirror. Kieri's court clothes fit near enough, he thought, though the royal tailor was busy with pins and needles, picking out a seam here and resewing it there. Dorrin had told him of her own reaction to seeing herself in ducal finery in a palace mirror. Now he saw himself transformed from the sunburnt mercenary captain fresh from the South into a . . . the word "fop" rose to mind, and he pushed it down. A court gentleman. The short bloused pants, the stockings, the ribbons and buckled shoes with their ornaments.

"You'll need a new plume, m'lord," the tailor said through the pins held in his teeth. "That one's beyond repair." He spat the pins into his hand at last. "Now let's see how that robe drapes."

The robe—not Kieri's robe now but his—lay on his shoulders as if made for them. In that dimension, he and Kieri had always been alike. The deep burgundy, Kieri's—his—arms in silver on the back, the fur edging to neck and sleeves. Deep inside, a moment of recognition followed by laughter. As a boy, he had looked in the mirrors at Horngard more than once, imagining himself in the formal robes of nobles—though there it would have been a surcoat over long trousers tucked into tall shiny boots, not this. But here he was, where he had once longed to be—and then given up any such notion. Change. Transformation, as Dragon would have said.

"It will do well enough," the tailor said. "To remove the fur at the bottom and raise the hem a finger might be wise, but not necessary. It will be ready, m'lord, on the day."

At the ceremony itself, when he knelt to pledge a duke's fealty to his king, the last remnant of desire for Horngard vanished. He had no regrets for having given Dragon the ring he'd held secret all these years. Fox Company, the North Marches, the gnome tribe that now looked to him . . . that was enough for any man.

The dukes settled themselves in one corner of the reception: Mahieran, Marrakai, Serrostin, Verrakai, and now himself, Arcolin. "A full hand of us once more," Mahieran said, clapping Arcolin on the shoulder. "And I hope, Jandelir, you're soon to wed and provide yourself an heir. Unless you have one hid somewhere."

"Alas, no," Arcolin said. "But I take your point."

"Duke Verrakai's got a Marrakai squire—" Mahieran began, but Marrakai put up his hand.

"You do not want that one," he said. "And it's not because I mislike your character, Jandelir." He turned to Dorrin. "From what you've said this visit, she's bound for the Bells or Gird's Hall in Fin Panir; isn't that right?"

"Yes," Dorrin said. She looked more at ease this visit. "She's not ready to settle down; she's got a touch of Paks-fever."

Arcolin laughed. "I'm not looking for a wild girl," he said. "Nor yet a soldier. Someone steady enough to manage an estate while I'm gone, who won't mind being up there in the north with a military training camp, yet young enough . . ."

"We do have a list," Serrostin said. "Though perhaps we should apologize for making one without asking you, but after . . . events . . .

everyone's been concerned about pedigrees this year, and we want you to be safe."

"Safe?"

"You haven't told him?" Mahieran said, turning to Dorrin. "Even after the king made the proclamation?"

She shook her head. "My lord, you know it would have been unwise: what if the message were intercepted in Aarenis before it reached the duke?"

"True. Well, then—"

The story he told chilled Arcolin's blood. Beclan proved to have active magery, stricken from Mahieran and now Dorrin's heir? His mother still confined to the Mahieran city house? If a Mahieran could have active magery, who else? Surely not the king—no, but the king's brother, and many more in families humble and high both.

"Even though it now seems it is not a matter of mageborn blood—or anything to do with Verrakai," Serrostin said as the tale ended, "we sought to find potential wives for you who were not related within five generations to Verrakai or Konhalt. My children qualify, but all the girls are married or already pledged. Please do not be insulted that our list is taken from lower nobility."

"I'm not insulted at all," Arcolin said. "I had not thought to seek a high marriage in any case."

"Well, then. There are two barons west of you who have daughters you might consider; they don't come to court, but their fathers declare them sensible young women. And a niece of Duke Gerstad Elorran, a widow. Of course, you may have your eye on someone else, but—"

"Thank you," Arcolin said. "Are any of these ladies at court now?"

"As a matter of fact, they are." Serrostin's eyes twinkled. "That was another reason to put these on the list."

When one of the king's messengers called him to the palace, Arcolin thought it must be a question about gnomes, recruitment, magery, or the search for a wife. Instead, he found a royal courier with the king.

"Your Captain Selfer sent a courier to Fiveway and demanded this be taken by one of mine with all urgency—his courier waits there for your answer and hopes to return over the pass before it closes for winter," the king said. "I do not know the message. Read it to me."

Arcolin pulled the roll from its tube and glanced at it. "Sir king— it is what I feared might be true but was not confirmed before I left. The Duke of Immer has Andressat's youngest son—"

"Andressat—the old man I met last year?"

"Yes. As I said before, rumor had it his son had disappeared, supposedly between Andressat and Cortes Cilwan. He was taken somehow— is now captive of the Duke of Immer. The Duke of Immer also has the necklace which is part of the regalia you hold and has moved up the western branch of the Immer. He controls Immervale and Lûn and will probably take Cortes Cilwan sometime this winter. Andressat's daughter and son-in-law, ruling Cortes Cilwan, have fled to Andressat." He looked at the king. "Sir king, Vaskronin has sworn to flay Andressat's son alive if Andressat does not yield his holdings . . . and if Vaskronin has Cilwan and Andressat—which Siniava never captured—he is well placed to threaten the pass. Selfer has spoken to those who saw the man use magery, whether of his own talent or by blood magery, he does not know. Selfer asks my permission to make contract with Foss Council as representative of the Guild League—with whom we had the contract this past summer—to serve through the winter as necessary."

"And will you then go south to command them?"

"That is your choice, sir king."

"*My* choice!" Mikeli looked grim. "My choice would have been to come to my crown in peace, for my cousin Beclan to have escaped peril, and for magery to lie quiet through my reign." He stopped abruptly. "Kings have few choices, my lord Duke," he said, in a quieter tone. "We have necessity. You must not go south now. I need you in the north. If your Company can hold the pass, well and good; if not, I need you and the forces you have in the north here. It is not a matter of distrusting Duke Verrakai, but of needing two experienced in war in my councils."

"I suspect, sir king, that Vaskronin waited until I had left to make his attack, knowing I would be far away."

"Then let us hope your young captains have wits enough. If word can still pass the mountains, tell your Captain Selfer to make what contract he will with the Guild League."

Arcolin wrote notes to Selfer, to his banker, and to the Foss Council magistrates he had known before, giving permission for Selfer to make the contract and do all other business necessary. "I will be down as soon as the pass opens in spring," he added at the end. "If you can find a gnome trader in Valdaire, ask if he can take word to the prince of the Aldonfulks in these words: 'That which we spoke of is begun.'"

The king summoned another courier and sent him on his way south "with all possible speed." He turned to Arcolin. "And should we move troops to the south end of the kingdom now, lord Duke?"

"No," Arcolin said. "There's much to do—and more to learn—before we move troops. Vaskronin is wily, and he has control not only of the Immer from Immervale down to the sea but of the coastal cities as well. What if this is a feint, meant to make us think he will attack overland? He might instead mount a fleet to sail out of the Immerhoft into the Eastern Ocean and come by boat all the way up to the falls of the Honnorgat with no hindrance. Pargun and Kostandan both traded to the south by sea. He will have heard of at least one river port. If he's heard that Pargun was defeated, he might plan to land in Pargun and march overland."

"I will need to talk to Duke Verrakai and you both within the day," the king said. As Arcolin took his leave and turned away, the king added, "And do not forget to find a wife and get your heir."

When Arcolin found Dorrin, he showed her Selfer's letter; she agreed with his advice that no troops be moved yet. "Supplies," she said. "We should have stockpiles of supplies ready for either invasion route, and right now the stores are full. I'll see about moving them. When did the king want to meet?"

"After dinner," Arcolin said. "And in the meantime I'm supposed to find a wife and get an heir."

Dorrin laughed and shook her head.

Their meeting with the king lasted only two turns of the glass, as he approved moving supplies to the south and east, north of the river.

"We have the winter, at least, to prepare," Dorrin said. "If Alured—Vaskronin—comes by land, he cannot get an army over the pass before winter closes it, magery or no."

"Could he melt the snows with it?" the king asked.

"Not over such a space," Dorrin said.

"And he will face resistance from the Aldonfulk gnomes," Arcolin said.

"And by sea?"

"If the northern gales have begun, they would never make it around the Eastbight."

"Then, Duke Verrakai, you and Duke Arcolin organize supplies in those locations; I will give orders for the Royal Guard to assist as needed."

This year, unlike the last, Arcolin felt perfectly at ease meeting women he might want to marry. None awoke the fire he remembered from his youth and Aesil M'dierra, but Aesil was past childbearing now, even if his passion had not finally worn out. He could not expect to feel the same, he told himself. He must be sensible and look for the qualities his wife would need.

Some seemed too young, too inexperienced, to leave as mistress of a remote domain full of soldiers. Duke Gerstad Elorran's niece, though clearly a strong-minded woman who could manage a kingdom, made it clear she preferred a city life and was happy running her former husband's business. "I grew up in a duke's household," she said. "My mother was Uncle Gerstad's sister and ran his household as he never married. And I mean no insult to you, my lord, but it is not the life I would lead."

Kieri's banker in Vérella, a man he had known for years, brought up marriage as well. "I'm sure you've considered breeding an heir," Ser Onagan said. "And I'm sure some prestigious doors are open."

"So they are," Arcolin said. "But beyond an heir I need a woman of sufficient maturity and strength of character—"

"Not likely among the dukes," Onagan said. "With all respect, my lord, you were not born a duke—have you considered a lady not of the peerage? A woman of good family and character, of substance, of course . . ."

"Indeed I have, but I know scarcely any," Arcolin said.

Onagan gave him a shrewd look. "You are a man of loyalty, my lord, and so your former commander said when he told me he trusted you with funds and missions of importance. Perhaps you loved unwisely in your youth?"

"Perhaps I did," Arcolin said. "The lady returned no favor, and over the years I thought of no one else—until it seemed too late and I had no need of heirs, having no estate."

Onagan nodded. "And now you do. So . . . I am senior in my guild; I know every guild's master in the city save the Thieves' Guild—they have some ruffian again in place of that thief the Marshal-General favored. I knew *that* wouldn't last long. Anyway—with your permission, I might let it be known that you plan to wed."

"My time is limited here," Arcolin said. "I need to see to my domain, and sooner rather than later."

"Haste today makes tears tomorrow," Onagan said. "True in marriages as in trade. Take enough time, my lord; I don't doubt your seed still sprouts."

Arcolin laughed. "You are ever wise, Master Onagan. Of your courtesy, inquire if you will, and meanwhile I will continue to meet the ladies the gentlemen at court wish introduced."

Over the next two hands of days, Arcolin met still more women recommended to him. Besides the young and inexperienced, this one was a vicious gossip, that one presented a list of her luxurious requirements, yet another—though smiling with him—he overheard sneer at his age behind his back. Rahel, from near Marrakai's domain, had a pleasant voice and sweet temperament but proved to have no head at all for numbers, and he wanted a wife who could at least keep simple accounts. Liris was simply too stupid; Marda was afraid of gnomes and shuddered at the thought of meeting them; tiny Virian, scarcely sixteen winters, could surely not bear a child safely any time soon. Calla, a wealthy merchant's daughter and a widow with a young child, appealed more: she also had a pleasant voice and keen intelligence, but she seemed quietly content as she was, living with her parents in their large house. Would she really be willing to leave that comfort for the north? Would any of them?

Finally, one crisp autumn day, the king invited a crowd to picnic on Mahieran lands, including the women Arcolin mentioned as still under consideration. Arcolin rode beside Dorrin, behind the other dukes, as they left the city.

"How's the wife hunt going?" she asked.

"Not well. Either I am too critical or they are."

"Mmm. Well, I can make no suggestion. Though as I told Beclan, Lyonya has many pretty girls."

"I don't want a girl," Arcolin said. "But surely there's some woman in this realm who is mature enough to be a true helpmate and young enough to bear."

"You could adopt an heir, if you found a widow with a likely child."

"How do you feel about Beclan as *your* heir?"

"He's going to make a good duke someday," Dorrin said. "But of course, he grew up in a ducal household far healthier than mine was."

"I would still rather sire one," Arcolin said. "But if I don't live to see one grown—"

"You're not that old," Dorrin said.

"Old enough to feel it on cold mornings," Arcolin said. "And your idea of adoption may be sensible. If I can find the right woman."

"Jandelir . . . are you truly over M'dierra?"

He felt heat rise to his face. "You knew?"

"Of course," she said. She did not say what he could see in her gaze, that Kieri and the other captains had known as well.

And probably, he thought gloomily, half the Company. Too late now to be embarrassed. "Then yes, I am. I am not comparing these women to her, if that's what you were thinking."

"Not that—you're too fair a man for that—but just the existence of someone else might keep you from seeing what's before you. The real difficulty, as you say, is finding someone with the skills you feel your wife needs and someone young and healthy enough to bear you children. Have you then considered—instead of adoption of a widow's child—hiring a more experienced steward? Who's your second up there now?"

He told her about Captain Arneson. "But he's recruit captain; he can't spend all his time on the domain."

"So you need a proper seneschal, not just a steward. It's changed since Kieri began it. Ask your banker or man of business. Then if your joy lands on a younger, less experienced wife, your land will not suffer for it. Look for your joy, Jandelir, not merely your business—and for hers, as well."

His heart lifted, and he looked at the women that day differently, less analytically. He still wanted nothing to do with the gossipy, the coldhearted, or the greedy, but both Rahel, with her numerical confusion, and Calla, with her child and comfortable home here, slid into his mind. Both were warmhearted young women slightly beyond first youth. Both had lost a first love—Rahel's betrothed and Calla's young husband, both to fever. Both seemed comfortable not only with him but with other men. Both had brothers who were soldiers. Rahel's older brother had once squired Duke Phelan, and Calla's older brother was in the Royal Guard.

His helpful sponsors, the other dukes, made it possible for him to have some time alone with each of those.

"Are you truly courting me?" Rahel asked, when he sat down near her. She was turning the heel of a small sock; she'd told him before she was knitting for her older sister's coming child.

The bold question startled him; she had seemed shy before. "I am seeking a wife, yes. Are you seeking a husband?"

She blushed. "I still wish to marry and have children, lord Duke, but . . . I am not pursuing you."

"You are not?" He was surprised to find himself disappointed.

"You must know," she said, "that I find you comfortable and not as . . . as frightening as I thought you would be when my father spoke of you and . . . and the possibility. But he said it must be your

choice, and I should not . . . do . . . anything." She put down her knitting and plucked at a leaf that had fallen on her skirt, tearing off
small pieces.

"Rahel, I am seeking a wife, but a wife who wants to be *my* wife,
not just *a* wife. It is not about what your father wants, but what you
want. If you have another in mind—"

The red on her cheeks deepened.

"You do, don't you?"

"It is impossible," she said, more softly yet. "And I would be a
good wife to you, lord Duke, truly. I keep my promises."

"You must keep them to yourself, as well," Arcolin said, thinking
of Aesil, but without pain. "Rahel, your happiness is in your hands.
I do not ask—"

"It has been three years and more since Davor died," she said.
"And I did love him. But last spring—my lord, he is not suitable; my
father will never consent—and I know I can forget him, if you . . ."

"Did you ask your father?"

She nodded, fingers pleating her skirt. "He said he had better in
mind for me."

"In the law, you cannot be forced to marry," Arcolin said. "Gird
protects you from that." He sighed and arched his back, easing it.
"Rahel, you are beautiful, and all your conversation has been pleasant; you seem kind and gentle as well as capable."

"Except with accounts." Her voice sounded choked; he realized
she was near tears.

Arcolin shook his head. "Dealing well with numbers is one thing,
but that skill can be hired. Dealing well with people counts more in
a family, and that cannot be hired. Do not cry; people will talk. We
had a trick in the Company: pinch your lip beneath your nose, hard."

She stared at him, eyes swimming with tears. "Pinch?"

"Do it."

She did.

"Now listen carefully. You are a young woman of quality. Unless
you chose out of grief some rogue who will mistreat you, your father
will eventually agree that an honest man who cares for you and you
for him is a better match than a noble—even a duke—who chooses
you as he might choose a horse, on the basis of marketable qualities."

He let his voice carry humor into the last of that. She gave him a trembling smile. "I will tell your father, Rahel, that although you are a remarkable young woman, I am just not able to envision you as my wife. And that I have told you so, and that you are naturally sad . . . but only one or two tears, my dear, or he will wonder too much. How about your lady mother?"

"She—she said Tamis was good enough."

"Then surely your father will come to the same opinion when ambition fades. For him, it is all my decision—and think, Rahel—he told you not to do anything. He knew I might not choose you, and then you would be free."

Her eyes widened as she thought about that. "Then—"

"Then wait here until I have spoken to your father, and go to him. You will make your Tamis a good wife." Arcolin stood up, gave her a formal bow, and went to find her father.

The man was not far off, of course, trying to pretend he had not been watching. "I come with less than joyous tidings, my lord," Arcolin said to him. "Your daughter is remarkable—a good heart, graciousness, gentle in every way—but for all that, as she is young and in many ways innocent, I find myself . . . well, to be frank, I cannot wed her. It was no lack in her but in myself—my years as a mercenary, in fact. She deserves a gentler man."

"I see." A keen look out of the man's dark eyes. "She did not beg you not to choose her?"

"No. She told me frankly she found me less frightening than she'd expected. I realized then that to gently bred young women, a man my age, with my experience, *would* be frightening. Yes, I have been at court; I am not the swaggering lout that some people think soldiers are, but the fact is, I spent four hands of years and more as a hired killer. And that is still my occupation; I am just back from another season of it. My stronghold in the north is full of similar men; my vills are populated largely with retired soldiers, men and women both. A better wife for me—a better duke's wife for my people—will be someone less sheltered than your daughter or others like her."

The man nodded. "I understand, my lord Duke. But I had understood you did not plan to marry a soldier, as Duke Phelan did."

"No—his and Tammarion's was a rare match; I cannot wait, at my age, for such a thing to happen to me." He sighed and looked Rahel's father in the eye. "I hope you will believe me, my lord, that this is not an insult to your daughter or your house, but—I truly believe—the course of wisdom."

"I am not insulted," the man said. "Will you then propose to the widow?"

"I will talk again with her, make plain the situation she would have with all those soldiers around her, and if she declares herself confident, then yes: I will. She is older; she worked in trade with her husband—"

"She has a child—"

"Yes. And if her child proves of good character, I may adopt the child; otherwise I will foster it and provide for its future. But that is still uncertain, as is my understanding of her."

"Well, then." The man put out his hand, and Arcolin shook it. "I wish you well, my lord Duke, and—though I may be disappointed in my hopes for my daughter, I call you honorable for speaking so plainly about the roots of your decision. Now I see Rahel sitting alone and looking pale. She needs her father, if you will excuse me."

"Indeed, my lord," Arcolin said with a bow.

The widow Calla was not far to seek, though out of sight of Rahel. She had her child with her, as if to make clear her status as a widow, and a friend sat nearby. When she caught sight of Arcolin, she gestured to the friend, who glanced at Arcolin and then left. Calla gave him a wide smile. "My lord Duke, have you come to sit with me?"

"Yes. And this is your child?"

"This is Jamis, yes." To the child she said. "Jamis, make your bow to Duke Arcolin." The boy stood—a sturdy child of five or six winters, dark-haired and blue-eyed—and made an awkward bow. "M'lord," he said. "Ark-lin?"

"Good day, Jamis," Arcolin said. He folded his legs and sat down.

"I sense that you are narrowing your choices," she said. "So the gossip goes, but the look on your face says you are still not completely certain."

"You read me well, sera," Arcolin said.

"Is it my gifts or my will that you question?" Here was no incipient flood of tears, whatever his answer; she was clear-eyed and steady.

"Not your gifts—and not the strength of your will, but its direction."

"Ah. Then it is convention like a sword between us, my lord Duke. Though merchanters are less bound by rules than nobles—or our rules may simply be different—it is still true that women are taught not to declare first."

"Sera Calla, are you afraid of me?"

"Afraid?" Her eyes widened. "Why should I be? Of your rank? A thief would frighten me, but not a duke. Of your history? You are a soldier, and as a soldier you have done much violence, I'm sure. Killed people, commanded others to do so. My brother is a soldier— I know what that means. But what I know of you, from others and from meeting you myself, gives me no reason to fear you."

"And you would not be afraid in the north, when I am on campaign and most or all around you are rough soldiers?"

"Not at all. All around me in my father's work—and in my husband's when he was alive—were rough commoners, some of them soldiers. Soldiers are people, after all, before they are soldiers." The look she gave him then softened something that had hardened year by year since Aesil's refusal. "Are you that concerned about me, lord Duke? And not just about my qualifications? Then let me tell you— against society's rules as it may be—that I like you well. Very well. Well enough to trust you with not only my life but my son's. If that will not bring you to a decision, then—I will go. But I will regret it."

"You like me . . ." He could not hide the surprise in his voice.

She nodded. "And respect you and esteem you for those qualities you have, which is to my mind the more important. I have met rogues in business whom I could not help liking though I knew they were rogues and not to be trusted—but I would never consider marrying such a one. You, I had heard of and admired from afar before I met you, and meeting you was like meeting an old friend. Trust, my lord Duke. That's what I offer."

Joy boiled up through his former confusion. He realized he was grinning at her like a foolish boy. "Then, my lady, we should make this formal: Sera Calla, will you marry me?"

"Indeed I will," she said. She glanced at her child, now looking from one of their faces to the other in puzzlement.

"Do I need to speak to your father?"

"Oh, no. I'm a widow; I'm my own woman. We should tell him, but—no more. And you aren't worried that marrying a merchant's daughter will injure your prestige?"

He laughed. "Kieri married a soldier. Besides—it doesn't matter to me. Does a marriage soon suit you?"

"Very well. We will want to be in the north as soon as possible, won't we?"

"'We,' not 'you.'" He put out a hand to the boy. "Jamis, I am pleased to see you. We will be going on a journey together."

"Indeed so," she said, when the boy looked at her, still puzzled. "You and I, lad, are going north—north beyond anything we've seen. It's an adventure!"

"Ad-venture? Like this picnic?"

"That's right. Only bigger. We won't know what's coming around the next turn of the trail. Isn't that exciting?"

"Leave Granna and Grandda?"

"Yes. But we'll visit sometimes. Now come, Jamis. We're going to walk around with Duke Arcolin and make our manners before going back home to start planning the trip." She turned to Arcolin. "I can ask Cyntha to watch him for a while, if you want."

"We're not in a hurry," Arcolin said. "I'll walk slowly enough." She took his arm and gave her other hand to her son. They strolled around; Arcolin saw—and was sure she saw—the knowing looks others cast at them. Duke Marrakai's lady was the first to approach. "Duke Arcolin—and—"

"Lady Calla," Arcolin said. "She has consented to marry me. And her son, Jamis."

"I am happy for you both," she said. "And hope you are both as happy as you look now, for the rest of your lives."

After that, it was greeting after greeting, but they stayed only so long as necessary; the king himself gave them leave to depart.

Immediately after the wedding, the king called Arcolin in for a last conference. To his surprise, Dorrin was there, along with High Marshal Seklis and the Marshal-Judicar. Something about Beclan, he surmised.

"No," the king said. He leaned back in his chair and gave Arcolin a measuring look before continuing. "Duke Arcolin, Duke Serrostin has told me that you now know about the resurgence of magery in this kingdom. Did he also mention the situation in Fintha?"

"No, sir king."

"Magery has appeared there, and though the Marshal-General convened a council to consider revising the Code, there has been . . . unrest." He turned to High Marshal Seklis and nodded.

"The Marshal-General is determined to change the Code," Seklis said. "And that has not set well with some of the Marshals in Fintha and many of the people. To them the Code is Gird himself, his very words."

"Though we know it has been revised over the years," the Marshal-Judicar said.

"They've had children killed, in Fintha," Seklis went on. "And one or two Marshals who were in favor of the change. There've been attempts on the Marshal-General herself, rioting in marketplaces. It is not quite a war there yet, but it may become one."

"Which would be a disgrace—Girdsmen against Girdsmen? I would have said unthinkable before this."

"What about here?" Arcolin said. "Tsaia's as Girdish as Fintha."

"Not . . . quite," Oktar said. "The Code as administered in Tsaia is not the same as in Fintha; that saved Duke Verrakai's life, as well as that of Beclan and the prince."

"There has been very little open opposition to the king's decree," High Marshal Seklis said. "And that was not to change the Code— which he has no authority to do—but to defer all cases until a decision by the Marshal-General unless magery is used to commit another crime."

"What I want from you," the king said, "is an accounting of anyone, child or adult, in your domain who shows mage powers and your best estimate if those powers are innate or imposed by someone else."

Arcolin could say nothing at first; the thought of near war, of trouble spreading east, filled his mind. "I have seen nothing I recognize as magery in my Company or on my way here," he said at last.

The king nodded. "We think it is very rare, showing itself mostly in children. We do not know why the gods have chosen to bring it back at this time. But we must prepare for more and prepare the people so they do not panic."

"That is the best we can do until Gird speaks to each of us," the Marshal-Judicar said.

"I know a man Gird speaks to," Arcolin said, surprised to hear the words come out of his mouth. "I met him in Aarenis; I stood his sponsor to the Fellowship."

"A crazy man?" the Marshal-Judicar asked.

"No." Arcolin told them quickly about Arvid and his conversion, including Paks's part in it, and that Arvid had left Aarenis with his son to go to Fin Panir.

"Gird talks to a thief and not to Marshals?" The High Marshal sounded indignant.

"Arvid would say you should not envy him," Arcolin said. "I have never seen a man so shattered and then remade. If he made it to Fin Panir, he is one the Marshal-General should ask."

The High Marshal shook his head. "She might—but would the others listen? We have had glib-tongued thieves before in the Fellowship—and in fact the results of our expeditions to Kolobia now indicate that Luap himself was not the paragon we thought him. He twisted Gird's own words to his use."

The Marshal-Judicar held up his hand. "But Seklis—consider. What do we know of the others of Gird's day, but by stories and Luap's writings? We know the Fellowship has changed, the Code has changed. Were all Gird's followers perfect? I doubt it. Gird himself changed: that much we are sure of. Paksenarrion—and all honor to her now—changed from a soldier who was not Girdish, to a Girdish paladin-candidate, to a craven who nearly died, and finally to a paladin. How can we say a thief could not change? I met this Arvid when he was here in Vérella, and there was something about him . . . If any thief could change, *he* could."

The High Marshal scowled, then shrugged. "I suppose. But I still say most will not believe him."

"I daresay many people did not believe Gird at first."

Arcolin followed this argument with amazement—still shocked by the news that magery was recurring, and that the king's own brother displayed it. The king now held up his hand, and both the Marshals subsided.

"The point is, my lord Dukes, that we have a potential division we did not have before and one that has implications should we be invaded. You both have military experience—you best understand, I believe, what the stakes are, if this becomes known and the people rebel. How, then, could we withstand this southerner?"

"You must not give him what he wants," Arcolin said. "Sir king, that would be the worst—he himself has magery. Magery may not be inherently evil, but the Duke of Immer has chosen evil already."

"Help us decide, then, how best to handle this problem."

Arcolin glanced at Dorrin, who was staring at her hands as if deliberately not taking part.

"Sir king, if it were up to me . . . I would find something that could be the cause of this resurgence."

"Duke Verrakai—" said the High Marshal.

Arcolin shook his head. "No, High Marshal. Something else. Who was first to show magery here?"

"She—"

"No, sir king. Kieri Phelan. I was told that when he drew that elven sword in the Council chamber, light came and the Bells chimed."

"Yes, but that was *elven* magery—"

"Was it? How did that happen? A paladin of Gird named him the heir and gave him the sword to try: even if the display was elven in kind, it came from a paladin's act. Duke Verrakai, how did you come by magery at your age?"

"It was blocked when I was at Falk's Hall, but . . ." Her expression changed. "Paksenarrion released it."

"You see?" Arcolin said. "A paladin of Gird, under Gird's guidance, brought magery back—first in King Kieri, his own innate elven magery—and then in Duke Verrakai, of a family of magelords."

"I suppose you could look at it that way," the High Marshal said, looking at the Marshal-Judicar.

"And if she influenced this thief," the Marshal-Judicar said, "then his hearing Gird's voice . . . but wait. What about the others? Had she met Beclan?" He looked at Dorrin, who shook her head.

"If Gird wanted magery back in the land," Arcolin said, "Paks may have been the one to bring it, but she might not be the only one. Or, once introduced, it might spread without that, at Gird's will."

"That's true." The king looked around the room. "So—if we have a reason to think Gird brought the return of magery, will that help the people accept it? Would it work in Fintha?"

"It might," the High Marshal said. "And I suppose you think I should tell the Marshal-General about this thief?" He looked at Arcolin.

"Yes, High Marshal, I do," Arcolin said. "As you said, how often does Gird speak directly and clearly to any of us?"

A hand of days later, Arcolin and his wife and her son rode north, a new wagon behind them, the gift of her father, wagon and team. It was half full of her things and half arranged for her and the boy to ride in when they tired. To Arcolin's delight, Calla had continued to show the same combination of good sense and joy that he felt himself.

"I could never be a soldier," she said, halfway through that first morning of the trip. "I was not formed for that. But this—riding into something new and strange—this I did always dream of. The very idea of the north fascinated me as a child. Seeing your troops come through every year, marching from one unknown to another, made me restless at heart."

"Will you then want to visit Aarenis one day?" Arcolin asked.

"Possibly," she said. "Though I suspect one end of the unknown will be enough for me—there's so much to learn. Your people, the land, how best I can help you . . . that will keep me busy a good while. And Jamis, of course." She glanced at the boy, who rode perched on a sheepskin on a steady pony led by one of Arcolin's troops. "He has asked for a pony many a time, but we had no place for him to ride in the city, and no one free to lead him about. Look how happy he is."

Just then the boy turned to wave at her and call out, "Mama—I'm not holding on!"

CHAPTER FORTY-TWO

They arrived in Duke's East by noon on the last day of their journey, the weather having cooperated. Everything looked as it should. Arcolin stopped and introduced Calla to Kolya and the mayor in Duke's East. Calla admired everything, and he could tell that Kolya, often so reserved, was delighted with her. Arcolin arranged to hold Duke's Court in two days' time and sent a messenger to Duke's West to let them know. From the town to the stronghold, the road had been tended—the crown smoothed, the ditches cleaned out. He could see recruits drilling off to the east.

"Dattur, do you want to go directly to the new gnome hills?"

"No, my prince. I would not delay your return to your home, and I think they will come to greet you here anyway. They have not seen me for three years. More."

"Very well." Arcolin had not imagined the gnomes would come to the stronghold unless they needed something. He could, however, understand how a *kteknik* gnome might prefer to return to the group in the company of their prince, proof he was no longer *kteknik*.

Everything was in perfect order in the stronghold itself. Young Jamis stared as the gates opened, soldiers saluted, and trumpets blew. Calla, now riding beside him, smiled, apparently delighted with the ceremony. Grooms were ready to hold their horses as they dismounted.

"Is the captain here?" he asked the guard corporal.

"No, my lord. He's with the recruit cohort. They made a day-march today. I'll send a messenger—"

"Yes, do that. You may tell him I'm married now, and I will introduce my lady to him and the Company this evening."

He led Calla and Jamis through the entrance to the inner courtyard. "Our quarters are here," he said. "Officers in residence also have quarters in this court and usually eat together."

"It's huge," Calla said. She looked around. "And our own well?"

"Indeed. There's no river here for water, but we have several wells both inside and outside the walls. Some of this is storage space—" He waved at the east side of the courtyard. "Let me show you to our quarters after I speak to the staff." They were waiting by the door: steward, cook, others. He introduced Calla, "My wife, Lady Arcolin, and her son, Jamis," and she greeted each by name. Then they went upstairs.

"There was no time to send ahead and have the rooms prepared," Arcolin said. The starkness of the rooms struck him as never before. No woman or child had lived here for tens of years, and that showed in the bare, cold, unwelcoming spaces.

"No matter," Calla said. "It will not take long to make them comfortable. Is there someone who can help me?"

"Do you not need to rest and refresh yourself?"

"I am not so old as that," she said with a grin. "A bath later would be delightful, but now I want to get the new bedding out of the wagon and into this room. And for Jamis?"

"Across the passage there's a smaller room." It had been a nursery when Kieri's children were born. The smaller room, dustier than his own chamber, needed cleaning, furniture, and bedding. Soon servants bustled up and down the stairs, bringing items from the wagon. The cook sent a meal up to Arcolin's office, as Calla wanted to be upstairs where she could direct where things were put.

Faster than Arcolin expected, Calla announced that the two rooms were now ready. Jamis's bed, reassembled, stood in the corner of his room with a quilted cover of Girdish blue; he had a chest for his clothes and a table and chair of his own. He whirled around and around, arms wide. "It's *big*!" he said. "And I have a fireplace!"

"Then put your clothes away," Calla said. She led Arcolin to the room that had been Kieri's, then his alone, and was now theirs. Despite the autumn chill, she had opened the shutters, and he could see that the room looked warm and welcoming: new mattress plumped up under the new bedclothes, bed curtains drawn back to the posts, striped curtains beside the window, the patterned rug he'd admired in Vérella now spread on the floor. Near the fireplace, she'd had servants put a tub, a towel rack, and ewers of hot water.

He had just dressed again after bathing when Arneson came to report on the recruit progress. With him was Kaim, Count Halar's son, who had served as Arneson's squire this past campaign year. He looked at the boy, liking what he saw at first glance—a sturdy, bright-faced lad. After Arneson introduced them, Arcolin said, "I need to speak to Captain Arneson; wait for us downstairs."

"Yes, my lord," Kaim said; he bowed and left.

Arcolin took Arneson into his office while Calla finished with Jamis and readied herself for dinner.

"We didn't expect you this soon, my lord. Congratulations on your new title," Arneson said. "If I'd known, I'd have had the recruits parade for you."

"Kieri used to come back north only within a few tendays of their departure for the south," Arcolin said. "But though I'm required to attend Autumn Court, I see no reason to stay in Vérella through the winter when I could be up here. If I am assigned to the Royal Council, I might stay, but not now. How was it this year?"

"We've had no real problems," Arneson said. He gave a concise account of the recruit cohort's progress, his assessment of Kaim's potential and then asked, "Any word at all from your Sergeant Stammel?"

"No. As the dragon and Stammel's own letter told me, he has left and does not want to be found. The dragon assures me he went to a safe place, a healthy place, and has settled into village life there. The dragon would not tell me more."

"I'm sorry," Arneson said.

"I was . . . but now I'm relieved. If he's happy where he is, that's enough for me." Arcolin took a swallow of water. "How are the gnomes settling in? Do they visit?"

Arneson shook his head. "No, my lord. Once they'd moved in over there, they vanished. We never see them. Of course, we don't do maneuvers in those hills, as you requested. No orc problems at all, nothing. There's a peculiar line in the vegetation, as if someone mowed a path short; I suppose that's the boundary line you told me about."

"Yes. You've heard I arrived with a gnome as well as a wife—"

"Yes, my lord. I wondered if your—if these gnomes had sent an emissary to meet you in Vérella."

"No. It's a long story." As he told Arneson about it, Arcolin thought how incredible it was—a thief meeting a gnome in Fin Panir, then showing up running errands for one of the junior captains in Valdaire. "And then," he said, "Dattur told me this was his tribe and I was their prince."

"Prince!"

"Yes. I had to tell the king, of course. I was just a count then, in the court of Tsaia. Luckily, the king thought it was amusing."

"Not the gnomes, though, I'll warrant," Arneson said. "What do you think will happen with them, now that you're back?"

"I don't know. I've been practicing gnomish with Dattur, of course, and trying to learn what their Law is. Normally, a gnome prince does not leave the stone-mass in which they live, but I must. I'll need to designate a leader for them."

"What are things like in the south?" Arneson asked.

"Do you miss it?" Arcolin asked without answering the question.

Arneson stared at his hands a long moment. "Sometimes. The smell of the orchards . . . the foods . . . and the markets . . . I have no complaints, my lord. I am fortunate to be here and have this position. But Valdaire—you know yourself—the morning light on the mountains—"

"Oh, yes," Arcolin said. "You know—I think I told you—I'm from the south originally myself. Not Valdaire, but I love Valdaire. And this is very quiet."

"I've come to love this, too," Arneson said. "I like the quiet—and it's never as hot. The people here have been wonderful to me; they understand me, and I understand them. And I do enjoy working with recruits."

"Has Valichi dropped in to give you the benefit of his wisdom?"

"Once or twice, early on. The last time, he smacked my shoulder and said it was high time I made my own traditions, and I haven't seen him since."

"That's good. Val was recruit captain so long, I was afraid he might nag you too much." Arcolin took a breath. "The situation in the south has worsened—not so much while I was there as what I heard from a courier some days after I arrived in Vérella. The new Duke of Immer abducted Andressat's youngest son—" He told the rest of it; Arneson listened intently. "King Mikeli is concerned, of course, and I understand the Guild League even more so, as you may imagine. By report, the man has powers similar to those of magelords. Whether they come from within or by blood magery, we do not know. I will need those recruits next year for certain."

"Yes, my lord, I understand."

"I must speak with Count Halar again before taking Kaim down there. It's likely to be a bloody year."

"If I may—send the lad home for Midwinter. He hasn't asked, but a chance to be with his family for a while may clarify for him and his family both what they really want for him." Arneson rubbed his chin. "He's a good lad: a hard worker, obedient, no trouble, and should make a good officer someday. But I'd say a year young to see the worst of war in the south if that's what's coming."

"Will he sour with another year up here? Would you have him?"

"Yes, of course I'd have him. From his side . . . I don't know. That age . . . he's matured a lot, seeing what the training is really like, but for all that we don't recruit them that young."

A tap at the door; when Arcolin looked up, Calla was there. "I put Jamis to bed, and the cook's called dinner. Shall we eat here or—"

"Downstairs," Arcolin said. "Captain, this is my wife—and this is Captain Arneson, who commands the recruit cohort."

Arneson stood. "My lady—my honor."

"I'm glad to meet you, Captain," Calla said, coming forward. "By your accent you're from the south, I think?"

"Yes, my lady."

Arneson paraded the recruit cohort after supper, and Arcolin inspected them, finding—as usual in this stage of training—many things to comment on. They looked much like any intake and would be ready, he was sure, for their first campaign season in the spring.

As he came into his quarters, he heard Calla's voice from the kitchen—she was chatting with the cook, and both sounded relaxed and happy. He went on upstairs. Servants had removed the bathing things; the fire burned bright, and candles gave even more light. The room no longer bore any trace of Kieri except the big bed itself—and with its new furnishings, it might have been any bed.

"You are gone, bright ones," he said to the memories of Tamar and the children engendered in this bed. "Be at peace. Our joy will not diminish your memory."

That night, when Calla nestled against him, his last doubts vanished; his past life made sense, the decisions that had led to this. He knew peace and security could vanish, he knew life might still bring them both pain, but he was not ungrateful enough to ignore this respite. Even the dragon, he thought, as he drifted off to sleep, might count him wise in that small way.

Next morning, Arcolin breakfasted with his recruit captain; Calla had, she told him, a busy day planned for herself and Jamis. He himself planned to ride out to the hills with Dattur to meet the gnomes. When he came to the forecourt with Dattur, he found the estvin and four gnomes waiting for him. They wore gray with an elaborate pattern of braid running down the front of their jackets. He could read the gnomish now: Arcolinfulk. His name. His people.

"Greetings, rockbrothers," Arcolin said in gnomish. The gnomes bowed, and he bowed in return. "It is my honor to see you again in this place. I have studied your speech with the help of Dattur." He gestured to Dattur.

"That one *kteknik*," the estvin said in Common. "It is not to wear the tribe's garments."

Dattur took two steps forward, confronting the estvin. "My prince names me belonging. Aldonfulk accepted him as prince and on his word gave me clothes. And you know me, Frakkur."

"Name forbidden." The estvin looked up at Arcolin. "This one *kteknik*."

"You were *all kteknik* by Dragon's word," Arcolin said, in gnomish again. "You had no stone-right. I gave stone-right. Now you wear a uniform naming your prince. Who is your prince?"

The estvin prostrated himself, as did the others, once more kissing Arcolin's boot. Dattur, to his surprise, kissed his other boot. "Lord, it is that the lord Duke is our prince."

"Yes," Arcolin said. He wondered how they'd learned of his elevation, but this was not the time to ask. "And as your prince I say none of you are *kteknik,* nor is this gnome I met on my travels, Dattur, who was of your tribe before."

Still holding Arcolin's boot, the estvin said, "This one was cast out by our prince that was."

"And restored to the Law by your prince who *is,*" Arcolin said. "Is it that the estvin argues with the Law?"

"No, my lord." The estvin kissed his boot again and backed away before standing. "As the prince commands."

"Then welcome one returned from a long journey and much danger, one who has performed great deeds and services for his prince," Arcolin said. "I bid you accept him once more."

The estvin bowed to Dattur, who returned the bow; each of the others performed the same ritual.

"I would come to you and see the progress you have made," Arcolin said. "It was my purpose to do so today, in hopes of finding that you prospered."

"It is our joy," the estvin said. "We have prospered indeed in your favor, O prince."

On the ride to the west hills, Arcolin watched as the little procession of gnomes jogged along, covering the ground as fast as his longlegged chestnut could walk. As they neared the hills, he saw a change in the outline and a beaten path leading alongside a stream, then, closer, the narrow line in the turf, a slash through brush. When they reached the entrance, one of the gnomes took charge of Arcolin's horse, and Dattur followed the others underground. Arcolin pulled the scarf Aldonfulk had given him from his saddlebag and hung it around his neck. The estvin bowed twice, then led Arcolin within.

The rest of that day he spent with the gnomes, partly under stone. They apologized for the roughness of the excavation so far, but to Arcolin it looked amazingly finished. "The great hall we have not begun," the estvin said. "We will need more workers, and we wished to ask your preference for it. If you will be indwelling with us, or not. That which is large enough for us would not be large for you."

Arcolin chose his words carefully. "I would do my duty to you, my people, but I must also do my duty to my king in Vérella and my other people, who are spread from here to Valdaire and beyond. I cannot therefore indwell with you as your prince ought. By the Law, I must be your prince; you can have no other, is it not?"

"It is so," the estvin said.

"Then by the Law, I must appoint one of you to be a guardian until I return. While I am here this winter, I will come often to you, and learn more of each of you, before making that appointment." Dattur had suggested this. Arcolin thought Dattur, with his experience of the outside world, would be the best guardian, but he realized that imposing an exile on those remaining might cause trouble.

The estvin bowed.

"Now I will hear a report of the tribe," Arcolin said. "Births and deaths, illnesses and injuries, recoveries, what stores you have of food, and so on."

"None have died, O prince," the estvin said. "One babe has been added to the tribe but will have no name until Midwinter, if it please the prince. It is the custom." The estvin clapped his hands, and one of the others brought a book. "The records, O prince, and if the prince cannot read—"

"But slowly," Arcolin said. "The symbols are still new to me."

"Then I will assist as the prince asks," the estvin said.

The gnomes had planted seeds from the grain he had sent with them in the spring and harvested that grain and wild grasses as well. They had snared rabbits and other small game—every one entered in the book—and begun the cultivation within the excavation of things Arcolin guessed were edible fungi of different types. Not all wore the new uniforms, the estvin explained, eyes cast down, as there had not been time to grow the . . . whatever it was they made cloth from. Arcolin decided he did not want to know. The women and children, and some of the men, still wore the cloth Arcolin had given them, but all who met the outside world went properly attired.

"You have done well," Arcolin said, when the account ended.

"It is by the prince's mercy," the estvin said. "It is a great debt."

"It is no debt to a prince, to have the people prosper," Arcolin said. Once more he thought, as he had the previous winter, of what might have been . . . gnome children dead in the snow.

The estvin's brow wrinkled. "It is strange—"

"For both of us," Arcolin said. "But not a bad thing."

"No." The estvin sighed. "My prince . . . when you think of someone to be your . . . your hesktak . . . you should consider that . . . that one who came with you. Datturnaknitunak."

"Advise me," Arcolin said.

"It is hard to say. It is . . . he was . . . he was should have died, but . . . but his living . . . it is not that kapristi think luck, but favor of Law is not luck."

That was sufficiently tangled that it took Arcolin a long moment to figure it out. "He told me he was taken away and left—"

"Yes. One who died later took him. The prince before ordered it. Ordered not kill but leave to die. Datturnaknitunak is—was—one seeks truth. Prince before said not looking, not talking. Datturnaknitunak would look, would tell. Not . . . obedient to prince. Said to Law."

"Did you know this before Dragon came?" Arcolin asked.

"Some." The estvin looked down. "It is shame. We believed—we thought we believed—the prince spoke Law. Fear ruled, not Law. So . . . you should choose him."

"Would fear rule you again?" Arcolin asked.

"I . . . not know."

Arcolin nodded. "You know I am a man of war. You know I understand courage?"

"Yes, prince."

"When you came to me last winter, you were afraid."

"Yes, prince."

"But you came. You were afraid of Dragon, and of me, but you came. And when I offered refuge, you were afraid, were you not?"

"Yes, prince, but—but no other choices."

"Always other choices," Arcolin said, a direct quote from their Law. The estvin looked up at him. "*Always* other choices. You could have chosen death, but you chose life and the risks of life. I say to you: that was courage. Every one of you who came—you kapristi and your kapristinya and the littlest of the children among you—you all had courage greater than your fear. You came into a human place, among humans who had not the Law, and lived among us from winter into spring and then moved here, to new stone, stone you knew had been infested with orcs. That is courage greater than fear."

"The prince is merciful."

"The prince intends to be just," Arcolin said. Quoting again from the Law, he went on. "Kapristin deal not in mercy, but in justice—is it not so?"

"It is so!" The estvin's eyes were shining now.

"The prince will not have confusion about this," Arcolin said. "For the Law is the Law, and even a human—even one such as I, newly learning the Law—can recognize justice. Because the prince is human, the prince will need what we call a judicar to guide the prince in matters of Law, until such time as the prince has learned it perfectly, but the prince will rule."

"Yes, O prince!"

"And for this, the prince will also take the words of the estvin into account. For a prince who must travel abroad needs both a steward—a hesktak—and an advisor in the Law. And it is in my mind that they should not be the same person."

"It is so, my prince."

Dattur reappeared with the other gnomes who were in gray. All bowed.

"Would you see everyone?" the estvin asked.

"Not today," Arcolin said, hoping that was the right answer. "I must go, to prepare for holding court for the humans of my realm tomorrow. Perhaps I should wait to greet you all until all are formally dressed."

The estvin bowed again. "That would be appropriate, O prince. The cloth you gave us was indeed appreciated, but we are most comfortable in the clothes of our princedom."

"I will come every fiveday to see what your needs are," Arcolin said. "If a need arises suddenly, send someone to the stronghold. I do have other news to share. Unrest in Aarenis seems certain to spread north—" He explained about the regalia, the Duke of Immer's ambitions, and the return of active magery among some families in the north. "Duke Verrakai and I think it possible he might come up the Honnorgat as well; the Aldonfulk prince might agree to help defend the pass above Valdaire, but only humans remain to guard the Honnorgat. You should be safe up here—the Duke of Immer wants the regalia, not our cold hills, and there will be recruits and veterans to defend the villages and strongholds."

The gnomes, as he'd expected, did not react. "We grow stronger," the estvin said. As Arcolin turned to leave, the estvin said, "O prince—will it please you to let us keep your stole in a place of honor? It should not be seen in the light of day."

Arcolin lifted it off and handed it to the estvin, who bowed again. "When you come next, O prince, you will have your throne."

Next day, Arcolin met with the village councils of both Duke's East and Duke's West, settled those disputes the councils had set aside for his return, and told them about the possible threat. Veterans who had retired after Siniava's War nodded. "Always thought he'd be trouble," one said. "But we'll give him trouble if he comes up here."

As winter deepened, Arcolin traveled to Burningmeed to hold Duke's Court and then to visit his neighbor to the east. They discussed the possibility of a southern invasion up the Honnorgat. Arcolin kept careful watch for any signs of magery in his domain, but saw none other than the gnomes' continuing use of rock magery in their new stone-right.

CHAPTER FORTY-THREE

Chaya, Lyonya

By autumn, both elves and humans had become accustomed to the king's ability to generate an elvenhome. It was not so large as the Lady's had been, though no one knew if it would expand to that size in time. With practice and Arian's help, Kieri had found a way to damp the light completely at night. He suspected it was not the way Orlith would have taught him, but none of the elves remaining in Lyonya knew how—or admitted it. He could make it more permeable, as well, but he could not lessen its effect on his subjects.

"I'm not *trying* to lay a glamour on them," he said to Arian one morning. "It just has that effect. I've wondered if that's an effect of the elvenhome itself. If the Lady, for instance, did not intend the intensity of the glamours she laid."

"The elves are certainly more cooperative," Arian said, grinning. "Surely you don't mind that."

"What worries me is that *everyone* is more cooperative. Not that I want to deal with troublemakers every day, but honest disagreement keeps commanders—and I assume kings—from making stupid mistakes. No one is right all the time. That's why I have a Council. I want my Council members to say what they think, even if I don't agree."

"Could you tell them that? Maybe if you say you want disagreement when they feel it, they'll cooperate by disagreeing."

"I had not thought of that," Kieri said. He stretched. "And then there's all that mess in Tsaia and Fintha. King Mikeli wants to know if we have magery emerging here . . . and how would we know, with so much elven blood in the realm?"

"I'm more concerned about those elves showing up in Fin Panir," Arian said. "That must be where my father came from, so why did they not come here as well?"

"Animosity toward my grandmother, according to Amrothlin," Kieri said.

"But she's dead."

Kieri stiffened. "Maybe . . . maybe they do not know. When was it they arrived in Fin Panir? It could have been before the Marshal-General knew about the Lady's death. If they think she's still alive—"

"They would think my father still alive," Arian said, eyes wide. "If he was reporting to them, they will expect a report."

"In their own time, which is not our time. I know the Marshal-General said the king she spoke to seemed in haste, but haste to them is not the same as haste to us. It may be they will arrive here next year or ten years from now and think it but a few days."

"I would like to meet them," Arian said. "For my father's sake and for my own." She patted her belly, clearly bulging now. "And for these, who elsewise will have no family but the four of us."

"And how is your sense of them now? To me they are clouded by your own taig."

"Healthy, growing, and very, very active." Arian shifted in her chair. "They do seem . . . different since you came back with the elvenhome. They would respond to it, I think."

Autumn continued into winter; Arian's pregnancy progressed normally, according to both human and half-elven midwives. Kieri could not use his elvenhome ability to travel, as the Lady apparently had, so his brief trips to check on the various projects removed the elvenhome protection from Chaya, to his annoyance. Arian, he felt, should be protected in the elvenhome at all times. His councilors regained the ability to disagree with him, but at the same time he began to see the stamp of his own vision more clearly on the taig and on the projects he had begun.

Along the scathefire road to Riverwash, the ugly hard-burnt ash surface darkened and softened a little. The route west from Chaya to the Tsaian border was smoother on the way back than the way out; tree limbs fell out of the way, and the track seemed to widen of itself. Only the stone outcrops resisted the elvenhome influence—but once clear of undergrowth, were easier to work.

Kieri found himself thinking about the magelords enchanted in Kolobia, as he had before. Could they be connected to the outbreaks of magery in Tsaia and Lyonya? Mikeli had shared Arcolin's notion that this was all coming from Gird, through Paksenarrion. Yet Gird was not a high god and had never concerned himself with elves, so far as Kieri knew, so . . . how could he be involved in Kieri's growing powers? He touched his ruby. How could Falk, for that matter? *Someone* chuckled in his mind, and he smiled in response. Whoever, and whatever, and however, the great changes had come, and were still moving in the world.

CHAPTER FORTY-FOUR

Immerdzan, Aarenis

The Duke of Immer reviewed his plans. This winter: Cortes Cilwan along the river and Rotengre to the north. He could cut the Northern Trade Road. He could invest Dwarfwatch, which—as his spies told him—had once more been vacated in the peace following Siniava's War as too expensive to garrison.

At one time Aliam Halveric and Kieri Phelan had used that pass, though not—he thought—to move large numbers of troops. How many troops would he need to keep Phelan's attention on his southern border? At the least, a few spies could go over and learn what they could of Lyonya and southern Tsaia, reporting back in the spring.

He spread his hand across the map before him. Was it too ambitious, this plan? Should he go at it piecemeal, tackling first the Guild League cities one by one? But that, he was certain, had been Siniava's mistake. Phelan had defeated Siniava with boldness and planning; Siniava had given Phelan time to plan, time to gather allies. He himself, with his mentor within . . . surely boldness would serve him best. Phelan had just fought a war against Pargun; he must be tired now.

So . . . a feint, but a strong one, against the western Guild League, to draw Fox Company in and keep them occupied defending the pass at Valdaire. A fleet—even now assembling at his orders—to sail around the Eastbight and up the Honnorgat. A force to pin Phelan in southern Lyonya, so that his force could invade on the river.

He reviewed his forces. No one knew where all his warriors came from; no one knew what ships dared thread the dangerous shoals outside Slavers' Bay or what cargo unloaded or loaded there. Coastal caravans kept well inland from it, the caravan masters well paid to see nothing and tell less.

It can all be yours. That voice whispered to him night and day now: praise, warning, advice, promises. So far, in the years since he had accepted the gift, it had led him truly, if slower than he wished, from one triumph to another. He had not always understood its reasons—why, for instance, he had not been given leave to slay Kieri Phelan in Siniava's War—but in the end Phelan's reputation had protected him from others' suspicions.

Why not, he wondered now, assassinate the young, inexperienced Fox Company captains while their commander was away? Why not kill all the mercenary commanders? If their troops were in disarray . . .

Not yet. That was clear enough, and he had learned not to disobey. *For now you want the cities to think they can trust those companies.*

What, then? Send spies to infiltrate them?

Patience. You are not as old as I.

No, but he would be. He had been promised that. Life beyond life, without aging. If not immortality as the elves knew it, still life far beyond other men. He would see the other kings die, and then . . . his vision blurred to the glory of it. Himself, in a radiant glow, crowned with the mightiest of all crowns, and all bowing before him.

No one would ever command him again.

Except me.

Who was part of himself now. That, he told himself, was different.

He bent his mind to the practicalities of war and issued orders. It had begun.

Cortes Andres

"My lord Count!"

Andressat looked up from his work. One of the scribes—Hastan—was waving a scroll as if it were a torch. What could he have found?

Hastan came nearer. "My lord, you know the rumors from the north—"

"Which rumors?"

"About the magelords in the mountain. The Girdish expedition found them, far to the west of Fin Panir."

Andressat now had an idea where Fin Panir lay, west of Vérella. West of Fin Panir, in his imagination, was a vast empty wilderness . . . but then, he had once thought all the North a tiny place, kingdoms no bigger than Andressat, and the reality . . . had been different.

"What about the rumors, Hastan? And what are you holding there?"

"Pedigrees, my lord. During the Girdish rebellion in the north, one of the Finthan lords sent a list of all the noble families and their relationships back to the south in case local archives should be lost."

"We have something of that in the list of those who came from Old Aare."

"Yes, my lord. But this is some hundreds of years later, and it mentions, in the holdings of one family, 'jewels of great power, once the pride of Aare, which have been sent for safekeeping to the east, as far from Gird's raiders as feasible.' This may be the regalia said to be found by Duke Verrakai and now in the king's treasury of Tsaia."

"What family?" Andressat asked.

"Here—" Hastan spread the papers out on another table; Andressat came over and looked where he pointed. "The Sier of Grahlin was the Finthan king's close relative and actually in closer descent from Declan of Valdaire. My lord will recall that the realm was vacated before the Girdish rebellion. By this, Grahlin had possession of the regalia. He was killed at the Battle of Greenfields, along with the king; his widow sent the jewels eastward, believing that even if Tsaia fell to the Girdish, a noble in the east might hide them."

"Why not send them south?"

"Ah." Hastan smiled. "We have a good history of the Girdish wars in Fintha and Tsaia, my lord. Girdish forces dominated the south of both realms, blocking access to Valdaire. The jewels, as you know, cannot be hidden in a pocket. They were originally housed in a golden casket, and that is how they were transported. According to this, they were sent to the easternmost name she knew, Verrakai, to hold in trust until, it says here, 'a king will rise again with both power and right.' The jewels are listed, along with a scroll giving the same history and Grahlin's pedigree. Except that we know of no scroll and the golden casket is missing, they are the same we know to be part of the regalia King Mikeli holds."

"And the Duke of Immer now holds the necklace from that suite," Andressat said. "And my son." He closed his eyes a moment; he could not help it. Cortes Cilwan had fallen; the Duke of Immer's army was poised on Andressat's border. He was surprised they had not invaded yet, but perhaps subduing the lands they'd conquered so quickly would keep them busy through the winter. Even—though he had scant hope of that—the next spring. Though what his son must suffer in that span—if he was not already dead—broke his heart.

"There is more, my lord," Hastan said, shuffling the scrolls to put another on top. "This . . . we thought of Prince Mikeli's as being the most complete listing of those who came out of Aare, but here is another. Declan of Valdaire's pedigree claims him to be a descendant of Mikeli's elder brother—thus a prince of Old Aare—by a child brought to Aarenis as a suckling by his mother. And here, my lord, your own line connects. With all respect, my lord, your right to that necklace is as clear as Grahlin's."

For only a moment, Andressat's heart leapt at the thought that he might, after all, have royal blood, but he put that aside and shook his head. "I am no magelord, Hastan. I have no magery, nor did my family before me that the record shows. If those jewels had power, I would have no idea what to do with them. Immer has magery—"

"Evil magery, my lord!" Hastan said. "Only evil, like Siniava."

"Probably. But I know from Duke Verrakai and Tsaia's king that blood magery controlled the other regalia. If, as we both think, Immer is a blood mage, then he could control the necklace."

"Verrakai, you told me, did nothing with the regalia but hide it with blood magery," Hastan said. "They did not use it. Perhaps the necklace cannot be used that way."

"Perhaps. We shall hope so. Come spring, we must get this information to those in the north. Somehow." Past Immer's spies and agents . . . how? He must find a way, just as he must defend Andressat no matter the cost to his son and himself. "I wish Count Arcolin were still in the south."

CHAPTER FORTY-FIVE

Chaya, Lyonya

Kieri woke to a room full of elf-light as silvery as the Lady's had been. At once, he realized it was both his and another elf's. Facing him, across the foot of his bed, was a tall figure, clearly elven, wearing a crown of silvery metal set with pale stones that glowed. His arms were folded, his expression stern.

Even as his heart stuttered and then raced, Kieri realized there must be another unblocked pattern in the palace. He felt no pressure from the other's glamour—was it his own elvenhome protecting him?

"You might have come at a better time," he said, glad to find his voice steady. Arian, he could tell, was still asleep.

"I would not have come here at all if someone had not blocked the patterns in the public rooms," the elf said. He sounded annoyed. "That was foolish. And discourteous. I am lord of the western elvenhome."

Kieri scowled. "And I am king of Lyonya. We had good reason to block those patterns." And again he wondered why this one, every bit as hazardous, had not been blocked. A question for Amrothlin, when he had dealt with the elf.

"And I had good reason to come here," the elf said. "An urgent reason. Rise, dress yourself. I must talk to you."

As arrogant as the most arrogant of the other elves he'd met. And where were the King's Squires? Kieri fought his anger down. "Over there—" Kieri pointed. "—is the bathing room. You may wait there while I dress."

The elf raised his brows. "You are ashamed of your body?"

"Ashamed, no. Are you? If you choose to disrobe yourself, then you may stay."

Beside him, Arian stirred. Kieri put a warning hand on her shoulder and squeezed a little. She lay still at once.

The elf stared a moment, brows raised, then shrugged and moved to the bathing room, disdain in the set of his shoulders. Kieri bent to Arian's ear. "It's an elf-lord, from the west, he says. Showed up here; apparently there's a pattern we didn't know about. I'm getting up."

"We knew they might show up any time," Arian said. "I'm getting up, too. Where are the Squires?"

"Elven magery, I expect." He swung out of bed and put on the clothes that lay ready on a chair. Arian threw back the covers and levered herself out of bed on the other side. She, too, dressed as quickly as she could. It took her longer, which Kieri knew annoyed her. He stood where he would block a view of her if the elf should be discourteous enough to peek.

When Arian had tied her hair back, Kieri walked to the door of the bathing room and found the elf staring at the bathtub with an expression between amazement and amusement. "Do join us," Kieri said, with an edge to his voice. He stepped back from the door, and the elf followed, his eyes widening when he saw Arian.

"You're—you're *Dameroth's* daughter! And with child!"

"And my wife and queen," Kieri said.

The elf turned to him. "And you're . . . Flessinathlin's grandson?"

"Yes," Kieri said. Arian moved closer to him.

A spate of elvish, too fast and complicated for Kieri to follow, in a tone between exasperation and distress. Then the elf quieted, gave a short twitch of the shoulders, and met Kieri's gaze. "I see," the elf said. "I did not know the Lady had agreed to this match."

"Is there a reason why you should have known?" Kieri asked.

"I would have thought so," the elf said. "When was it that you wed?"

"The Spring Evener," Arian said. "And our engagement was announced, with the Lady's consent, at last Midwinter."

"Flessinathlin is more fool than I realized," the elf said. "She knows—I will speak to her—"

Kieri shook his head. "You do not know she died?" he said; though he had suspected the elf had not heard that at Fin Panir, he was still surprised.

The elf flinched as if someone had hit him. "Died! She is dead? When? What happened?"

"Last spring," Kieri said. "Not long after our wedding." He told it as concisely as he could, ending with "several elves, including Arian's father, were killed defending the Lady." He paused, startled by the elf's shift of expression. Was that grief? Tears in those strange eyes? The elf said nothing; Kieri went on. When he finished, he said, "I thought all elves would have known."

"So . . . that was why I could not reach the elfane taig . . ."

"That was gnomes," Arian said. "The Lady gave up the elfane taig; the gnomes will have destroyed the pattern there, I'm sure."

"She—I never thought she would do that!" The elf looked more closely at Arian.

"You spoke of a reason why you came," Kieri said. "Would it be related to your visit to Fin Panir?"

"You have heard about that?"

"Yes, but no details other than you wanted the Marshal-General to waken the sleeping magelords."

"It is necessary. We must close the rock, and we cannot while they are there. The magery that holds them prevents it."

"And you think someone here can do it?" Kieri asked. "Why?"

"Not you alone, perhaps. As I sense the spells, they were woven of multiple mageries: elven and human, and of the human, both mageborn and something . . . other. As you are half-elven, you must have at least two of these mageries. And I was told you know a mageborn in Tsaia—"

"Yes," Kieri said. "But she owes allegiance to Tsaia's king, not to me. I cannot command her. And without knowing how a spell was contrived—"

"It *must* be done!" the elf said, his voice rising. "The Eldest has told us it is the only way to keep iynisin from more destruction."

"Eldest?" Arian asked. "An Elder other than Sinyi or rockfolk?"

The elf stared at her. "I cannot say," he said after a moment.

"An Elder with whom one might touch tongues?" she said. "An Elder who values wisdom?"

"You know . . ." The elf looked at Kieri, then back to Arian. "You *both* know. Have you—?"

"Yes," Kieri said.

"Then you must—at once—you must try—"

"No," Kieri said sharply enough that the elf stepped back a pace. "No, not at once. What you tell me suggests great risk. A trifold magery, or even more, to be unwoven at a distance—"

"You must come; I will take you through the pattern, both of you—"

"No!" This time Kieri let his anger show. "Arian is with child. We have lost one child to malice; we will not lose these to carelessness or haste. And what of the mageborn, if they are awakened? Have you thought where they will go, how they will be received, what they will do? I see by your expression you have not. You see them as impediments to be removed, but if they wake, they are people—people who must have a home and a purpose."

"But . . ." The elf looked at Arian again; his expression softened. "We have much to talk about, you and I."

"Do we?" Arian asked. She eased her aching back a little.

"You are tired," he said, as if that were a surprise.

"I am carrying two babes," Arian said, her tone sharp, "and they both kick like mules. Now that you have said what you came to say, and Kieri has given his answer, perhaps you will wait until morning— or after—to continue this."

The elf startled, then—to Kieri's surprise—gave Arian a smile of such sweetness that he seemed a different person and bowed. "My pardon," he said. "You are right; you cannot travel, nor should you attempt great magery or be in the presence of it until after your babes are born. If it is no longer until this is done than it has been since I came to Fin Panir, that will be soon enough. There are indeed things you must know, Arian—and you, Flessinathlin's grandson—but the health of those who carry life comes first. If I may—" He reached out his hand. Arian stepped forward, and the elf touched her hair lightly. "Peace and health to you," he said. He bowed to Kieri and then with-

drew, his elvenhome light contracting to a point that vanished sound-
lessly.

"That was risky," Kieri said. "After what we know of some elves."

"He was not evil," Arian said. "I am sure of that. Neither I nor
the babes took harm." She smiled at him. "Now if you will help me
out of all this, perhaps I can get some sleep before dawn."

"I should wake the Squires," Kieri said, when he had helped her
back into her sleeping robe.

"You should come to bed," Arian said. "The sheets have chilled
already."

I n the morning, the Squires appeared as usual to light the fire. They
did not mention having fallen asleep, and Kieri decided not to tell
them. Last night's meeting seemed almost dreamlike, though he was
certain it had been no dream. Arian slept on until—when he had
dressed for arms practice as usual, she woke abruptly and stared at him.

"We did have an elf here last night, did we not?"

"Yes. And I intend to find out why that pattern wasn't destroyed."

"What about the magelords?"

"Not our problem for now," Kieri said. He picked up his sword
and belt. "Would you like any help before I go down to practice?"

"No, thank you. In another two tendays, though, I may need you
and two Squires to get me out of bed. Go on, now. I'd rather not have
anyone watching this." She grinned at him, and Kieri bowed, then
left the room.

All during practice he considered who to question first on the
problem of the remaining patterns. How many were there? One in
every bedroom? He met the steward on his way back from practice.

"How did you determine there were none of those elven patterns
in the bedrooms?"

"The elven lady, sir king. She asked to come upstairs to see if the
patterns were upstairs as well as down. Of course I said yes, and she
told me that none had been put upstairs. I asked if she was sure, and
she said yes." He looked worried. "Was that all right? Did she . . .
um . . . steal anything?"

"No," Kieri said. "She lied. There was a pattern in my chamber."

"Sir king! I'm sorry, I didn't—"

"I don't blame you," Kieri said. "You could not know. She was an elf; she could have laid a glamour on you—and anyway, why would you suspect her?"

"I didn't . . . I really thought—"

"Of course. But we will have to find how many there are—"

"Did something happen?"

"An elf visited. Nothing happened but that. I'll talk to Amrothlin." He would more than talk to Amrothlin; he would demand answers, but that was not the steward's worry.

He was finishing a leisurely breakfast—Arian had sent word she planned to breakfast upstairs—when Amrothlin appeared, looking flustered, and followed by last night's visitor, still wearing a crown but not clothed in light. Kieri sat back, eyeing the pair with no great favor.

Before he could speak, Amrothlin apologized. "I did not know, sir king—Merithllyn offered to check the upstairs as I was searching for patterns down here—"

"And you did not think of this when I told you what happened in the place my mother died?"

"No, I swear it. It had passed from my mind."

"Um." Kieri looked at the other elf, wondering what the proper term of address was for a "lord of the western forest" who wore a crown.

The elf bowed. "Lord king, I have known Amrothlin for longer than your life, from before your mother was born. I believe him to be telling what he knows."

Which was not the same as the truth, necessarily. Kieri broke open a roll and spread jam on it.

"There are things you must know," the visitor said. "Things Lady Arian must know."

"I am not," Kieri said, around a mouthful of jam and bread, "going to risk our children to travel or attempt great mageries I do not know how to control."

"And you are right to be cautious. By your leave, lord king, let me explain." He turned to Amrothlin. "Unless the king needs you, you are free to go."

Kieri held up his hand. "By your leave—I prefer Amrothlin stay. Please—sit down. Will you have food or drink? There is plenty."

"No," the elf said. "I broke my fast with Amrothlin at the inn where elves gather. But thank you." He sat, folding his hands very deliberately; Kieri's eye was caught by the great ring he wore. "It is necessary that I tell you a tale that is long in the telling, but I will make it as short as I may, with the promise of telling it in full later. It is the tale of Lady Arian's birthright from her father . . . and from me."

"From you!" That escaped before Kieri could stop it. He remembered then what Arian had said seasons ago.

"Yes." The elf held his gaze. "Her father, as you know, was elven, but fathered children on humans only while he lived in the Ladysforest. Dameroth, as you knew him, was one of my sons. She, Lady Arian, is my granddaughter, as you are Flessinathlin's grandson. My quarrel with Flessinathlin began long before, and that, too, is a tale you must know, but perhaps not now. What you and she must know now—before your children are born—is that her father carried the elvenhome gift, as your mother did."

Kieri could not move for astonishment. Finally, into the silence that the elf allowed, he said, "You . . . sent your heir—your single heir—here? Why?"

"He is—he was not my only heir," the elf said. He looked at Amrothlin, then back to Kieri. "I saw no reason to limit the elvenhome gift with so few elvenhomes left. I foresaw that Flessinathlin would fail, that her line would fail; I hoped my son would take over the Ladysforest and restore elvenkind here. But he is dead. Now I see that you have the Lady's own elvenhome gift, and that is a wonder to me. I had not known such a thing was possible—a half-elf creating an elvenhome."

"It was a surprise to me, too," Kieri said.

"You have no one here to teach you how to use it," the elf said. "It has not come to full power. I would help you with this, if you wish."

If he wished to have the full power of an elf—of course he did. But why would an elf make such an offer?

"I would not offer such help," the elf said, as if he'd read Kieri's mind, "but that Arian is my granddaughter, and your children are my great-grandchildren. We treasure children; I must see them protected and safe." He paused and then added, "And . . . they have inherited the elvenhome gift. Did you know that?"

"I was not sure," Kieri said. "We hoped for it, since I will not live as long as elves do and the land needs what the Lady gave it."

"They will be stronger than you," the elf said. "If they survive. Amrothlin has told me of the attacks by the traitor elf as well as iynisin. Arian should have more protection than you can give her. Accept, please, my offer of help. And for your children, if not for you, assistance in training them in their elven magery as they grow."

Kieri thought about it. He needed to know more about his own magery, and the local elves claimed they could not teach him. The children would need help even more than he did as they grew. But accepting help from this elf meant becoming dependent on someone whose ambitions he could not fathom. Best meet that head-on; he could not hope to outwit an elf with subtlety.

"Your offer is gracious," he said. "But—with apologies to you and to Amrothlin—" He nodded toward his uncle elf. "—my experience with elves has included enough contradictory behavior that I am . . . wary. You know more than I, that is clear. You are older, more powerful. I swore an oath to this land to protect as well as rule . . . I will not lightly give up that charge."

The elf's eyes flashed; his face stiffened in what Kieri knew must be outrage. Then he calmed again. "I . . . understand, I believe. You dealt with your grandmother. She was not entirely reliable. Nor were all her elves. You do not know—you cannot know—my honor. Yet we have need of each other. If you are to rule and protect this land as you hope, you need to advance in your mastery of the elvenhome. If I am to see my lineage succeed here, so will your children. I do not dispute your right to rule. I do not dispute my granddaughter's right, through her father. Can we begin with that?"

Kieri nodded slowly. "We can . . . but you must forgive me if my trust comes slowly. You have not shared your name; you know mine."

"Ah. My name is long and difficult to say—" The elf uttered something that slipped past Kieri's ears in a ripple of sound like running water. "It is my history as well as my name. In a shorter form, which even elves use, I am Machrynalýthnyan, and my domain is known as the Lordsforest."

Kieri repeated the short form, noting the stress on the next to last syllable. "I thank you," he said, "and would welcome assistance in protecting Arian from iynisin if you think another attack might come—"

"Indeed, I am certain it will, though I cannot know when," Machrynalýthnyan said. "You defeated one whom you did not destroy; it will have told others about you, and as it hated Flessinathlin, it will hate you. I propose that I send four elves skilled in battle, experienced with iynisin. They can arrive where I found Amrothlin; the elves have placed a pattern in their inn, so it will be wise of you to obliterate all other patterns in this palace. Amrothlin and I can locate them for you now."

"Uncle," Kieri said, looking at Amrothlin. "Are you able to find these patterns yourself?"

"Yes, sir king," Amrothlin said. "I truly did not know she lied—"

"I believe you," Kieri said. He turned to Machrynalýthnyan. "Then, my lord, if you will do me the courtesy—in my concern for Arian, I ask that you return at once to send those guardians for her, and Amrothlin will search the palace high and low. Will that suit?"

"It will, my lord," Machrynalýthnyan said, equal to equal. "They will have a seal like this—" He held out his ring showing a design carved into the stone. "They will speak this word to you: Watersong."

"Watersong," Kieri said. "Thank you."

"The other matter," Machrynalýthnyan said, "I will not speak of until Lady Arian has recovered from the birthing, but—when the children are born—will you tell me?"

"Yes," Kieri said. If he trusted the elven king by then, which would depend on those he sent to guard Arian. Surely the man wouldn't want to harm his own granddaughter.

Arian was not best pleased when Kieri told her he had accepted the offer of additional guards. "He may be my grandfather, but are you sure we can trust him?"

"Amrothlin says yes. He was fostered there for a long time; he insists the king is honest." He reached out and stroked her hand. "Do you dislike the king that much?"

"No. But . . . I don't know him. I won't know these elves he sends. I'm used to ours." She shook her head. "Never mind. It's these two— my balance is gone, I can't sleep through the night, and I'm sure it's affecting my mind."

"All will be well this time, Arian," Kieri said.

T he elves arrived before nightfall, early as that came in winter, showing the correct seal and giving the correct password. They greeted Kieri respectfully and, when he introduced them to Arian, bowed low. Amrothlin knew one of them, Kiliriathlin, from his time fostered to the elven king. Kieri asked him to stay in the palace, meeting the Squires and learning the layout of the place, while Amrothlin took the others to meet the Ladysforest elves.

At Midwinter, Kieri went to keep vigil in the ossuary, wondering if he would have another adventure like the last, but the night— long, dark, and cold—passed quietly. He was ready at dawn to return the Seneschal's greeting and went inside quickly to reassure Arian.

As the days lengthened, the local elves and the visitors kept guard together, always some in the palace, night and day. Iynisin did not come. At the half-Evener, as the year before, a storm blew in, and with it a message from the Sea-Prince of Prealíth, carried by one of the forest rangers.

I have word from one with whom I have had dealings, in the times before, but with whom I wish no dealings now, that he is intent on mastering all lands, and will have the crown he is sure is his. He thinks me still his ally, but I fear him. He is not who he was since he came back from beyond the Eastern Ocean. You say you escaped from there; you will know what I mean.

No other name. But it must be Alured the Black the Sea-Prince meant. Beyond the Eastern Ocean . . . was the memory of horror. Baron Sekkady. Kieri shuddered once, then reminded himself: he was free now. He had been free a long time. But . . . Alured there? And "not who he was"? Had Alured met Sekkady? Surely Sekkady was dead by now. His heir, though—surely he had had an heir, and his heir was like to be as vile as Sekkady.

The thought sprang into his mind in one vivid image: how Sekkady might outlive an aging body—how a magelord might outlive an aging body—as Dorrin had learned. Could Alured have been taken over by Sekkady? But why would Sekkady choose a pirate? If it could be, if Sekkady came near . . . for a moment the lust for revenge rose in him again, the thought of Sekkady at his mercy, a chance to kill, once for all, what had so tormented him.

Falk. Only the one word, but Kieri knew what it meant. Falk had never sought revenge on the tyrant who had enslaved him or the brothers who had lived in luxury while he suffered. To be Falk's knight . . . Kieri touched the ruby he wore, and turned his attention to the message.

He plans a feint to the west, but will attack both over mountains and up the great river. I have sent word to Kostandan. The rest of the scroll was a crude map with a line across the mountains from a square marked "fort" to somewhere in southern Lyonya. The map showed the coastline of the Eastbight and north to the Honnorgat in careful detail, but inland only crudely. Aarenis was the wrong shape, and the Immer drainage nowhere near reality, with four cities marked at equal distances along it. The man must have drawn it from hearing it described, not from seeing it or any good map. But the "fort" lay north of the circle for Rotengre . . . Kieri's mind leapt to Dwarfwatch.

Snow pummeled the windows, coated the courtyard, veiled the view beyond. Kieri tried to remember his own trip across the pass at Dwarfwatch when he was Aliam's squire, but the wounds he'd taken getting Aliam out alive and the fever that had followed left him no clear notion where that pass came out. Not too far from Halveric Steading . . . where Estil and the family were alone, all the soldiers having come north with Aliam.

He could do nothing in the teeth of this storm. Aliam was days away in Riverwash. He could but hope that Alured had not sent any substantial force across the mountains before the pass closed.

CHAPTER FORTY-SIX

Aarenis

Spring came early to the island, bringing the tangy fragrance of flowering white-bush, the bleating of newborn goats, the chink and scrape of hoes working house-gardens. Stammel, on his way to fetch water one morning, stopped short. Smoke. Not the village's cookfire smoke, but a more acrid smoke from somewhere at a distance. He knew that smell. The smoke of war . . . death, destruction, ruin.

"What's wrong, Matthis?" asked Rimmel.

"Smoke," he said. "The wrong smoke. Tell everyone: douse all fires here." It was too late, he knew, to pretend no one lived here; enemies would already have seen cookfire smoke rise pale in the morning sun against the slopes of the mountain. And enemies already knew their way up from the sea; they had been here before. "Pack up," he said. "What I told you—" Someone cried out, a youngster he thought by the sound—panic in that cry. Stammel said, "Be quiet," in a voice that no recruit had ever disobeyed, and none here disobeyed either.

"We can't be sure they'll come," Rort said.

"We can't be sure they won't," Stammel said. Another gust of wind from the east brought a stronger whiff.

"I smell it now," Rort said; others muttered agreement. "It's early for pirates."

"They're closer," Stammel said. Two other villages lay between them and the coast; it was the smoke of the nearer one burning, he thought. "Gather the children; form your groups. You know what to do—" He had told them, argued with them, told them again, all the summer long, all the autumn. Insisted that they find a place, carry supplies up, practice leaving.

"How long—?"

"If you go now, maybe long enough." Stammel set down the yoke with its buckets, turned, and went back to the shop. He could hear Cadlin inside, the clink of his tools as he picked them up and packed them into a leather bag.

"It's now, then," Cadlin said. Not a question.

"Yes," Stammel said. He felt his way past the shaving horse almost as quickly as if he could see and reached up to take the crossbow off its peg. He reached again for the sack of bolts and met the sack coming down in Cadlin's hand.

"You should come with us," Cadlin said, his warm, callused hand on Stammel's shoulder. "You are a better leader than anyone else."

"We have one bow," Stammel said. "And one archer. And you are a better leader than you know. Tell them what they know to do, and keep them moving."

"There's always a chance pirates won't come this far," Cadlin said.

"If they don't, I'll climb up and tell you it's safe," Stammel said. They both knew better. Cadlin hesitated, his feet shuffling on the floor. "Go now," Stammel said, putting all those years of command into his voice. "They need you."

"Gods keep you, Matthis," Cadlin said, and was gone out the door. Stammel waited out of sight, listening to him organizing the villagers—it was taking too long, so much longer than a disciplined troop of soldiers . . . but the climb up from the sea grew steeper and should slow the enemy down. They would stop to eat and drink; they would stop to loot and rape.

He stroked the crossbow, checked that he had a second string curled into the sack of bolts, counted the bolts—Cadlin had made him more than he remembered. And all the while the bustle and scurry and noise of the villagers gathering what they could carry, dropping things, children beginning to cry, women scolding, men barking gruff orders, the baaing of goats and sheep, the grunting of pigs . . . anyone would know there was a roused village up ahead.

When they were gone—not quite out of hearing on their way up to the caves—he hung the sack of bolts over his shoulder, took his own supplies—oil, water, bread, cheese—and walked out into the village street, in and out of houses, to be sure no child was hiding under a bed, no one forgotten. The wind brought a stronger smell of smoke but as yet no sound.

He had chosen his place the summer before, with the help of several small boys who thought it was a great game to play at being soldiers and to keep that a secret from their mothers. An outcrop of rock at the end of a ridge, separated from it by a rift the boys spanned with a plank. The track up the mountain turned here, to go around the outcrop. If his sight had been clear, he would have been able to see anyone coming up the track, and then look down on them as they turned, and turned again the other way, to continue up to the village.

He hoped—he had to trust—that he was still the Blind Archer. All he could see was a blur, lighter by day and dark by night. The invaders would not be fire-shapes like the dragonspawn. But the gods would not have set him here unless he had a purpose. That he was sure of, though he was not sure who stood before him until that person moved or spoke, and he could not name the gods he believed gave him purpose.

He felt his way across the plank and pulled it free, hauling it up onto the top of the outcrop with difficulty. Then he sat down on the rock he had chosen and ate a little bread, drank a little water. He felt lighter, the old battle excitement rising again. That surprised him; he had not expected to feel it. The sun warmed his face; he smelled, under the smoke, the rock and the aromatic bushes that grew near it. He touched the foxhead ring on its thong around his neck, thought of putting it on his finger . . . thought of throwing it away, so those who found his body would not know who he was, or take it to use. Finally, he left it on the thong. He was, at the end, a soldier, and he did not really care who knew it.

Before he heard anything with his ears, the stone beneath him shuddered once. Earthquake? But before he had taken five breaths, he heard voices from below carried on the wind, men's voices complaining, and took the stone's movement as a warning.

The notches he'd chiseled in the stone reminded him where to stand, how far he could move without being seen. This outcrop gave him three places from which to shoot, and he could move between them without being seen—at least until they outflanked him and came from behind. That would happen, he was sure. But if he made it sufficiently costly, they would be slow to expose themselves. And they did not know the details of the land. When they'd come before, they'd simply come up the trail the village folk used to trade with the fisherfolk below.

He spanned the crossbow and set the first bolt ready, then moved his head a little . . . could he see anything? Unbidden, for he had not prayed for sight for a long time now, he found himself naming the gods and asking their mercy for the people of the village. The High Lord, Tir, Alyanya of the Flowers, Gird and Falk and Camwyn and Esea Sunlord and Barrandowea Sealord, as the locals had taught him.

The gray blur he had known so long shattered into bright shards of color and movement—nothing like the sight he remembered. It sickened him for a moment—too bright, too confusing, but there— there was movement flicking from one place to another. Stammel blinked, struggling to make sense of what he saw. There, armed men— not there now—over there—not there but another place . . . He blinked again and again and finally understood that what he had was vision as different from what he had known before as the ability to see the fire inside the dragon. Whatever moved flicked in and out of sight, moving from one window, as he thought of it, to another.

And he could use it.

The men toiled up the steep trail toward the outcrop, where it turned. Most wore leather jerkins over their shirts, short dark leather trousers, and low boots. Long hair, braided behind with colored yarn or ribbons. Stammel remembered Alured the Black, green ribbons and other gewgaws in his braid. He thought one or two might be wearing a breastplate or a mail shirt. They had curved blades thrust through belts, a long dagger in one hand and a short pike in the other. With them were two slaves, roped together and carrying coils of rope and bundles of what looked like sails. Something to put plunder in, Stammel thought.

All but the slaves wore some head covering, but only three had a metal helmet. The others wore cloth wrapped around the head or a leather coif. Good protection against thrown stones or the light arrows they'd expect from hill peasants with no training. A crossbow bolt might penetrate even the metal, depending on its quality, and would certainly pierce a leather coif. The cloth—if thick enough—might withstand a bolt, but it would surely hurt.

Stammel could not be sure how many there were; his fractured sight and the scrub and twisting path made that impossible. He picked up the cow's horn and blew it. The man in front stopped and looked around, but he was not quite close enough yet. Crouching low, Stammel moved to the far end of the outcrop and blew the horn downward into the ravine, where he knew from practice the sound would echo as if coming from there. Three short blasts, as if in answer to that first long one. He picked up one of the round stones piled nearby and threw it as far away from the trail as he could. It hit and rattled down onto others.

Then he moved back to his first position. Some of the men had taken cover behind rocks that would screen them from the ravine's mouth but not from above. All those he could see, in the flashes of sight, were looking toward the ravine. If he climbed a little way down to his right—not as protected a position—he could take one of them at an angle that would make experienced fighters move to his left. He remembered his play with the village children. He could be seen from those positions if he didn't duck fast enough, and returning to the higher ground would be tricky. But worth it.

He eased over the edge of the outcrop, dropped into a hollow, and then clambered up the next boulder, all with his eyes shut to block out the unnerving jerky flashes of sight. Then he looked. Sure enough: five men visible, all facing away to their right. He placed a bolt and aimed carefully, all the while wondering if this was what the gods meant in giving him sight. Should he have claimed the Blind Archer's name? He touched the trigger, and the bolt flew true, striking the man he'd chosen in the side, piercing his leather jerkin. One of the others stood up, looking at the tumble of boulders lower down, and Stammel took a second shot, this time hitting the man square in the chest. Then he flattened himself on the rock behind the thin screen of bushes.

Yells from below. Stammel slid backward down the boulder he was on, back into the hollow, and decided to take the more difficult climb up into the cleft behind his main position. He made it safely back to the top and peered out carefully. For a moment the shards of vision jerked around, but then steadied. A man in a metal helmet with the edge of a metal breastplate peeking from under a surcoat with some kind of fancy design on it was pointing out where Stammel had been . . . or close enough. He had no good shot at this obvious leader. Stammel moved to the ravine end and looked again. Now three men were exposed, moving cautiously toward the boulders below what had been his hiding place. He could not see the leader at all. He chose his target and whispered "I am the Blind Archer" as he touched the trigger.

That bolt too flew true and struck the man in the ribs; the man screamed. The others whirled around, staring back the way the bolt must have come. Stammel picked up the horn again and blew an obvious signal: two and two.

That brought the man with the helmet and breastplate into view again. Stammel guessed that he thought his protection sufficient, for he stood spraddle-legged on the trail below, yelling orders to his men in some foreign tongue. Stammel's erratic vision cleared abruptly, as if he were falling toward the man; he could see every detail of the man's face, his clothing, his hands, thumbs hooked in his belt . . . and the edge of his breastplate showing just above the belt—a half-plate, they called it in the armorers' shops. It protected only to the waist or a little above and never included a back plate. Cavalry wore it sometimes, as full frontal protection made riding harder.

"Thank you," Stammel murmured to whatever gods were listening. Some surely were, to help him this way. He wondered which . . . but it did not matter, if he kept the villagers safe. He aimed carefully . . . and the bolt flew home into the man's gut. Stammel winced as the man cried out and folded around the wound. He knew what damage it would do; he had seen it often enough.

Shouts from below. Stammel belly-crawled to the middle shooting spot. Another troop coming up from below, and this time four of them had crossbows. He took a long shot at the man in front; the bolt hit a metal breastplate and did not penetrate. Two of the men with crossbows raised them and shot at him, but their bolts shattered on the rock. Back to the first spot. Someone was standing up, calling to the oncoming troop. Stammel shot him in the side.

It occurred to him that if he had had one more trained crossbow-man, the two of them could have held off the intruders for the rest of the day. Well . . . he had known from the beginning that he was not to train any of the villagers. The gods had given him a chance to be a soldier once more, to protect people he had come to respect and even love, and that was all the grace he needed. He sat with his back against the protecting rock and drank some water, ate a little bread and cheese. No use feeding a dead man, he told himself. Then he eyed the rest of the bread and cheese. No use feeding the enemy, either. He ate as much as he wanted, crawled to the edge of the cleft, and re-lieved himself.

A hard noise from behind made him turn around in time to see two more bolts drop from the sky and shatter on the rock. A volley of four, by the four broken bolts. He flung himself back to his own bow, grabbed his sack of bolts, the water bottle, and the last hunk of bread, and slid back to the cleft just as another four bolts hit the rock a man's length from the first. They weren't stupid: they were working along the line from which he'd shot, and they were expert enough to land the shots behind the jagged rocks that topped the outcrop.

He heard voices but could not distinguish the words; he hadn't understood the language he'd heard before, either. There were two places in the cleft where a dropping volley could not harm him, but both could be found by men entering the cleft at one end or the other—and he'd be cornered in that event. Yet he could not think of any alternative. He had no armor; a dropping bolt would likely be fatal. Well, he expected to die . . . but he'd rather kill the enemy. And they could not have an infinite number of bolts.

The plank he and the boys had placed across the cleft, that he'd pulled over when he came, was still on his side of the cleft. It had a crossbow bolt in it. Stammel felt its underside. The bolt had not pen-etrated the thick wood, and the plank could cover most of his body . . . but would it be better to let them think they'd killed the shooter?

He wasn't sure. He peeked out the narrowest of the gaps. Men were coming out of the boulders . . . gathering on the trail. The wounded had been dragged into a row and killed. The bloody gashes of their throats gaped. The commander—the man in the metal breast-plate that went all the way to the groin—seemed to be arguing with another man wearing a metal helmet. Their arms made expansive gestures. Stammel assumed it was an argument of "go on" versus "give up, cut our losses."

Maybe they would give up. Maybe this time they would give up, and by the time they came again, he would have a better plan. It was at that moment he heard a noise behind him and rolled over. Someone was in the cleft, climbing. They were checking to be sure he was dead.

Stammel spanned his crossbow and slithered over to the cleft as silently as he could, staying back from the edge enough that he would not be seen from below until the climber's head topped the rock. One climber or two? And what weapons did they have? Had they climbed with those swords or the short pikes? The crossbow was certainly not the ideal close-quarters weapon, and he had only a dagger in addition.

What he could hear most was heavy breathing and the bump of body parts on the rock. Two climbers . . . three or four man-lengths apart. They could alternate looks at the top of the rock for any hint of where a live enemy might be. They were far enough apart that a single defender could not attack them both; it would take too long to span a crossbow and reload. Stammel shrugged. It would have been nice to have a stupid enemy for once.

The only good thing was that they were grunting and panting as they climbed. One seemed to be faster than the other; Stammel hoped their own noise would cover the slight sound he made moving toward the sound of the faster climber. He dared not look over . . . but when the top of the man's head showed at the edge, he thanked the gods that the man wore only a leather coif. He rolled, the full strike of his arm bringing his dagger down on the top of the man's skull. He felt it penetrate leather and bone; the man grunted, lost his grip, and fell, the dagger stuck in his skull.

Stammel grabbed the crossbow, ready for a shot, and rolled to the edge of the cleft; he could see two more men, not just one, and the one standing in the bottom of the cleft had a crossbow. Stammel leaned out a little and shot the higher one just under the arm; that one too lost his grip and fell. The third had his bow spanned and ready. Even as Stammel rolled away from the edge, the bolt struck his left shoulder from behind, spearing through his shoulder blade. The man below yelled. Others answered.

Stammel struggled back to the shelter of the taller rock and tried to span the bow one-handed. He could not reach the bolt in his shoulder to pull it free. He knew the bolt had hit his lung; he could feel himself weakening and fought the urge to cough. But it was not in him to give up. Every moment he delayed the attackers was a moment more for his people to get clean away.

The first man over the lip of the cleft got a crossbow bolt in the chest . . . and the next man, red-faced in a rage, ran toward him, his short pike aimed at Stammel's chest. It was the end. Stammel grinned at the man, as he had always grinned at the enemy, as the point went home. *Thank you,* he thought through that last pain.

The man who killed the old fellow on the ledge wrestled his pike free of the body, then tossed the man's crossbow down to his fellows below and searched the body. No money, of course. A ring on a thong around his neck—he yanked that off. "Hurry up, Tegar!" someone called up to him. The crew was moving; Tegar left the corpse for the carrion eaters and climbed back down as quickly as he could. One man, to kill so many—he must have been a soldier once. Tegar looked at the ring he'd taken. A foxhead seal. Fox Company *here*? Or just one of their veterans? He shrugged and jogged up the trail to catch up with the others.

With the rest he climbed the last stretch to the village, but had no breath to call out about his find. He took several steps more, coming close to the captain. Silence. No more horn calls; no more bolts from the rocks. No doubt the villagers had fled, but they would have left behind what villagers always left behind.

In the crooked lane between two crooked rows of houses a man stood, dark in the brilliant sunshine glaring off pale rock walls. The air shimmered with noonday heat. "I found a ring," Tegar said, when he could speak. "It has a fox—"

"Shut up," the captain said. He was staring straight at the man in the lane, and Tegar could read the tension in the captain's shoulders. "Who are you?" the captain said to the dark figure in the lane. "Are you the headman? Tell us where the gold is and I might let you live."

"You killed him," the figure said. Heat waves rose off the stone; an incongruous smell of hot iron, like a forge, stung Tegar's nose.

"If you mean that crazy old fool with the crossbow, certainly," the captain said. "I don't know what he thought he was doing . . ."

"What he always did," the figure said. "His duty. Tell me: are you wise?"

The captain gave a harsh bark of laughter; Tegar felt a sudden cramp, a twisting in his mind as painful as a twisted knee. *Don't laugh,* he wanted to say, but he could say nothing. "Wise?" the captain said. "That's for fools to think on; I don't need wisdom. I have swords at my command—"

Flame blossomed in front of them: impossible flame, a spear of flame brighter than the sun, and it pierced the captain and all directly behind him. Only the fourth man had time to scream, and only briefly. Through the flame, Tegar saw the dark figure of a man change to another, much larger shape shimmering with heat, and could not move. Such things came in tales—they did not exist—could not. As one after another of the crew, touched by flame, became fire as well, Tegar stood as if his feet had grown into the rock.

"You," the voice said. Tegar shivered as if in cold, but sweat poured from him. "You took—"

Tegar threw the ring; he heard it clink on the stone.

"—his life," the voice said. "That was not wise." And before Tegar could beg for his life or cry out, the flame wrapped him round. He never saw the dark man with the oddly patterned skin and the yellow eyes pick up the ring and one particular unburned crossbow and swallow them.

Already the carrion eaters' wings made a column over the place of death, and some were feeding below; three strutted boldly toward Stammel's body, but they scattered with alarm cries as the shadow of much larger wings moved over the rocks and settled on the end of the ridge above the trail down to the sea. The dragon shape ignored the bodies below, those beside the trail, and those in the cleft of the rock. One only interested the dragon, who put out a long questing tongue and tasted.

"It was a chance," the dragon said aloud, as if the corpse were still a live man. "I did not know they would come, and your commander will rightly blame me that you had no help. You hid your thought from me until too late; I was too far away. But you were faithful, and they will know." The long tongue wrapped around the corpse and drew it slowly in.

The next morning, the wizard appeared at the entrance to the cave where the villagers were hiding. "He is gone, and so are the pirates," the wizard said. "Come down."

"He is dead," Cadlin said. "I wish—"

"He saved you," the wizard said. "And as a reward, he was taken away."

"Away?"

"I found blood. I found bloodied weapons. I think the gods took his body."

"He knew," Cadlin said.

"Possibly," the wizard said. "But it was his choice." They were near the village now. "I cleaned up a bit for you. There were bodies in the street; there are others below. These here I burned."

The scorch marks and a faint smell of burned meat were obvious. "Where do you think he was killed?" Cadlin asked. The other villagers were moving in and out of their houses.

"I know," a boy said. "I know where he was; he played a game with us, and he said up on those rocks—"

"That's where I found the other bodies," the wizard said. "Below those rocks. And on top, a dead man who wasn't Matthis and . . . his blood."

"I wish he'd come with us," Cadlin said. "I'd rather we lost every house in the village than him. He was a good man."

"Yes," the wizard said. "He was. But you are safe now, for a while at least, and I must go again. Fare well." He turned and walked up the trail away from the village, past those still streaming in with their bundles and jugs and children.

Tsaia, North Marches Stronghold

The dark-skinned man with flame-colored eyes waited outside the stronghold gates—the sentries being wary of strangers—and Arcolin knew without a doubt who it was and why he had come. He bowed.

Impossibly, the man extended a hot red tongue and plucked from his throat first a crossbow, which he laid on the ground, then a ring, and then—with a curious sort of gulp, spat forth a shape that expanded and became a corpse; he held it in his arms like a beloved friend.

"Stammel," Arcolin said.

"Yes. It was his choice. He died saving those among whom he lived."

Rage as hot as the dragon's tongue rose in Arcolin's heart.

Before he could say anything, the dragon said, "Your anger is just. I did not know in time; I did not protect him."

"Why?"

"I do not know, other than he chose to act alone; he did not call on me. He sent away those who might have aided him. I saw once, from a distance, that he was training them . . . I thought for war, but they told me after it was to run and hide."

"He chose death, you mean."

"He chose not to risk the others," the dragon said. "If he had chosen death, he could have died before." He held out his arms. "Will you take him?"

Arcolin felt tears running down his face. "Yes," he said. Stammel seemed heavier without life in him; Arcolin almost staggered under the weight. The dragon picked up the crossbow and the ring and put out an arm, just under his own, and together they walked back to the gates.

They cleaned the body and dressed it in uniform once more—the uniform Stammel had sent back over a year before. Arcolin fitted the foxhead ring on Stammel's heart-hand, and they laid his body on a plank to carry it out to the Company burial ground. Arcolin sent word to the villages, where veterans who had fought alongside Stammel now lived. Solemn-faced recruits who had known Stammel only from veterans' tales stood at attention in the courtyard when his body was carried past.

As they came through the gates, Arcolin saw in the distance a shining helm glinting in the sun and a red horse galloping toward them beside a road already crowded with people from Duke's East. Arcolin held up his hand, and they all halted until she rode up.

"I hoped you would come," Arcolin said.

"How——?" she began, and then shook her head. "Afterward," she said.

With the veterans, she sang the "Ard hi Tammarion," so long the traditional death song of the company that Arcolin had never considered changing it. The dragon-man came forward and looked Paks in the face but did not ask if she was wise.

"Sister and daughter," he said. "Blessings." Out came the tongue. "Honor me, if you will."

"Blessings," Paks said, and touched her tongue to the line of fire with no hesitation at all. Arcolin heard gasps from the others.

The dragon did not stay after the funeral rites but changed, there in broad daylight, in the sight of all. Then he rose into the air and glided away on dark wings.

"Dragon wants everyone to know dragons are back in the world," Paks said.

"It is not the first time you met," Arcolin said.

"No—but how did you know?"

"It did not ask if you were wise," Arcolin said. "As far as I know, that is what it asks everyone on first meeting."

"It called me, summer before this last," Paks said. "I thought it was the gods' call at first. I left the Marshal-General staring after me when I rode away. Maybe it was . . . but what I met was Dragon."

"You don't know its name?"

Paks shook her head, still looking into the bright sky where the dragon had been. "If it has a name, as we know names, it is not a name we can say. And I do not know why it called me, what that meeting was for. Nor do I know why Dragon calls me sister and daughter, though . . . it feels almost like family to me. And yet I know—" She scratched her head. "I know my father is a sheepfarmer up above Three Firs and my mother is the daughter of another sheepfarmer. My brothers and sisters are their children, as I am."

"Um. Perhaps Dragon considers all paladins as family?"

"Perhaps. But please, Captain, tell me what happened to Stammel."

"I know only what Dragon told me," Arcolin said. "I should never have let him go—and yet I could not refuse him what he wanted." He told her of the dragon's earlier visit, the offer of a job, and Stammel's decision to be the dragon's archer. "I thought he would come back at the end of it, truly."

"I did not even know he was blinded," Paks said. "I wish . . . perhaps I could have . . ."

"I hoped you would come," Arcolin said. "We thought—I thought—after the Marshals could not heal him, that perhaps a paladin could. But . . ."

"But Gird had other plans for me," Paks said. "Nothing so important as Stammel, to me. If I had known, I would have come." She sighed. Arcolin looked at her closely. Were those silver hairs among the yellow? It had not been that long. "And perhaps that is why I was not given to know," she said.

"You will stay for a night at least, will you not? I would have you meet my wife and son."

"As the gods allow," Paks said. "I would like that. It was none of my business, but I never thought you would marry—and you have a son—a babe?"

"Her first husband died; Jamis is this tall—" Arcolin held his hand out. He led her into the inner courtyard and up the stairs. Calla was supervising Jamis's daily stint of study—the boy was just beginning to read—and Arcolin made the introductions. Jamis's eyes widened. "You're a . . . a *paladin*!" he said. "And your mail really is shiny!"

"Jamis!" Calla said. "Be polite."

Paks shook her head. "I was a big sister long before I was a paladin, milady. Jamis, would you like to see my horse?"

Jamis bounced off the chair, then looked at his mother. "Go along," she said. "But come back quickly; I'm sure Paksenarrion has other things to do today than play big sister to you."

Arcolin went back downstairs, watching Paks chatting with the boy—listening, rather, as he shed his shyness and began telling her everything about his life as fast as he could. Her horse stood quietly in the courtyard, bare now of saddle or bridle, with a worried groom standing nearby.

"He won't move, milady," the groom said.

"He's waiting to give this lad a ride," Paks said. Jamis, looking up at the tall horse, clutched her hand harder.

"No saddle?" he said. He sounded worried. Though he rode his pony more confidently now, he had never ridden bareback.

"You don't need one," Paks said. She scooped him up and deposited him on the horse's back. "Sit up straight now, like your father. And you don't need reins, because the horse knows where you need to go." She nodded to the horse. It took one careful step and paused. Jamis looked scared, but stayed upright. Another. Another. Jamis's mouth relaxed, Arcolin saw, and the horse gradually lengthened its stride, circling the forecourt.

"It's—it's fun!" Jamis said, turning to look at Arcolin. "Even on a big horse."

"A very special horse," Arcolin said.

"And now my horse wants his dinner," Paks said, as the horse came to her and stopped. "Sorry, Jamis, but you must come down. Another ride later, maybe."

Arcolin took the boy into his arms and set him on his feet. "Back to your books, lad; your mother's waiting."

The rest of that day, Arcolin was aware of Paks moving about the stronghold. Most of her comrades were in the South; few up here had been Stammel's recruits, and most had not known him, or only briefly. He wondered if that was worse for her. He wished he had old comrades with whom to reminisce about Stammel.

She came in to supper with Captain Arneson; the two of them

seemed already friends, chatting easily about the recruits' progress. During supper, Arcolin asked her when she had last been in Fin Panir.

"I came from there, on my way to Lyonya; the Marshal-General gave me messages for both the kings. I had just delivered the first to King Mikeli when I felt a call to come here. I cannot stay long; I must get to Chaya soon after King Kieri's children are born, and quickly."

"Is there trouble?"

"Not to concern you or this domain, my lord," Paks said. She shook her head then. "But who knows what may flow from any occasion? You know about the reappearance of magery in both Tsaia and Fintha?"

"I heard, on my way through Vérella. Is it all the same, or is some blood magery?" Arcolin asked. "Or a gift of some god, as you paladins have?"

"No, my lord. As far as we can discern, it is all natural magery, what the magelords had. Born magery, showing in children as young as five or six winters, though more often in those at the change, twelve to fifteen—sometimes in those older. Your Marshal will hear, if he has not already, of the Marshal-General's concerns in this matter."

"He knows," Arcolin said. "But no one seems to know why it came." He paused, fiddling with a napkin ring, then went on. "Some of us thought it might have come from Gird through you, Paks—the first magery anyone remembers seeing was Kieri with the sword when you gave it to him. And you helped Dorrin regain her magery. After that it was Beclan, her squire—"

Paks frowned. "I don't think so . . . though who knows how the gods work? I had no part in saving Kieri Phelan or Dorrin Verrakai from the perils of their early lives, but I am sure Gird and the High Lord did. A paladin is but the tool the gods use. The eldest of Elders might know, but Dragon does not explain."

"Dragon's essence, he tells me, is transformation," Arcolin said, remembering that conversation.

Paks tipped her head to one side. "But who wakened or sent or released Dragon?" she asked. "He did not tell me."

Arcolin felt a shudder down his backbone at the casual way she spoke of the dragon. "Perhaps . . . perhaps he just *is,* and none of our words—sleeping, waking, sending—mean anything to him."

"Perhaps." Paks yawned. "Excuse me, my lord, but eating and sleeping both mean something to *me.*"

A few days later, she said she must leave the next dawn; Jamis began to cry, throwing his arms around her. Paks hugged him then set him down. "When a god calls, Jamis, a paladin must answer. If the gods will, I will return—and meanwhile, you are fortunate in your mother and father and in having your own pony. Think of those things, and spring coming. You will make friends and learn as much as you can. Will you do that?"

He nodded, solemn-faced now, and took his mother's hand.

Arcolin was up before dawn to bid her farewell. As he'd promised, he woke Jamis, and with Jamis and Calla stood in the courtyard to see her come lightly down the steps and across the inner court, her mail glittering under her surcoat, saddlebags over her shoulder. They followed her through to the forecourt, where her mount waited, saddled and bridled, red coat gleaming as if in summer sun though no sun yet lit the place.

Paks greeted the horse; the horse nudged her with its nose, and then she tossed the saddlebags up; they clung without tying. She turned to Arcolin. "You were the best captain I could have had," she said. "And Matthis Stammel was the best sergeant. Gird's grace rest on you and yours. Milady Calla, I am so glad to see my captain wed to someone who loves him . . . and you, young Jamis, are like to grow into a fine man."

Jamis nodded silently. She mounted and rode away, out through the stronghold's gates, down the road to Duke's East, out of sight. "*Will* she come back?" Jamis asked.

"I don't know," Arcolin said. He put out his hand; Jamis took it, and Calla took his other hand. They walked back inside to the smell of breakfast cooking.

CHAPTER FORTY-SEVEN

he queen lay propped against pillows in her bed, eyes bright and a smile as wide as the kingdom on her face. The king came and sat on the stool a Squire placed for him beside the bed. Tucked into Arian's arms were the two most beautiful babies Kieri had ever seen. The room smelled fresh with the good-luck herbs the midwives had strewn.

"Our children," she said to the babes. "Here is your father."

Beyond expectation, they looked at him, eyes appearing to focus. One—the girl—had wisps of pale reddish hair; the other—the boy— had light brown. Their arms moved, tiny hands opened. He offered each a forefinger; the hands clenched around his fingers. It was only the infant grip . . . but he felt more than that, more than he had felt with his other children. Surely no babes just born could recognize anyone but their mother.

"They are our hope," he said. "And you, my queen?" He wiggled his fingers loose from those grips and stroked Arian's hair.

"I am well. More than well, rejoicing in them and in you." She grinned. "And I suspect you feel in them what I do. Both of them. My grandfather was right."

Kieri nodded. "I was not sure it would survive their birth. Though it survived mine. And they have it from both parents." He sighed. "Which makes it all the more important to see that they have guidance in its use from earliest childhood. I suspect some elves will not be pleased if they do have that ability. Your grandfather is re-signed, I think, but others—and certainly the iynisin—will see them as enemies."

"My grandfather will aid us," Arian said. When he did not an-swer, she put out her hand to touch his. "I know you do not want to be his vassal, Kieri, but he is our best ally for now. The guards he sent have not sought to usurp your authority over the Ladysforest elves, have they?"

"No . . ." Kieri shook his head. "But—you know why I distrust even honest elves."

"And you have reason to do so, but—are you not more able with your elven magery now, thanks to their instruction?"

He nodded. "So I am, and I have exercised it out of their pres-ence, as far as I dared go away from you in this critical time." He grinned. "I have even used it in ways they would not approve—so I must admit my instructors do not control me."

"What did you do?" Arian asked.

"Nothing evil, I promise," he said. "But if a king may not wake and put back to sleep a rosebush in thanks for his queen's safe birthing—" He reached down and picked up the roses he'd laid there. "Aliam told me the Lady did much the same in his stead-ing, and it is too early for roses." As he held them, their fragrance poured out, filling the room for an instant as if they stood in the rose garden in summer, then faded, no more than three roses usually pro-duced.

Arian smiled. "Thank you. I am glad our children will have that scent at the root of their lives." She frowned a little. "Kieri . . . if you can wake and put to sleep the roses, do you think you now know how to wake those sleeping magelords?"

He shook his head. "I doubt it," he said. "They sleep by someone else's spell, and how to unweave another's spell is still beyond my understanding. At least a trifold weaving, your grandfather said. And yes, I may have some elements of mageborn talent, but I know nothing of its use. Dorrin has no idea what would set magelords asleep for hundreds of years. I wish Paks would come from wherever she is and tell me more about what she saw."

"Or someone else on that journey. Maybe the Marshal-General could send one of the Marshals who were there."

"Maybe. I confess I would like to have those magelords when I consider what Alured the Black might do. If he has been invaded—or if he willingly harbors one of the Verrakaien or their like—we will need those with experience in warring with magery. We had paladins with us in Aarenis when we defeated Siniava, and yet it was a near thing. Alured, I believe, is a more dangerous opponent than Siniava. From what Paks said, those sleeping magelords seem to be mage and warrior both."

Arian looked down at the babies, her face stiff with worry. "They must have time to grow, Kieri."

"Exactly. And this realm has suffered enough from the scathefire. We must not ignore the danger; a few magic-wielding warriors would not come amiss. They would have been of use in that battle winter before last. Or if Alured chooses to come to the north by water . . . I can all too easily imagine him storming our new port with whatever magery he's acquired: his own, or that of an ally. By Arcolin's letters, uncanny things happened down there the last few years." Kieri shook his head and leaned over to kiss her. "But nothing, my love, matters are much as this: you here, alive and well, with our firstborn alive and well in your arms."

Arian glanced down at the babes, now both asleep. "I had best get my rest while I can. I suspect both of them will be keeping us awake for years to come."

Kieri chuckled. "We will have help with that, but—if you allow—I will take them to their cradle." Arian nodded, and he scooped up one babe at a time, a little surprised at himself for remembering how to hold a newborn. He laid them in the double cradle built for them, and when he turned back from the second, Arian was already asleep.

The sound of hooves on stone came through the window. Kieri reached the window overlooking the courtyard just in time to see a tall figure in a Girdish-blue surcoat over glittering mail on a red horse ride through the gate. So much for rest.

ACKNOWLEDGMENTS

As always, many contributed to the research in this book as well as others in the group. Their contributions made it better; errors are my fault. David R. Watson of New World Arbalest graciously lent books from his library and gave advice on weaponry, as well as serving as an alpha reader for some sections. The other alpha readers, pressed into service over the holidays, did their usual amazing job of pointing out what still needed to be done. The group of fans who read and comment on the Paksworld blog looked up details from past books for me, and their commentary gave insight into some issues. Choir members provided much-needed support when things weren't going well and helped me keep focused on the ultimate goal. Former editor Betsy Mitchell, a strong supporter of the Paksworld books from the very first, continued to advise on this one right up to her retirement, and current editor Anne Groell has done an extraordinary job of taking over, including reading all the previous Paksworld books. No writer could be better served. And finally, thanks are always due to my husband, Richard, and son, Michael, without whose patience and willingness to take over the other work there'd be no time to write.

ABOUT THE AUTHOR

Former Marine ELIZABETH MOON is the author of many novels, including *Echoes of Betrayal, Kings of the North, Oath of Fealty,* the Deed of Paksenarrion trilogy, *Victory Conditions, Command Decision, Engaging the Enemy, Marque and Reprisal, Trading in Danger,* the Nebula Award winner *The Speed of Dark,* and *Remnant Population,* a Hugo Award finalist. After earning a degree in history from Rice University, Moon went on to obtain a degree in biology from the University of Texas, Austin. She lives in Florence, Texas.

www.elizabethmoon.com

ABOUT THE TYPE

This book was set in Apollo, a typeface designed by Adrian Frutiger in 1962 for the founders Deberny & Peignot. Born in Interlaken, Switzerland, in 1928, Frutiger became one of the most important type designers. He attended the School of Fine Arts in Zurich between 1948 and 1951, where he studied calligraphy. He received the Gutenberg Prize in 1986 for technical and aesthetic achievement in type.